The Bloodline

By
James Morse

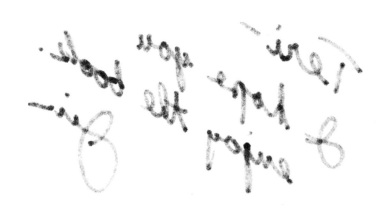

Copyright © 2010 Author Name
All rights reserved.
ISBN: 0615589170
ISBN-13: 978-0615589176

DEDICATION

I grew up like most—believing in the faith that I was handed at birth with little need or reason to question it or explore further. But as I grew it was obvious that there was much more to the stories and religious doctrine than met the eye. Satisfying that curiosity led to writing this book. But the luxury of chasing mysteries can only come from having certainties in life. Those certainties came early from my parents who instilled in me a solid grasp of reality and what was really important and true in life. The continued love and acceptance of my wife and daughters has given me a boundless belief in the future and made this book possible. For this, and the fun we have had on the journey, I am forever grateful. –the Author

1

I am too much of a skeptic to deny the possibility of anything. -- Aldous Huxley

Hark the herald angels sing ...
Jen Manton looked nervously from the choir to Danny, fidgeting in the pew. It didn't matter that her son's face had been on the front of every newsmagazine and tabloid in the past six months, he was a six-year old, it was Christmas Eve, and he was ready to get on with the real event of Santa's arrival and ripping open the presents. Jen wondered whether all the commotion the last few months had ruined Christmas forever for her son, or for her, for that matter. She glanced over at her husband. His eyebrows were furled tight. She knew Rick was sharing her concerns. Jen could sense the glances and behind-the-hand whispers of the curious and the faithful who packed the church.
Peace on earth and mercy mild, God and sinners reconciled ...

Jen couldn't remember last year's Christmas Eve service. It seemed like a long time ago now. She knew it was more crowded this year and wondered if everyone was there just to look at her family.

With angelic hosts proclaim, Christ is born in Bethlehem.

Inside the church, the body heat generated by the shoulder to shoulder overdressed worshipers made the air stifling. The portly minister was rising to deliver his sermon, and didn't seem to notice. Jen was not inclined to listen closely, and let her mind drift to the family's upcoming vacation plans.

"On this Christmas Eve we should all pause to remember that it was God who sent His Son to us to save us from our sins. There are many external influences that make us forget that blessed fact. True Christians should not be tempted to stray from their beliefs for that which is simple and easy to behold," the reverend announced, gently waving his arms.

The words jolted Jen from her thoughts of warm ocean waters. Rick had been right. Coming tonight wasn't a good idea. This no longer sounded like the standard Christmas sermon warning of the danger of forgetting the religious nature of Christmas in the press to buy presents and attend office parties. Now it seemed like every word was directed at her. Jen was thankful that Danny seemed unaffected by it all.

Rick glanced over at her with his 'I-can't-wait-until-this-is-over' look. She returned the glance and nodded in agreement.

Rick's glance lingered. His wife was the only child of an only child. But the stereotypes that brought to mind did not fit her. Her parents had divorced at an early age, and her mother had raised her in the hills of central Pennsylvania to believe that she was special and loved. There had not been enough money to spoil her and, with the long hours her mother had worked to support them, there was no time to pamper her. By her mother's example, Jen believed that all people were born equal and that rewards came only through hard work. Through sheer determination she had graduated from nursing school. Tonight, he could still see the spunky and determined co-ed he had fallen for, romanced and married eight years ago. At thirty-one, three years his junior, she took her natural good looks and intelligence for granted. Rick knew he was lucky to have her as a mate. And tonight she looked wonderful.

With her last minute gift wrapping completed, Jen had spent the day pampering herself. Jen still considered it a treat to go to the hair salon, have her nails done and shop for a holiday dress at somewhere other than the discount stores. They had had typical financial struggles. An apartment at first. Two cars. And then there was a mortgage. And then Danny. But somehow they were making it. It would be smoother sailing from here on out.

Although Rick regretted the loss of privacy that followed going on the television talk shows, the generous "stipends" they paid had certainly changed their financial situation for the better. The sparkle in Jen's impatient eyes rivaled the sequins on her designer Christmas sweater. Perhaps the inconvenience of their fame was worth the hassle. Perhaps.

The Mantons had seen the television news crews pulling up as they had entered the church. Jen had insisted that they go early to get a seat near the back. Rick had forgotten that he had hinted at his family's Christmas Eve plans to a reporter for Channel 6 in an interview earlier that week. *I won't make the same mistake next year,* he vowed. So he and Jen both knew that there would be a gauntlet of cameras to move through as they left. *Let's get this over with.*

Jen was thankful as the sermon, probably the first one she had ever critically listened to, came to an end. As the minister wished the congregation a parting merry Christmas, the Mantons stepped into the aisle and moved toward the exit, the aisle seemingly parting for them.

"Merry Christmas, Mr. Manton," said a young woman who held out a white orchid.

"Thank you. Merry Christmas," he stammered as his hand waved off the flower in a practiced gentle motion.

"God bless you, Danny," urged another.

They kept walking until an elderly woman blocked the aisle. "I know you are busy, but when you could find the time, my sister has cancer ..."

"I'm so sorry. We will keep her in our prayers," Jen stated firmly, moving around the forlorn woman.

Other voices were awkwardly loud, but equally sincere and respectful. Rick and Jen had learned to keep walking and smiling through encroaching crowds. Weeks before they would have stopped to listen or try to give answers. But they found that they didn't know the answers. There was not a solution to every mystery. There was not enough time. They couldn't give these people what they wanted.

When they reached the exit, the brisk wind in their faces gave them a breath of relief before a muffled chorus of "It's them" triggered a wall of bright lights. With the protective parents flanking Danny, they put their heads down and began shuffling forward as if warding off the wind would also ward off the lights.

"Could we get a shot here?"

"Do you have any special Christmas message for the viewers of America Tonight?" The voices were louder than inside, and they had lost the ring of respect. The Mantons, nervously smiling, kept pushing forward.

"Danny, do you still believe there is a Santa Claus?"

Rick grimaced. He knew they had better throw something to the sharks or it would get worse. He held in the sarcastic retorts he was mulling over, and pulled his family together in front of the cameras. The photographers jockeyed for position and hushed when Rick held his hand up. "Ladies and gentlemen, we wish you all a merry Christmas. Your viewers should celebrate Christmas the same as they have in the past, with whatever beliefs they have. That's what we intend to do. So with your cooperation we'll start that right now. Thank-you."

"Merry Christmas," Danny chimed in, still not certain whether all this fuss over him and his family would delay Santa's arrival.

Jen, still seething over the last intrusive question, smiled through gritted teeth as she ushered her family through an opening in the throng.

A voice boomed from the back of the throng. "You should be ashamed of yourselves for going along with this hoax."

Not everyone had taken their story the way it had originally been intended. Rick put his shoulder down and pushed his way through the wall of cameras, his eyes darting around. *There's always a few in the crowd*, he thought, regretting that they had not spent the money for a bodyguard tonight. *It's Christmas Eve, for Chrissakes*.

A vendor with a makeshift cart on the sidewalk near the street was holding up T-shirts with a photograph of the Mantons on the front. Jen couldn't make out the caption. Their lawyer had told them that there was no way to stop that kind of stuff. They were now 'public figures'.

The reporters followed them to the parking lot, in futility throwing out questions. The Mantons reached their new car and scurried to get inside.

"Whew." Jen wriggled into the seat of their new Volvo and straightened the lap of her new coat. She loved the feel and smell of the leather interior. They could have afforded better, but Rick was still too practical to spend an exorbitant amount on a car. The top of the line Volvo was a good compromise. "You would think those poor slobs would at least get Christmas Eve off, wouldn't you?" There was a lot more she wanted to say, but she was acutely aware of Danny's attentiveness from the back seat.

"You would hope. Buckled up, Danny?"

"Yes, Dad." Everything was easier with Danny the closer Christmas came.

Rick glanced over his shoulder and backed out. Even in the parking lot, where common courtesy was often suspended, the holiday drivers seemed to delay to allow the Mantons to pass. *Embarrassing, but I could get used to it*, Rick chuckled to himself. Inside he hoped that this kind of adulation wouldn't last much longer.

They paused at the entrance to Chestnut Street. Christmas Eve light traffic, they could easily make a left turn for a change. No cars except for two idling their engines eighty yards up the sloping street. Reaching for the radio switch, Rick started to swing the car left across the street.

"Rick ... car coming." Jen, the ever diligent co-pilot saw one of the two cars lurch forward, its rear wheels squealing.

"What a clown," Rick muttered. He easily hit the brakes before reaching the center line. He'd let this jerk race by. *Must be closing early at the local bars.* But the speeding car veered toward the stopped Volvo and kept accelerating.

"What the hell," Rick mumbled and laid on the horn, at first in anger, then, realizing they were going to be rammed, in a last attempt to ward off this lunatic.

"Danny, cover up! Head down! Head down!"

The car smashed into the front right corner of the Volvo, flinging Rick and Jen forward as the airbags exploded, slamming them backward into their seats, stunned.

Eyes blurred with his own blood, Rick called out. "Jen! Danny! All he could hear was the roar of the two car horns as if they were two animals locked in mortal combat. He could see the bright headlights of another car pulling up quickly. Very close. *Not an accident*, his dazed mind screamed.

The camera crews were still packing their gear at the sound of the crash. Like a reflex, the camera lights were back on, and the pack dashed across the parking lot, angling for the best view of the only news the film crews thought they would have that night.

A terrified cry came from the back seat. Rick could tell Danny's hurt cry from his scared cry. This was a blend of both. He was reaching over for Jen when the passenger door behind her was yanked open.

"Just stay put and no one will get hurt." The voice was nervous and angry.

Rick's eyes began to focus on a thickset man roughly pulling on Danny's arm. His movements didn't seem right. Something was strange about the rescuer's face. It was waxy looking. It was plastic! Rick realized the person was not wearing a protective mask of a firefighter, but a Halloween costume. Rick was looking into the caricature face of President Ben Dailley.

"What are you doing?" Rick demanded groggily. He shook his head to try and clear his mind. *Can this be happening?*

Danny's scream intensified to terror as the attacker tugged violently on Danny's collar. "I said shut up! Shut up!" the voice demanded.

Dream or not, this was all wrong. Rick was suddenly looking down the black steel barrel of a street assault rifle. Still not certain that he wasn't hallucinating, Rick's anger surged. As the masked man jerked at Danny again, pulling him through the gap in the shoulder harness, Rick lunged through the opening in the front seats, and grabbed for the barrel of the gun. The last thing he saw was a blast of fire as the weapon discharged in his hand.

*   *   *

Christians in Hong Kong were doing their last minute gift shopping. In living rooms throughout America, families were sipping eggnog, greeting relatives. In Germany, *die kinder* were opening presents with the first rays of morning. Around the globe radios and televisions in the background interrupted the quiet reverie of Christmas with the staccato beat of a news bulletin. They turned up the volume and leaned close for the news:

> *"We have just received a report over Associated Press wires that in Norristown, Pennsylvania, at seven-thirty two, Eastern Standard Time, Jen and Daniel Manton, the only two known descendants of Jesus Christ, were victims of what appears to have been a terrorist attack. First reports from the scene indicate that Daniel Manton has been kidnapped at gun point, and that Richard Manton has been critically wounded by several rounds of gunfire. He is being transported to Franklin Memorial Hospital in Philadelphia. There is no known motive for the attack, and no one has yet claimed responsibility. We now take you to the scene where, incredibly, we have been informed that we have live footage of the attack ..."*

*   *   *

Nine months earlier in southern France

The heavily scarred, thick, wooden door of the cathedral was swung open by a smallish man in a black smock. He was not surprised to see the three visitors.

"Bonjour, Monsieur," said the two men in unison.

"Bon matin, Professeurs."

Professors Stephen Hershner and Kathleen Fahey were professional scholars and, between them, were fluent in six languages, none of which was French. They had already used up most of their working French in greeting the priest who stood before them. As he continued to speak, they nervously relied upon their young graduate student, Brijette, to translate the conversation as they stepped out of the already intense morning sun into the darkness of the vestibule.

"He says he is pleased to meet you and is thrilled, but still ... um," she paused and rubbed her chin thoughtfully, "ah ... perplexed, I think that's the word, by such interest of Americans in his little church so far from nowhere."

'Far from nowhere' was a good description of the rustic village of Rennes-le-Château, in the Languedoc region of southern France, nestled between the foothills of the Pyrenées Mountains and the blue Mediterranean Sea.

"Please tell him that we appreciate his…cooperation," said Fahey, biting off the last word.

Languedoc was the subject of many fantastic legends in French folklore. Hershner and Fahey had studied every one of them for the last six years leading up to this moment. They strained to look into the dark corners of the cathedral as their eyes adjusted.

The priest leaned close to them and raised his furry gray eyebrows and spoke in English, "Ah, you are looking for Father Saunière's secret, non?"

He was correct. Of all the arcane history of Languedoc, what had captured the curiosity of the professors was the story of Father Saunière, a lowly priest from Rennes-le-Château, who, in the early 1900s, rose to great notoriety and influence within the Catholic Church, and Parisian society as well. His rise was purportedly due to his discovery of something of vast religious significance which he parlayed into money and power. But his finding was a mystery, at least to the general public, which only saw an undistinguished country cleric inexplicably living *la bonne vivre*. Alas, at an early age, Saunière suffered a stroke and mutely took his secret with him to his grave. The priest's unjustifiable rise to power gave new life to the belief that somewhere in the hills and valleys surrounding Rennes-le-Château lay the secret which had caused this unlikely region to be home to more than its share of bizarre events that molded history.

Fahey leaned close to the priest's face and raised an eyebrow of her own. *"Oui,"* she stated definitively.

The professors were tracking Saunière's secret along a broken historical trail marked by a cryptic Latin phrase, *Et In Arcadia Ego*. The words popped up consistently, but seemingly at random, over many centuries. They were hidden in the works of a master painter. They were found on tombstones and church walls. They were in popular poems and in medieval arias. There was no rhyme or reason to their appearance, but it was always in connection with Languedoc. Hershner and Fahey pursued the phrase like bloodhounds, each sighting providing further revelations that convinced them that it was the road to a discovery of explosive historical significance.

The priest smiled at Fahey knowingly. He leaned a little closer and hissed, *"Bon chance."*

Fahey stared at him and then turned her face to Brijette. Her eyes asked for an interpretation.

"He says, 'Good luck,'" she relayed without interpreting the priest's inflection which indicated that she would need lots of it.

Et In Arcadia Ego. The words by themselves didn't make sense, either grammatically or in substance. In English the phrase translated: *And In Arcadia I ...* The professors knew that it had to have a hidden meaning, but whatever it was, it was indecipherable to them. So far.

As the priest turned and headed toward the altar Brijette turned to the professors and added unnecessarily, "This way, please."

Fahey looked at Hershner and rolled her eyes. Hershner did not share his colleague's impatience. He was too enthralled to be finally exploring 'ground zero,' as they had jokingly referred to the cathedral for months. He did share with Fahey a large degree of arrogance in their belief that they could find the key to this puzzle which had eluded the local population, as well as historians, for centuries.

Like many others, they had always suspected that the cathedral, the fulcrum of medieval life in Rennes-le-Château, must have once held a secret cache. They had relayed their suspicions and a request for diagrams to scholars at the Université de Toulouse. But the return investigation, which included detailed sketches and photographs of the cathedral in its modern condition, had revealed nothing meriting inquiry. But their insolence was fueled later that year when one of their graduate students, digging through dusty volumes of architectural studies while studying for a semester in Paris, had discovered a series of photographs from the inside of the cathedral at Rennes-le-Château prior to an extensive remodeling conducted in the 1890s under the watchful eye of Father Saunière. Before this accidental strike, there was no documentation whatsoever of the interior of Cathedral de la Madeline. The professors' examination of the photographs was exhilarating, in scholarly terms. The aged brown and yellow photographs showed a slightly revised layout to the cathedral. There in the center of the church, on the floor in front of the altar, which apparently had been moved forward in the alteration, lay a raised granite statue of a medieval clergyman in deathly repose. Its stone hands held a book, most likely a Bible, the professors surmised. To their great excitement, above his head was a curved scroll. They studied the photographs under microscopes. Only partially visible due to the angle of the photographer, but as clear as day when magnified, the visible part of the scroll was inscribed with the letters, *Et In Arca* ... . Hershner and Fahey knew immediately how the scroll read. *Et In Arcadia Ego*.

Arcadia. A province of ancient Greece which was renowned for its peacefulness and tranquility, and whose name came to be associated with those qualities wherever they were found. Perhaps it reflected the desire of those who were inflicted with the troublesome secret that Saunière last revealed. When measured by the ill-fated inhabitants of Languedoc, it seemed more of a curse than a treasure.

Now, after months of one-sided negotiations in letters to the regional Catholic authorities, Hershner and Fahey knelt at the altar and rubbed their hands over the smooth flagstones on the floor.

Brijette interrupted their reverie. "The Father says he needs to deposit the check before work begins."

Fahey gave out an exasperated breath as she sat her oversized combination camera bag and briefcase on the nearest pew to retrieve the check which, to Fahey, was for an exorbitant amount. They had had no leverage when bargaining with the Catholic Church to come to Rennes-le-Château to move the altar and, archeologically, exhume the grave they expected to find underneath.

The priest looked sheepish and mumbled in French.

"He says it is Church policy and, besides, he must pay the workmen up front," Brijette explained in a patronizing tone. Americans could be so impatient.

"Whatever, whatever," said Fahey as she handed over the cashier's check drawn at the Banque du Lyon.

The priest took the check, examined it and nodded slightly. Fahey returned the nod grudgingly. With a broad smile the Frenchman turned, and, with a torrent of words, waved for them to stay put.

"He says he will get the workmen," Brijette reported dutifully.

"I think I got that," Fahey retorted sarcastically, giving Brijette a look which said, 'Don't push it.'

The translator's pouting lips needed no interpretation. "We may as well sit," she said as she retreated to the far end of the front pew. Hershner nodded to Fahey and they continued to roam the altar area, stooping again and again to probe the tiny cracks of the massive flagstones with their fingers.

It took the six workmen a full hour just to move the massive altar on wooden rollers. On the uncovered floor underneath the altar the outline of the statue was still visible on the covering stone. Fahey's camera flashed and clicked continually as the workmen took a break and watched on in amusement at the professors' antics.

"Whatever was here, Saunière took great pains to cover it," murmured Hershner.

"But did he put it back?" Fahey said from behind the lens. "There. Got it." Fahey put the camera back in the bag on her shoulder. "Could we get back to work?" she announced, to no one in general.

Brijette gave Fahey a haughty look and began an excited discourse to the workmen, complete with hand gestures. At the end, they all gave a hearty laugh and picked up their tools.

"What did you tell them?" asked Fahey.

"Oh," Brijette replied coyly, "I just explained how important you are."

Fahey opened her mouth to retort, but Hershner stepped in, "Kathleen. We are almost done here."

The workmen crouched and laboriously began cramming their iron bars into the cracks. Hershner cringed at the destructive scraping sound. But, once they had leverage, the crew slipped their fingers into the small gaps they created and gently lifted the stones free.

Below the flagstones was a layer of dirt and dust. The youngest worker knelt and swept the area revealing a massive stone. He swept to the sides until square edges appeared. On the sides were notches, apparently for lifting.

"The crypt," whispered Hershner, unnecessarily.

Brijette, back in control, was exhorting the men to proceed carefully. "*Attentions. Soyez prudent!*" she barked briskly as they counted, *un, deux, trois*, and swung the large stone to the side. Her tone changed as she looked into the opening in the floor. "*A Dieu,*" she groaned. She had been prepped to see a coffin.

Looking up from its barren stone grave was a discolored skeleton, fully intact. Its hallow eye cavities stared up blankly. Its crooked yellow teeth grinned hauntingly. The crusty remains of a grand altar cap laid grotesquely across the skull. Its arms were crossed over its chest, clutching within them a dried leather satchel.

The cathedral was silent as Hershner and Fahey pressed forward through the workmen to inspect their treasure. They stood in awe.

"Who was he?" Brijette whispered. The professors did not answer. They didn't know. The name had not been visible in the photographs and no other record existed to reveal the identity of the unknown man, apparently a high ranking clergyman.

"Don't touch it," ordered Fahey, pulling out her camera.

After his partner had clicked a dozen shots from different angles, Hershner pulled on a pair of rubber doctor's gloves and knelt over the hole. Carefully placing his covered hands on the relic, he lifted the top wrist bone of the deceased guardian. The entire arm lifted up. He could almost sense Fahey's heart beating as loudly as his own as he laid the arm aside and gently picked up the other. The collection of onlookers leapt back as the arm snapped loose at the elbow. Hershner looked at Fahey. It happens, he shrugged. Fahey nodded and Hershner laid the hand and forearm to the other side and slowly lifted the sack free of the bony ribs where it rested.

Fahey took the satchel in her now rubber-gloved hands. She knew that even the oil from her fingers could start irreversible damage to this rare artifact, whatever it was. She set it on a cloth spread on the flagstone floor, and gingerly tried to part the opening at the top of the bag. The leather was crusty and split open. Flecks of gold leaf lettering flaked off the side, unnoticed by the professors who mistook it for dirt.

Gently, as if disarming a bomb, Fahey reached in and began sliding out the contents. It contained scrolls and leather bound volumes that appeared to be Bibles. Cautiously, she unrolled a scroll. Hershner was pressed shoulder to shoulder with her. They both knew that further examination should be conducted under scientific conditions. But the laboratory was back in Boston and, like children at Christmas, they couldn't wait another minute. They opened another scroll, peering at the ancient writings. Then a Bible. And another. Not a word passed between them. Neither looked at the other. Finally Hershner spoke.

"Kathleen, we have found it."
"Yes.　God help us all," she breathed.

     * * *

Southern France.   1205 Anno Domino

"It is as magnificent as they say," Brother Bernard Delacroix whispered in reverence as he looked across the bustling square to the massive, recently-completed cathedral dedicated to the blessed Virgin Mary. Nôtre Dame.

Although he was thirty-two years old, middle aged for the year 1205, it was his first venture to young and vibrant Paris, the country's fastest growing municipality. Though it was emerging as a religious center, the teeming city was not yet an archbishopric and the Church's power was both supreme and non-existent, depending on which dark, muddy alley was traveled. Delacroix had been thrilled when he was summoned to report here to meet an emissary from Rome.

Delacroix crossed the square slowly, hoping to soak in every detail of this moment. His eyes scanned the glistening facade adorned with chiseled saints, peaceful and passive, seemingly unconcerned with the hideous, menacing gargoyles which peered down at them and the masses in the cobblestone place, vivid reminders of the alternate terminuses that awaited the souls of those who fell from the Church's grace.

Cupping his hand above his eyes and squinting into the late morning sun, Delacroix leaned backward and looked up at the delicate spires. It was half again as tall as the cathedral in Orléans.

The front doors were open and the monk entered carefully. Inside the door the clatter of the street was muffled. The air was cool and still and smelled of spices that had been burned at the dawn mass. Delacroix was overwhelmed by the presence of his Lord. Lowering his squat body to a knee, he bowed his head deeply.

"Brother, may I help you to a more comfortable place?" said a soothing voice, breaking Delacroix's prayer. Delacroix looked up at a younger monk, dressed in a brown robe similar to his own, but not as worn. "This is the entry way," he continued, obviously familiar with the cathedral and the look of beatification on Delacroix's face.

"Of course." Delacroix rose slowly. He had been in prayer for nearly ten minutes and had not noticed his knees stiffening. "Thank you," he said, when offered a hand.

"Your first visit to Nôtre Dame?" the guide asked, softly.

"My first to Paris," replied Delacroix. "I have been summoned to meet the emissary from His Holiness."

"Ah, oui, there have been many summoned this month. They are meeting now. I shall see if they will receive you, if you wish?"

Delacroix blinked at the younger man. He was surprised that someone so young could relay his arrival to men so important. "Yes. If that is how it is done?" he stammered.

The monk smiled. *"Certainment."* He had seen it many times. And he himself would feel the same way if he were summoned to an audience with a cardinal, or perhaps an archbishop. But high-ranking officials had been flooding to Nôtre Dame for the last two years, even during construction, and he was no longer apprehensive of mere bishops.

"Follow me, *s'il vous plait*." The guide walked purposefully across the back of the church and turned down an open hallway that ran along the side of the nave, where the masses would sit in rows of polished wooden pews. Delacroix hurried to keep pace, eyes glancing sideways between the pillars to absorb the wonderful structure.

"And your name?"

"Bernard Delacroix. Of Orléans."

"You may wait here," the monk stopped abruptly and gestured from the passageway to the front row of pews.

"Merci," Delacroix said as he shuffled toward the pew. The monk watched him go. He liked this part.

Delacroix stared at the pew. It seemed to vibrate with color. Before entering the row, he turned toward the altar to kneel. He froze where he stood, mesmerized by the brilliant glow of the intricate stained-glass window which seemed to capture and multiply the rays of the sun still rising over the Seine River. The warmth of the colors penetrated his mind. The Rose window of which the priests had spoken. It was everything they had proclaimed. Each hue was more vivid than he had ever seen. Tears welled in his eyes. For that instance, he truly believed that he was beholding heaven's entrance.

The monk chuckled and turned to go inform the bishops that Brother Bernard Delacroix, of Orléans, was properly prepared to appear before them.

"Am I worthy of such blessings, My Lord?" gasped Delacroix, barely able to catch his breath, recalling his lowly beginnings. His parents and four siblings had died in a wave of dysentery that swept northern France when he was an infant. By the grace of God he had been spared the fate of countless hundreds of plague victims who were buried in a mass grave on the outskirts of Orléans. Punished by disease for their unnamed sins, they could not be buried within the blessed cemetery of the Holy Catholic Church.

As Delacroix's mother lay in the throes of death, he was baptized with the Christian name Bernard for the beloved Saint of Clairvaux who had reformed the monasteries of northern France one hundred years before Delacroix's birth. His mother's last sight of her remaining living child, the only one who, miraculously, escaped the fevers that had taken her others, was as the nuns cradled him and quickly left the rough wood hut in the forest which had been assembled for those whose lives were painfully draining from their bodies. He was raised in the orphanage of the parish and he did not question that he owed his life to the mercy of his Savior.

Delacroix turned out to be a bright, precocious boy who flourished under the strict guidance of the nuns. His obvious desire to please caught the attention of Father Mihicl who supervised Delacroix's instruction in reading and writing, an honor not usually bestowed upon the child of cursed parents. By the time Delacroix was fourteen he had absorbed everything Father Mihiel could teach him. He could read Biblical texts in Latin, Greek and Hebrew. He could also read and speak fluently in French, Italian and most Germanic languages.

Delacroix's talents were a blessing and a burden. After taking his vows at age sixteen, he was assigned the tedious task of duplicating the Bible and missives from the Holy Father at the broad tables in the southern wing of the cathedral where the sunlight was best. With his extraordinary talents, he eventually replaced the aging Father Mihiel and supervised the monks who were more experienced, but less skilled. It was not hard labor, but the repetition was mind-numbing, and Delacroix chafed for a more rewarding task. After ten years in this post, Delacroix requested that he be allowed to minister directly to the masses and spread the Word of God that he had so thoroughly studied. His requests were rebuffed. He was informed that his service to the Lord was most valuable where he was. Although Delacroix had hoped for a different response, he had not questioned the wisdom of the Church.

As the years passed, Delacroix served the parish and the Church well. On occasion he had traveled to the archdioceses in Lyon and Rouen to counsel the staffs of the archbishops, but only on matters within his displayed talents. By virtue of the lack of visibility of his position he easily avoided the pitfalls that befell his brethren. There were no accusations of improper demands for tithes used for personal pleasures, no young girls of the flock who had become with child after closed session spiritual guidance, and most importantly, no political friction with any of his brethren. Consequently, Delacroix was held in high esteem as incorruptible, an attribute not always found in those who also were deemed intelligent. So at age thirty-two, when the years of deterioration to Delacroix's eyes had progressed so that he could only read by the midday sun, the Bishop had finally recommended that his request be granted. Now, Bernard Delacroix, abject orphan of Orléans, was to meet messengers of the Pope himself for a special assignment.

Interrupting his reverie, Delacroix barely heard a voice whisper, "Bishop Morceau of Lyon, the Legate to His Holiness, awaits."

Delacroix rose and followed the monk, nervously, through a labyrinth of hallways. When they reached a high, double set of doors, they stopped. "May God be with you," the monk whispered in parting. Delacroix could only swallow and nod.

The monk swung open the door and Delacroix took a deep breath and marched in. Crossing the stone floor, he approached a dais with three men perched in throne-like chairs. His words were never truer than as he fell to his knees in front of the middle chair and hoarsely stated in Latin, "Your Grace, I am your humble servant."

The red-faced, thin man looked down on the brown knit cap which could not cover all of Delacroix's balding head. He smoothed his flowing, white, silk robe across his lap. The Bishop's high, large hat was adorned with the cross of the Pope, distinguished by its three graduated cross bars, proclaiming his authority.

"Brother Delacroix, thou art highly praised among your superiors. Thy service to His Holiness, despite your roots in heresy, has been to the glory of God."

Delacroix's misfortunate origins were always a qualifier to his accomplishments. The harsh truth that was inescapable brought Delacroix back to reality. He raised his face to the messenger of the Pope.

"Thou has been chosen," the Vatican emissary continued, "for an appointment of great importance for His Holiness. As thou knowest, the servants of the Church in Languedoc are less devout than as required by God."

Delacroix didn't know any such thing, but accepted this statement as truth. He had generally heard of heresies committed in this vague region known as Languedoc, but he could not distinguish them from rumors of heresy in numerous other kingdoms and regions.

"At large in the Pyrenées, and spreading to the sea, where the heresies of the past were believed to have been extinguished, there remains the smoldering embers of blasphemy. It is through disciples such as thee, with beliefs firmly founded on the Word of God, that the flock can be led back to the true path. Therefore, by the power of His Holiness, Pope Innocent the Third, I hereby ordain thee as Father Delacroix to the diocese of Rennes-le-Château to carry His Word and restore faith to a region led astray by the forces of evil."

Delacroix was overwhelmed by the decree. He had never heard of Rennes-le-Château, but knew this was the opportunity for which he had prayed. He did not know that hundreds of priests and brothers like him, those who were dedicated to the Church's literal, and at times self-serving, interpretation of the Holy Bible, were being given similar "honors" and were being infused into Languedoc to stem the rising tide of heresy. The trip was long for the crude modes of travel of those times, and under different circumstances such an illogical and inefficient transfer would not have been considered. But the Church believed that the absolute purity of the northern French clergy was needed in an area where heretical thought seemed to overcome even the most devout. Delacroix humbly accepted his assignment.

"Thy will be done, your Grace."

"Now, we have much work to do to prepare you for your important work."

"I will do my best to serve His Holiness."

"We are certain that you will. I present to you Bishop Hanford of St. Etienne and Bishop Pantelle of Grenoble," he stated, motioning to his sides. They nodded slightly as Delacroix bowed.

"We have been sent here by His Holiness to insure that the priests that we are sending to Languedoc are properly warned of what they will be confronting." He made it sound sinister. Delacroix nodded sincerely. He was standing in the center of the large hall, and was not offered a seat.

Hanford leaned forward. He was rotund and pale and his breath reeked of sour garlic. "In Languedoc, the Holy Catholic Church is infested with sects that practice heresy. Where you are going, Rennes-le-Château, the largest and most influential sect is the Cathars. It's a Greek name. *Cathari.* It means 'the pure ones.' Even their name reflects their heresy. They think they are above us." His lip curled in a sneer. "And above Our Lord," he added as an afterthought.

The information was shocking to Delacroix. The panel was delighted to see the disgust registered on his face.

"Languedoc is also beset with Jews, and the Cathars have openly intermingled," Hanford said the word slowly for maximum effect, "with the murderers of Christ for as long as anyone can remember. The Cathars outwardly profess the Christian faith, but, with their actions, deny the divinity of Christ."

"Now, now, Bishop Hanford," interrupted Morceau, who was clearly recognized by the others as senior to them. "That may be putting it a bit harsh.

"I must say that the Cathar people are an educated lot. Many can read and write at least their names," added Hanford as a token gesture toward fairness in his comments.

Delacroix nodded thoughtfully. Literacy was a rarity that he greatly admired. The written word was one of God's richest blessings.

The bishop continued, "Precisely because they are educated, we think they can be saved. We hope that by being provided priests such as you, Bernard Delacroix, that we can reverse this malignant course on our southern shores."

Delacroix nodded, adopting their hope.

"But you must be aware that these people are not merely innocent misbegottens," Pantelle interceded. "The Cathars have strayed impermissibly from Church doctrine when they persist in their heretical assertion that they are descendants from a bloodline of the Jews' King David. Some contend that they are the children of our Lord Christ! This cannot be tolerated." The bishop pounded the broad arm of his chair.

"The Church demands obedience to it, the declarant of the Message of Christ. This preposterous claim of a royal Jewish throne threatens our authority. Will the Cathars follow the divine wisdom of the Holy Catholic Church, or will they rally to the blood pretenders of a Holy Throne? The Church cannot risk the answer to this question."

As Delacroix's back began to ache, he was informed of the history of the struggle with the heresy in Languedoc. In 1165 a council had been convened in Albi, a hotbed of Catharist support. In the castle of Lombers, ten miles south of Albi, Cathars were prosecuted for heresy for the first time. The gathered bishops and abbots of neighboring Narbonne province condemned the Cathars, or Albigensians as they would later be called in reference to their first condemnation site, for several counts of heretical beliefs. But, by Delacroix's appointment, the power of the Church had dwindled in Languedoc to such a degree that the condemnation was more in word than in substance, and, in most villages, the Cathars continued their practices, often within the very cathedrals financed and maintained by the Church. They were crypto-heretics, attending mass and taking the sacraments while refusing to relinquish their non-conforming ideology. Despite their advanced intellectual culture, the Cathars were politically naive that such peaceful coexistence could last forever.

The three clerics continued, as if in a debate over which could provide Delacroix the most comprehensive warning. "It is quite ironic," mused Morceau, "and a source of much regret, that many of the Cathars are also members of the Order of the Knights Templar."

Delacroix was surprised that he could still be shocked. The Knights Templar had served for over a century as the military arm of the Vatican. He couldn't believe that even they had been infested with heresy. The Knights Templar represented a class of nobility respected throughout Europe. Every learned boy in France knew their history. The order had been formed by Godfroi de Bouillon, who, in 1099, had led the greatest of all the crusades to the gates of Jerusalem where he had seized the Holy City and restored the Holy Lands to Christian authority. After his triumphal return to France, he created the Order of the Knights Templar to escort subsequent pilgrimages to Jerusalem. Throughout the next century, despite onerous self-imposed restrictions on the behavior expected of their member knights, the order grew in number and influence.

Morceau had known that this news would be disturbing. "Bernard, we understand that the Knights Templar are held above reproach by our people. But we now have evidence that, even while the Knights Templar have appeared to be a strong and forceful ally of the Church, the exalted Godfroi de Bouillon also formed, ten years before marching on Jerusalem, a secret society known as the Prieurć de Sion." The Brotherhood of Zion.

"Have you heard of it?" inquired Hanford.

"Certainly not, Your Worship."

"Good. These Brothers of Zion heartily joined in the pronounced desire to reclaim Palestine, but they also harbored many tenets of the Cathars, most notably the belief in this royal bloodline emitting from Our Savior. The Brotherhood of Zion served as the secret administrative arm of the Knights Templars and spurred the return to Jerusalem. But it was not merely to recapture the ground on which Christ was crucified and resurrected. It was to fulfill its members' assertion of a royal heritage and claim the Temple of King Solomon in Jerusalem for themselves. They say the Temple was rightfully theirs."

Delacroix had known that the Order of the Knights of the Templar had drawn its name from its quest to regain the grounds that held the ruins of the Temple of Solomon, but he had believed, as had everyone until now, that they were claiming it for all of Christendom.

"For a hundred years, the Church has been willing to overlook the blasphemous rumblings attributed to the Knights Templar as long as the order served the will of the Pope and carried forward the Christian banner," said Hanford.

In fact, in 1139, in an early attempt to appease the knights and earn their allegiance, Pope Innocent II issued a papal bull decreeing that henceforth the Knights Templar would pay all allegiance directly to the Vatican, and were deemed free from all local secular or religious influence, including the possibility of excommunication.

"But the grandest of the Knights Templars' conquests are many decades behind them," Morceau added condescendingly. "Jerusalem was retaken by Moslem hordes in 1187 and what have our vaunted Knights Templar done to reclaim it? Their attempts to liberate the Holy City have failed. Now we know why. God is aware of their heresy. He can no longer distinguish between them and the infidels from the deserts. But the knights have all retained a generous share of their plunder in these unsuccessful crusades, and, throughout their home villages, have developed fiefdoms where the protection of the knight's castle often overshadows the less direct blessings of the Church. As the power of the Knights Templar grows, their belief in this bloodline becomes less secret, and their boldness and defiance of Rome increases," concluded Morceau.

It was true that by the thirteenth century, the Knights Templar had become emboldened by their autonomy. They were their own independent European empire. The Church was again disturbed by the Catharist leanings of this once loyal servant, now corrupted by power and wealth, but it was not prepared for direct confrontation. The Knights Templar, even with their glory years behind them, were far better suited with their armies and castles to defend themselves than the peace-loving Cathars who had joined their ranks in great numbers in Languedoc. So in an effort to strengthen their control, the Church assigned clergy, such as Delacroix, well-grounded in the accepted True Word as contained in the Holy Bible, to the troubled land.

"Do you understand your mission, Bernard Delacroix?"

"I believe so."

"What questions do you harbor?"

"Is the entire Order of the Knights Templar so afflicted with this curse?"

"We fear so."

"Then why do we not attack it here in northern France. We could begin saving the knights today."

In his spiritual fervor, Delacroix had unknowingly asked a troublesome political question. As Delacroix was obviously naive, the panel forgave him and hid its displeasure with the question. The heresy of the Brotherhood of Zion existed throughout France wherever the Knights Templar existed. But by themselves, they were only a religious nuisance. That would change in the century to come when the Church would see fit to disband the order, but for now, it still served a purpose for the Church. The Knights Templar and Brotherhood of Zion were only a threat when combined in number with the Cathars who were only populous in Languedoc. For the panel, this was not a matter of saving individual souls, it was a matter of preserving power.

"The situation is more grievous in Languedoc," Morceau vaguely responded. He would allow no more questions and rose. Raising his hands above Delacroix's shoulders he led the panel in prayer.

"May the grace of Our Savior lead thee in righteousness as thou goeth to those that have fallen and needeth salvation. In the name of Our Father, Amen."

"Amen," joined Delacroix.

"May God be with you, Bernard Delacroix."

*   *   *

2

God offers to every man the choice between truth and repose. Take which you will, you can never have both. --Ralph Waldo Emerson

Rrrrring.
"Hello."
"Mrs. Jennifer Manton?"
"Uh-huh." Telephone solicitations at night used to annoy Jen, but she learned it was less disruptive just to play along until the opening line had been spit out. Besides it was Double Jeopardy and she didn't want Rick beating her to the winning question while she wasted her concentration on a telemarketer.

"This is Professor Stephen Hershner of the Boston University School of Theology. I have my colleague, Professor Kathleen Fahey, also here on the speakerphone."

"Uh-huh." Different approach, but these guys better learn to pick up the pace if they want to survive on the phone banks.

"What is encephalitis?" Jen whispered excitedly with her hand on the receiver. Rick looked back at her and she smugly nodded at the television.

The voice on the phone interrupted her celebration. "We have some very important findings concerning your family background that we need to discuss with you."

"Thank-you, but we're busy now." That was polite enough and long enough that Rick wouldn't accuse her of being unnecessarily rude.

"Mrs. Manton, we are not selling anything. We have concluded a lengthy research project and your family lineage is a key component of our findings." Professor Hershner had anticipated a credibility problem and quickly forged ahead. "We would like to schedule a meeting with you to discuss your family's role in this as soon as possible."

Okay, get to the punchline, Jen thought. For no money down you're going to tell me ... she kept watch on the television.

"What is the Van Allen radiation belt?" she whispered.

Rick would concede another night to his wife, master of all trivia.

"Look, I'm sorry, but I'm really not interested."

"Mrs. Manton, this relates to your maternal grandmother, Claudette Dupere, and her descendants of the Vassimont line." It was awkward, but Professor Hershner could tell that he had to get his proverbial foot in the telephonic door. It worked. The line was silent, but had not clicked off.

Jen held the phone, speechless. Her grandmother had passed away sometime twenty-some years ago when she was a young teenager. Her memories of her were as vivid as if he had seen her yesterday. On countless weekend visits, Jen had had her grandmother all to herself at her grand white Victorian home in the country. She recalled the slow walks past budding vineyards into the center of the small town in the hills of north central

Pennsylvania. By listening intently to her tales, she knew she would be rewarded at the dilapidated grocery store with whatever candy bar she desired, no matter when supper was to be served. She remembered her stories, almost legends by then, of how her father and her Grandfather Vassimont had brought grape seedlings from France, hiding them in the linings of their trousers as they passed through Ellis Island. Jen had no idea if the stories were factual, but if Grandma Dupere said it was true, then it was so.

"Where did you get those names?" Jen asked haltingly. Although the names were significant to Jen, she knew that in the Internet age, it was information that probably could be dug up by a scam artist.

A female voice spoke into the speakerphone. "As we said, Mrs. Manton, as part of the university's grant we have been conducting a scholarly analysis of the roots of Christian theology, and your family tree comes into question." Fahey was as subtle as a baseball bat. "Although we believe our search has been exhaustive we would like to confirm a few items with you."

"I'm listening." Jen didn't like this intrusion into her privacy nor the inquisitorial tone of Fahey. But she wanted to get to the bottom of this scam. "Shoot."

"Look Mrs. Manton, I know this sounds strange, but believe me, we are who we say we are and we know that our findings will be of utmost interest to you. It is a little too complicated to detail on the telephone, and we would prefer to meet with you as soon as possible to discuss our findings and verify our research on your family tree."

Maybe I've inherited some money from my long lost relatives in France. Jen hopefully searched for some rhyme or reason to this call. "I'll tell you what, I'll meet you at a Starbucks across from where I work after my shift tomorrow. You bring some proof of who you are. If you aren't up-and-up I'll walk out with my coffee and you've wasted your time."

To her surprise, the supposed professors agreed. Jen gave them directions and hung up the receiver.

"Who was that?" Rick was stumped on the entire 'Western Civilization' column and appreciated an excuse to stop.

"Not really sure," Jen said, paying more attention to the next category than her husband. She knew he was looking to create a distraction. "They claimed to be some professors working on some research project. I told 'em to call me at the office."

"Professors? Really?"

"I don't know. Probably going to show up with a cart of Tupperware ... c'mon, last chance, 'Irish Literature' ... I'm ahead by a million by now."

"Great." The only Irish literature Rick had ever read was on the back of a Jameson's bottle. He slouched back to admire his wife at work.

* * *

On the Rhône River

Father Bernard Delacroix couldn't decide if it was better to stand and look at the sky, or lay by the side of the barge and watch the current run by the green banks. He had tried both ways and had been violently ill with both. It was true that floating down the Rhône was much quicker and less strenuous than walking, or even riding, but the newly ordained priest wasn't sure it was worth the pain in his stomach that once again was pushing its contents upward.

It had taken him three weeks, resting on the Sabbath, to walk from Orléans to Chalon-sur-Saône, nearly two hundred and eighty kilometers. He had now covered that much distance in four days as the Saône had blended into the Rhône and pushed the barge southward toward the Mediterranean Sea.

"How are you doing, Father?" the captain of the barge asked. With powerful forearms from years of pushing the barge back up this river with long wooden poles, the oarsman looked rougher than he was. Actually, years of traveling the river, and a native intelligence, made him as cultured as anyone Delacroix had met, or would meet, on the entire trip.

The captain was honored to have the spiritual presence of Delacroix on his boat. Whatever bad happened on the river was attributed to bad luck or curses, and having a clergyman on board would certainly temper both. The oarsman worried however, that the periodic vomiting of the priest did not portend only good luck.

"Not so well," Delacroix answered truthfully. "How much further to Avignon?"

The oarsman eyed a hard scramble set of shacks along the west bank. It told him their location. "Aye, I'd say we should be there long before sundown."

"I think I should leave you there," said Delacroix.

"But you paid to go to Arles," protested the captain. He did not want to refund any portion of his fee. Arles was only a few hours past Avignon anyway.

"I shall not ask for a refund." Delacroix had anticipated the objection. "But I believe that the roads west are as good from Avignon as they are from Arles," he explained, momentarily forgetting his nausea with the thought of getting back on land.

"Wouldn't know. Where you headed, Father?"

"Rennes-le-Château."

The oarsman shook his head. "Never heard of it."

"It is in Languedoc."

"Mon Dieu, Father, why are you going there? They aren't Christians, you know," the man said, showing his displeasure with Delacroix's plight.

"They most certainly are Roman Catholics. I am to lead the parish there," Delacroix said proudly, with a hint of defiance.

"Ah, maybe, but they are Cathars first," the oarsman said. "You know about them, don't you?"

"I have been informed," Delacroix replied flatly.

"Then you know that they deny the Lord's crucifixion and resurrection."

Delacroix hadn't recalled that rather significant detail and his face showed it.

"Aye, and they are obsessed with the struggle between God and Rex Mundi."

"What is that?" The Latin phrase was foreign to Delacroix.

"Who," corrected the captain. "It is the devil. They actually see him, I'm told. For them life is a daily contest between God and this anti-god. So they use the teachings of Our Lord to hold him off."

Delacroix didn't want to say that such beliefs were not totally aberrant from his own. Weren't the Lord's teachings supposed to ward off evil?

The captain spat into the river. "I even heard from people coming up the river from there that some of them refuse to kill and eat fowl or beast. And Father, I cannot tell you the stories I have heard of the deviate sexual practices ..." The captain glanced at the priest. He had gone too far, and retreated to a safer subject.

"Some of them Cathars are said to take vows of poverty and chastity. Without entering the priesthood! And everybody knows that they will not swear oaths using the name of God. Now Father, how can the Church maintain order in the face of such heresy?"

By now, Delacroix, too, was nodding his assent.

To some extent, the charges of blasphemy were true. Many Cathars abstained from sex, wealth or meat. They believed that oaths using the name of God were irreverent and should be avoided. Homosexuality was not unknown. But in reality, the Cathars were harmless pacifists. In a modern era they would have been dismissed as eccentric individualists. They had drifted to the Cathar thought in a passive rebellion against the generations of neglect and abuse inflicted upon them at the hands of Catholic administrators such as the panel that had indoctrinated Delacroix. As a consequent of the religious oppression upon them, the Cathars were liberal in their belief that God was benevolent, and that other religions and philosophical thought should be tolerated.

"Are they not merely naive?" Delacroix asked the question that had been gnawing at him since Paris. He liked to see the best in people, and this was his way of excusing their heresies. He could be bolder now in the safety of this barge, far from official eyes.

"Naive?" The boatman mulled over the possibility as he pushed hard on the oar to steer the barge toward the middle of the river, and to miss a shoal that Delacroix could not see. "Yes. I suppose you could look at it that way. They don't seem to hurt anybody. Except for going to hell," he added quickly, glancing at the priest.

The barge passed over a swirling current and bobbed rapidly. Delacroix's stomach revolted at the motion. He fell to his knees and vomited over the side.

The oarsman grimaced. "Maybe departing at Avignon is a good idea, Father."

*　　*　　*

Starbucks

As Jen slipped on her jacket she congratulated herself on telling the so-called professors to meet her at Starbucks. She always went there anyway after work for her reward. Decaf latte. She hadn't given last night's conversation much thought since she had completed her route in Final Jeopardy, but what thought she did give it was skeptical. This way she wouldn't feel so foolish if they didn't show up as she fully expected.

Jen wasn't surprised when Angie, the Starbucks server, called out to her when she walked in. Her frequent visits, and prominent name tag, made familiarity easy. But this time Angie leaned over the counter, conspiratorially.

"Coupla people asking for you," she whispered. "They look like a couple of real partyers." Jen knew she meant just the opposite.

"Professor-looking types?"

"Down to the brown Hush Puppies and horned-rim glasses. The guy would be kind of cute, out of corduroy, anyway. They gave me these cards." Angie handed over two sturdy manila business cards. Jen glanced at them. They looked legitimate. Red raised crests above their names, proclaiming their affiliation with the Boston University School of Theology.

"Which ones are they?"

"Last booth. I'll bring you your decaf."

Jen took a breath. Something to break up a routine day, she thought and walked through the shop to the last booth.

The professors saw her approaching and awkwardly half rose in the booth. They had an air of, academia, was the only word to describe it. Hershner spoke first, "Mrs. Manton, we appreciate this opportunity."

"No problem. How was the drive?" There was no reason not to be civil. He looked to Fahey to shake hands, but the severe woman was already seated, clicking open the clasps of her well-traveled briefcase.

"Fine, thank you." Hershner was apparently the friendly side of this duo. He shook hands with Jen. Fahey looked up and stuck her hand out as an afterthought.

"What can I do for you?" Jen gave them until her latte was ready to explain what they *really* were up to.

"As we stated, we have been researching the roots of Christianity," Hershner proceeded cautiously.

Fahey jumped in and picked up the pace. "Actually, 'researching' doesn't do our project justice. We have spent the greater part of the last six years conferring with theologians, coordinating professors and graduate assistants in six different universities. We have supervised investigators and archeologists in three countries, in formulating our theories and developing our theses."

Fahey appeared to be on a timetable herself. "Having uncovered conclusive evidence establishing an unaccepted and later disavowed lineage of Christ, it was a logical extension, although not necessary for our publication, to trace those roots as far as possible. We were a bit surprised that the line did not end. Statistically you would have expected that."

Jen resisted the temptation to say 'Huh'? "What does this have to do with me?" she asked firmly.

"Centuries of historians and theologians believed that Jesus Christ had descendants who fled to southern France to escape persecution. Those families flourished. Historically the growth of a large Jewish community along the Mediterranean coast is well accepted and supports that belief. That kingdom, 'Septamia', as it has been called, waned as time went on. It was believed that its people were extinct or at least had dissipated into extinction for statistical purposes. However, our contemporary archeological findings from the Middle Ages have revealed evidence that the line did not go completely dormant as had been believed. We have followed those family lines, which were well documented by a French secret society, through the Vassimonts to your maternal grandmother, Claudette Dupere." Fahey looked proud.

Jen was still confused by the explanation, but didn't want to appear as baffled as she was.

"So you're telling me that I come from one the oldest lines of Christians from this Jewish Kingdom?" This would be quite a story for Rick. She always told him they should go to church more often than Easter and Christmas.

Fahey looked disgusted. Hershner leaned forward. "No. Mrs. Manton, we are telling you that you are a direct descendent of Jesus Christ."

Jen leaned back and smiled. "Right. And there is Elvis two booths over." She didn't know whether to laugh with them at the afternoon's diversion or just get up and run.

"Here's your decaf," Angie announced. Time was up.

"Professors, I'm afraid I have some business to attend to. If you'll excuse me."

"Mrs. Manton, I know this sounds far-fetched, but please allow us..." Hershner was likable enough, but Jen had had her fill. She didn't even know what she was fixing for supper yet.

"Far-fetched? I think you are both ... well, I don't know what your angle was in coming here, but I'm not buying." She stood up.

Fahey didn't seem to care and was packing her papers as efficiently as she had pulled them out. "You know that we're going to the press with this anyway?" It was more of a threat than a question.

Jen glared at her. She had her limits.

Fahey continued, oblivious to the stare, "We've spent eight years on this project. It's history. It's public knowledge. We've prepared a draft of our theses for the New York Times and we're meeting with the editorial staff next week to discuss publication. We felt we owed you the courtesy of knowing what was coming."

"What is coming! My God, you both are crazy."

Hershner saw Fahey bristle. He didn't come here to start a fight. This had gone even worse than Hershner had feared. He could sympathize with Jen's disbelief. He had the same feelings early on in their research.

"Mrs. Manton, why don't you look at what we are going to give to the Times? I've got copies of the parts that relate to your family. Please. Just look at it. You can see everything we've developed."

"Whether you want to or not," Fahey couldn't resist a last jab.

Jen reluctantly took the thick folder that Hershner held out. Curiosity and cats, she mused. She purposefully turned her shoulder to Fahey and spoke to Hershner. "I'll take a look. And I've got your cards. But don't hold your breath."

*   *   *

On the road to Rennes-le-Château

Newly ordained Father Bernard Delacroix led his donkey slowly along the dusty, winding path into the village of Rennes-le-Château. Even by standards of the thirteenth century, the trail was rough. His only worldly possessions, a reddish-purple ceremonial robe and a brown cotton sackcloth identical to the one he was wearing, were bundled in a burlap blanket, and strapped to his lower back to brace against the rhythmic jarring as the tired beast picked its way along the rutted trail.

At a turnoff from the path, Delacroix pulled lightly on the leather reigns to stop the weary animal. She was more than willing to comply. Delacroix leaned forward and slung his leg behind him and slid his pudgy frame to the dusty ground. The grateful donkey drifted to a few tufts of long grass growing in the shade of a wiry shrub. There was no need to tie her up. She wouldn't stray farther than the grass until she had to, and then reluctantly.

Lifting his wide-brimmed straw hat, Delacroix wiped tiny beads of sweat from high on his forehead. He stiffly walked to the side of the trail. He had been traveling for three weeks now. His body was used to his prior sedentary life. The trip on the barge down the Rhône to Avignon had been miserable at times, but, looking back, had been sheer comfort compared to his last five days of his journey, primarily uphill from the cooler coastlands into the arid foothills leading to the now looming mountain range.

Delacroix enjoyed the magnificent view until he looked down. In front of him the ground dropped precipitously into a dry ravine hundreds of feet below. He timidly backed away from the edge to admire the scenery without fear. He was not used to heights. This land was not at all like the lush and fertile, but relatively gentle, hills of the Loire Valley that surrounded his church in Orléans, now some three hundred kilometers distant. He knew in his mind that he would never return there.

Moving into the shade of an ancient oak tree that leaned away from the floor of the valley, the product of years of wind gusting out of the mountain passes to the broader northern plains. Delacroix gazed at the panorama before him, amazed by the stark beauty. To him this region did not look at all like the France he knew. It was dry and rugged. And with each day that he traveled south the rocky passes grew steeper. Gnarled trees dotted the northern sides of the canyons where the first travelers, centuries before, had wisely started the first trails partially shaded from the strong southern sun.

This is what Delacroix thought Spain would look like. It made sense that it would, it was only another days' ride to the border. Languedoc was not officially a part of the Kingdom of France, but its people lacked cohesiveness and power to be truly independent. They shared a common language with the French and homage was grudgingly paid to the French King, as well as the Holy Father in Rome, just as was mandatory in northern France.

A hot, dry, breeze from the canyon blew into Delacroix's face. In the distance, to the south, he could make out a village, which, by the directions he had received the night before, had to be Rennes-le-Château. It was not an impressive sight, visible only because it perched on a small, steep hill in the middle of the broad sweeping valley. The priest squinted hard and identified the square silhouette of what had been described to him as the village "cathedral." By northern standards it did not justify such a grand description. To Delacroix it merely looked like a large church although it was faced with an imposing Gothic facade that made it appear grander than its size warranted. But it had survived the judgment of time and had stood as a landmark in the area for over two hundred years.

The cathedral hovered at the end of a line of box-shaped storefronts that constituted the town square. In orderly streets, circling the sides of the hill, stood rows of low-lying stone houses where the more prosperous merchants and village notables lived. On the outskirts of the villages lay a vaster section of ramshackle wooden and dirt huts of the serfs and servants.

Had Delacroix's eyes been stronger, he also would have seen a massive man-made stone castle wall high on the foot of the mountain on the far side of the valley. In the low afternoon sun, the gray stones brilliantly reflected the rays, and the white glow could be seen for miles. The castle, and manor behind its walls, was simply referred to as "Blanchefort." It was no longer known whether the castle, whose name meant roughly "White Fort," was named after the Blanchefort family which had occupied it for centuries, or whether the family had taken its name from the gleaming castle walls which were built generations before last names were of common usage for non-nobility.

In the shade of the oak, the dry wind quickly cooled Delacroix. There was less humidity here than in the lowlands, making up in comfort for the increased intensity of the sun. Delacroix kicked his legs from side to side and waved his arms in a last attempt to loosen his aching muscles. He had heard that there were hot springs in the mountains. He hoped it was true. A hot bath would feel wonderful.

The donkey looked ruefully over her shoulder as Delacroix began the awkward process of crawling back into riding position. Bouncing his generous torso onto her back, Delacroix wrapped an arm around her neck and, lying flat, swung one leg across her hind quarters and pushed himself upright.

With no haste in her steps, the donkey plodded back onto the trail. Both donkey and rider hoped to end their journey before nightfall.

The parish that Father Bernard Delacroix was inheriting consisted of numerous small hamlets in addition to Rennes-le-Château. News of the appointment of a northern priest was warily received by the parishioners. He was replacing a very popular clergyman who had served in a non-threatening manner for eighteen years before going blind and dying of what, centuries later, would be known to be diabetes. Delacroix was acutely aware of his predicament as he saw the spires of the cathedral draw nearer. By this time, however, he was so tired that any trepidation was secondary to rest.

The centerpiece of Rennes-le-Château was its cathedral which had been built in 1059 on what was then the edge of the village. It had been consecrated to Mary Magdalen. Although the building did not impress Delacroix, particularly having just visited Nôtre Dame, its size and beauty was remarkable for this location so far from the traditional centers of commerce. A series of thin, twisting spires rose from the facade. Lining a sweeping arch over the main entrance were three foot tall limestone statues of the major saints and apostles. Narrow stain glass windows ran the length of both the east and west sides. Although covered with a film of dust, patches of color hinted at the brilliance that one would behold inside.

Delacroix's mule clomped up to the flagstones in front of the cathedral. The front door swept open and a troop of brown-robed brothers, notified of the priest's arrival by a swift child one hamlet to the south, swept forward to greet their new appointed leader.

"God greets you to our humble village, Father Delacroix," called out the brother in the lead. He was tall and thin with an angular face. He was not the oldest in the group, he looked to be still in his twenties, but, because he was the quickest among them, had been unofficially installed as their spokesperson.

Delacroix was exhausted and merely replied, "I am thankful to be here."

"It is a thankless journey, yes?" said the brother. Without pausing for an answer, he continued, "I am Brother Francois. Please come out of the sun."

Delacroix gratefully entered the cathedral as Francois rapidly introduced the others. The interior was dark and cramped by the new standards for the great cathedrals such as Delacroix had seen in Paris. The walls, stained dark from smoke from animal fat candles, were adorned with round wooden carvings of the stages of the cross depicting the events leading to Christ's death. Rows of rough hewn wooden pews, made smooth by decades of wear, were closed packed together. Only the radiant colored light angling sharply from the stained glass to the floor added life to the drabness.

Francois led Delacroix through the cathedral, expounding on attributes of the cathedral and, in the same breath, the town in general. Delacroix tried in vain to absorb the details.

At the rear of the building a stout wooden door opened onto a covered causeway that ran to a sprawling stone monastery that housed the order of brothers, who, though not sworn to poverty, as was becoming fashionable throughout Christianized Europe, lived a meager existence, though not significantly harder than the rest of the populace.

Mercifully, Francois led Delacroix directly through the complex to the priest's quarters which consisted of a separate combination sleeping room, study and grotto in the rear southern corner. The monastery was austere compared to what Delacroix had left in Orleans, but he was not discouraged, rationalizing that the conditions would steel him to the task he had been given.

"High mass has been scheduled for tomorrow to celebrate your arrival," Francois informed Delacroix. "With your approval," he added, before mischievously continuing, "unless, of course, you prefer to conduct it at sundown."

Delacroix began to protest, but stopped, quickly recognizing the jest in Francois face. Puzzled, he said, "Tomorrow will be fine, Francois."

"I thought so." Backing out the door, Francois offered, "If you need anything within our humble means, just call out and I will see that it is provided."

Delacroix stared at the door as Francois closed it behind him. He said a silent prayer that God would grant him wisdom to know whether the loquacious brother could be trusted.

Brother Francois knocked on Delacroix's door long before the sun had peeked over the eastern foothills. Delacroix was awake and dressed and accepted the offer to be escorted to the dining area, a long row of rough wooden tables adjacent to the kitchen in the rear of the monastery. Delacroix was ravenous and didn't mind Francois' continuing talkative mood.

After a silent blessing of the food Francois offered, "If it pleases you, Father, I will tell you of those that you will meet today."

Delacroix was already rolling a large mouthful of steamed oats in his mouth and merely nodded. It was sufficient encouragement for Francois.

"Most certainly mass will be attended by Sir Frederick Lancel of Blanchefort." Francois paused to look for a flicker of recognition by Delacroix. There was none. The intelligence reports of the Church provided to Delacroix had not gone to such detail.

Satisfied that he was the lone source of information, Francois continued, "Lancel is the most powerful man in the valley. His holdings include the majority of the surrounding farmlands and forests. His wealth is vast." Francois seemed to be building toward something important. "He is the maternal grandson of Bertrand de Blanchefort, the fourth grand master of the Order of the Knights Templar."

The mention of the Knights Templar secured Delacroix's attention. "Go on," he said, reaching for the tankard of warm, fresh milk.

"The grandfather, Bertrand, who is now deceased over three decades, came from a Cathar family."

Delacroix nodded to indicate that he was not ignorant of the Cathars.

"Bertrand persuaded the Cathar landowners to donate tracts of land and wealth to help create the Knights Templar. He of course, was grand master, and with this wealth he built the castle Blanchefort which is on a hilltop a short ride from Rennes-le-Château. His grandson is said to carry many of the same ... characteristics ... of his influential grandfather."

"He is a Cathar?" inquired Delacroix.

"Yes."

"And a Knight Templar."

"Yes," answered Francois. "The grand master."

Delacroix nodded thoughtfully. Perhaps the situation was as bad as forewarned.

"The knights are always generous in their donations to the Church. Lancel insists upon it, we are told," Francois said. He was treading carefully now. "You know that as servants of the Pope, the Order of the Knights Templar is exempt from tithing."

"It is the same where I came from." Except that Delacroix knew that Knights Templar in the north rarely contributed more than a pittance to support the local parishes.

"Of course, of course," retreated Francois. "I just wanted to let Your Highness know that Cathars are not enemies of the Church. At least, not around here."

Delacroix eyed Francois suspiciously. Time would tell. Francois wisely changed the subject to the strength of this year's crops raised by the brothers.

At dawn the cathedral bells pealed in a long familiar code that informed the distant farms that mass would be held at noon. Word was spread. Daily chores were suspended. All would attend. This was not a ceremony to shake hands and get to know the town. The ritualistic mass followed closely those being conducted throughout Europe, beginning with a lengthy chanting of the monks, followed by readings in Latin and responsive prayers.

Lancel's presence was conspicuous in the front pew that, for generations, had been reserved for his family. Delacroix took it as a good sign that he had even come to the unscheduled mass.

The mass with a twenty minute prayer by Delacroix, in French, extolling the divinely inspired wisdom of His Holiness, the Pope, and the necessity for obedience to the Church's directives. Having listed intently, the parishioners reverently backed out of the cathedral, genuflecting and returning to their interrupted tasks.

Having conducted his own official inauguration, Delacroix retreated to the monastery. He was to wait for a length of time sufficient to allow the village notables to assemble in the entrance of the cathedral. It was a part of the time-honored ritual. He was anxious, not knowing what to expect from the heretics he had been indoctrinated that he would encounter.

Francois tapped on his door and entered.

"Are you ready to meet the people, Father?" he asked.

"Yes, Brother Francois. Are there many?" Delacroix was not experienced in this part of the job and was anxious.

Francois could see the uncertainty in Delacroix. The news was not good. "Why almost every land or shop owner in the valley awaits."

Delacroix did not try to hide his grimace.

"We shall keep them moving, M'Lord. And the Knights Templar are generally men of very few words. They shall not engage you long," Francois assured him. "Others can be wordy," he apologized. Delacroix wondered if Francois included himself in the "others."

Delacroix said a silent prayer and reentered the rear of the cathedral. His arrival was announced with the booming baritone of the largest of the brothers. The gathered crowd shuffled to attention and lined up behind Lancel. Without further ceremony, Francois introduced Delacroix.

"Father, I present to you, Sir Frederick Lancel of Blanchefort."

The knight was tall by medieval standards, nearly six feet, made all the more imposing by his long, shiny black hair that hung in loose curls down to his shoulders. A trace of an old scar crossed the dimple in his left cheek which gave him an air of danger tempered by friendliness.

Lancel bowed slowly, causing his white scarf emblazoned with the unmistakable cross of the Knights Templar to hang at the feet of Delacroix. "Welcome, your Grace, to Rennes-le-Château."

Raising to full height, Lancel was eye to eye with Delacroix who was standing two steps up on the altar. Lancel flashed a smile which caused his scar to disappear into his dimple. "I hope our dusty roads have not treated you too irreverently. Each spring the rains wash up entire carts which had been lost in the bottom of our ruts."

Delacroix startled at the mysterious comment until he realized that it was meant as good-natured small talk. Hardly the harsh reception he had been anticipating. "I'm afraid I did find it a bit challenging," stammered Delacroix.

Lancel roared with laughter. "Challenging? Your Grace's kindness is only exceeded by his nimble tongue." To Delacroix this handsome knight, his supposed antagonist, seemed perfectly at ease. And the comfort seemed genuine.

"If you please, your Grace." Lancel turned his head and issued a sharp command that startled Delacroix. "Joseph, come." Instantly, a young boy, barely three years old, deliberately marched forward, a solemn look locked on his face. "My son, Joseph."

The boy still had his baby fat, but he also had the dark good looks of his father. With a slight tap on the back of his head Joseph bowed low. He had a miniature version of his father's scarf that hung to the ground.

With a forced deep voice, Joseph raised up and huffed, "Welcome, your Grace, to Rennes-le-Château." He then looked up at his father and flashed the grin that had been passed down to him at birth. Recovering quickly, he returned his mock scowl as his father nodded his approval.

"Hopefully, your Grace, this weed won't be too much of a burr in your sandal," said Lancel.

In spite of his recent warnings Delacroix could not help but feel relief by the sincere, but comical display of Joseph. He placed his hand on the boy's curly locks. "I shall welcome a strong, young knight to lend a hand in the Lord's work."

Cognizant of the numbers behind him, Lancel terminated the conversation. "Good day, Father. I am sure that we will be meeting again soon."

Joseph stepped forward and repeated, "Good day, Father." Then he hesitated before blurting out the rest of his speech, "Meet again soon."

Delacroix smiled. His contact with children had been limited in Orleans. It seemed less rigid here. It would take some adjusting, but it did not feel uncomfortable to him. "And good day to you, Joseph. I look forward to meeting with you again."

Joseph beamed as he turned to follow his father out of the room.

A string of knights, landowners and merchants followed for introduction, all subservient to Lancel either by rank or economics. When the cathedral was nearly emptied an hour later, Delacroix was eager to get off of his feet. A priest was not high enough in rank not to greet the members standing up. He was dismayed to see the front door open slightly to allow another new face to slip in.

Delacroix heard Francois groan lightly. He was glad to know that the younger man was also tired of standing. But as the person in front of them moved on, Francois leaned over and whispered into his ear, "That one that just came in. He will talk until your ears turn to turnips."

Delacroix slumped. It was the worst possible news.

The line had dwindled now to the latecomer who approached Delacroix and turned his shoulder slightly and leaned in.

"Good afternoon, Brother," he said to Francois. The brother did not bother with an introduction.

"Jacques Boulanger," said the man, nodding slightly in a modified bow. "Metalware. Not blacksmithing. Fine metalware. For trade."

"It is a pleasure to meet you," Delacroix said, trying to put a dismissive tone in his voice.

Boulanger looked at Francois. "Brother, I need just a minute with the Father. Alone." Delacroix protested. "Monsieur, I am certain that we will be able to talk another day."

"No, Father. Just a moment. Really." He looked imploringly between the two and did not move.

"Just a moment," Delacroix said, more to Francois than to Boulanger.

"As you wish, M'Lord," responded Francois, retreating out of ear shot.

He was a smallish man, in his mid-thirties, which was middle-aged for the century. He had deep-set blue eyes that would have been becoming except for the way they darted restlessly, giving Delacroix a feeling of unease.

Boulanger got quickly to the point of his visit. "I saw Frederick Lancel leaving the cathedral. You should know that he, and those of his ilk, those Knights Templar, believe that they are above the word of our Lord. They claim divinity, you know?" he whined. "I do hope you have been warned of the heretics in our midst."

The bluntness of the statement surprised Delacroix. He responded impatiently, "I have been apprised of the circumstances here."

The tone did not deter Boulanger. "I'm sure. But if you want to know what's really going on, I can tell you. In my business, I get around."

"That will be helpful," said Delacroix, looking to Francois for relief. Francois was leaning against the wall, rubbing his feet, and did not notice.

Boulanger leaned in farther. "We hear that the Pope has finally had enough of this royal bloodline talk. So you should know that Lancel of Blancheforte is the leader of the Prieuré de Sion. He claims he is a direct descendant of Our Lord Jesus Christ."

Despite himself, Delacroix could not help but listen.

Boulanger continued rapidly, "He'll be good to the Church on his face. Oh, very good. And he'll have you thinking he isn't part of the bloodline. But the society still holds their secret meetings every month. And if you're not one of them, you better not go near. I have seen the blasphemy that goes on."

Francois shuffled noisily toward them. "Father, your other duties beckon."

Delacroix looked at Boulanger who, to the priest's shock, winked.

"If you need me, Father, Francois here knows my shop."

"I thank thee for thy counsel, Monsieur. The Church shares your concern with those that have strayed too far from its teachings."

Delacroix watched with confused thoughts as Boulanger turned and limped out of the cathedral.

"Ahhhh," sighed Francois. "Dear Jacques Boulanger. I am certain that he had no kind words for Sir Lancel. But I'm sure that he didn't tell you that he was once a member of the Prieuré de Sion. He has been Lancel's enemy for years now, ever since it was discovered that his claims were counterfeit."

Delacroix turned to walk back to the monastery where he hoped to rest. Francois followed alongside.

"Tell me, Brother Francois," he asked, "do you find this Prieuré de Sion dangerous?"

"Father, I have lived here all my life and I have seen no danger. In fact, all of those in the brotherhood are all Knights Templar. I don't see how Rennes-le-Château would survive without them."

They slowly paced a few more steps. "But don't you know that it is heresy...this bloodline they speak of?" challenged Delacroix.

Francois stopped and the men faced each other. Francois' face showed his confusion. "Heresy? Why I never thought of it that way, M'Lord. They cause no harm." Francois looked at the floor. "Heresy?" he mumbled, but did not speak further.

It was the first time Delacroix had seen Francois speechless, and, somehow, it was uncomfortable.

"Never mind now, Brother. Perhaps there is much we can teach each other about your land." He put his arm on Francois' shoulder and they returned to the monastery.

*   *   *

Shortly after dawn on the third morning after his arrival, Delacroix knelt for his morning devotion in the grotto dedicated to the blessed Virgin Mother. His knees ached on the cold slate floor as he peered up at a crude, but colorful painting of Mother Mary. She was dressed in blue, the color of royalty that had long since been decided was what she had always worn. Around her head was a golden halo that reflected the glimmer of light in the entryway behind Delacroix. He did not notice the contrast between the smooth layers of heavy oil and the rough, two-panel wooden board on which it was painted. It was not as fine as the works he had seen in Paris, nor even as nice as he had grown up with in Orleans. But he had not expected as much in this far off village. For a man of the cloth, it was the symbolism and the peacefulness of this secluded nave that provided strength and inspiration.

On the panel opposite the Holy Mother, was another painting of a woman, apparently by the same local artist. Its presence troubled Delacroix. His concern was not with artistic quality. The painting was equally crafted, but Delacroix knew by the beauty of the subject, and the flowing red gown, that it was the likeness of Mary Magdalen. Delacroix had seen her likeness in churches throughout France. She was revered as a companion of Christ who stood at the foot of his cross on the most holy of days. But now Delacroix was informed that in Languedoc, Mary Magdalen was worshipped on almost the same level of devotion of the Virgin. He was warned to watch for such shocking heresies.

This morning, however, Delacroix was praying for guidance. He purposefully turned his shoulders to more directly face the likeness of the Virgin Mary. Since his arrival in Rennes-le-Château, he had been faced with contrasting tales. It was hard to decipher friend from foe. Some of the sources were incredible. Others forthrightly confirmed the warnings of the archbishop's emissaries. But still others were only interested in soliciting Delacroix for the lucrative contracts needed for the parish's subsistence. They would tell him whatever they perceived that he wanted to hear. Delacroix was to report back to the archbishop, but as of yet, the only conclusion he had drawn was that he was hopelessly confused and dismayed. He had always wanted to administer to the needs of a parish, not spy upon its people.

Delacroix's prayer was interrupted by one of the brown smocked brothers who hesitantly announced that Sir Frederick Lancel had arrived and was asking to meet. Delacroix replied that they could meet in the study in a few minutes, and turned to complete his prayer.

As Delacroix was signing himself the silence of the grotto was shattered by a loud voice.

"I found him!" Joseph had bustled into the entryway. "Good morning, m'Lord."

Delacroix was prepared to deliver a stern lecture for such a violation of the sanctity of God's house, but as he turned he saw the grinning little boy bow deeply, lose his balance, and fall over onto his palms. Delacroix heard the strong rustling of leather pantaloons as Lancel turned the corner. His face was red.

"Forgive me, Father. This boy has missed the guidance of a firm hand." Lancel was glaring at his son who was still on his hands and feet and was peering up under his armpit.

Instead of quaking with fright, Joseph lifted his head up, and whinnied his best horse imitation. In spite of themselves, both Lancel and Delacroix laughed out loud.

Quickly regaining his fatherly composure, Lancel commanded, "Joseph, on your feet. This is the Lord's house. We pay respect here."

Joseph, even at this tender age, knew the limits of his father's patience. "Yes sir," he said cheerfully and rose rigidly to attention. Lancel looked at Delacroix with the ageless look of a helpless father.

"Never mind, Sir Frederick. I am glad to see the boy knows his way around God's house. I am sure his knowledge of the rules will follow." Delacroix recalled none too fondly the strict requirements imposed on his every move as a young boy. Although he was inclined to issue the same code of conduct, he recoiled at personally enforcing it. Joseph looked up at Delacroix skeptically.

"We apologize for the intrusion, but we came to town yesterday and my mare became lame." Lancel rode only mares. He had learned on his expeditions for the Church that they were quicker and more nimble than the larger and more impressive steeds. "We spent the night at the inn."

"May we be of assistance?" Delacroix asked, speaking for the entire abbey.

"Thank you for your offer, your Grace. Last night I was able to negotiate for a fine mare that I've had my eye on for some time. Then as it turns out, my mare is not lame. She had picked up a thistle in her shank that we did not discover in the dark. Now I have an extra mount."

"Good fortune." Delacroix was slightly uncomfortable with the small talk.

"What my father meant was, will you come for a ride with us into the mountains? It's great fun. He said you could come," Joseph explained earnestly.

"Boy! I shall speak for myself." Joseph retreated to attention.

Delacroix began to offer an excuse, thinking that this was another attempt to curry favor.

Lancel was insistent. "Father, you have come to the most beautiful countryside created on earth. But you cannot see it well from Rennes-le-Château. I know that you come from the grand city of Orleans. I have been there, and it has its charm. But the view from these hills, well, it was sculpted by God. We would be honored to lead you on some of the best paths to see His work. I swear I will not take you on the goat trails you traveled on the way to our fair village."

Joseph's eyes were pleading. Delacroix did long to explore the surrounding area, but had not had a moment of spare time since his arrival. Yet he was wary of going into the woods with the knight who was supposed to be the instigator of the heretics. As he pondered the offer, Joseph's face registered his mounting disappointment. It confirmed to Delacroix that this strange proposal could not be a plot for treachery or bribery. He would risk taking the excursion. He told himself that, if nothing else, he would get to know his chief rival so as to report to the Archbishop his findings.

"I will be honored to accept your guidance," Delacroix replied.

Joseph's face froze as he tried to interpret the response. He looked up at his father who nodded and smiled. His young body could barely contain his excitement. "Can I ride with Father Della ... Della ...?" Joseph stumbled over the name.

"Father Delacroix. And the answer is no. We will let him see the countryside without the chatter of a little imp."

When Delacroix informed the senior brothers of his plans, they were aghast. Out of hearing of Lancel, they protested Delacroix's decision. It was inappropriate to be seen socializing with the leader of the Knights Templar. The appearance was not good to the townspeople, they argued. Delacroix had expected this reaction, but their pettiness only reassured him that a day away was a splendid idea.

* * *

Although the morning was less than an hour old, Rennes-le-Château was buzzing with activity. Sunlight dictated when work would be done. But the merchants and customers all paused to stare as Lancel and Joseph pranced by on the new mare, followed closely, and less confidently, by the new priest on the old mare that all knew belonged to the knight. Not a word was spoken by the on-lookers until the riders left the square. They would speak of little else the rest of the day.

Lancel did indeed know the best paths. Narrow, but smooth, they wound up the steep, rocky hills. Testing the new mount's responsiveness to the bridle, father and son would gallop ahead and await Delacroix on the side of the trail, often studying something they had spied in the bushes or in the distance. Where there was room to ride side by side, Lancel would identify terrain features and describe to Delacroix the location of hidden hamlets and the best streams from which to refresh. Joseph, riding in front of his father on a specially prepared saddle, was quick to point out every movement in the woods and every call of a bird.

"Did you hear that Father Della-craw? Did you? That was spotted grouse. Wasn't it Father?"

"Yes, perhaps, Son."

"They're real good eating. Have you ever had one Father?"

Delacroix smiled at the youthful enthusiasm. "I can't say that I have."

"Let's have him over for the next hunt, Father," he said, looking over his shoulder. "Then he could have one." Joseph felt sorry for such a deprived man who had never tasted spotted grouse.

"That's a fine idea," Lancel agreed.

As the path narrowed in the higher elevations, Lancel took the lead. Delacroix ambled behind, looking at the broad back of this influential knight and his chattering son. This tranquil scene was certainly not what he had expected.

After riding for an hour the trail led deep into the mountains where the larger trees covered the path with a canopy of leaves that cooled the air. Before the sun was directly overhead, they had reached a long, narrow lake that reflected the surrounding peaks in its crystal clear blue waters. They dismounted by a stream that flowed from thundering falls and fed the lake. Delacroix's experienced mare clomped quickly to the water.

Lancel untied a satchel from his impatient horse and slapped its rear. Brushing dust from his leather pants and reaching into a flap on his leg, Lancel suddenly pulled out a wide, thin-bladed knife. Delacroix stepped back warily as Lancel reached into the pouch and withdrew a large ball of cheese. Holding the cheese in one hand, Lancel swiftly sliced a large slab of the cheese and, pinning it to the blade of the knife with his thumb, held out the knife to offer it to the priest. Delacroix hesitated in reaching for the cheese and looked up into Lancel's eyes.

"Fromage. It's old," Lancel responded, misinterpreting the clergyman's hesitancy. He was giving the cheese his ultimate compliment. It was not too young and had ripened properly. Its pungent odor indicated it was fit to be consumed.

Delacroix blushed at his unjustified fears and delicately lifted the cheese from the blade. Lancel dug into his sack and removed a squat loaf of bread which he ripped in half and handed to Delacroix before strolling toward the lake.

Food in hand, Delacroix followed Lancel's lead and sat on the smooth, pebbly shore of the stream and ripped at the hard crust with his teeth. Joseph sat at his father's side, mimicking his every move. After a rigorous mouthful, all three leaned over the stream and cupped handfuls of clear, cold water. This was the highest elevation to which Delacroix had ever ascended, and the thin air intensified all of his senses. Food and water had never tasted as refreshing.

"May I go swimming, Father?" Joseph asked after hurriedly eating his portion. Lancel knew that 'swimming' meant splashing in the shallow waters.

"Certainly."

"Do you want to swim, too, Father Della-craw?" Joseph struggled with his name. "It warms up after you get in."

"Joseph, I'm afraid that men of the cloth are not allowed to swim. But the Bible does not prohibit that pleasure to young men."

"Oooh," said Joseph, realizing how harsh of a life this man had. No grouse. No swimming. He resolved to be extra nice to the unfortunate soul. "If I catch any frogs, I'll let you play with them."

"Why thank you, Joseph."

Joseph quickly peeled off his dusty garments and plunged into the waist-deep water. At another time

Delacroix would have been aghast at the boy's nakedness, but in this setting, the natural innocence was fitting.

Delacroix feared that now that the boy could not hear, Lancel would begin the lobbying efforts that Delacroix expected. Instead they sat silently, watching Joseph splash and squeal. After a long period of reflection for both, Lancel cleared his throat.

"Bishop Delacroix. I know that as a holy man, you believe in the power of the church."

Delacroix braced for a confrontation, but Lancel was not referring to the institution of the Church, he was talking about buildings.

"But for me and Joseph, we are nearer to the Lord Jesus up here amidst his wonderful works than we ever could be in a cathedral. Look at that mountain peak. Do you not feel the Lord's majesty? Breathe the air. Do you not want to thank God for every breath?"

Lancel lapsed back into silence. There would be no argument of positions. No threats of action. Only a man and his son paying homage to God and nature. Delacroix looked at the craggy rock outcroppings framing the soaring peaks. He filled his lungs with the fragrant pine scented breeze. He would not argue these points with Lancel.

The trip back to Rennes-le-Château was as revitalizing as the trip out had been. Delacroix returned, renewed to face his perplexing challenges. He bid a heartfelt thank you to his guides.

"You will join us for the hunt, won't you?" Joseph inquired.

Delacroix learned on the trip that the words of the son were indeed the words of the father and there was no need to look further for approval of the invitation. "I would be delighted to attend. I look forward to tasting the largest spotted grouse in the woods."

Joseph looked relieved. There was hope for Father 'Della-craw.'

As the months passed, Delacroix shared other excursions to the mountain lakes and streams with Lancel and Joseph. He attended their next hunt and, to the eternal chagrin of Joseph, no grouse, spotted or otherwise, were scared up.

In the informal settings, Delacroix found no reason to mistrust Lancel. In fact, he found him to be the most articulate and knowledgeable person in the region. He was certainly likable. Their visits became more and more entertaining as the men felt comfortable with each other. And despite the distance to Blanchefort, Joseph seemed to be underfoot on a daily basis, either chasing the chickens in the monastery garden or quizzing Delacroix on empirical questions, such as how God made clouds and why He made roses have thorns. With certain exceptions, the taste of real life after the repetitive rigors of Orleans was sweet to Delacroix.

* * *

The Manton home

Maybe it's some kind of instinct, Jen pondered. Maybe it was the sincerely disappointed look on Dr. Hershner's face as he walked out. Hell, maybe it was the official looking cards and the intimidating presence of professors that never leaves a student. Whatever it was, Jen couldn't help thinking about the bizarre meeting. The professors seemed so legitimate. She had glanced at their folder. It looked scholarly and thorough. And they had gotten her last four generations right, which were all the ones that Jen could trace in the family Bible. But she had no way to verify any of it. It looked legitimate, right up to the point that they said she was a descendent of Christ. Christ! If they would have said he was descended from great wine growers, or great wine drinkers, or mass murderers even, she could have dealt with them. But this was farcical. She'd have to forget about it.

And she did. At least until the following Wednesday morning when the telephone rang.

"Hello."

"Mrs. Manton? Jennifer Manton?"

"Yes." Jen rolled her eyes. Not morning telemarketing.

"My name is Jim Gilliam. I'm an editor with The New York Times." Gilliam never was comfortable with the 'Religion Editor' mantle. "I'm calling about a meeting we had yesterday with Professors Stephen Hershner and Kathleen Fahey."

"I'm familiar with them." Surely this newspaperman would tell her that they were well-intentioned but severely misguided.

"They told me that you would be, but you need to know some more about them."

Good, here it comes. It is all a hoax.

"Despite the unbelievable nature of what these professors are claiming, I have to tell you that they are some heavy hitters in the educational ranks. You've probably never heard of them, but the research and articles coming from them at Boston University is pretty much accepted as gospel in theological and archeological circles."

Jen hadn't expected this. "So they can propose any crackpot idea they want and no one challenges them?"

"No, that's not what I mean at all. Everything they publish is well-substantiated. Supporting artifacts from archeological digs, carbon dating, analyses of ancient documents. That sort of thing. There has never been anything controversial about their methods or their findings."

"Until now."

"Well, half right. They told you about their theory of a bloodline of Jesus?"

"Sort of."

"As I understand it, the possibility that Christ had children has been accepted in some circles for decades. You won't ever hear about it in a church service, but an honest preacher will tell you that the Bible doesn't absolutely preclude it either. The controversial part is you."

"Me?"

"Right. Although the legends of a line descending from Christ have existed for centuries, it is Hershner and Fahey's recent findings in some rundown cathedral in southern France that expose the possibility that the line survived the persecutions of the Dark Ages and Middle Ages and actually survived to modern times."

"And...?"

"You're it."

"It?"

"Yes. I've seen the family trees the professors have developed. They're pretty in depth and thorough. About what you'd expect from these guys. And it looks pretty convincing, at first blush anyway, that the last known branch of the tree goes right to you."

Jen was overwhelmed. She searched for a way to minimize what he was hearing. "So there are probably thousands, no millions of us, that are descendants of ...well, in the tree, right?"

"That's kind of what you'd expect after two thousand years. But no. The professors admit that it is quite an abnormality that only one branch, and a very small one at that, would endure, but their research shows that to be the case for now unless they can find some other line."

Jesus Christ! Jen wasn't sure if she was swearing or just repeating the name. "So what am I supposed to say?"

"You know," Gilliam confided, "we were kicking that around ourselves yesterday in the pressroom. The research is just fine without your name, but for pizzazz you can't beat the headline you'll make. You're the difference between a debatable theory and a major news story. And that isn't lost on our boys at BU who wouldn't mind a little publicity on the streets."

"So what do you want from me?"

"Well let's start with an interview. I've got copies of everything that Hershner and Fahey brought. You take a look at them and we'll go from there."

"I've got a husband who is going to need some convincing."

"Yeah. Dr. Fahey had that checked out."

Figures, the witch. "And I've got a boy, too."

"So Fahey hadn't found everything. The last descendent, eh? Mrs. Manton, I look forward to meeting you."

3

You cannot petition the Lord with prayer. -- Jim Morrison

"Ah, Christ!" With a swipe of a wiry, but powerful, forearm, the stack of papers was swept off the table and crashed against the far wall of the kitchen. "Goddammit!"

A sleepy-eyed woman walked into the room, squinting to shut out the early afternoon sun blaring through cracks in the disjointed blinds. Her dyed-yellow hair hung down in tangled permed curls onto her crumpled polyester teddy. 'Tina' walked up behind the angry man and wrapped her arms around him, pressing her large bare, breasts against the prickly hair on the back of his head.

"What's wrong, Keith, Honey?"

"Incompetence! That's what's wrong," he raged.

Keith Carney was a lost soul. He was far too anti-social to fit within accepted society, but also way too intelligent to effectively lead the amoral organization that he now headed. He had been thrilled, although he could not show it, when his predecessor had been sentenced to prison for the next decade for a botched strong arm job than ended up being a murder, second degree. He had been the obvious brains behind the organization for years. Now he was fully in charge. At times the money that could be made leading these hoodlums was obscene. But the drawback was that his schemes, while organizationally brilliant, often collapsed under the weight of the slow operatives he had to employ. Musclemen were not often rocket scientists.

"The Sons?" she inquired sweetly.

"Of course. Idiots. Brain dead idiots!" His hand shook as he failed in his first attempt to ignite the lighter. She rubbed her breasts back and forth across his shoulders as it flared on the second attempt and he lit the cigarette.

"All they have to do is collect the money. A monkey could do it. But, no. The restaurant is run by a 'nigger' so they have to rough him up." Carney blew out a long stream of smoke. "The asshole dies and now the police are crawling all over the place and everyone on the block is squealing. We can't go back in there for years. Those morons just blew a half a million a year. Half a goddamn million!"

Tina dragged her fingernails down Carney's long, hard neck. His shoulders relaxed. She liked his body. Hard. Pale. And she liked the drugs that his unreported income could purchase. It allowed her to live without worries like those racking her 'boyfriend.'

"What about that TV show? How's it doing?" she cooed. She wanted to be sure that her source wasn't too close to drying up.

Carney stiffened. That was another one he didn't like to think about. "I know that Bible-thumping hypocrite is ripping me off. I know it." He stubbed out the cigarette.

It wasn't helping. "The bastards I have to put up with ..." he groused.

"But you've got plenty of 'toot,' don't you, Honey?" If the cocaine stopped coming, Tina would be out of there. His body wasn't that good. Hers was.

"There's always plenty of that," he replied, mind on other schemes.

"Then let's not worry about anything this morning," she said, sliding her cool hands inside of his unbuttoned silk shirt. Early afternoon was 'morning' to Tina.

Carney closed his eyes as Tina scraped her long nails over his nipples.

"Your boys are very bad," she whispered.

"Imbeciles," he responded, quietly.

"And I haven't been much help either," she cooed.

"You bitch."

"Yes, I am, Keith. I am bad, too."

Silently the couple rose and retreated into the dark bedroom. The bed squeaked as she landed on it.

"I'm sorry Keith," her muffled voice said into the pillow.

Carney did not reply. He picked up a belt draped over the chair by the bed and stared at Tina's bare buttocks cocked up toward him. He could still see red stripes from last night. Normally he would go easier, but the accounting had pissed him off. He swung hard.

*   *   *

The monastery

The clatter from outside startled Delacroix awake. Feeling his way across the pitch black room, he pulled open the wooden shutters and squinted at the brilliant glare of a trail of burning, fat-dipped torches that dotted the road leading out of Rennes-le-Château. As his eyes adjusted, he made out the silhouettes of his parishioners leading over-loaded rattling oxcarts and impatient horses. Their hurried pace gave the scene an air of urgency. Excited children pulled protesting cattle on frayed ropes.

Delacroix checked the position of the moon. Odd. It was the middle of the night. Closing the shutters to the cold night air, he crossed the room to the stool where he had left his clothes. He did not have much furniture and had quickly mastered the room and most of the monastery in the dark. Puzzled, Delacroix slipped into his loose leather boots. He gathered his robe around him as he hurried through the halls to the brothers' communal hall where a group had already gathered, lighting their smaller candles from the master on the wall.

Francois saw Delacroix approaching and called out, "Your Highness, we have been given word of saqueadors."

Delacroix was not familiar with the term. It sounded Spanish, and by Francois's tone, it was a bad development.

"And what are these ... saqueadors?" Delacroix inquired cautiously, reluctant to reveal his ignorance once again.

"Plunderers. Murderers. Ungodly men who forage from beyond the Pyrenées. They pillage villages in Languedoc and, after they have stolen their fill, retreat to the Spanish side of the mountains."

"Hmmm," nodded Delacroix, sympathetically. The world was inflicted with many evils. "Does it happen often?"

The gaggle of brothers, timid souls by nature, nodded their assent. Francois gave them a scathing look. He had the exclusive ear to Delacroix and would maintain it. "In the higher villages it is common." The brothers could not help but nod vigorously.

Francois continued. "But they have not come to Rennes-le-Château for over a decade."

"What have we heard that causes the commotion outside?"

Francois eyes widened. "A messenger awoke us. He said that Clarbonne has been sacked this evening."

Delacroix recognized the name of a small village, actually a mere collection of poor farmer's houses, which was part of his parish. It was twelve miles to the south, deep into the mountains. He had not yet visited it.

"Only a few escaped with their lives." Now Francois was embellishing the story.

Delacroix's brow furled in displeasure. He wrung his hands in contemplation. "Why doesn't King Phillip stop this?"

The brothers looked nervously at the ground, embarrassed by the unknowledgeable question.

"Your Highness," said Francois delicately, "the King of France is not, shall we say, 'concerned' with the tribulations of our region. As long as the Spaniards' raids stay in Languedoc, and do not cross into Bordeaux or Dijon, he will not act. And the bandits know this. As long as they do not pillage from other Spaniards, and the Church, I might add, their Queen is likewise unmoved. We are, so to speak, left to fend for ourselves."

Delacroix edged from the group toward the door where the noise in the road had increased. He pulled it open and surveyed the increasing panic.

"How far north must they go? Where do they flee?" he asked into the night.

"Blanchefort, M'Lord," Francois stated factually.

Delacroix repeated, thoughtfully, "Blanchefort." He now realized that the trail of lights was leading on the path to Lancel's castle, and not the most direct path to the north. He turned to look to Francois. "And what do we do?"

"We are probably safe here, M'Lord. But it is not certain. So we hide the Church's relics. We take our livestock to Blanchefort. We do not want to give the saqueadors any temptation to violate the sanctity of the Church."

"No, we would not want to do that," agreed Delacroix. He stood silently at the door, watching the eerie moonlit procession straggle by. The brothers swayed and murmured nervously behind him. They were afraid that their new northern leader would not approve of the usual evacuation to Blanchefort. Francois held up his hand to quiet them.

"Shall we proceed with the precautions, Your Highness?" he asked.

Delacroix slowly shut the door. He looked down at the stone floor rubbed smooth by decades of observers before him, searching for wisdom in its cold polish.

"Indeed."

*   *   *

Delacroix and Francois stood on an upper balcony of the monastery and surveyed the final exodus of the brothers and the livestock. The sun was just rising above the purple eastern foothills.

"Brother Francois, you have disobeyed my order that you go with them to Blanchefort," Delacroix reminded his younger assistant.

"Ah, yes, M'Lord," replied Francois foxily, "but I have followed my higher order to assist you and provide for you."

"And who gave such an order?" Delacroix inquired lightly, not entirely disappointed that Francois had remained behind.

"I do not recall," Francois said, watching the dust of the cattle drift over the valley.

Delacroix smiled to himself. It was nice to have a friend as well as an assistant. He glanced toward the now vacant village. "Tell me. Did Father Varnes before me flee to Blanchefort in such times?"

Francois cast a shocked look aside that told Delacroix that he was not comfortable with the subject.

Delacroix retreated. "I do not ask to disparage his holiness, and certainly not his courage, Brother. I only inquire so that I may better understand this strange and puzzling land."

Francois answered while continuing to look out the window. "We all went to Blanchefort, M'Lord."

"Was it unsafe here?"

"Perhaps, yes. But perhaps, no. In any event, it seemed wise and we saw no reason not to follow a path that had been set before our time."

Delacroix allowed a respectful amount of silence to intercede. "You understand that I feel that I must stay here. The people need to see that the Church can stand alone. It too, in time, can provide safety." Delacroix still was unsure as to whether Francois agreed with the principles instilled in him by the emissaries in Orléans. He had certainly expounded enough on them to the parishioners, and even more certainly to the brothers. Francois had never expressed disagreement.

"M'Lord. We assuredly shall be safe here. There are places we can hide where even the mice cannot find it. And the people will know of your bravery. But there is one area in which you cannot compete with Blanchefort." Francois smirked slightly.

"And what is that?" Delacroix demanded, affronted by Francois' temerity.

Francois turned to face his superior. "The food will be much better up there," he said, waving a hand toward the distant hills. Then he cocked his head and crunched up one side of his face. "What does one prepare when all the food is gone?"

Delacroix stood open-mouthed. He may have had a sense of humor, but in the strict upbringing in Orléans, it had never been allowed to surface. He didn't know how to react. And Francois knew it.

"You'll see. You'll see," cried the young assistant as he fled the room.

Delacroix looked at the back of his assistant as the door closed. In delay, he laughed to himself. He had a lot to learn about these free-spirited people.

Within the hour, Delacroix and Francois were deep into their task of hiding the Church's relics in deep, hidden crypts under the floor stones. As they lowered a wrapped fresco of the Virgin Mary and Mary Magdalen fleeing the shores of the Holy Land, they heard a low distant rumble.

"Is it the saqueadors?" asked Delacroix.

"No," replied Francois. "The Spaniards come like rats in the night. You do not hear them." He cocked an ear. "No, it is the Order."

Delacroix followed Francois into the street. They looked up the road to Blanchefort and saw a tight column of dust rising to the sky. Within minutes a column of horses appeared. Perched on their backs were the Knights' Templar, banner unfurled and brilliant flowing white gowns flapping behind them. The blood red crosses on their broad shields caused Delacroix to gasp at the display of raw and divine power. The soldiers of the pope. It was a sight that few saw and none forgot.

The column slowed and approached the steps of the monastery. Lancel was in the lead and rode to within feet of the clergymen.

"Greetings of God, Bishop Delacroix. Brother Francois, " called out the knight from his mount. The process of dismount while in full gear was cumbersome and awkward. It was only done so when necessity demanded, and that did not include the usual deference that Lancel would have extended the leader of the parish.

"God's blessings to you, Sir Lancel," returned Delacroix.

"You have been warned of the approaching saqueadors, I am informed," stated Lancel.

"Yes. I am appalled. We have not heard of these atrocities up north," stated Delacroix, sympathetically.

Lancel snorted. He was keenly aware of the King's policy of indifference to the problem. He did believe that Delacroix had never heard of it. "They are a burden we must bear. But the Bible grants leave to smite thine enemies, does it not?"

"Indeed it does, Sir Lancel," agreed Delacroix. "Are you to confront them?"

"Yes." Lancel nodded to his men. "I dare say that we shall be fortunate to confront them. I fear we shall have to pursue them first. The account we have received is that they have slaughtered over a dozen innocents at Clarbonne. They must know that eye will be taken for an eye."

"As God wills," assented Delacroix, shocked by the report.

Lancel's frisky mare reared slightly. Lancel calmed her. He had more to say and was searching for the words.

"Father Delacroix, thou knows that your presence is welcome in my castle?" he said, half question, half statement.

"Yes. Thank you for your kindness. But I believe it is suitable for the presence of the Lord to remain in Rennes-le-Château at all times. Particularly in times of danger. I mean no disrespect."

Lancel nodded. He in turn would respect Delacroix's integrity. "I understand, Your Highness." He tightened his grip on the reigns. "But should you change your mind, come suppertime, the invitation stands."

"Brother Francois informs me that my stomach will regret this decision," grinned Delacroix.

Lancel smiled broadly at the humor. "We shall make up for it another day." He kicked his horse gently on her flanks and the column began to move forward to the hills.

"Sir Lancel," Delacroix called.

Lancel stopped his mare and turned. "Yes, Your Highness."

"Do you not want to seek the Lord's blessing for the battle?" Delacroix knew that such ritual was standard for soldiers leaving for conflict in the north.

Lancel looked at Delacroix uncomfortably before responding, "No." After a pause, he added, "It shall not be necessary. Good day, M'Lord."

Delacroix and Francois watched the column move into the middle of the road, and, having passed the monastery, continue their gallop.

*   *   *

The Knights Templar had been gone two days when a single rider came speeding from the Pyrenées foothills. He charged to the front door of the monastery. The approaching hoofbeats had echoed through the silent village and Delacroix and Francois were quick to run to the road to greet the rider.

Jumping from the panting horse was a young man that Francois recognized as the eldest son of one of the senior members of the Order.

Francois grabbed the boy's shoulders, "Boy, what word? What word do you bring?"

The boy shook his head excitedly and tried to speak, but could only expel from his lungs the accumulated dust of the trail.

Francois hurried inside to fetch water. The boy sat on the steps and panted in rhythm with his horse. Delacroix could not read the boy's emotions through his exhaustion. Francois was quick and soon the boy was pouring a waterfall of cool water down his throat. He sputtered and exclaimed, "They are all dead."

Delacroix looked at the boy in horror as the young face broke into a grin. "The Order surprised them last night where they encamped. They were like sleeping grouse and we captured them with nary a wound."

The boy took another drink and continued. "They still had the things they had stolen from Clarbonne. They even had with them a young girl ..." He looked to the ground and shook his head and deeds he could not speak.

The anxious clergymen did not push him. After a moment he looked up again. "Lancel conducted the trial. At dawn we hung them. Thirty of them, I thinkest. We did not have enough ropes to do it all at once, so we hung them in five rounds while the doomed watched."

Delacroix grimaced at the description, but did not condemn the deed.

"Lancel allowed the youngest three to ride free after they had witnessed the executions. He told them to return to their homes and inform the other Spanish rodents that such will be the fate of any who approach Rennes-le-Château." The boy beamed with the news. "I was sent ahead to inform the people that they may return home and plan the celebration."

Francois, relieved and weary on the stale food in the monastery, hugged the boy. "Drink and be on your way, Lad."

The boy poured the rest of the bucket over his head. "One for my mount, and I shall fly."

After the boy's hurried departure, Delacroix and Francois retreated into the monastery. Francois was jubilant.

Delacroix did not share his enthusiasm. "Brother Francois, it seems that we should be thankful to God for his deliverance."

Francois did not notice the edge in the Bishop's voice. He continued merrily, "Oh, but we are."

"Then shouldn't the prayers of thanksgiving come through the Church?" intoned Delacroix.

Francois stopped. "M'Lord ... what are you saying?"

"That a celebration of victory is a pagan ritual and unbecoming of Christians."

"Why I couldn't agree more," he said, enthusiastically, placing his hand on Delacroix's arm. "I am certain that the boy stopped here to inform us so that we could begin preparations for a mass of celebration. You shall never see more devout men than the Knights of Order Templar. Only after they have spent the day in prayers of thanksgiving will the feasts begin. M'Lord, have no doubt, but that their first allegiance is to God."

Delacroix blushed at the correction he was receiving. With the unsavory descriptions he had been given of the Cathars and the Knights' Templar, he had envisioned an orgy of drunken debauchery. He was beginning to learn that the character of the people of Languedoc was not as certain as had been represented.

* * *

Francois had been right. The Knights entered the village the next morning, and, before even returning to Blanchefort, entered the cathedral in anticipation of a celebratory mass. The brothers had scurried back from Blanchefort the night before and the relics and artwork was hurriedly restored, festive banners raised. Breaking only when nature called, the knights, only two dozen strong, spent the day on their knees, uttering prayers in French and Latin, offering thanks for their God-given victory.

Delacroix observed them in equal shares of awe and confusion.

That night the grateful villagers of Rennes-le-Château prepared a feast around a roaring bonfire that lit the skies for miles. Every utensil that could be banged, strummed or blown was produced for a cacophony of music. Hogs that were being saved for weddings and holidays were slaughtered and the Knights, as well as the brothers, ate well.

Delacroix approached Lancel as he stood gazing into the roaring fire in the village square. He held a large wooden tankard, engraved with hunting scenes. A head of foam indicated that his mug had been filled again with a strong, dark beer that was being served a bit too young. Women danced with partners around the fire, casting hopeful looks in the direction of the handsome widower.

"God has been merciful," said Delacroix in a formal greeting.

Lancel turned. His eyes were red with exhaustion, emotion and a tankard of brew. "What we had to do was not merciful, Your Highness." Lancel did not take lightly the duty he had just performed. The kicking of dangling legs, even those of his enemies, did not give him pleasure.

Delacroix understood. He had always dreaded the public executions in Orleans, and had always searched for some duty that would cover his absence. "You performed the Lord's will."

Lancel exhaled, drunkenly. Many barrels of beer had been tapped. A brazen woman danced by and shook her long dark locks within inches of his face. Lancel laughed, but waved off the invitation.

Lancel and Delacroix stood side by side, feeling the heat of the fire on their faces. They were an incongruous pair to lead Rennes-le-Château. Lancel, tall, straight and keen of vision, Delacroix, small, slumped and squinting. But each held a clarity of mind and with that, mutual respect for the other. They watched the orange flames silently.

As the stars beamed through the smoke of the fire the night chill set in. The party was degenerating and Delacroix sensed that his presence was no longer appropriate. The Lord had been sufficiently praised earlier. He turned to Lancel. "It is time for me to retire."

"Mine was hours ago," added Lancel, tiredly.

"You have no reason not to sleep well. You have done all that was asked of you, Frederick."

Lancel turned at the informal address. He raised his eyebrows to Delacroix.

"Bernard," said the priest, answering the unspoken inquiry.

Lancel nodded. "Good night ... Bernard."

Delacroix began to turn away, wondering if this informality was an advance that should have been reserved. Despite the display of devotion at the day-long mass, there were many questions yet to be answered. He decided to ask one before he left.

"Frederick. The day that you left to pursue the saqueadors, you gave me grave pause. You did not ask for the Lord's blessings. Yet you have been abundant in giving Him praise. I do not understand why you do one, but not the other

Lancel turned to Delacroix and shook his head. "I do not believe that the Lord grants his power only to those who clamor for his attention," he said. Then, leaning in heavily, he whispered, "But I also believe that I should thank Him abundantly if He chooses to do so."

Then he smiled his broad smile.

*   *   *

"Gentlemen. Gentlemen!" Lancel called over the roar of the crowd gathered in the great dining hall of Blanchefort. Slowly the noise subsided to a few scrapes of chairs and clearing of throats.

"I call to order this gathering du Prieré de Sion," he stated somewhat quieter, but still with enough force to carry to the back wall and beyond.

Huddled in the damp passageway at the rear of the hall stood the footmen and servants of the powerful knights assembled in the room. It was good duty for them. After their masters had supped, leftovers and long simmered bone broth would be generously dished out. In their anticipation, no one concerned themselves with the shadowy figure who crowded the door, occasionally peering inside. He must be new, they surmised. He does not know that the officious quarreling of the Brothers of Zion, and the feast that was served concurrently, could go on for hours before it would be their turn to eat. They rolled dice and played card games, careful to keep their voices down, lest they disturb the important undertakings inside.

Jacques Boulanger kept his back to the stable hands. They smelled of horse manure. And he was there to witness the heretics, not to learn the peasants' arts.

"Brother Sigmund," Lancel called out, "will you lead our prayer?"

The Knight Templar and member of the Brotherhood of Zion rose. Boulanger recognized him from the meetings he had openly attended years ago when he himself had asserted his claim to membership. Sigmund, the owner of vast tracts of land to the north of Rennes-le-Château, had joined Lancel in his ouster. Boulanger glared at him, unseen.

"Our Father of heaven, Our Father of earth, ..." began the knight in a booming baritone.

That's it. Boulanger had not been able to recall exactly how they had begun every prayer. He had told the new priest that it was blasphemous, but the actually words, 'Father of Earth,' would be damning. He smiled inwardly and leaned forward to listen closer. Sigmund was praying for forgiveness, mercy, and good weather, all standard pleas to the Lord Jesus in 1209.

"... until we rejoin our family in Heaven ..."

That's one, too. I think, pondered Boulanger. He would have to emphasize the phrasing to be sure that Father Delacroix understood the blasphemy.

It would take creative talent for Boulanger to make anything damaging out of the next two hours. The majority of the meeting consisted of squabbling over a plan to build a new stone millery outside of Blanchefort, closer to the swifter river that ran through the village. There were various reports on crops and the amount of taxes that could be expected in the spring. And verification of the gossip concerning the statuesque brunette in a local hamlet who was now with child even though her husband had sailed out of Marseilles over six months ago. Boulanger became impatient as his stomach rumbled in protest that it was not receiving the food that the nose was smelling.

As Boulanger groused, a signal was surreptitiously given and the stable hands flooded to a door that Boulanger had not even noticed. He would be last in line.

He looked from the hall to the line. His stomach won out and, for this day, his eavesdropping was completed.

*   *   *

"Thank you for your counsel, Monsieur Boulanger," Father Delacroix stated. He was growing used to the weekly visits by Boulanger, the way one got used to mosquitoes in the bogs. And the nosy man was providing him with information that he had no other way of obtaining. While Brother Francois was helpful, historically, this Boulanger was not shy about his gathering techniques.

To Delacroix, despite the wealth and power, Lancel seemed content to allow the Church its sovereignty. He was generous in his donations and supportive of the monetary requirements imposed from Rome, even despite his exemption, as a servant of the Pope, from locally imposed tithes. The Knights Templar of the region, who gave their secular allegiance to Lancel, attended mass regularly, and had made no criticism when Delacroix laced his prayers with the dual themes of divine Papal wisdom and obedience to the Church.

Despite the respectful relationship, Delacroix had been ordered to report on the dealings of the Brothers of Zion. Boulanger was a necessary evil. But as far as Delacroix could discover, the purpose of the meetings of the Knights Templar was to provide fraternal support and generally run the valley. Boulanger substantiated the prevalent rumors that the society was limited to those who claimed to be descendants of Jesus Christ. While this claim was blasphemy, such a contingency not being allowed for in the Bible, it was dichotomous with the behavior of the members. They seemed as reverent as the people Delacroix had seen shepherded in Orleans. To their credit, they were certainly better educated. And, like Lancel, they supported the Church well.

As directed, Delacroix reported all of his observations and the hearsay reports of Boulanger in his periodic letters to the Archbishop. Whereas he hoped that his weekly exhortations of obedience to the Bible would be heeded by the Brothers of Zion, he also could honestly report that the region should not be deemed as much of a threat to the Church's power as had been feared. Since Delacroix received no contrary instructions from the Archbishop, and certainly no direct communications from the Vatican, he believed that he was fulfilling his mission.

In many ways, he was.

*   *   *

"Honey, let's just hear him out. If we're not convinced, no harm done. We can have a good laugh over this later." Jen had to change her role from skeptic to reluctant facilitator after she had broken the news to Rick as a not-too-casual aside at dinner. He was even more incredulous than she had been and directed most of his disbelief at her for agreeing to have Gilliam come to their home.

"I'll hear him, but as soon as he asks for money, ppphhht, out he goes."

Gilliam hadn't stopped to worry about how to present himself or his incredible news story. But his appearance was perfect for not arousing the Mantons fears any further. He looked the part of a preoccupied journalist. His rumpled shirt was in need of a pressing and the elbows of his worn tweed jacket had seen better days. He did not look like he was out to sell anything.

After a brief introduction by Jen, acting as the nervous intermediary, Rick jumped in. "Mr. Gilliam, you need to know up front that we are not particularly religious nor interested in our family trees ..."

"No, no, no, I understand. And call me Jim. You're really going to be interested in this." Gilliam plunged ahead like a child showing off his pet worm, oblivious to the apathy and revulsion of the parents. He pulled out two large manuscripts.

"Hershner and Fahey gave me permission to go over these with you. They would have done it themselves, but apparently you all didn't see eye-to-eye. Believe me I can see why. Where should I start?"

"I've told Rick the bottom line, that the professors believe that my family line from France is connected to the family line of ... well ... Jesus." Jen could still barely say it.

"Like I said, we aren't regular church-goers, but we do know that we've never heard anyone even suggest that Jesus had children, so I think you better start with that hurdle."

"Sure. First off, let me tell you that I'm not all that religious myself. I used to be a hack on the police beat in the City. Stick around long enough and you get to be an editor of something. But I'm not the religion page editor. We took this story from those guys. We think this is going to be bigger than just a section headline. Much bigger. And second, these aren't my theories. But they do look awfully convincing. Enough so that we hope to start a four-part series by early next week. We're trying to break down these theories into something the average reader can digest. I guess you two can be a good test."

Gilliam launched into his trial run. "We're going to pitch the newly discovered family line of Jesus Christ as the subject of the first known cover up. All Christians know that their religion is based on Jesus and the Bible. But when it gets right down to it most of us don't really know the first thing about either one, historically speaking. We are raised to believe that the Bible is the word of God. And we assume that it is pretty contemporaneous with the events it's describing. But the truth is that the first four books of the New Testament ... Matthew, Mark, Luke and John ... the books that describe the life events of Jesus, weren't written for thirty to seventy years after his death by apostles that never even met him. Many of your average Christians are surprised to hear that. But when these books were first written, they weren't recognized as anything divine. Heck, the different apostles don't even agree on a lot of the details. The belief that they were infallible evolved over time. During the first three centuries the Christian church was very loosely organized. The various leaders formed councils to cull through all the competing works and letters attributed to apostles and saints. The writings were studied and debated and eventually some were selected to make up the first Holy Bible. At the Council of Hippo in 367, I believe."

"I've heard of that," said Jen. Rick wasn't surprised.

Gilliam continued. "Theologians agree now that the selection process was rife with the political pressures of that time, just like our congress is today. We'll never know the whole story, but historians have copies of some of the works that were rejected. Quite a few of them. The theologians call them the Apocrypha. By looking at what was rejected, it isn't hard to imagine the editorial slant being applied."

"So do the rejected books say that Jesus had children?" Jen prodded.

"Not in so many words. What they do tell is a different concept of Jesus. Instead of a Virgin birth followed by a simple life with no apparent political affiliation, some of these rejected writings emphasize the royal blood of Jesus, descending from Abraham through King David, the greatest of the Jewish kings. They tell that Jesus' ministry was swept up by a wave of hope from the Jewish people awaiting their Messiah, a title which at that time was interpreted as a ruler-king and not necessarily a god or savior. They even go on to detail a different version of the Crucifixion as well, some versions matching the Koran, the Muslim's holy book, in saying that Christ walked on earth as a mortal for many years after his supposed death."

Rick raised an eyebrow and looked at Jen for some confirmation of this theory. She nodded. She had heard of it.

Gilliam continued. "You can see why the heads of the Church back then wanted this kind of talk stopped. They had built their power on an organization that spread the *message* of Christianity, but here are these other works portraying Jesus as a mere human with a royal bloodline.

And in those days royal blood was true power. If descendants of Jesus were to come forward with that kind of claim they would be a formidable contender to rule the Christians. Back then, say you're a peasant that can't read or write. Who are you going to follow? The ones spreading the message or the ones claiming to be descendants of Jesus Christ? Obviously this was a threat to the Church. Hence, the descendants are edited out and the cover up begins. After a few centuries, who's to know?"

Rick, struggling to absorb the details, wasn't sure Gilliam had yet gotten to the point. "Okay," he said, gathering his thoughts. "So the Bible was selectively edited a thousand and some years ago. A cover up, they say. So how do we know there was a bloodline? Actual children?"

Gilliam waved his hand over the paperwork in front of him. "Hey, we're still not even at the really controversial stuff. Hershner and Fahey have been working for years on a hypothesis that Jesus had children with Mary Magdalen."

"The prostitute?" Jen's disbelief was coming to the surface.

"Yes. That's exactly how you're supposed to remember her. But the professors are convincing in their interpretation of the rejected works and the original gospels written in Greek to show that she wasn't branded a hooker until centuries after her life. Nowhere in the Bible does it say Mary Magdalen was a prostitute. It points out that she was present when Jesus was first anointed, an important symbolic event for a rabbi. It says that she was one of the few present at the Crucifixion, and that she was the *first* to see Jesus after he arose from the dead. When you look at where she shows up, you get a feeling that her role was somewhat more important than that of devoted camp follower."

Gilliam gave them a smug tilt of the head as if to say, 'See how this falls into place?'

"The disciples were jealous of Mary Magdalen," he emphasized. "Jesus is quoted many times in the Bible defending her and declaring his love for her. Now that sounds to me like she could have been the wife as Hershner and Fahey contend. They say that the marriage of Jesus and Mary Magdalen is described in the New Testament when Jesus performs his first miracle and turns water into wine at a wedding feast in Cana. But they believe that the marriage part of the miracle story was conveniently edited out as part of the cover up."

Gilliam paused and waited for a sign to go on. "The professors also point out that the Bible is strangely quiet on Jesus' lack of a wife, a very strange circumstance for a middle aged rabbi in that age. Jesus never proclaimed that he was celibate. Celibacy didn't come into practice in the Christian religion until centuries after his death. But as time goes by, the celibacy of the Church is implied to Jesus. Pretty effective way to foreclose any possibility that Jesus might have a family, wouldn't you say?"

"Well, what proof is there that he did?" Jen challenged.

"That's the question. Historical sources reveal a long-accepted legend that Mary Magdalen, the Virgin Mary, a Joseph of Arimathea, and their families, fled from what is now Israel after the crucifixion to escape persecution." Gilliam turned to Jen. "Joseph of Arimathea. Ever heard of him?"

"Sounds vaguely familiar," Jen said truthfully.

"That is all it should. He is only mentioned once in the Bible, as the rich man who was given the body of Jesus when he was removed from the cross. Ask yourself, who was this guy to be given this honor, or burden, without being referred to anywhere else in the Bible? No explanation. Zip-o. It seemed like another of the suspicious omissions, so the professors reexamined the early Greek texts of the Bible and found evidence that Joseph of Arimathea was the father of Mary Magdalen. But, sure enough, these parts are deleted from the official Bible. Why would they cut them out?"

Neither of the Mantons attempted to answer.

Gilliam lightly jabbed a finger on the table. "Because it supports the whole theory that the immediate family of Jesus fled together to escape persecution. If the legend is only that an unknown Joseph of Arimathea and the two Marys escaped in a boat, that is a pretty easy story to ignore. It makes no sense. But if your own Bible admits that Joseph of Arimathea is the father of Mary Magdalen, and admits the union of Mary Magdalen and Jesus, then the whole thing ties together. Wife, father and mother-in-law running from the mobs of Jerusalem. The legend is substantiated. A royal bloodline exists! This is the last thing Church officials of 300 A. D. want to get out of hand. So they edit the books, and remember, there aren't that many books back then, and they cut out anything they don't like."

"Okay, say there was a cover-up. How does it get to us?" Rick pressed.

"The legend, which we now know is supported by the disfavored Greek texts, was that Joseph of Arimathea and the two Marys followed the prevailing winds across the Mediterranean and landed in Marseilles, France."

Jen cringed at the first hint of a connection to the homeland of her family tree. "Any truth to it?" she asked.

"Hard to prove one way or the other. But for centuries the French have claimed that Mary Magdalen's relics are still in France. There is an urn with fragments of bones and skull located at a church in a small village called St. Maximin. And the crusaders certainly believed it was Mary Magdalen's bones, and made pilgrimages there to pray for protection. No one knows when the story first arose. But no other country is claiming her. She wasn't exactly a hot commodity, especially after her profession was officially declared. It's hard to conceive a motive for claiming her as your resident if it wasn't true. Going against the Church for the sake of tourism wasn't a smart practice in the Dark Ages. Yet she had to die somewhere. We know where almost all of the apostles died, but again, official Church chronicles are silent on this, as they are on a lot of points we would consider crucial today."

Gilliam paused to make sure his language wasn't offensive to either of the Mantons before charging on. "There is other evidence that Mary Magdalen fled to France with children of Jesus. Historians have verified the existence of a Jewish kingdom, called Septamia, that arose at just the era of their arrival in southern France. This kingdom extended along the French Mediterranean coast into Spain and flourished for centuries. And its rulers claimed a royal bloodline from King David. They didn't make a big deal out of Jesus. But the blood of King David had to have come through him. And to show its significance, the Bible, in the very first chapter of the New Testament tracks the lineage of King David down through Joseph, the husband of Mary."

Gilliam saw their skepticism. "You know, the section that has the long string of so-and-so begets so-and-so. Why do you suppose they would open the New Testament with all of that if they didn't think it was what was most important to the people of that time? Royalty was a pretty substantial assertion in those days, so it doesn't appear that this is fiction or a mistake in translation."

"So Hershner and Fahey found some proof of all this?" Jen asked.

"Who's that?" Gilliam said loudly.

"What do you mean? Hershner and Fahey, the professors," Rick corrected.

"No. Who's that?" This time Gilliam pointed past the Mantons to a window curtain behind the couch. It was swaying, but there was no breeze in the house.

"Danny?" Jen asked.

They heard a muffled laugh behind the couch. Rick leaned over the back and looked down. "Come out from back there, it's dusty."

"Oh thanks," Jen said, rolling her eyes.

Danny scrambled out on all fours, giggling.

"Mr. Gilliam, this is our son, Danny," Rick introduced. "Danny, this is Mr. Gilliam from the New York Times newspaper."

"You bring the newspaper?" Danny asked with awe to the person that he thought made the pre-dawn deliveries.

"No Danny, he writes the articles that go in them," Jen clarified.

"Wow. You write a lot."

"Well, Daniel, I don't write all of them. Nowadays I hardly get to write anything."

Danny was not used to being called by his full name unless he was in trouble. But the friendly tone of the stranger's voice told him he had nothing to fear. "Did Mom and Dad do something bad?" It summed up Danny's knowledge of his parent's reaction to the newspaper.

"Not at all, Daniel. Not at all. They're helping me write a story about your family." Gilliam looked skeptically around the room to see if he had overstepped his bounds.

"Can I help?" Danny offered.

"Not an hour past your bedtime, you cannot," Jen stated, and then, for effect, added, "Daniel."

"Aw Mom."

"Your mother is right, my boy. You need your sleep so you don't get all wrinkled like me," joked Gilliam. Reaching for his pocket, he added, "But you take this official New York Times pen, and if you think of something in the morning that I should know, you write it down."

"Wow. Thanks," said Danny as he took the cheap souvenir pen and closely studied the name and newspaper logo stamped on the side.

"Off to bed with you," Rick ordered lightly.

"I'll escort him," said Jen, knowing Danny's curiosity would override the command. They headed up the stairs toward his bedroom.

Danny's eyes betrayed his fatigue. As Jen firmly tucked him in with a gentle lecture to stay put he questioned the impact on him of what the grown-ups were so intently discussing. "Do I have to go to Sunday School now?"

"You know Bruiser, that might not be such a bad idea. There are a few things we might want to learn there."

"That's okay Mom. They have good snacks there anyway. Good-night. Tell Mr. Gilly-man I want to see where they make the paper."

"I'll tell him. Now you get some sleep."

"Quite a family you have, Rick," Gilliam said downstairs.

"Thanks. I'm pretty lucky."

"My daughters are grown and off to college. Seems like only yesterday they were that size," Gilliam reminisced.

Jen wasn't gone long. But even in a few minutes of small talk, Rick's assessment of Gilliam firmed up. He could be trusted.

"Did you go on?" Jen asked.

"Not without my interpreter," Rick kidded.

"Good. Now you were saying that Hershner and Fahey found proof of this bloodline," Jen prompted.

"Now, all history during the Dark Ages is a bit sketchy, but the claim of a royal bloodline persists in France, particularly in a Christian sect known as the Cathars. The Cathars dominated the Order of the Knights Templar. You know them as the crusaders you saw in books as a kid. Stalwart men in long white robes marked with bright red crosses. The knights have a secret order, translated roughly as the Brothers of Zion, who all claim to be descendants of Christ. At first the Knights Templar keep their belief in this royal bloodline under wraps, if you will. But as they gain more power and wealth from their conquests and plundering they get more vocal."

Gilliam paused and both Mantons nodded that they were following and that he should continue. He stretched his neck and rolled his head. "Kinda dry from all the talking. I'm used to being the one taking notes."

Rick and Jen simultaneously offered a drink. Any threat that Gilliam posed had dissipated.

"How about a beer?" Gilliam responded to their offers.

Rick joined Gilliam with two cans of Budweiser. He thought he might need one, too.

"Thanks. Where was I?"

"The Knights Templar," prompted Jen.

"Right. Not surprisingly, in the thirteenth century, the Pope senses that these claims to be descendants of Christ as a threat to the Church and he calls for a crusade. But he doesn't want a trip to Jerusalem, he calls for the elimination of all Cathars and any of their supporters, including Knights Templar. He also kicks off the start of the Inquisition which was so handy that the Church kept it around for the next two hundred years to deal with all suspected heretics. This crusade is a bloodthirsty affair and the Pope almost succeeds. But it was easier to kill the people than it was the concept and a claim to the royal blood of Jesus persisted through the Brothers of Zion which apparently survived the crusade in some diminished fashion. Much smarter this time, the order stays underground and has survived to this day, albeit with conflicting claims as to who is the true holder of the royal bloodline. Rick, your family line was one of those contending for the throne, so to speak."

"So it sounds like I'm in one of many lines from this secret society in France that could claim to be descendants, right?"

"Yes, up until Hershner and Fahey's recent discovery. They followed their leads throughout southern France. They knew that the Nazis had searched for something in the woods and hillsides of that region when they controlled it during the war. There was something there. They just didn't know what. Their efforts were rewarded when an old servant of a long since dead Bishop, in the region which included the village of Rennes-le-Château, told them of a small crypt that was accidentally discovered during the remodeling of the village's medieval cathedral. The crypt was located under a tomb of an unknown priest and had been undisturbed for eight hundred years. The crypt contained a number of ancient parchments that the Bishop, for reasons unknown to the servant, hid from the Church officials. Hershner and Fahey took one look at them and knew why the bishop had stashed them." Gilliam paused for effect, obviously relishing the suspense he had created.

"Why?"

"They contained the missing link. An entire library of the royal blood lineage beginning with the son of Jesus and going up through the purge of the Knights Templar. It also named the survivor of the slaughter of the crusade who was of royal blood. It was easy to match that survivor to the competing lines of the Brothers of Zion and determine which one was valid. They followed it to the present and, as luck would have it, you're it."

"Unbelievable," Jen murmured. Gilliam gave her a startled look. "Oh, not the research. Unbelievable that it's me."

The Mantons spent the next two hours poring over the manuscript of Hershner and Fahey. It was in research paper form with footnotes and citations crowding the commentary. It was scholarly and convincing. Had his family not been the ending to this tale, had he read the four-part series in the Times, Jen would have accepted it as just another example of life being stranger than fiction. Even Rick had to admit that the existence of this bloodline was believable, even logical, as it was laid out.

Gilliam's open honesty and frankness appealed to the Mantons. It was amazing that in a few short hours this absurd proposal that she was related to Jesus, really related, had become plausible.

It was past midnight when the session wound down.

"So what do you suppose this all means for us, Jim?" Rick inquired.

"I'm not sure. I suppose it depends on how the articles are accepted. Hershner and Fahey hope that the theory is controversial and, hence, profitable for them. Certainly the Times hopes it will sell enough papers to cover all the editing this baby will take. If I were to guess, I'd say we might make some big ripples in some circles, but that generally the public will only give it a short span of interest. I would expect that your family will be a curiosity for a while and you'll get a number on interview requests. In fact, I'd like to scoop everyone else and do some personal interest pieces. Would you mind if we did an interview, took some photos? I'm sure I could get the Times to spring for dinner and drinks."

The Mantons agreed, both secretly excited about their anticipated notoriety. Little did they know how far off their humble expectations would be.

As they closed the door behind Gilliam, they looked at each other with exaggerated faces.

"Can you believe that?" Jen said, slowly shaking her head.

"So do I get my feet washed tonight?" he teased.

"Don't hold your breath. You only think you're married to a saint. I know better."

* * *

Rick walked nervously through "BobRick's", the restaurant he and his brother had co-owned and managed for three years now. He found his brother in the cramped office in the back.

"Hey, Bob," Rick started awkwardly, "I've got something coming up that you're going to get a kick out of."

"You finally got that beautiful wife of yours preg-o again?"

"No. This is something weird." Rick hadn't told anyone yet of his being 'discovered' and hadn't settled on a pat speech.

"Are you okay?" asked Bob.

"Yeah. But Jen got this call a week ago from these professors from the theology school at Boston University ..." Rick began. Bob raised an eyebrow. In all their life, the phrase 'theology school' had never just popped up.

Looking for an adverse reaction, Rick continued, "And they've done a ton of research about Jesus having children and descendants." The topic was getting uncomfortable for Rick. Religion had always been off limits except for an occasional, 'Going to church for

Christmas?' type question. Bob looked at him uneasily, but it was his little brother, so he would give him a little room to ramble.

"Well, anyway, these professors did some research in France, where some of Jen's relatives are from, and they think they've found a connection," Rick said, almost apologetically.

"Connection between what," prompted Bob, indifferently.

"Between my family and Jesus."

The look was puzzled. Bob finally snorted, "What the hell are you talking about, Rick?"

"What I'm saying, and believe me, I didn't believe it at first either, is that these professors have traced a bloodline from Jesus to Jen. And Danny."

Bob slowly lowered his pencil and carefully placed it between the pages of a ledger. His hands slid back and forth against the edge of the desk. "So you're saying that they're related to Jesus. Jesus Christ. The one in the Bible, right?"

"That's what they're saying, and the New York Times is going to publish it, probably this week."

Bob laughed nervously, awaiting the punchline. None came.

"That's bullshit, Rick," said Bob. "What are you really getting at?"

"I'm serious. Jen and I met with an editor from the Times, and they're going to publish this work in the paper that proves that Jesus had kids. And they trace it to her."

Bob feared that his little brother was losing it. "Did you pay something for this?" he asked.

"No. I'm telling you, they showed me the thesis, or whatever it was, and it looks legit."

Bob looked disgusted. "These people say Jesus had kids and you're one of them?" He paused for effect and reiterated his first opinion. "Bullshit."

"C'mon, Bob. You've got to look at this stuff." Rick could understand his skepticism. He wasn't sure he bought it himself, but he didn't like the challenge to his word. Even if the story was, by any definition he held a week ago, crazy. "Jen believes it." That was his trump card. His wife's level-headedness was universally acknowledged. It had the desired effect and Bob tilted his chair back.

"You are really serious about this?" Bob said after a long pause, still obviously in disbelief.

"Yes."

"And it's going to be in the Times? The New York Times?"

"Yes. Probably this week."

Only the shuffling of feet interrupted the long silence that ensued.

"You should read the materials. It makes sense. You'll see," he offered, hopefully.

"Let me finish payroll."

"Sure, Brother."

Rick was painfully aware when Bob finished payroll and started into preparation for the lunch hour without talking to him. The usual rush that followed kept him occupied, but Bob's continued silence in the afternoon ate at him. It was Bob's turn to cover the evening meal and Rick was due to go home. He needed something from his brother. Since birth, validation by the older sibling had been an unspoken, but necessary component of their lives.

"So, Bob. I gotta go. What do you think about ... what we were talking about?"

"Your Jesus thing?"

"Yeah." Rick knew from Bob's tone that a lecture was to follow.

"I've got to tell you, as your brother, you're in over your head. I know you have never been a church-goer, and that's been okay by me," said Bob, thoughtfully. "That's not my call."

Rick thought of protesting. They did go to church. Admittedly, only on the holidays with his brother's family. But he knew Bob was much more dedicated about it and even served on one of the church's various boards. "Kind of ironic, isn't it?" Rick interjected, without commitment.

"No. No. It's not just ironic. That's what I'm trying to tell you. It's wrong and it's insulting," Bob said, still softly.

"Insulting? How so?" Rick said defensively.

"First off, there is no record whatsoever that Jesus had children. Nothing. Don't you think that it would be mentioned somewhere in history? Second, for you, or anyone, to say you're related to Jesus is ... foolishness. But it mocks everything we believe in."

"I can't explain the whole thing, Bob. But the professors and the editor from the Times really made sense. It is well researched."

"Then why is it only coming up now, two thousand years after the fact?" Bob said, more exasperation creeping into his voice.

"They said that their research goes back to reinterpret some older versions of the Bible. I don't know for sure. I guess a lot of it was passed down through the Middle Ages where it got lost until recently," Rick explained.

Bob was agitated at his brother's insistence. "I'm telling you, someone is suckering you. It happens all the time. A picture of Mary weeps tears. The Shroud of Turin. These things always look realistic at first. But you dig deeper ..." He shook his head, sadly. "It's just not right, Rick."

"What can I do about it? They tell us that we're it. The end of the line. I didn't invent this."

"They tell you that Danny and Jen are blood relatives of Christ?"

"Yes. The only ones they can find," Rick explained.

"And you believe that?" Bob said sarcastically.

"Yes, I did.... I guess I do."

"But a week ago you didn't even truly believe in Jesus, did you?"

"It's different."

The two stood by the side of the cooler. Bob broke the short, uncomfortable silence.

"Look. You're family. And I love Jen and Danny. You know that. But if you go on with this ... I don't want any part of it. I'm not telling Gina and the kids that their aunt and their cousin are divine. Count us out of this charade."

"Oh Christ, Bob," Rick said reflexively before he realized his words.

Bob looked at him smugly. "You really think people aren't going to laugh at you?" And he walked away.

Rick thought about chasing him to further the argument. The research. The facts. But he barely knew what he was talking about. It was futile for now. He turned and kicked the cooler.

* * *

Jen could sense when Rick had had a bad day at work. He had been quiet and immediately taken Danny up on the standing offer to 'shoot hoops'.

The phone rang. Jen welcomed the distraction. Her day had not been the best either.

"Hello."

"Jen. Gilliam here."

"Oh, hi Jim. How's the story coming?"

"Everyone here is getting excited about it. So we pushed it up a week. We're hitting the stands tomorrow," he replied.

"Really?" Jen said absently, her mind racing. *Tomorrow...* She had actually expected Gilliam to call and say that the whole story had been canned for any number of reasons. It still didn't seem real.

"Yeah. I thought you better know as soon as possible because I'm sure that once this gets picked up on the wires, you're going to get a lot of interview requests. I'm sorry I couldn't give you more warning."

"That's all right," Jen said, mentally reviewing her week.

"Well, you may want to be prepared. I think this is going to generate a lot of interest. The layout looks great. I have to admit, I looks like a helluva story, now that I see it in print. I'm having some copies messengered to you as we speak. They should be there shortly," Gilliam said, matter-of-factly.

"Great. We've been anxious to see the story. Kind of hard to know what to tell people, you know?" Jen said.

"I think you'll like it."

"Thanks. We'll call you after we read it," promised Jen.

"Great. Talk to you later." Gilliam hung up.

Jen looked out the kitchen window. Rick was in the driveway with Danny. She smiled at the male bonding ritual.

"Okay. Now this is important, Dan-O," said Rick in his best coaching voice.

The boy's eyes were wide, absorbing every word his Dad said without prompting.

Having Danny had changed their life. Gone were the spontaneous, carefree moments. But working as a team the daily chores got done as little Danny blossomed into a little person, every bit as full of intelligent mischief as his adoring parents. As a toddler, Danny behaved instinctively to his parent's demands, but within seconds he returned to his rambunctious behavior, as if his grin would absolve him from all rules. He loved his mother dearly, and couldn't imagine that any mother could be 'more beautifuler' or kinder. In Danny's mind, his father was an indestructible big buddy who was not afraid of anything, including bending Mom's rules when she was away.

School was a mixed blessing for Danny. He inherited an innate intelligence, so the work was not a problem, but he chaffed under the restraints of being inside, trapped in a chair, seemingly, to him, for the entire day. With the recess bell, he was the first to sprint out the door and, after ten minutes, the last to drag back in.

Rick dribbled the ball slowly. "Just before Iverson runs the back door alley-oop, he either gives a look to the center or he gets a look from him. But they don't say a word." They had covered alley-oop plays a hundred times. It was Danny's favorite.

"Right," Danny responded, seriously.

"Not a word. You'll tip it off if you say anything. Just a look." Rick rolled his eyes toward the house. "Like that."

Danny looked at the house.

"No, Danny," Rick laughed fatherly. "I'm telling you to go that way. And I'll alley-oop you."

"Oh," said Danny without embarrassment. "I got it."

"Okay. So let's try it," Rick said as he rolled his eyes toward the street. Danny jerked into action and ran an exaggerated circle around the top of the driveway toward the street, and headed for the basket, staring at his father the whole way.

Giving a theatrical look toward the house, Rick passed the ball about six inches above his son's eyes.

Danny jumped and grabbed the ball with both hands. He came down on both feet and shuffled forward until he was almost under the six-foot high basket. Sticking his tongue out, he heaved the ball with his entire body. The shot hit the backboard hard, and with no surprise to his father, ricocheted in. Danny clapped his hands and jumped wildly.

"Way to go, Seventy-Sixers!" yelled Jen from the back porch. "How about some dinner?"

Danny looked at his Dad reluctantly, torn between his stomach and being with his Dad.

"What's bugging you, Big Guy?"

"Justin and his brother were picking on me. If I had a brother they wouldn't do that." Rick thought of the comfort he felt with having a big brother as a protector when he was Danny's age.

"Sorry. But a little brother wouldn't do you any good against them," Rick said while drying off.

"I wouldn't have to play with them then."

Rick chuckled as he thought of the fights he had gotten into with his brother, always on the losing side. "We'll see, Dude."

A sibling wasn't in the cards for the time being. Jen wanted a serious run at her career. Rick was content with his one sports-minded son, and hadn't disagreed. It certainly helped the finances.

"Let's eat. We can shoot some more later, Sport," Rick offered, to alleviate the dilemma.

"All right," Danny yelled as he motored for the house.

As Rick clomped up the back stairs, Jen told him Gilliam's news.

"Tomorrow, huh?" Rick said thoughtfully. "Good. I'm tired of waiting for this thing to break."

"It's only been two weeks, Rick," Jen reminded him.

"I know, but I just want to see it in print to make sure everything is legitimate, you know?" he explained.

"I feel the same way. I told Gina. She had a fit," Jen said.

"I figured she would," he said. "I told Bob today. He kind of came unglued, too. I'm sure we're the topic of discussion tonight. I just hope that after everyone sees the article they'll understand that it really isn't such a big thing."

"I'm beginning to wonder."

*   *   *

The messenger arrived within the hour. Gilliam had enclosed five copies of the section that was to be released. Rick and Jen tore open the envelope and leaned over the same folded-in-half copies. The headlines were big, but not sensational. They scanned the opening paragraphs. It obviously covered the whole front page of the supplement.

"Open it up," urged Jen.

Rick took the top copy and spread it on the kitchen table.

"Oh ... my ... God," whispered Jen. On the top of the right side was a six inch photograph of the three of them that Gilliam had arranged. It was a good picture. The header above the photo simply said, The Descendants of Christ. The caption below read, "Jennifer Manton and her son, Daniel, with husband, Richard, at their Pennsylvania home. See Feature Story on Page 6."

They both stared speechlessly at the familiar likenesses looking up from the page. Rick slowly opened the section. It went on for pages. Historical timelines. Maps of France and Israel. Photographs of Hershner and Fahey at Rennes-le-Château. A Knight Templar on a horse. A chart of the bloodline through the middle ages.

And, on page six, as promised, a full page, with more photographs, featuring the lives and personalities of the Mantons, right down to their favorite foods.

"I don't believe this," said Rick, trancelike.

"This," said Jen, holding up the paper, "is embarrassing." A slight lilt in her voice said that it was an acceptable embarrassment.

They read the feature section silently. Finally Rick sat back and exhaled deeply. "You know, when we were looking over the thesis it looked so ... authoritative. I guess I didn't stop to think what it would look like with us in the story. I mean, this makes us look like some kind of celebrities, don't you think?"

Jen shook her head. "I never thought this would really come out like this." She leaned over for a better look at the photographs. "God, that's us. All over The New York Times!" She sat down.

Rick sat in a chair next to her. He snickered quietly. Then harder.

"What's so funny?" Jen asked, annoyed.

Rick looked at his wife and chuckled, "We're famous."

*   *   *

The phone rang at five o'clock in the morning. Jen answered it, automatically dreading that it was bad news from someone at that time of day.

"Mrs. Manton, sorry to disturb you so early this morning ..." the voice said.

Jen responded reflexively, unsure who would be addressing her by her formal title at this time of day. "That's okay."

"This is NBC Morning News, and we'd like your permission to do an interview in your home this morning for the seven o'clock broadcast."

Jen blinked her eyes. "What?"

"On the descendants of Jesus story. This is the Richard Manton residence, isn't it?"

"Yes. Yes, it is." Jen struggled to think clearly. The story. "I'll have to get back to you. Not this morning, though."

"I'm afraid the truck is already on the way, Mrs. Manton."

Jen didn't understand if the statement was inviting more comment or not. "I'll have to talk to my husband."

"Is he there?" the voice asked.

Jen wasn't sure if there was a protocol for such pushiness. "You'll have to call later," she said firmly, followed closely by "Good-bye." She hung up.

"What was that?" her husband asked, face down in his pillow.

"NBC."

"Huh?" came the muffled voice.

"NBC News is sending a film crew over," Jen said, wide awake.

A hand pulled the pillow back. "Now?"

"That's what he said."

"Ugh."

"Come on celebrity. If you're going on the national news, you'd better get in the shower."

Rick sat up and threw his feet onto the floor and scratched his head. "NBC."

Before either had showered, the phone began to ring non-stop. It was the same line from each. National. Regional. Local. Everyone had a film crew on the way. Would they give an interview.

"Rick, we've got to say something, or these people will be camped out in the front yard all day," Jen said after the last call. It was the fifteenth or sixteenth. There was no point in counting.

"I guess we could give them a few pictures out on the sidewalk and answer a few questions. Just easy ones." he said, shrugging.

The phone rang again. Jen let her husband answer it.

"Rick Manton. ... Yes. ... My wife and I will answer a few questions at eight o'clock." Rick was definite. Then his face furled. "I don't know. ... We'll see." He hung up.

"Don't know what?" Jen asked.

"What about Danny? They want to interview him, too."

Jen set her makeup down on the counter. She looked at him in the mirror. "I guess we need to think this thing through. I don't think he's ready for all this."

Rick frowned, "Like *we* are."

Within the hour the street looked like a circus had arrived to set up. Rick told the first crew that they would be out at eight. A crowd of neighbors were gathering, as well. Those who had not read the paper feared some tragedy had struck the young family. When they were told the news, they scurried off to see the Times.

"Dad," Danny squealed, "look at all the TV trucks! They're really here to see us."

"Just for a few minutes, Son," Rick said, studying the throng. "They are just curious because of Mr. Gilliam's article. It's nothing to be worried about," he added hopefully.

"I'm not worried. It's cool. Everybody at school will see me on TV."

"Yeah, that's cool," his father agreed absently.

The phone rang three times before the answering machine clicked on. They had stopped picking up an hour ago.

"Rick. Jen. Its Jim Gilliam returning your call," the speaker announced. Rick had called and left a message as the publicity surge had become overwhelming.

Rick picked up the receiver. "Jim, thanks for calling. It's crazy here."

"Here, too. The phone is ringing off the hook. Everybody is focused on our story. Nothing else happening in the world, I guess. What's going on there?"

"Every news station within a hundred miles of here has a film truck out front. It looks like a civil war reenactment. We told them that we'd answer a few questions at eight." Rick glanced at his watch. He had seven minutes. "But now we're kind of rethinking that. We think it is going to overwhelm Danny. Hell, I'm overwhelmed."

"You know," Gilliam said, "one of our editors here got a call from a friend of his, an entertainment agent, that said you guys should have an agent. I laughed it off when I heard it, but if it's as crazy as you say, it might not hurt."

Jen was standing close by, holding back the curtain a crack and peering outside. Rick covered the phone and whispered, "Jim could get us an agent."

Jen turned quickly. "Do it," she said without hesitation.

Within minutes Sid Flink, entertainment agent, was on the phone. There would be no press conference until he could be chauffeured from his Long Island home. If they hired him. Fifteen percent of any money paid for interviews, photographs, etceteras.

Jen had brought the upstairs phone to the kitchen and listened in with her husband. "So if we don't get paid anything, we don't owe you anything?" she confirmed.

"You'll make money, don't worry about that," Sid stated confidently. "If you don't .. you don't owe me a thing."

Jen looked at her husband. "What's to lose?" she said under her breath.

"Deal," said Rick, conscious of the time.

Rick sent word out to the news crews. They milled around unhappily, but no one left. Sid Flink arrived, as promised, within three hours, and took charge as if he had planned for this fiasco on a Sunday mid-morning. After a brief meeting with the whole family, he escorted them onto the front porch. Deftly, Flink handled the mob of reporters like the experienced agent that he was and allowed only innocuous questions about the Mantons' home life and ancestry. He deflected any questions concerning the bloodline back to The Times staff and any inquiries about the Manton's religious beliefs he put off limits as 'personal.' The Mantons were relieved to have his intervention.

Flink seemed to know intuitively when the crews had enough film for their desired sound bites for the night's news and called a hasty end to the conference and led the Mantons back indoors.

"Sid, I can't thank you enough," Jen said.

"I agree," added Rick.

"Just doing my job," replied the agent. "Now, I get down to the real work of sorting out your offers."

"What offers?" the Mantons said in unison.

"Oh, they'll be coming," Flink proclaimed. "We gave 'em just enough today to make 'em hungry for the Manton family."

Jen and her husband looked at each other. It sounded ominous.

Flink continued, unabated, "I'd keep this week wide open, if I were you. This story will only be hot for a short while, so we need to be ready to maximize your asking price."

"Asking price? For interviews?" asked Rick.

"Sure. You ask the market price. Today you're hot. Tomorrow, you're not."

"I dunno," said Rick slowly. "Is this right?"

"What do you mean? Right?" Flink said, incredulously. He was not used to unsophisticated clients. "If you win the lottery, poof, you're a millionaire and there are still homeless in Manhattan. So is the lottery right?"

"But we haven't done anything," added Jen.

"Look," said Flink with a wave of his hand. "The networks want to interview you. You let 'em do it if they pay you. They decide if it is worth it to get the ratings. They make money, you make money. Nobody gets hurt. How many times can you make a profit and say that?"

"I guess it is like winning the lottery," agreed Jen, reluctantly.

"Maybe we were due for some good luck," added Rick.

"Good," said Flink, enthusiastically. "Now you're thinking straight. Let me go back to my office and start calling around. Here's a stack of my cards. Refer everybody to me. I'll call you by the end of the day, and I'll betcha we have some good money on the table."

The Mantons beamed. It sounded so simple. "Okay," said Rick.

"But nothing sleazy," said Jen.

"The best," said Flink, heading out the door.

* * *

Southern France 1207

After two years, Delacroix was well pleased with how the parish had prospered under his stewardship. It had been a period of no famine or pestilence, and he attributed these blessings of God to the piety of the Church's constituents. Whereas the tension caused by the existence of the Brothers of Zion was always present, Delacroix perceived the prosperous times as a sign that the status quo was acceptable to God and the fathers of the Church. His relationship with Lancel and many of the lesser Knights Templar had naturally strengthened as they worked for the good of Rennes-le-Château in the constant struggle for survival in a harsh time.

Delacroix learned Lancel's history bit by bit while attending the many hunting expeditions captained by Lancel. Most of the information came from Lancel's hunting companions. Lancel rarely spoke of himself, and never of his past.

Reportedly, Lancel's marriage had been arranged by his father when he had turned twenty years old. His bride-to-be was a mere fifteen. At a time in his life when his interest was focused on crusading in far-off adventuresome lands, the thought of marriage to one of the spindly and dull prospective daughters of nobility in neighboring provinces filled him with dread. All that changed when he first laid eyes upon Solange DuClois. She was stunningly beautiful; slender with long auburn hair which framed in curls her narrow face of smooth, pale skin. Her wide-spread blue eyes flashed with mischievousness and laughter. The resulting marriage was a joyous affair.

Lancel quickly learned that he would not dominate this young girl. Solange had a wit, charm and nerve that equaled her important husband's. And although such behavior was frowned upon, she could ride her large steed like a veteran knight. She would often challenge Lancel when they were alone in the countryside, away from the eyes of the serfs whose land they owned. To his chagrin, her steed always outraced his mare in the open fields.

Solange was strong, but her willowy build was not suitable for childbirth. Her first pregnancy, at age seventeen, resulted in a miscarriage late into her term. The whole village mourned, but she was young. Certainly there would be other children.

But Joseph's birth was also ill-fated. After excruciating labor for an entire day, the large baby was stuck in its mother narrow birth canal. Upon seeing his emerging forehead begin to lose color, the experienced midwife, using the limited resources of the age available to her, inserted a pair of broad metal pliers into the womb opening and clamped on to his temples. As Joseph was wrenched from Solange he appeared barely alive. But when the cold night air struck him, he screamed, a joyous sound to all. His bluish body began to turn pink as he kicked and stretched. He was a strong, healthy child.

Lancel was enthralled to be presented with a son, but the ordeal had caused internal bleeding in Solange. With bare medical knowledge of internal organs the doctor's methods and herbs were insufficient to stem the flow. After only a brief glimpse of her son the delirious, exhausted mother lapsed into unconsciousness. By morning her bed was soaked in blood. Her devoted husband held her limp and pale form in the warm embrace of his strong arms until her last breath weakly rattled from her chest. He never said a word as he laid her gently on the bed and tenderly kissed her forehead.

Walking ghost-like past the sobbing attendants, he took his sleeping son from the midwife, and cradled him tightly in the arms that seconds before had rocked his dying mother. He looked at the peaceful face of the infant, so like his mother's, and swore that he would never let harm come to the boy. Joseph had opened up one sleepy eye, and, seemingly knowing that it was his father, gave a deep sigh and went back to sleep.

Lancel had never overcome his wife's death, and he didn't seem to want to. He would never marry again, and rejected any advances toward that goal that came from well-intentioned matchmakers. A shrine dedicated to Solange, established just inside of the manor's entrance, was never without a bank of burning votive candles. On many moonlit evenings, the outline of the fearless knight could be seen through the door, kneeling silently at the foot of the flickering flames.

Among many things that Delacroix admired in Lancel was the manner in which he raised Joseph. He did not lament the tragedy that had befallen his wife, and did not shun his son to the many manor attendants who would have eagerly accepted the task. Joseph was his life. He guided him with a firm hand, yet was careful to cultivate inquisitiveness. He was tolerant of the boy's playfulness, a trait that Joseph had obviously inherited from both of his parents. And he was taught to be respectful of God and the Church.

Delacroix also grew tremendously fond of Joseph. He saw in him many of the traits he had had as a boy, but was never allowed to express in the confining atmosphere of the Orleans monastery. A bond of mentor and student was cemented between them during their frequent fishing trips to nearby streams flowing out of the mountains. At times, while the trout had sequestered to the bottoms of the rapids, Joseph would lament the pure and noble standards that his father expected him to maintain due to his heraldry. Out of respect for their friendship, or perhaps from a fear of knowledge, Delacroix had not questioned him further. He would not break their trust. It was customary that a priest remain at his assigned post until death, and Delacroix welcomed the opportunity of growing old and watching this delightful lad mature into a fair and devout leader in the likeness of his father.

*   *   *

In the fall of 1207, upon return from a particularly rewarding outing, Delacroix received a lengthy dispatch from the Archbishop notifying all dioceses in Languedoc of the growing concern of His Holiness, Pope Innocent III, to the rise of the Cathars. The letter advised that tolerance of heresy was made at the peril of the souls of the Cathars and all who associated with them. Explicitly the Archbishop ordered that the parishioners were to be warned that consorting with heretics would be the source of eternal damnation. Prayers for the deliverance and salvation of the miscreants were to be included in every mass henceforward until the situation was rectified. And for that purpose a papal legate was being sent to Languedoc to oversee the measures.

Delacroix was perplexed. He had seen no evidence that the situation in his diocese was worsening. In fact it seemed so workable that vigilance such as this did not seem necessary. Yet again he accepted the disclosure as truth. It would not have occurred to him to suspect that the Church would have any motive in raising the people against the Cathars, other than attaining their salvation. He would do as he was commanded.

Delacroix was planning to attend the evening supper at Blanchefort. He had a standing invitation whenever he had been on a recent hunting or fishing trip with father or son to bless the bounty and join in the partaking. Joseph had reminded him of his obligation as they had parted at the crossroads to the church and castle. The young boy was proud of the amount of the catch that day which made the burlap carrying sack almost too heavy for a five-year old to carry. Delacroix would go early and address this matter to Lancel. Certainly heading off any further escalation of tensions with the Cathars and the Knights Templar was within the Archbishop's intent, he wrongfully assumed.

Delacroix now rode a horse to visit Blanchefort. The size of his diocese, and the steep hills separating its hamlets, made foot travel impractical. He had become a much better horseman in the last two years, although he would never be mistaken for a cavalryman. He left earlier than usual to arrive before the feast began.

Even with the rising sun the field workers were busily tending the rows of grape vines. "God's greetings, Andre," Delacroix called out to one of his parishioners that he recognized. He was one of the brightest boys in the village who had an amazing mind for memorizing Bible verses and trivial information, starting with the best ways to raise his grape seedlings into thick, lush plants laden with large pump fruit. The beautiful vineyards inspired Delacroix.

As he trotted along the rough trail, Blanchefort was visible at each rise and opening in the trees. The castle walls were imposing, even more so as they were approached and the sharp rise of the final ascent could be appreciated.

The trail steepened as Delacroix reached the bottom station of an enormous pulley that was used to haul supplies up the sheer side of the hill. A hemp rope was looped around a wooden dowel, almost one foot thick, and stretched up the cliffs to the castle walls, virtually unseeable from the low angle. At the top of the castle wall was an unloading station and the engine for the massive lifts, an eight-foot high, wooden, cylindrical cage, driven hamster-like by strong-legged serfs, when the occasion called. On behalf of his huffing mare, Delacroix wished that the pulley was used for visiting dignitaries.

After five minutes Delacroix mercifully dismounted and led his horse for the last fifteen minutes of the trek. He was always glad to breach the last rise and see the top of the circular arch of the castle entrance. The metal hooves of his mount echoed merrily as they crossed the bridge which had been dropped over the dry moat.

Even more impressive than the outer walls, was the vast vista of the castle grounds once the narrow main gate had been passed. It easily could have held a village the size of Rennes-le-Château, and, of itself, was a functioning city. The few goods that could not be grown or fashioned within the castle walls were purchased in Rennes-le-Château. And, other than a simple, stone chapel for the daily devotions, the spiritual needs of the people were administered from Delacroix's monastery.

Delacroix took a deep breath to signal the end of his climb. The warm sweet smell of the bakery wafted through the air. He smiled. It was much better than the putrid smell of the hog and cattle butchery that often, but necessarily, fouled the entrance even though it was tucked in the far corner of the bailey.

Plodding past the well at the heart of the square, Delacroix sympathized with the mud-encrusted cattle, yoked in heavy wooden collars, straining in never-ending circles to pull precious water from deep beneath the hill's surface.

Blanchefort was staffed with hundreds of servants and caretakers who lived in huts at the bottom of the hill. For the most part they were serfs who had shown some ability to master a skill that was needed at the castle. And any job at the castle was usually desired over working the dry rocky fields. All who worked on the castle grounds ate their noon meal there. It increased their incentive that the whole complex run efficiently and profitably. And under the watchful, prodding eye of Lancel, it did.

There were no merchants or middle-class at Blanchefort. The land-owners and extended families of Lancel occupied various wings of the manor, which, on one entire side, was also the castle wall. The rest lived outside the walls, and walked up the hill every day to their jobs.

The main square was alive with activity, and Delacroix did not pass unaddressed. He was greeted courteously at the front door of the impressive two-story manor by a servant who was not surprised to see the frequent visitor. He was led through the feast hall to a study in the rear.

Lancel was straining to read a leather bound text. When he heard footsteps he pulled off a pair of eye spectacles and rose. "Father, always a blessing to have you join us. I hear you've taught Joseph a fancy sailor's knot from Normandy. Perhaps I should not spend so much time surveying the serfs and more at the shoreline."

"In another year it will be Joseph tutoring both of us. He's a bright boy," replied Delacroix.

"We are grateful to his sainted mother."

"Sir Frederick, I have come to speak to you of a grave notice I have received from the Archbishop."

"Sir Frederick? This must be most grave, Father. Pray, tell."

"It has been unspoken between us of your association with Cathars and engagement with the Brothers of Zion." Delacroix paused, but Lancel did not offer comment. "I have found no root to question your fealty to the Church."

"And there should be no question." Lancel closed his book.

"There is none as to you. But there arises in Languedoc, a continued heresy which is supported by these people and these blasphemous beliefs."

"I know not what this could be." Lancel sounded more defiant than doubtful.

"You are aware of the condemnation of Catharism at the Council of Lombers."

Lancel nodded. He was well aware of the decades of persecution that had followed the travesty that the Church had considered a trial. It was a subject that could easily raise his ire. His furled brow reflected his displeasure with this breach of etiquette between them.

Delacroix continued, "His Holiness is informed that it is the belief of the Brothers of Zion that its members are the blood children of Our Lord. A papal legate is being sent to supervise the efforts in Languedoc to correct such thought."

"Father Delacroix ... Bernard," Lancel said, grimly. "We have shared many good days afield. We have supped and drank together. You know what is in my heart. You know that the Knights Templar fear God and love the Church. So we have not held discourse on this undertaking as our positions are opposed. I will not deceive thee now. The Brothers of Zion celebrate our kinship to Our Risen Christ. We are the descendants of King David."

Lancel paused to assure that Delacroix heard his conviction on this point. The priest began to speak, but Lancel raised his hand to continue. "We have rejoiced in this knowledge as did our fathers and our fathers' fathers. We know that the Church does not accept us as we accept the Church. But our beliefs are true. It was for the vengeance of our Redeemer that the Knights Templar marched on Jerusalem to reclaim the Temple of Solomon. We marched to reestablish our heritage, for ourselves, if no one else. Can we deny that which God has bestowed upon us? We cannot. But we welcome the spread of the Savior's message throughout the world. We wish to live in harmony with the Church. I pledge to you my word that there is no insurrection within the Knights Templar nor the Brothers of Zion. As to the Cathars, I see not what complaint there can be of them. Are they not as meek as the sheep in the field?"

Delacroix knew that Lancel was a man of immovable convictions. But he also knew that the Church was divine and its leaders unbending. It was necessary for the salvation of those who were ignorant of the true path of God that he correct their erroneous ways.

"Sir Frederick, you must examine your beliefs. You will see that they are inspired by evil and you must turn away from them. I have seen the people of Rennes-le-Château and Blanchefort. They respect you, and they will follow your guidance. Your mistaken belief in this bloodline of our Lord shall lead them all to damnation." Delacroix may as well have tried to make the mountain streams run uphill.

Lancel did not lose his patience with the challenging words. "Father Delacroix, the Brothers of Zion have known twelve centuries of persecution for their beliefs. For us, it would be evil to deny our heritage. We cannot now be swayed."

"But how can you reconcile that the Bible is supreme and this claim of children of Jesus also be true when it is nowhere sanctioned?" Delacroix debated.

"Bernard, do not betray what has passed between us on such a stance. Have we not spent hours, nay weeks, discussing the phrases of the Bible that can be interpreted in opposite ways? What of our discussions of the slaying of the Moslems in the conquests of the holy lands as contrary to the commandment that 'thou shalt not kill'? Surely you cannot hold that the Bible excludes as possible that which is not mentioned?"

"But children from Mary Magdalen! Surely such an event would not have been overlooked?" Delacroix would admit to ambiguities in the Bible due to human ignorance, but he could not admit that The Book itself was fallible.

Lancel continued, patiently. "But what are we told of Mary Magdalen? In the great masses we are told that she was a whore. A woman of several sins. In every city on this continent there are homes for fallen women. The Church has named these refuges "Magdalens" to remind us of the lady's sins."

Lancel walked to the mantle where a massive Bible sat, it edges well-worn. Lancel laid his large hand upon it, gingerly. "But as we learn to read the Lord's words, we find nowhere is Mary Magdalen anything but the devoted follower of Jesus." Lancel's eyes flashed to Delacroix. "Why is her name so slandered? Think, my Brother. Why are we not told that she escaped to France? We of Languedoc know what the papists in Italy will not admit." Lancel's voice filled with emotion as he reached out and grasped Delacroix's forearm. "She blessed our shores, Bernard. With my own hands, I have touched her bones at Saint Maximin. Was all of this, which you know to be true, my friend, also overlooked?"

Delacroix could not think of any passage in the Bible that addressed any of this directly. Cornered, he relied on doctrine. "The Holy Father is divinely inspired. We cannot question the proclamations of the past."

"My accepting Brother," Lancel said, shaking his head. "The Pope serves at the will of the King of France. Should the Church contradict the wishes of the throne, the king shall have the papal see moved. It will happen in our lifetime." Lancel had correctly predicted the direction of the future, if not the timing. Early in the next century the papacy would be installed in Avignon in response to such a feud.

"It is unthinkable."

"Ah, but it is." Lancel could not diffuse the conversation now. "We will not accept the word of a pope and discard all else. We choose to base our beliefs on our reading of the Holy Word, and what our fathers have told us."

Lancel's answers to these questions displayed the depth of the heresy that Delacroix, until this moment, had not fully grasped. Yet the conviction of this learned man caused him to pause and consider the unthinkable. Perhaps the Bible was not infallible? Perhaps the reputation of Mary Magdalen was soiled by those who sought to persecute the holy children brought to French shores? But to Delacroix, faith was absolute. He concluded that the whole tale had to be preposterous and the conversation demonstrated how badly a good man such as Lancel was in need of spiritual guidance.

Delacroix's troubled look was obvious. Lancel had faced this argument many times before and knew that he had Delacroix at a disadvantage. He did not press the topic. He liked the priest and needed the support of the local Church.

"Bernard, we should not concern ourselves today with problems that are eternal. Come, we have fish to eat and the wine crop has been freshly stomped. Please do sup with us."

Delacroix could not hate Lancel for his beliefs, they were too naive and artless. But he did fear for his friend's soul as this dogma had to be rooted in evil. He vowed to work to save his soul. "Of course. But we shall unite in our prayers for wisdom, shan't we?"

"Indeed. I can always use more of that." Lancel was glad to put this episode to rest. "Now where is this secret stream of which Joseph resounds, where the fish leap from the water in quest for your net?"

Laughing together, Lancel and Delacroix strode shoulder to shoulder toward the great dining hall.

* * *

New York City

"Good evening, Ladies and Gentlemen. As tonight's guest we are pleased to have the Reverend Johnny Hanner." Larry King was sitting forward, staring into the camera. "Reverend Hanner has hosted his syndicated television and radio program, 'Eternal Hope' since 1972. It is estimated in that time he has had close to a half billion viewers. In addition Reverend Hanner has provided spiritual counsel to our last eight presidents of the United States, beginning with the administration of Richard Nixon. Welcome, Reverend Hanner."

The camera backed up to reveal Reverend Hanner sitting across the mahogany desk from his interviewer. He was dressed in an expensive dark suit with a conservative red tie. On his lapel was an American flag. As usual, Hanner's full head of silver hair was perfect, swept back and shiny from the spray that held it rigidly in place. He was still a youngish sixty-five years old. His brief smile flashed white teeth which seemed all the more brilliant against his dark tan. From years of practice he had his television appearance down to a fine art.

"Ah thank-you, Larry." Hanner spoke with a heavy, slow, dignified southern drawl. Those who knew him well knew that he saved the accent for public occasions and television appearances. He believed it was the suitable image for a fire-and-brimstone preacher.

"And of course we send our greetings to your lovely wife, Linda Sue." Hanner's wife was an integral part of 'Eternal Hope', fawning over his prayers as a dutiful wife would honor her husband. She was a role model for millions and her fluffy bleached blonde hairdo and puppet-like makeup made her recognizable across the land.

"Yes, she is sorry she could not be here tonight, but she is at a fund-raiser for the children's hospital in Memphis."

It was enough small talk for King. "Reverend Hanner, you've been on this show many times. As you know, we invited you back this time, not as in the past for your views on current political issues, but to discuss the maelstrom created by the New York Times story printed earlier this week of the existence of a bloodline from Jesus Christ."

"Larry, it's always a pleasure to come on your show. Ah am certainly happy to be here to bring to light the fallacies of that story which, in mah opinion, was recklessly published."

"Now you've come out publicly quite critical of the research of Professors Hershner and Fahey. If I may summarize, you take these theories to constitute an unsubstantiated attack on the Christian religion. Is that a correct statement of your position?"

"Yes, Larry, that sums it up quite well." Hanner continued without a prompt. "This far-fetched theory is not founded in historical fact, let alone theology. It was quite irresponsible for a publication of the Times stature to publish it. Quite frankly, and Ah hesitate to say this," Hanner was not hesitating at all, "upon impartial review of these series of articles it appears that both the professors and The New Yahk Times were more swayed by profit motive than by serious intellectual research. They knew that these wild claims would generate intense interest which, in their world, equates to obtaining donations and selling newspapers. They have been quite successful in that regard to the detriment of the American Christian public."

King knew that Hanner would use his forum for pontificating and was well-prepared to refocus the interview. He had built his show's popularity on lulling his guests with cream puff questions before sneaking in a hard one that would prompt a sensational response that the guest would later regret, but could hardly recant. "Reverend Hanner, as you are aware Professors Hershner and Fahey were on this program yesterday. I have to say, they made a pretty convincing case for their theories and had the research, at least to my untrained mind, to back them up. Do you have any historical facts or data that you can point to that refute their theory that Jesus Christ had children and that his bloodline exists to this day?"

"Heh, heh, heh." Hanner chuckled theatrically as he made a movement as if pulling his chair closer to the desk. He smiled the familiar smile that gave comfort to millions of viewers every Sunday morning. "How can you factually refute something that isn't based on known facts to begin with? If you tell me that you saw a UFO, and you give me a letter from your great-grandfather saying that he saw the same UFO, what could Ah possibly have to prove that you are both wrong? Ah have the rest of the world that didn't see your particular UFO. So who is wrong and who is right? The same is true here. These professors from Boston," he pronounced the city with disdain in his voice, "have taken a few historical myths and woven a tale among those myths to conclude that Our Lord had children. Yet the rest of the civilized world has known for over nineteen centuries that that is not true. So who do you believe? The two thousand years of known facts or the current theorizing two thousand years after the fact?" Hanner had not risen to his position of national prominence by being stupid. He had the ability to break down the most complicated issues into a simple phrase, usually while in prayer, that could speak to his audience long after the television set was off.

"That may be true, but the Bible is silent on whether or not Jesus had children. Isn't it logical that a rabbi in that day and age would have children? Shouldn't the Bible tell us why if he was making such a break from tradition?" prodded King.

"Again, Larry, that sounds good on the surface, but those of us who have spent our lives studying the Bible don't expect all the answers to be there. We never claimed that they were. That is part of the beauty of the Holy Bible. The New Testament doesn't proclaim that Jesus had a red Lincoln-Mercury," Hanner paused and smiled for the camera, "but does that mean that he had one and someone is trying to hide that fact from posterity? Of course not. If the Bible does not say Jesus was married, and does not say he had children, isn't it more logical that it is silent because those things never occurred?"

"True, Reverend, but the argument is that early Christian writers may indeed have commented on the marriage and children of Jesus, but those were edited out in later centuries. Isn't that possible?"

"Certainly anything is possible." Hanner paused to let his watchers nod their agreement as he knew they would be doing.

"Seriously, there is a great deal of theological scholarship on the inadequacies of the early Christians' selection of the books to be included in the New Testament. Why do you feel that these theories should not be explored to see if they have any credence?"

For the camera Hanner bristled at the questions. But his responses were ready. "First of all, the attacks on the various holy councils that insured that only the Word of God was sanctioned are primarily motivated by those with a political agenda to forward. Romans authored many books that proclaimed Christ was one of many deities only equal to their pagan gods. The Greeks championed their gods over Jesus. And some Christian sects went too far and proclaimed Jesus a god unto himself. These holy councils, where the greatest scholars of those early centuries were gathered, were called to weed out the incredible claims that were arising from religious manipulators of that age. We can be thankful for their work. Had the books of the Bible not been selected and sanctified back then, well, we all may have gone home tonight and prayed to our statues of Jesus, Zeus and Apollo."

Hanner was on a roll and was, ostensibly, answering the questions. "Secondly, Christians of faith do not need to see these theories explored. The Word of God has been sent to us through His Son, Jesus Christ of Nazareth. If Christians suspended their faith every time another attack on the Message of God occurred, we would never have time to pursue the teachings of Christ."

"But what would be so harmful to Christianity if Jesus had fathered children?"

"Ah'm glad you asked." Hanner said this as if the question were a surprise. He had planned on it. "The Mantons are a prime example of the evil that arises from this so-called theory. We now have these people," Hanner said, referring to the Mantons, "appearing, Ah hear, on 'The Lorrie Waters Show' as the new purveyors of the word of God. Ah don't know about y'all, but Ah'm offended. Are their views to become the new, revised Holy Bible? And what of their children and their children's children? Will they revise the message as each sees fit? The Word of God is Holy. If it is allowed to be altered generation to generation then really all you have is a monarchy, not a divinely inspired religion. And that is what the Mantons, Hershner and Fahey and The Times are all advocating here."

"We have the Reverend Johnny Hanner with us tonight and he has some strong opinions of the newly discovered bloodline of Jesus. We'd love to hear your opinions on the phonelines, right after this word from our sponsors."

Rick hit the MUTE button on the remote.

"That isn't fair." Jen was steaming. "He makes it seem like we've concocted this thing to start some new religion. We didn't invent my family tree. It could have been anyone else in the world, it just happened to be us."

"I know, Jen, I know."

"He'd probably be singing a different hymn if he was the end of the bloodline instead of us. He would probably rewrite the Bible."

As a hot topic, the bloodline story exceeded everyone's predictions. And Gilliam was right, the human interest element of seeing living, breathing relatives of Christ had made the Mantons overnight sensations. Every television network in the country wanted a news clip of the only survivors of the bloodline. Particularly their photogenic son. At first, no one cared if the bloodline story was fact or fiction. The public wanted to see what these Mantons looked like.

Sid Flink naturally had recommended the most monetarily lucrative offers. They had just signed for an interview with Lorrie Waters, the glamorous hostess of the hottest up and coming television newsmagazine. According to the commercials, which aired hours after the deal was cut, the Mantons were scheduled to be on coast-to-coast television in three nights. There was no reason not to take the offers. The Mantons firmly adopted Flink's motto that if they weren't making money off of anyone else's misfortune, there was no harm done. Maybe they didn't deserve such luck, but then again, why not? Good things happened to other people. This was a balancing of their lifetime luck scale, they mused.

The commercials were over and Rick again pushed MUTE and restored the sound.

"Hello, Birmingham, Alabama. You're on the air."

"Hi, Larry. I'm glad to see that you haven't gone all the way to the left on us. I couldn't believe that you had those east coast liberals on your show and let them ramble on about this bloodline claim. I agree with the Reverend, you might as well have a show on UFO sightings if you believe that."

"So you don't believe that it is possible that Jesus had children?" King tried to inject some controversy into each call.

"Of course not," the caller continued. "There is no mention of it at all whatsoever in the Bible. I think the Mantons are just some used car salesmen trying to make a buck off of this."

Jen was out of her chair. "You idiot!" she yelled at the screen.

"Thank-you for calling. Topeka, Kansas, you're on the air."

It didn't get much better that night for the Mantons. The supporters of the bloodline theory had called in the day before. Hanner had the floor to himself and the self-described 'back hills preacher' attracted a large following which wasn't hesitant about expressing the belief that the bloodline claim was an affront to everything they had been taught since birth. The only caller that could say anything on the Mantons behalf sympathetically concluded that they must have been duped by the smarter professors.

Jen switched the set off. "I'm always amazed at how closed-minded some people can be."

"Some take their religion more strongly than others," Rick offered. He had always thought Jen was slightly closed-minded herself on the matter of religion, but it had never mattered enough to him that he had told her so. He felt it was all a matter of perspective. And to him peace with his wife was worth more than philosophical debate. "Let's hit the sack. We want to look good for our interview tomorrow morning."

"Rick, did you ever think this thing would get so big?"

"No. I still can't believe it."
"Me either."

$$*\quad *\quad *$$

Washington D.C.

"God damn it." The Oval Office echoed with the curse.

President Ben Dailley clicked off the Larry King Show from across the room. He had been Commander in Chief of the United States for nine months and had a hard enough time handling the *anticipated* issues. Now this political grenade was bouncing his way.

"I don't give a goose's crap whether Manton is the grandson of Christ, Buddha or Mohammed," he railed at window.

His first year wasn't supposed to have been this difficult. In an upset he had been elected on a conservative platform while dozens of his fellow Republicans nationwide had been thrown out of their Senate and Congressional seat by voters that were demanding change, any change. The opposition was determined to flex their newly retrieved muscle at every opportunity, making Dailley's life miserable. His campaign promises had fallen like leaves in the resulting storm.

Now his staff was telling him that the public wanted to know his stand on this ridiculous business of whether the Christian church should recognize the alleged descendants of Jesus or stick with the message it had been preaching for two millenniums. He had been elected on the promise that he had a formula to reduce taxes without touching Social Security benefits. But Congress wouldn't cut back on their pet projects and now the deficit was splitting wide open again. As had been predicted for years, the only sacrifice to appease it was Social Security. He had compromised on minimum wage increases and illegal immigrant penalties. He had quieted down on the right to bear arms and abortion. Just when he felt besieged on all fronts and now the people wanted to know his stand on the foundation of the country's majority religion, and the staff was feeling his anger.

Dailley turned to the only other person in the room. "Why the hell would I know if this is bullshit or not?"

"Ben, let's look at the voters." Joe Thorne was Dailley's chief of staff and had steered him through political swamps for over twenty years, including three terms as governor of Florida. He always spoke in terms of 'voters' and not 'public opinion.' The latter did not concern him.

"Our polls say that seventy per cent of the voters believe that your lack of position on this Manton thing means that you support its credibility. That is not a good thing with our conservative donors. The liberals, on the other hand, are transforming this into an *intellectual freedom* issue. Sort of like the abortion debate: it's not the bloodline, but the right to believe in the bloodline that is important."

The President cringed at Thorne's comparison with the dreaded abortion issue. This was another nightmare.

Thorne continued. "But the bottom line is that the majority of Americans will see whichever direction you go as pandering to one side or the other. Your silence is making them edgy."

"It's only been a week since I heard of this whole cock-and-bull story."

"Issues break fast."

Dailley paced. "Say that I come out against this bloodline. Then what happens if these stuffed shirts up in Boston come up with more proof? What do I say then? The press is holding their breath for the next Dailley flip-flop." Dailley stopped and glared at Thorne. "Aren't they?"

"We know that, Ben. But we also know that we were elected by the voters that support traditional family values and school prayer. The Mantons are viewed as another challenge to their long-standing Christian philosophy. We haven't delivered for the Moral Majority and the polls are starting to reflect it. We are losing our base. But they seem to be drawing a line in the sand here."

In Dailley's experience, Thorne was never far off base. But he also knew that it was he, and not Thorne, that had to handle the questions from the press. He had learned from experience that if he took positions that he hadn't fully comprehended or believed in that it came back to haunt him. This certainly fit into that ill-fated category. "This is a lose-lose issue, isn't it, Joe?"

"You could call it that," Thorne agreed. As chief of staff, he certainly labeled it that way. He also knew that his boss rebelled at being *told* where to stand and often had to be *corralled* into the correct position.

"Can't I just hold off saying anything for now and leave it to the preachers and professors? Let them battle it out?"

Thorne feigned contemplation. This was where he wanted to go. "Oh, I suppose there isn't that much harm in laying low on this for a while. But as soon as some other scholar pops up with a good, historical refutation of Hershner and Fahey we should be ready to jump on the front of that bandwagon. All will be forgiven."

Dailley looked relieved. He didn't want to fight with Thorne again. The deficit and tax platforms had been confrontational and he wanted to avoid any more personal strife between the old friends. "Great."

"I'll put out a release saying that due to your immersion into the recent domestic issues and upcoming peace talks in Vienna that you haven't had time to fully review the articles and rebuttal. That sort of pooh-poohs the issue, which will keep our constituents happy, but not deny the theories in case the public mood makes a swing."

"Once again Joe, you've proven why I keep your irritating mug around here." The President smiled, relieved. "Are we going to be able to get the Gators' opener on satellite at Camp David?"

"I'll see to it."

*   *   *

Rennes-le-Château

From the pulpit, Delacroix administered the warnings of the Roman Catholic Church as he had been directed. Attendance by those suspected of being Catharist sympathizers dropped slightly in the next year, but generally they continued to support the Church and stowed their beliefs even farther from view. Lancel and the other Knights Templar that regularly attended did not protest the tone of the sermons. But the words did not have their desired effect. The knights did not abandon their affiliations with Cathars nor did they disband the Brothers of Zion.

To the rest of the villagers, albeit the minority, the habitual reminders that there were infidels in the community that could cause them all to burn in the fires of hell accomplished one goal, a resentment to the knights and the Brothers of Zion arose where previously there had been cooperation, if not outright admiration and respect.

Lancel could weather the animosity. He still held title to the majority of the lands. The feudal loyalty of the farmers and peasants could not be withdrawn. His contracts were still the highest prize of the village merchants, though they no longer bragged about them over ale at the village roadhouse. It was apparent to Lancel what was happening, but as he had told Delacroix, the bloodline of Jesus had long suffered from prejudice and oppression. This was minor. It too would pass. Despite pleas from Delacroix, the secret meetings and the heresy they fostered continued.

Whereas Delacroix felt the pressure and awkwardness that the conflict engendered with Lancel, little Joseph was immune to it. He still showed up at the priest's entry on a regular basis in search of a companion headed for the streams, or to pose a question that only the bright mind of an innocent child could ponder. Delacroix understood that these visits were approved by Lancel and were a sign that, despite the apparent schism, they both believed that the eternal struggle for survival would outlive this quarrel.

*   *   *

Rome   1208

Even in this far south in the country, the damp January air could be bone-chilling. Especially when the pressures of decision making that inevitably come with power, bore in.

The leader of a vast empire, yet he often felt trapped within this palace built for comfort of his predecessors. He rubbed behind his prominent ears, trying to massage out the headache, as he looked out the slightly steam tinged window. Past the concrete railings he could see the average citizens milling in the square below, hoping to catch a glimpse of him. They would not be rewarded today.

Pope Innocent III cringed as he heard a tap on the door to his study. He knew it was the contingent of French "advisors." Thirteenth century lobbyists. The meeting had been scheduled that morning. His Holiness dreaded these sessions. The Roman Catholic Church covered the majority of Europe, the British Isles and onto Constantinople, thanks to his efforts. Such power meant wealth and influence that was unfathomable to the people in the piazza. But it also meant headaches, because somewhere, at all times, there was a challenge to that power. And the French were a continual thorn in his side.

As a young man, Innocent, then Lothar of Segni, had planned for this office his whole life. It was the greatest political plum that could be reaped. And he had truly hoped that when the College of Cardinals had elected him, unanimously, at age thirty-seven, now some nine years ago, to succeed Pope Celestine III, that the secular turmoil would be minimal. He had been wrong.

"Your Worship," announced the doorman, "the Abbott of Grandselve."

Innocent was surprised to see Arnaldus Amalrici enter alone, without his usual entourage.

"Your Holiness," the abbot said as he knelt and kissed the papal ring on Innocent's hand which he had automatically extended. The pontiff had had arguments in the past with Amalrici, but they were over doctrine and he had not held the intellectual debates against the cleric who was the same age as he. From his years of study at the Université de Paris the pontiff was comfortable with the language, if not its people. He inquired, in French, about the journey, knowing that in the wet winter season, the trip must have been slow and damp. "And how did you find the roads, Arnaldus?"

"Terrible, as one would expect," the abbot replied.

"Then your business must be important," replied Innocent.

"Your Holiness, we have news of the Cathars in Languedoc."

The Pope rolled his eyes in disgust. He pursed his thin mouth even smaller. For years he had been beseeched by requests from the French King Philip to subdue the heretics in this bastard region which no country really seemed to want. He did not say this, aware that it was Amalrici's homeland, where he had been born to nobility before entering the monastery at Cîteaux. The "democratic" bent of the Cathars threatened the feudal system that supported the land-owners, and hence, the tax base of the king. If their beliefs were to gain popularity and spread, who knew where it would end. It was a threat to the Church, the French advisors had urged time and time again. But, he mused, did any of them ever have a plan for its cure?   "Yes.   Yes," Innocent said, impatiently. "They have been condemned, have they not? Have I not supported the Council at Lombers?," Innocent correctly reminded his visitor.

The Frenchman nodded. Innocent was not a man with whom one argued. What he said was true. But it had been over forty years since the famous council had been convened in the French castle of Lombers, just south of Albi, France, the stronghold of the Cathars at that time. Under the strict supervision of the local bishop, the Cathars were accused of several counts of heresy. And in Innocent's first year as pontificate he had issued the decree Vergentis which authorized the dispossession of the lands of heretics such as the Cathars. Indeed, Abbot Amalrici could not have asked for a better partner in ridding his homeland of the pesky Cathars.

"Certainly, Your Holiness." He continued cautiously, "And it has made the Cathars be more, shall we say, discreet. But still they persist. And I need not remind you that their ties to the Knights of the Templar grow ever deeper."

Innocent chaffed at the rebuke. "I am aware. I am aware," he huffed. More haranguing was not what he needed. He needed the warmth of the summer Italian sun. Pushing his floor length silken robes to his sides, he strode across the carpeted floor to a massive wooden cabinet in the corner. He swung open the elaborate door, inlaid with polished wood and jewels. "I have read these reports." He waved a hand at the neat rows of paper scrolls, including many written from a particularly verbose Frenchman, Father Delacroix of Rennes-le-Château. "Tell me something that is not known to me, Arnaldus," he challenged.

The advisor grinned. "Your Holiness. We have received confirmation that one of the legates, that only last fall, you sent to Languedoc, Pierre de Castlenau ... has been murdered."

The Pope's face furled in dismay. He had no great attachment to the representative that he had barely known, it had been Amalrici's choice, but he could not tolerate the affront to his papal control. "Who has done this deed?" he demanded.

"The circumstances are, shall we say, suspicious, Your Holiness," Amalrici continued. "But it can only be the work of Cathars."

"That is true," the Pope agreed, warily, surveying his options. He turned to look out the window again.

"The past condemnation of the Cathars has not been sufficient." This was not a new complaint, but Innocent did not chastise the Frenchman. He sensed that, for a change, he would be presented with a plan of action. He nodded, his high cap exaggerating his movement.

"Your Holiness, with the consent of Her Majesty, the Kingdom of France requests that these Cathars be, shall we say, eradicated."

Innocent could not stifle his laugh. This was the brilliant French plan. "And you shall tell me to rid Saxony of rats, as well," he roared.

Amalrici cowered momentarily, surprised at the unfavorable reception. Had he misjudged Innocent? "Your Holiness, we only ask that you, as leader of the Roman Church, lend divine blessing to this crusade."

"And what do you propose that the Pontificate shall bless," Innocent replied, placing the specter of his office in front of them all.

"Another crusade, your Holiness." Three years after Innocent had been crowned, he called for a crusade, the so-called Fourth Crusade, that had marched to Constantinople, in an attempt to unify the Roman Catholic Church with its Eastern Orthodox brethren. It had succeeded, in military terms, and a Latin patriarchate was installed. But without the collaboration of the Grecian clergy, his dream of a unified empire had crumbled in the ensuing years.

"To Jerusalem? To Constantinople?" Innocent, confused, was not anxious to extend his power to those fronts again. And what would it matter to the French?

"Mais non. A crusade to Albi. To drive the infidels from our Languedoc, just as the great crusades of the past drove the infidels from the Holy Lands."

"A crusade," Innocent said slowly, trying on the concept.

"The King supports, no, King Philip requests such a decree from His Holiness." By strengthening the allegiance owed to him by landowners in Languedoc, the abbot did not need to add.

"Who would lead such a crusade?" Innocent asked. "The Knights Templar cannot be expected to lead one against themselves?"

"Ah, but that is not correct. The Knights of the northern provinces are aware that the Knights of the south are infected with this belief that they are the descendants of our Lord Jesus. They will lead the charge to eradicate such heresy. In fact, we can recommend to you the services of Simon de Montfort l'Amaury."

Amalrici knew that the general from Toulouse was a favorite of Innocent. He had led one of the armies of the Fourth Crusade, and, unlike other of the generals, had sided with Innocent's in protesting the crusade's various diversions. In fact, Montfort had not yet been consulted on this matter. Amalrici would deal with that later.

"Montfort would know the region ..." Innocent said, thinking aloud. He paused in thought as Amalrici leaned in.

"And if it were to be sanctioned that those joining the crusade were allowed to keep, shall we say, a percent of that which was owned by the heretics, perhaps it would not take long to conscript an army for this crusade."

"A crusade," murmured Innocent, warming to the idea.

"The Albigensian Crusade," urged the abbot. "It shall be done."

*   *   *

4

Consciously, I was religious in the Christian sense, though always with the reservation: 'But it is not so certain as all that.' -- C. G. Jung

The program began with the familiar face and voice of Lorrie Waters. "Good evening ladies and gentlemen. Welcome to the living room of the most controversial family in, well, perhaps American history."

The Mantons sat glued to the television set in the very room where the piece had been filmed the day before. They didn't know which portions of the four hours of interview would be aired in the hour-long special. They both knew that they had said things that later, in retrospect, they couldn't believe they had blurted out. Waters had an uncanny ability to wring confessions and stories from even the most jaundiced movie stars. Network executives were predicting viewership of Super Bowl proportions for the "coming-out" of the Manton family. The Mantons proved to be little match for Waters' cunning charm. Fortunately for them, but unfortunate for the network, their life stories, up until now, were pretty boring stuff. Even the sleazy tabloids would have to inject an alien or two into their stories to bring them up to juicy industry standards.

"Good evening, Rick. Jen. Thank you for inviting America into your home."

Jen groaned as the camera swung to them for the first time. "God. Look how fat I look. Look at my hair." Jen certainly wasn't fat and her hair looked fine, but the shock of seeing herself on television gave rise to insecurities she didn't normally feel. On the screen the Mantons were sitting next to each other on the couch, Jen's hands in her lap and Rick with his arm draped over the back. Rick flinched at the sight as well. They looked like two nervous school kids talking to a probing parent before a first date. He knew he would never hear the end of this from his league basketball teammates. He thought that the video put twenty extra pounds on him as well.

"Sure."

"You're welcome." Again they groaned. It sounded so trite. But what could you say to that. *'Thanks for the $350,000 appearance fee my agent negotiated?'*

The Mantons were flabbergasted when Sid Flink told them that the myriad of talk show hosts were calling and bidding for the "virgin" interview with their family. He had previously advised them not to talk to any local media, other than Gilliam, of course. Now they knew why. To build the anticipation. To build the public's hunger for information. And to build the price their agent could command. The Mantons discussed between themselves whether it was right to accept money for an interview. They quickly came to a unanimous decision. This wasn't morals, this was show business. They weren't making money off of anyone's misery, so they thought, so *'why not?'*

As the bids came rolling in, going up in increments of $50,000, even this sliver of doubt evaporated. The final bid was the Lorrie Waters Show.

Sure, the lawyers had to work out the terms so the money would come from the network as an 'endorsement' so it would not look like 'checkbook' journalism. But Waters had the ratings, network support and, hence, the biggest budget. She wouldn't be outbid for presenting the first peek and the famous Manton couple, with cameo appearances of the son, America's first and only Crown Prince.

The show began slowly as had the interview. The mundane details of their lives had been edited. But when Jen's voice faltered as she recalled the struggles of her since deceased mother raising her alone, the camera was affixed on her wet, green eyes to insure that America knew that the descendant of Jesus wept. The producers knew when they saw the tapes that her wholesome good looks would provide the sex appeal that this story desperately needed. With some help with her wardrobe they projected her as the media's next Lady Di.

"Are either of you particularly religious? Or should I ask, were you before all this came out?" Waters evoked a laugh from everyone. She knew how to relax her prey.

Rick explained. "We are, of course, Christians ..." That caused a laugh from even the camera operator. Rick had a puzzled look at the interruption, then laughed hesitantly when he realized how odd that sounded from the only family in the world that would fit the newly-evolving definition of 'Christian.'

"I mean religiously, we are Christians. But I have to confess ..."

"Oh, not to me, Rick," Waters exclaimed as she slapped her hand on Rick's forearm and gave a light squeeze. Rick laughed nervously. The camera angle selected for viewing was tight on Rick's shoulder and the millions of viewers only saw a person who looked very uncomfortable with his surroundings. "Please go ahead. I was only kidding."

"Yeah. Well, I was saying that like many Christians we have not been very regular, attendance-wise."

"Christmas and Easter types?"

"Well ... yes."

"I'm sure that describes many Americans," Jen interjected. She didn't want them to appear to be complete heathens. She had always felt guilty that she hadn't given Danny much religious guidance. She had been born Catholic and her mother had held "The Church" in high regard even though she and Jen had rarely attended mass. When Jen had left for college, religion was simply not an issue. It wasn't that she had *fallen* away from her faith, she had just *drifted* away. When she met Rick, the topic of religion just never came up seriously. They were young, in love and too busy.

After Danny was born, Jen renewed her vow to again attend some church's services. With her husband in tow, they ended up at the local Methodist church, more due to its handy locality than any conscious philosophical decision. But, to Jen, the Methodists' services were undisciplined when compared to the Catholic masses she had grown up with. When Sunday mornings arrived it was easy for her to concur with any excuse her husband would proffer.

Sitting in front of the prying stranger, with all of America looking on, Jen felt pangs of conscience about the overall moral appearance of her and her good, but not overly religious husband. At home, in comfortable anonymity, Jen was making faces at the screen.

"What did you two think when you were first told of this amazing news? I assume that you didn't know?" Waters asked, eyes wide.

The on-screen Jen answered. "We were dumbfounded. Actually, like most people, we didn't believe it at first. When Professor Hershner and Professor Fahey first told me I pretty much walked out on them."

Rick's description of how Gilliam slowly converted them was conveniently edited. Waters' network and The New York Times had no affiliation.

"Do you now believe that you are a descendant of Jesus Christ of Nazareth?" Waters put on her "truly-don't-know-the-answer" face even though the whole world must have known by now after Gilliam's series of feature articles. Waters knew that television viewership did not necessarily correspond with newspaper readership.

"We have now had a chance to review and absorb all of the findings and theories of the professors, and although we don't agree with all of the theories, we have to admit that the research on the family tree, and the books they uncovered in France ... it's all very convincing. If it wouldn't have been us I would have accepted it without much question."

Across America some understanding heads nodded. That could have been us, they murmured, some fearfully, others wishfully. Others, contorted with anger, yelled their disgust at the outrageous statements coming from their set. Were the Mantons frauds or fools?

Jen clarified what they had gone through. "You have to understand that we had no way to evaluate what we were being told. But it apparently is being embraced by other scholars. Their research is quite thorough and in depth. And we've been told that these professors are well-accepted in their fields."

As the program broke for the lucrative commercials, households from coast to coast argued. Were Hershner and Fahey charlatans selling snake oil? Or were they respected scientists? The opinions widely varied and the answer usually depended on the viewers' religious convictions and not on the research that had been presented. For most the whole subject was too personal to be purely a matter of science. The future battle lines were being well-drawn as the network logo flashed, indicating a return to the controversial program.

The camera focused on Waters as her face twisted into her now famous look that foretold that a hard, serious question was coming. "So from what you are telling me, you believe you are true descendants of Christ. That the Lord's blood runs in your veins. Tell me, do you believe that Jesus is the Son of God, and if so, does that make you divine?" Waters' piercing stare followed the question.

"Whoa." Rick pushed his shoulders back and took a deep breath. "That's a hard one."

Rick had never believed in an eternal afterlife. All he knew was that his father had also died when he was young and he had felt nothing but loss. There was no return. No reaching out from beyond the grave. To him his father, and years later, his mother were gone. Their bodies were, as the priest had said, dust. And so they were. He didn't hold that tenet with bitterness, it just seemed apparent to him. Dogs were life. Cows were life. Even a tree was life. But their death or destruction was just a natural pattern in the ebb and flow of life. It was the same for humans. Life was precious and short. That was his religion.

It didn't bother Rick that others attended church, or even encouraged him to do so. His mother had been an avid church-goer most of her life. He had many memories of his family trekking in the car to church on snowy Sundays-closest-to-Christmas. After he was married, he and Jen would attend church on the rare occasion when Jen pushed it, usually Christmas or Easter. He could see the utility in having the back-up comfort of all that Christianity proclaimed. The concept of an eternal heaven where all loved ones were reunited sounded inviting. But his brief attempts to embrace it were rebuffed by the absence of proof. He promised himself that he would make a conscious effort not to pass his skepticism on to Danny. Everyone had the right to make their own decision on such affairs.

"Go on." Waters knew when to push. Yet, inexplicably, she inspired soul-searching truth.

"Jen and I feel differently on this issue, because of our religious backgrounds I suppose, but for me, deep down," Rick took a deep breath, "I never fully accepted the part of Christianity that said Jesus was the Son of God in the meaning we have today, like Danny is my son. Much of that is my lack of religious training, I know, but I always took it to be more of a metaphorical thing. A description. I never did understand the Trinity. I always just thought maybe I was the one who didn't understand it. So to answer your question, I thought Jesus was a great man. Probably inspired by God. But not God himself. So I don't think Danny or Jen could, or would, claim any form of divinity. God knows ..." Rick stumbled with the metaphor he had used so commonly before, "... that is, anyone who knows me knows I'm an average Joe. Maybe a little luckier than most, but you have to remember that I'm an accidental tourist in all this. It's not like we were exploring our family tree to prove this. It really landed in our laps. We're still trying to sort out what it all means." Rick felt he had given a polite answer. But all true.

"That sounds very Christ-like." The camera refocused on Waters. She posed theatrically as if in thought. "You know, like selected by a higher power? Take this mantle from me?" Waters had been well-briefed by someone with religious knowledge.

"I guess so." Rick hadn't thought about it either. But to many in America this very answer was taken as defiantly smug.

Most of Jen's follow-up answer to the same question ended up on the cutting room floor. Her beliefs were much more traditional and too boring to boost the Neilson ratings.

"So America has been waiting patiently. Where is little Danny Manton?"

"He's in his room, waiting to come down," Jen replied on cue.

The buildup was too great not to break into a commercial. "Let's get him out here, right after this break," said Waters.

Jen reached for the control and turned the sound down.

"You know, I never knew you felt that way about religion and Jesus," she said, sounding hurt by the fact that she heard it for the first time in front of a television crew.

"It isn't any big deal, is it?" Rick was sensitive to her feelings.

"No, but you never told me." There was some irritation in there, as well.

"It never really came up."

"But we go to church. Now and then, anyway. Don't you feel sort of, well, funny, about it?" she asked.

"About what? Going to church, or what I think?" Rick didn't mind discussing his beliefs with Jen. He didn't see it as a divisive topic. It was just his feelings.

"Both."

"Not really. We don't go that often. And I don't mind it. And what I believe is really just what I think. It isn't like I'm not Christian."

"It sure sounded like it."

"Nah. Nobody would take it like that. Lots of people are the same way."

"I don't think so. What about the guys you play basketball with. Most of them are pretty conservative.

You said some of them go to church. Don't you think they believe in Jesus?"

"Jen, first of all, we don't talk about anything that deep. Second, I didn't say I don't believe in Jesus. I just don't think that we've got the whole story. Frankly, I wasn't too shocked at what Hershner and Fahey were saying. I just wasn't sure I believed it." Rick was defensive about the questioning.

"It was just that I was surprised when it came out," Jen explained.

"Sorry. Show's back on." After he said it, Rick realized that he was the 'show.'

On the screen, Danny shuffled out and sat on the couch. Rick ruffled the back of his head and his mother patted his leg. Their affection was genuine and apparent. Danny was uncomfortable in his pressed shirt and neatly parted hair.

"Hello, Danny."

"Hi."

A few minutes of Danny's one syllable embarrassed answers had to be cut before Danny thawed out. It was his usual pattern. Once he got rolling, heaven help whoever he was talking to, to get a word in edgewise.

"What do you think of these people saying that you are related to Jesus?"

"Mom and Dad say it's all right. But the kids at school tell jokes and I don't like that. They tease me and call me Jesus Manton. Mom says to ignore them. Dad said I can punch 'em." Rick cringed when this came out in the interview, and now, alone in his living room with Jen, he cowered again. Somehow he knew that comment would make the televised segment. He still thought his pointer to Danny was sound, but he knew it wasn't the politically correct parental advice he should have given. Secretly he was glad it came out. He wanted to affirm his manliness. In Rick's mind, it was hard to appear macho sitting in your living room discussing religion. Waters had given him a knowing wink.

"Danny, what do you know about Jesus?"

"He was born on Christmas. That's why we get presents. It's like his birthday party. And he isn't 'lated to Santa Claus. He was God's boy. That was a long, long time ago. So he's in heaven now." It was simple and profound coming from this freckle faced imp.

"Do you know that he's related to you?"

"Mom and Dad said that is what the professors and Mr. Gillyman say. It's different than what they told us in Sunday School."

"What was that?"

"Miss Hiner said we are all God's children and all Jesus' children. Dad says this isn't the same. Mom says Jesus was like my great-great-great grandfather, but even older. And nobody else is related to him like us." With a close-up on the earnest face of Danny, the interview portion of the segment ended. The Mantons would lament Danny's innocent comment in months to come when insulted religious opponents would hurl this child's interpretation of a complex subject in their faces. Tonight they naively believed in honesty.

The segment concluded with Waters' light banner with her co-anchor. She expressed a sincere liking for the whole family. She praised them as honest and hard-working. Good examples of the "Christian work ethic," she summarized.

Waters' handsome, deep-voiced co-anchor fed her a closing line. "So Lorrie, what is going to happen next to the Manton family?"

"Hugh, that's a good question. Really, God only knows."

Rick shut off the video recorder and then the television. "All in all I'd say that was *pretty* fair."

Jen pouted. "I suppose. They have to pick some of the silliest comments to air though."

"She had four hours to choose from. I didn't think we came off too badly. Not like some of her interviews." They laughed as they recalled segments they had watched in the past with movie and television stars that had revealed idiotic tales of their lives. The Mantons couldn't have revealed anything that would compete. So they thought.

What neither of them could judge was the reaction around the country to what seemed to them to be their innocuous, comments. They didn't see the controversial storm rising as they tip-toed up the stairs.

"I'm sure not looking forward to Oprah." It was scheduled for Tuesday. "Yuck." Jen was still disturbed by her appearance on the screen. She would have to have her hair redone Monday.

"It'll only last a couple of hours. Not bad for another two hundred thousand dollars and all expenses paid to Chicago." The price had dropped significantly for the second negotiated 'endorsement.' In a month, their agent admitted, they would probably have to do interviews for free. They both expected the hub-hub to die about then and life would get back to a revised, but wealthier, normal.

Rick was bent over the sink brushing his teeth when Jen squeezed behind him. "Oh Ricky, are you going to confess to me tonight," she mocked in her best Lorrie Waters imitation as she patted his rear end. Jen would make him forget his moment of fame with an exhausting session of love-making. And with Rick's ego recently massaged by a world famous personality, he would respond in kind. Afterwards, as they lay perspiring, feeling the night air cooling their flushed bodies, they would laugh and kiss and talk of how they would spend their new-found money.

* * *

"Good morning, Jen," the receptionist announced, uncharacteristically friendly. Adult heads in the waiting room turned to watch her cross through.

She was late, for the first time ever. The morning had still been a zoo, with phone calls and camera crews and even a picket line on the street outside her house. She quickly entered the door to the back offices.

"Jen." She heard her name called out by one of the doctors.

"Dr. Robinson. How is it going here?"

"Crazy. But I'm probably not telling you anything." He looked at her face. Not as fresh as usual. "Hey, let's get a cup of coffee in you before the first patient."

They walked by the back window. The appointments secretary handed Jen a list of the day without a word. Jen glanced at her. She seemed preoccupied. Then she looked at the list. The day was full. There must be some kind of bug going around.

Uncharacteristically, the doctor handed Jen a cup of coffee.

"Jen, you have put us on the map," He said enthusiastically.

"Oh. How so?" Jen asked, blowing into the cup so that the steam moistened her eyes.

"Look at the appointments."

"I did. We are full."

"Do you recognize any of the names."

Now Jen took a closer look. Almost all of the names were new.

Mark read her look. "Yep. The phones haven't stopped ringing since you were on Lorrie Waters."

Jen blushed. She didn't know what the right response should be.

Dr. Robinson leaned in. "A lot of cancellations, too, you ought to know. Some people were pretty offended. But don't worry about it. They were our complainers anyway." Mark sat back, having let Jen know that he was on her 'side.'

Now Jen was flushed. She was distressed that patients had canceled because of her.

"Anyway," Dr. Robinson continued, "we all are pleased with this. Pretty damned amazing, isn't it?"

"Yes." Jen looked at the list. "Amazing."

The day was one that Jen would rather forget. The patients streamed in all morning. They were a mixture of star-struck and intensely curious. A few sought miracles, one openly requesting to take a plastic jar of water from the faucet.

"Hey, Jen, you want a sandwich?" asked Linda, a nurse that had worked with Jen since her first day. Her question meant that the food service van was in the parking lot. On busy days, it was a good option. But not for Jen today.

"No thanks. I don't think I'm hungry."

"Got some weird ones today, don't we?"

"You've noticed."

"Yeah, we're all getting the third degree out here. What are you like, did we ever notice anything special about you, on and on."

"Sorry."

"Hey, not your fault. Besides, we're having fun. Did you see Mrs. Covalt looking at your hair?"

"No," Jen said, suspiciously.

"We told her that we thought we had seen a glow like a halo around your head at times."

"You didn't?" Jen smiled at the ludicrousness of it.

"Yeah. And worst of all ... I think she bought it."

Jen's smile faded. It was mind-boggling.

"Anyway," Linda continued. "Since Dr. Nelson is out today, I doubt you got the word on the Ramirez boy."

"Willie?"

"Yes. The parents brought him in with a hundred and five fever."

"No," said Jen, fearing from experience what Linda was going to say next.

"I'm sorry, Jen. He died that night. We still don't know why."

Jen shook her head. A three month old. When a patient died, Jen, any health professional, felt that there was something more that could have been done.

Linda lowered her voice. "Jen, we've got a ten minute break between patients. Our only break today that I can see. I'll leave you alone."

Linda shut the door.

Jen stared out the window at another wing of the hospital. She mourned inwardly, bitterly. Sometimes everything we do is just not enough. *We were not enough to save Willie.*

Jen thought of her near-argument the night before with Rick. Although she didn't admit it to him, and maybe not to herself, she, too, was undecided whether God or a Supreme Being existed. At times the medical miracles that she had observed at the hospital were of mystical proportion, and it only made sense that there was a rational, logical force to the universe. But at other times, the suffering and randomness of tragedy that confronted her made genuine belief repugnant. The upbeat religious background she had received on the off-Sunday when her mother was not working had not steeled her for the cold harshness of reality.

At this moment, she was sure that none of it mattered to Willie's parents.

She looked at the list of next patients. Twenty four in the afternoon. And after that she could go home and hurriedly pack for Chicago.

*   *   *

Jen hurried down the aisles. Danny was a little too big to ride in the shopping cart seat, but, once in a while, he liked to ride in the compartment. Normally Jen frowned on this. She had seen too many cut lips and broken noses on kids that had been caught off-balance when the cart was stopped. But she was short on time today and had barely made the day-care center before it closed. If her business continued to pick up like today, she and Rick would have to come to some new understanding on that issue.

"Don't forget the Chips Ahoy, Mom," called out Danny.

"Okay, son," she replied, half impatiently, half in admiration at his tenacity. He had already reminded her once, and the whole point of the trip was to get snacks that he could take to the Kendalls where he was staying while she and Rick were in Chicago overnight.

"And the thick pretzels."

"Danny," she growled. He quickly turned his attention to the shelves of colorful boxes.

"Mrs. Manton?"

Jen did not recognize the voice and turned. It was a woman in her early sixties. She didn't remember her as a patient.

"Yes," Jen said with a smile.

The woman came forward and reached out her hand. Instinctively, Jen took it.

Tears welled up in the eyes of the woman. "Oh my God," she began to weep.

"Are you all right, Ma'am?" Jen asked.

"And is this Danny?" the woman said between sobs, letting loose of Jen's hand.

"Yes," Jen replied slowly, edging closer to the cart. Danny turned and his eyes grew large at the sight of a crying grown-up.

While Jen looked on in discomfort, the woman leaned over and tried to take Danny's hand. He quickly yanked it away and put it behind him.

"Ma'am, may I help you?" Jen stated forcefully.

"God bless you," she sniffed. "God bless you."

Jen put her hands on the pushbar. "Thank you, Ma'am," she said politely, but dismissive as she accelerated the cart down the aisle and around the end.

"Mom. What was wrong?" asked Danny.

"Nothing Danny."

"That lady was crying."

"She was happy."

"Oh," said Danny. "Bout what?"

"Danny, I've got to get this shopping done," said Jen, glancing behind her.

"I'm bored."

"We'll be done in a second."

Jen hurried through the rest of her mental list. Less than ten items, she headed for the express checkout lane that had only a small line compared to the others.

"Mom, look," said Danny, pointing to the magazine shelf. There was a picture of Danny and Rick smiling up from the cover of a pulp newsmagazine that Jen did not recognize. "It's me and you!"

"Yes it is," said Jen, wondering how and where they got the picture.

"Can we buy it, Mom?"

"I don't know ..." Jen replied, somewhat embarrassed.

"Please," whined Danny.

"Okay." Mom gave in. Hard to argue with a request to buy your own picture. Jen looked around, sheepishly, and realized that almost every customer in the long lines was looking at her or Danny. She quickly looked down at Danny.

The line moved even slower than usual. Interminable.

"Hi, Mrs. Manton, " the clerk said, brightly. Jen had seen this checker a hundred times, but she had never been addressed by name before, at least not until she had handed over her credit card.

"Hello," Jen stammered.

The clerk said nothing else and flashed the items by the scanner.

"Fourteen, fifty-three," the clerk stated.

Jen handed her a twenty.

Danny was down now and tugging on his mother's arm. She looped the plastic bag handles into her hand. Danny had pulled out the magazine and was clutching it tightly.

"Whore!"

The clipped shout came from behind Jen. The shoppers at the other counters heard it and turned, their eyes now frozen on her. Assuming the epithet was directed to her, she spun to face the offender. She glanced frantically from face to face. Nervous shoppers glanced at a man in his late forties, heavy set, dressed neatly, erasing his anonymity. Jen did not know him. She glared at him icily and he recoiled, castigated, prompting the other shoppers to scowl at him.

The checker looked mortified and fumbled with Jen's change. "You know, we have call and delivery available," she leaned in and whispered.

Jen smiled and squeezed Danny's hand tightly. Call and delivery. A good idea. She certainly wouldn't be shopping with Danny until this blew over.

Jen and Danny walked out, not looking back. A chorus of angry voices erupted as the nameless shoppers confronted the man who in turn confronted them.

*   *   *

Chicago

"I'm surprised that I'm not really very nervous. How about you?" Jen whispered after having her makeup touched up for the fourth time by the makeup artist.

"I could do without this," Rick squirmed as an eccentric-looking young woman fussed over some perceived shine on his forehead. He had resisted makeup for the Lorrie Waters interview and his pale appearance on the screen had reflected it. He reluctantly consented under the warm influence of Oprah Winfrey in their backstage preinterview.

After closing his eyes and mouth prior to one last puff of facial powder, he continued. "Like the producer said, we're not expected to answer any heavy theological questions. This is just a 'fluff' piece about us." Rick wasn't sure he had believed that piece of advice, but he felt more prepared, having gone through the interview with Waters. There hadn't been enough time since that interview for the hate mail to arrive, and, other than the perceptive flight attendant in first class, they had made it to the studio in Chicago incognito. Jen's tale of her trip to the supermarket had them on edge.

They waited behind the curtains, off to the side of the stage, looking for a cue from the assistant producer. He appeared to be listening intently to a message on his massive headphones. His arm was raised, palm facing them in a stop sign. Jen brushed off her husband's lapel and unnecessarily straightened it. He had been puffed and brushed and primped to perfection. Jen smiled nervously at him. They had bought the new suit two days ago and hurriedly had it tailored. She loved the look of power and control it gave him. Besides, Rick had already worn his one 'good' suit in the Waters interview. For herself, Jen had purchased a conservative, yet feminine royal blue skirt and jacket outfit. It was cut only slightly above her knees. The light blue scarf wrapped tightly in a roll around her slim neck accented her eyes. The producers were thrilled with her appearance, and at the sound and light test an hour earlier they made sure that the camera crews had tested and retested the best angles to get close-ups of her.

With a frantic motioning of his fingers, the assistant waved them on-stage. They headed for the bright lights, holding hands.

"Ladies and gentlemen, let's give a Chicago-style welcome to Jen and Rick Manton." Oprah's producers had pre-conditioned the crowd which responded with a raucous round of clapping and whistling. The Mantons stood, acknowledging the applause with bemused looks on their faces. As the noise died an undercurrent of hisses could be heard. The sound startled Jen and troubled her as much as the cheering had amused her. Neither seemed warranted. She still did not see what about this story should generate such emotions one way or the other.

The first part of the show was indeed, as promised, a happy combination of banter and anecdotes with the talk show hostess. They were asked about their church attendance and Danny's religious rearing, but they were framed in a more unpretentious manner than in the Waters interview. Winfrey seemed to genuinely understand their position.

"Do you two ever wake up and pinch yourselves and wonder how this happened to you?"

"Every morning," Jen chimed in.

"I mean, you were pretty much average middle-class Americans and now you're as big as, well, me." Winfrey's biased crowd cheered their approval of her humor. "When we come back, we have some members of our audience that are dying to ask some questions. Don't go away."

The Mantons were each handed a small paper cup of water. Winfrey sat down next to them on a hastily provided chair. "See that wasn't so bad. I love this kind of story that sells itself. Thanks for coming, but next time we get Danny, too."

"That would be great." Rick was feeling comfortable and leaned back just as the makeup artist appeared out from behind the props and began powdering his face as if he wasn't even there behind it. Winfrey asked them about their flight and other small talk. It seemed that the break was over in a flash.

"Thirty seconds!" echoed in the studio. Winfrey smiled her excusal and went down into the audience. An assistant took the half full cups from the guests.

"We've been talking with Jen and Rick Manton. Do you have a question for either of them?"

They fielded the first questions deftly, mostly directed to Jen. What religion were they growing up? Did they feel any differently now after hearing this news? Were they going to write a book? They were too relaxed as the middle-aged man approached the microphone.

"Do you believe in heaven and hell?" he stated softly in a cold tone. Winfrey kept a firm grip on the microphone and gave the Mantons a look that said, 'One little religious question can't hurt.'

Jen explained that, for her, these were terms that related to good and evil and not necessarily actual places. Rick said that he generally agreed.

The man placed his hand firmly over Winfrey's and leaned to the microphone. "Do you understand that you are causing the loss of hope for mankind by defiling the Word of God? You will go to hell for this!" The audience erupted in a frenzied shout, mixed between scorn and approval of these words. As Winfrey tried to wrench her hand free a woman stepped into the aisle, swinging a large black leather purse over her head like an ancient warrior and landed a solid blow to the man's head pitching him forward onto Winfrey. As beefy security guards sprinted down the aisle everyone rose to their feet and pandemonium erupted.

At first the Mantons sat dumb-founded, worried more for Winfrey than themselves. As they looked toward the audience a number of figures began moving forward, shouting insults.

"You lying devils. You trample on the name of Jesus for profit."

"The fires of hell await you."

"My God, how can you say these things?"

Just as quickly as the threatening figures emerged, a faction of others jumped in between them and the Mantons, placing their backs to the Mantons and turning to ward off the encroachers.

"Don't come near these blessed people."

"How dare you speak like that to Christ's messengers?"

As the guards dragged the man who had started the eruption from the studio, calm began to return. Groups were standing in the aisles and in front of the stage, glaring at each other. Slowly they began edging toward their seats. As the crowds thinned one of the protectors who had stood directly in front of Jen turned and, before Jen could react, knelt and kissed her shoe. "Mother Jen, forgive my sins and make me whole." She was clutching her foot in both of her hands and continued kissing between her pleas. Jen looked down in horror at the pitiful sight. She wanted to kick her foot free, but she did not want to hurt this woman who, seconds before, had guarded her. She knelt and placed her hands on the woman's shoulders. As she held her a shriek rose from a woman in the aisle who raced forward and fell on her hands and knees and began to crawl across the forestage.

"Please, me too, my Savior, I need thee." Another cry arose.

As midday America sat stunned watching, Jen wrenched her foot loose, and, taking Rick's hand, ran backstage as a dozen men and women shuffled forward on their knees, hands clasped and raised in glory.

Backstage Jen clung to her husband, both heads turned toward the stage to see if they would be followed. "My God, Rick, was that real? Were those people acting?"

"I don't think so. Winfrey looked awfully pissed off." He took a deep breath. "I didn't know what to do when that lady started kissing your shoes."

"I thought she was some nut case." Jen was too unnerved to use clinical terms. "I've seen plenty of that type. But when the others started crawling forward ... that gave me the willies."

They held each other in silence and watched a monitor suspended from the wall. It had no sound, but they could see the studio where uniformed security had arrived. The audience was subdued. A number of people sat, heads bowed, praying. The Mantons could not remember which ones were supporters and which were not.

"These people really believe we have some kind of power," he mumbled in disbelief.

A bustle of guards came through the curtains, Winfrey in the middle.

"Whew, folks. Sorry things got out of hand. This isn't supposed to be Geraldo." She looked flushed, but it was immediately evident that she was not displeased with the rowdy turn of events. This was big time ratings. "We're going to keep the guards in place for the rest of the show ..."

"You don't think we're going back out there, do you?" Rick said.

"Sure. It's safe. We can ..."

"No way. Those people are crazy. There's no telling what they'll do next."

"But you can explain to them that you're not God, that you're just a normal woman and it was by chance that you are in this position."

"No. You're explaining it just fine. Sorry." Jen was sorry. Winfrey had treated them fairly and he liked her, but this was too much.

Winfrey could see her star attractions disappearing. She appealed to Rick's manhood. "Wait. I understand. You could come out alone and explain it. Jen will be safe back here, I promise."

Jen was insulted by the offer. "We're a team. And we're out of here." She started looking in the direction of the dressing room where they had left their belongings.

The show's producer stepped forward at Winfrey's elbow. He had been unctuously friendly before. "We have a contract," he stated pompously. "If you want to get paid, you complete the show." It was not the right approach with the Mantons.

"And if you want to get your ass sued for almost getting us killed out there you go ahead and hang on to your money." Rick didn't know a single lawyer, but he couldn't let the threat pass without response. Surely Sid Flink would know an attorney.

"And we'll be glad to tell Lorrie Waters that the whole scene out there was scripted from the start." Jen knew the better threat to throw.

"Okay, okay. Let's stay friends," Winfrey had met her match. "You'll get paid. Tell you what, how about we just bring a telecam into the dressing room and finish this up one on one?"

"No. I think we've had enough." They began to turn as a couple toward the hallway. Three steps down the hallway they heard the producer's grating voice.

"Double the money."

Rick and Jen stopped in their tracks, but neither turned. It was dark in the hallway. Rick looked down at her. She had a mock look of surprise that one gets when they've just gotten a steal of a bargain. She looked up at him and reiterated the look.

　　　Rick turned his head over his shoulder. "Deal."

　　　For the next fifteen minutes the Mantons tried to explain their position. Jen reminded the viewers that she was not the author of the theories that these people found so inflammatory. They certainly were not claiming any divine status. Jen pleaded to rationality that this so-called royal bloodline only meant that an extended family of Jesus existed and it was not a challenge to Christian beliefs, at least not in their eyes. For the viewers that were prejudiced against the whole concept, this was deemed to be a further example of the Mantons' arrogant usurping of the role of interpreters of the Holy Scripture.

　　　But most of the millions of viewers would not remember the Manton's vain protestations of mortality in the well-paid closing interview. They were waiting breathlessly for the replays of the dark-haired woman in the red smock who had fallen to her knees and kissed the feet of her perceived savior. The show closed with a slow motion close-up of Jen reaching down and gently placing her hands on the woman's shoulders as she raised her face to Jen in bliss.

*　　*　　*

New Jersey

"Jesus, those people are crazy, aren't they, Honey?" Tina had learned years ago to call whoever her current boyfriend was 'Honey.' It cut down on mistakes. Keith Carney, if he noticed, hadn't cared. He never called her anything.

The credits on Oprah were flashing on the screen. Tina never missed the program. Carney, uncharacteristically, watched it with her this time.

"I mean, people are treating those Mantons like they are Christ himself," she added. Deep in her background there was an inkling of religious education. It was under many layers by now. "Did you see that?"

"Yeah," Carney replied vacantly. "Just amazing, isn't it?"

"Uh-huh," Tina added cautiously. She was rarely on the same wavelength with Carney, except in bed. "What was amazing?" she added.

"Those people adore them. Just plain fucking adore them."

"Yes, they do," Tina said. She had never heard Carney use the word 'adore' before. Big words made her nervous.

* * *

The next month was a blur to the Mantons. Contrary to their prior expectations, their celebrity status did not diminish. They had become unsuspecting lightning rods for public opinion. But there were no more repeats of displays that had occurred on Oprah because they no longer ventured openly into the public. There were no more live talk shows. At any price. They told their Sid Flink not to even bother relaying the offers. They reluctantly agreed to consider paid interviews, but to the networks their value was no longer as individuals, but as the subjects of the vitriolic campaigns of an outraged moral minority. Their story was nice, but it was tension and confrontation that drew sponsors. The requests for interviews without audience participation would be fewer and less lucrative.

Pickets in front on the Mantons house shattered the normal peace and tranquility of the suburban neighborhood. Fortunately, Rick had played basketball for years against a team from the local sheriff's department and had developed a camaraderie with the deputies who knew him as a regular sort. When the sheriff enforced a picket line restriction of five hundred feet from the Manton house, with no bullhorns allowed, the protesters lost their steam with the increasingly colder weather, at least on the front line.

They began receiving bags of mail every day. Much of it was routed to them through The New York Times, courtesy of Gilliam. There was a large percentage of unfavorable letters and a few that were threatening. It angered Rick that he was impotent to find his cowardly enemies. And other letters were just plain sick in the emotional pleas for healing and divine intervention. It unnerved Rick that his family may be in danger from one of these demented fanatics. It wasn't public knowledge where they lived, but it wasn't hard to discover. Norristown was small and within days every convenience store clerk and gas station attendant knew which direction to point sightseers.

Jen had raised the subject of installing a home security company which they did with their first appearance fee. It seemed prudent, but so far, other than the anonymous letters which they had turned over to the sheriff, there was no immediate danger. It was the threat of recognition that now cramped their lives. They could rarely leave the house without being spotted and stopped. Once in a while that was good. They had received free dinners, drinks and flowers from well-wishers. But more often than not, it was embarrassing. They were approached by lost souls looking for deities that could somehow solve their problems. Others openly showed their contempt. It would enrage Rick when the un-Christian epithets were loud enough for Danny's sharp ears. It fueled Manton's growing resentment of organized religion and was weakening Jen's faith. What had at first been a fortuitous lark was now seen by the Mantons as a living hell.

* * *

Jen came into the kitchen, squinting against the intense rays of dawn's light streaming in the window. The smell of the brewing coffee had drawn her from the warmth of her bed. Outside the ground was covered with frost, the trees were stark and barren, long stripped of their colorful fall leaves. The volume on the small portable television was barely audible so as not to wake anyone. It had been six weeks since the professors first called. The initial scrutiny was lessening. At least they could turn on the morning news now without fear of seeing bad photographs of themselves starring back. Rick was pouring through the Philadelphia News-Journal.

"Good morning, Hon."

Rick didn't look up. "Good morning." He didn't sound happy. She knew something was up. It had always irritated Jen that he woke up so damned cheerful. She needed a cup of caffeine before addressing the world civilly.

"Whatcha reading?"

"Us again. I was hoping that The News-Journal was above jumping on the bandwagon, but I guess their readership is down."

"Let's see."

Jen looked over his shoulder. He was reading the editorial page. The lead editorial had an ominous heading: "Manton Blood: Fraud or God?" Jen put her hands on Rick's shoulders and read on.

"There is no clear formula for anticipating the next issue that will capture the public's fascination. It will arise from a startling event or ironic twist of fate and there is no way of predicting what that incident will be. Jen and Danny Manton have now become the latest catalysts of history. To them the discovery of their astounding genealogy was a surprising, but not foundation-shaking revelation. But is it as harmless as it all sounds? From the undying clamor across America it appears that this may be one of those periodic defining events for which a ready public has been furtively waiting. People who had never examined their religious beliefs are now doing so and finding their upbringing seriously challenged. The Mantons are the lead actors in the drama which has caused many to doubt the very roots of Christianity. Religious leaders across the land bravely maintain that this scrutiny is good for Christianity, that it will bring a renewal of faith. But that seems to fly in the

face of public polls which show higher percentages of Christians than ever before are admitting that they were Christians by habit and not because they truly believed the story of Jesus' birth, death and resurrection as detailed in the New Testament.

Is the work of Professors Hershner and Fahey a gigantic hoax? As we said in this space before, their research is so far scientifically unrefuted. Are the Mantons divinely revealed descendants of Jesus Christ? We don't know. But from a historic point of view, this appears to be a turning point for the Christian religion. And possibly a fatal one."

"Oh, great," Jen whispered, defeat in her voice. "Every day I wake up hoping this will all blow over. Look at that. The end of Christianity. Caused by us. That is going to really bring the nutcakes out of the walls."

"There must be something we can do to down peddle this. It's getting ridiculous. Is there such a thing as counter-publicity?" He snorted a small laugh. They had been so bombarded with wild accusations the last month it was hard to take anything seriously anymore.

"You know what really ticks me off?" Jen was waking up now. "It's almost Christmas and we can't even go to the mall. I love malls at Christmas. I haven't even been able to take Danny to sit on Santa's lap."

"I don't think he's heart-broken about that. He wouldn't be caught dead on Santa's lap. His friends have all decided this year that they don't believe in him anymore."

"Well, I do! And I hate catalog shopping." She was on a roll now. "It's not like we're millionaires now." Jen stopped. Her lips crunched up and her chin began to quiver. Rick rose and took her in his arms.

"Babe, we'll get through this. We'll just have to celebrate Christmas at home. Next year we can plan on going somewhere away from all the cameras."

"Sure. Like where? The North Pole?"

"That sounds pretty good some days, doesn't it?"

Jen smiled through her tear-filled eyes and hugged herself against his chest. She felt his strength and knew that together they would survive this.

"Can we still go to Christmas Eve service like old times?"

Rick thought about it. It might be uncomfortable, but he was craving a little normalcy in their lives as much as Jen was. "I don't see why not," he fibbed. "Surely no one's going to hassle us at church on Christmas Eve."

"Let's go early. Get a seat in the back for a quick get away," she suggested.

"Anything you want, Dear."

*   *   *

5

If all our misfortunes were laid in one common heap, whence every one must take an equal portion, most people would be content to take their own and depart.
-- Solon

"Shut up, kid. Just shut up. Do you hear me?"

Danny was screaming in terror as loud as he could until the heavy, gloved hand clamped roughly over his mouth and nose. He struggled to breath.

"You can breathe when you shut your piehole." Danny's lungs wheezed his assent as he tried to suck in air. He was pressed down against the floor board of the back seat. Due to a child's amazing flexibility he had not been injured in the impact moments earlier. His head pressed against the bottom of the door as the car swung wide and sped around a corner. His eyes rolled wildly. He could not comprehend what was happening. He was dreaming of the presents that Santa Claus was going to bring. Maybe Santa didn't exist, but this was no night to be cynical. All he remembered was his Dad yelling for him, then this mean man grabbing and yanking him out of the car. He had been too scared to yell. Bright lights seemed to erupt from nowhere. He hadn't screamed until he was thrown into the car and it pulled away, its rear tires fishtailing furiously.

Danny looked at the man who sat above him. He was wearing a Halloween mask and he smelled bad. He saw Danny looking and raised his hand as if to hit him with the back of it. Danny ducked down and began to cry. He wanted his Mom and Dad. He wanted his Christmas dreams back.

He felt the car screech to a stop.

"C'mon, kid. Move, move, move." The door was pushed open and he was pulled into the street and quickly pushed into the floor of another waiting car. He looked out onto the street and saw another man wearing a mask, lighting a match and throwing it into the back seat of the car he had just been in. He felt the surge of the explosion as the man squeezed into the back seat and slammed the door.

"Nice and easy, Ron."

Danny lay quietly as the car pulled away, this time more slowly and cautiously.

"Stick your feet in here, Kid." The man with the matches was holding open a large cotton bag, just the kind Danny thought Santa would carry on his shoulder later that night. "C'mon. Get in it." When all but Danny's head was in the sack the man removed a roll of tape from his coat pocket and strapped a long piece over Danny's mouth. "Keep your nose near the opening and you'll be all right." Wide-eyed, Danny nodded. In a strange way he felt relief as the bag was pulled up over his head and the drawstring tightened until only a two inch hole remained. He prayed that the cover over his head would protect him from these boogie men just as the covers at home had done in the past.

*   *   *

Pope Innocent's summons to assemble the following year in Lyons for a holy crusade to Languedoc quickly spread throughout Europe. It was received with shock in Rennes-le-Château. In disbelief that such a drastic reprisal would be carried out, Delacroix and Lancel wordlessly agreed upon an uneasy truce. They galloped the fields in lively hunts. Over feasts their conversations were still challenging. But the subject of the bloodline and the possible Albigensian Crusade were taboo. The fishing trips of the priest and Joseph continued, seemingly all the more refreshing now that they were not taken for granted.

Delacroix's consorting with heretics was questioned by some villagers, instigated by Jacques Boulanger. But loyal Brother Francois rationalized the trips to Blanchefort as a continuing attempt to bring its occupants into conformity with the Church. And the villagers did not dare to openly question the authority of the priest, who, with the force of the Church behind him, provided the only potential protection from the wrath of the impending crusaders.

At Blanchefort, the Knights Templar assembled to lay plans for the defense of the castle. Throughout the centuries defenses from the roving bandits had been provided for the safety of the villagers. But this was a threat of a much grander scale. Now these same people who had benefited from the mercies of their landlord watched the knight's assemblage with unvoiced hostility and anticipation.

Not surprisingly, in response to Pope Innocent III's call, with a year's notice, contingents from all over northern Europe eagerly assembled the following June of 1209. Informed by Abbot Amalrici that he had been hand-picked by the pontiff himself, Simon de Montfort l'Amaury reluctantly agreed to lead the vast army, numbering almost thirty five thousand strong.

Thirsty for conquest, and the booty promised to them, the Albigensian crusaders set upon towns in central France where the Cathar heresies were only minimal. They moved southward with the ferocity of barbarians which had been unseen for generations. Farmlands were confiscated or destroyed. Entire villages were razed. Like a rising tide of destruction the crusade surged into Languedoc.

Delacroix was aghast by reports of the unexpected violence that did not seem warranted against the peaceful, but misguided, Cathars. He, and all others in the village, were relieved when subsequent reports told that the crusade was bogging down at Beziers at the mouth of the Aude river valley, the only viable path to Rennes-le-Château. The army was still over two hundred kilometers distant, with numerous villages and castles defending the path, and hopefully losing fervor. The danger was not immediate. It was hoped that the threat would completely lose momentum and dissipate before entering the exhausting Pyrenées foothills that, for centuries, had sheltered Languedoc from the foul weathers of the civilization.

*   *   *

Abbot Arnaldus Amalrici was pleased to read the missive from crusade commander Simon de Montfort l'Amaury. The commencement of the Albigensian Crusade had exceeded expectations. The year after the announcement had gone out had been fairly uneventful. There were no major outbreaks of plague, no wars of any consequence throughout Europe. Men of a marauding nature were antsy for adventure and conquest. The reports in de Montforte's letter of beastly violence and widespread plundering troubled Amalrici, only because he was sure that he would be hearing from Pope Innocent III on the acts of the crusaders. The pontiff was sometimes too intellectual, and soft. Saving souls was sometimes a dirty business, the abbot would have to explain.

He moved to the sunlight shining in the window. It was a beautiful summer day in the Narbonne valley. He should have been with the crusade in weather like this. But, after all, he was forty-nine years old and getting a little frail for such work.

Amalrici sat at his desk to read the rest of the lengthy letter. De Montforte was a good choice. He did not ignore details.

"We now approach Beziers, which we know to be a stronghold of the heretics. Behind the walls of its ancient fort, the entire village is sealed off. Whence my soldiers have rested and reassembled, we shall move to its capture. In this time, I inquire of the Revered Abbott, for guidance received from Our Holy Father, as to recognition of the heretics when commingled with the innocent. Until now only the Cathars have fought. At Beziers it shall not be so easy to distinguish friend from foe."

Amalrici chuckled. De Montforte was also a good commander because he was a simple man, trusting, and, in the hands of a cleric that comprehended the underpinnings for control of the secular world centuries before Machiavelli would articulate it in print, gullible. His fellow countryman still believed that he had been handpicked by Pope Innocent III. There was no reason to burst his bubble.

Amalrici sat at his desk and lifted the quill from the ink pot. He tapped it gently and slowly and examined it for just the correct flow before he began to write.

* * *

The young man stomped his feet in the hallway. Dust drifted from his loose clothing. The servant opened the door to Lancel's study and he entered.

"Your Honor, I bring word from Sir Thomas of Carcassonne." The messenger's face was coated with a thick grime of layers of dirt mingled with perspiration from the twenty-five mile ride. In the southern French July sun, such a ride was exhausting.

"Bring this fair man some water," snapped Lancel to the doorman who would quickly relay the order to the kitchen.

Turning to the young man, a boy, really, Lancel said, "Pray, tell, what brings you at such haste." He feared the news was not good. Sir Thomas, a Knight Templar whose castle was located further down the Aude River, to the north, had regularly sent reports of the stalled crusade. Such reports came slowly. Bad news, even then, traveled quickly.

"Sire, Sir Thomas has received word that Beziers has fallen."

Lancel closed his eyes. That was indeed bad. Beziers had been besieged for some time. And it was a mere fifty miles east of Carcassonne, near the mouth of the Aude at the sea. He had hoped that the crusaders would never gain a foothold into the river valley. Surely, they would be headed this way. Seventy-five miles.

"When?" Lancel asked softly.

"On the twenty-second, Sire." Two days ago.

The doorman returned with a large earthen goblet.

The thirsty messenger took the vessel and looked at Lancel anxiously.

"Drink," the superior invited.

After downing the cool liquid, the messenger wiped the back of his sleeve across his mouth.

"Sir Thomas has directed that I recite to you the details of the fall."

"Certainly." Lancel doubted that it could differ from the other stories of horror that had been delivered.

"The crusaders have slaughtered the entire town."

"What?" Lancel straightened. "What do you mean?" He prayed for some hidden meaning to the words.

"As you know, there were many Cathari in Beziers..."

"That is true."

"And with the entire city within the castle walls, they were able to withstand the siege for many weeks."

Lancel pictured the city in his mind from the times he had passed through it on the way to the coast on trading missions. It was many times larger than Blanchefort and easily held a population of ten thousand. "Yes."

"Upon the eve of the final breach of the walls, Commander Simon de Montfort knew not how to choose who to punish."

"So he killed them all?" Lancel concluded.

"Sire, he sought guidance from Rome on how to tell heretic from innocent."

Lancel blinked. "And what direction was given?"

"The Pope said, and Sir Thomas made me memorize this, he said, 'Slay them all. God shall know his own."

Lancel gulped for air in disbelief. This was his Church. The Roman Catholic Church of his fathers. Were they all to be sacrificed in this bloodletting? "Is there anything else?" he asked in resignation.

"Oui. They are headed south. To Carcassonne."

And then to Rennes-le-Château, discerned Lancel.

"Will that be all, Sire?" the messenger inquired. "I must return to prepare the defenses."

"That will be all."

The messenger turned to sprint out.

"Boy!" called Lancel, for the messenger now seemed too young for the information he had delivered.

"Yes, Sire."

"Tell Sir Thomas that the prayers of Frederick Lancel shall be with him."

The messenger smiled, thankful for the assistance. "Oui, my Lord," he said enthusiastically, and ran through the door.

                        *   *   *

The White House Residence Chambers

The red light blinked in the dark room as the phone gently buzzed. It was slowly picked up and the sleepy voice of the President of the United States said, "Yeah."

"Ben." It was Joe Thorne. Very few people had the privilege of calling Ben Dailley by his first name, or in the middle of the night.

"Yeah, Joe. What is it?"

"It's the Manton kid. He's been abducted."

"What?" said Dailley, trying vainly to shake the cobwebs from his mind.

"It's on all the networks. It was done in front of a bank of camera men outside their church," Thorne reported. He was getting his news, as he spoke, from CNN which was providing live coverage.

"And ... " It was Dailley's way of asking for more details.

"And they shot Richard Manton. He and his wife were both taken to Franklin Memorial." The scene on television was the emergency room door.

"God dammit," groaned Dailley, more in resignation than anger. "Who did it? Some nutcake?"

"They don't know," Thorne replied. "But from the film of it, it looks like a pretty professional hit. Well timed. Fast."

"They have it on film?" Dailley asked, incredulously.

"Just about the whole thing."

The phone line was silent as Dailley contemplated whether to go to the Oval Office's television room where the whole spectacle could be seen on nine televisions simultaneously. It was Christmas morning. He was looking forward to being with his grandchildren in a few short hours, a normal citizen for at least a morning.

Dailley sighed. "So what do we have to do?"

"I'll round up the domestic cabinet for a meet tomorrow. They're gone to hell and back for the holidays."

"Is it necessary?" Dailley asked, hopefully.

"Ben, there isn't going to be another damned thing on the news until this blows over. And that is not going to happen fast."

"Okay. But not until after lunch."

"Couldn't get us all together any faster anyway," Thorne agreed.

"Okay. I'll call you mid-morning," Dailley said.

"I'll release a statement to the press right away. I'll have you say that we're working with law enforcement, a shame, the usual."

"Sounds good Joe."

"Ben. One more thing."

Dailley grimaced. "What?"

"Merry Christmas," Thorne said flatly.

Dailley snorted. "Yeah. Same to you."

* * *

Intensive Care Unit

"Mr. Manton. Mr. Manton. Can you hear me?"

Rick could hear the distant sound of an unfamiliar voice. "Yes," he mumbled. His head pounded. Gotta wake up from this nightmare. Gotta wake up. He tried to sit up but failed.

"Mr. Manton, I'm Dr. Rutten. Don't try to sit up. We have just brought you out of surgery and you have some tubes hooked up to you. Do you understand me?"

After a long pause Rick's bandaged head slowly nodded forward once. He gasped it a dry, painful breath to speak.

"The nurse will get you a sip of water. Don't try to talk. You have some injuries to your face and arms, but as far as we can tell, they are not life-threatening."

Rick felt a hand pulling his head slightly forward and a paper cup touching his lips. He sipped the cool water and breathed deeply. Against orders, he whispered, "What happened? Where's my family?"

"Mr. Manton," a louder voice came from the other side of the bed. "I'm Deputy Heekin of the Highway Patrol. Sir, you were in a pretty bad car accident. Do you understand that, Sir?"

Rick nodded. "How's my family?"

"Sir, your wife took a pretty good jolt. She's not in real good shape. She is still in surgery right now." Rick's body went rigid.

Dr. Rutten's smoother voice came back. "We're sure she is going to make it through the surgery, but she has some internal injuries. It may be touch and go for a while."

"Danny?"

There was a silence as the doctor and patrolman glanced at each other. The doctor nodded. The patrolman's voice was softer. "Sir, I regret to inform you that your accident was a part of a kidnapping plot and your son has been kidnapped."

"Who? Who? Who?" Rick struggled to sit up again. Three pairs of hands gently restrained him.

"We don't know. Sir, I can assure you that we have every available car on the street, every available officer securing all routes out of the city. We have a good description of the getaway car and we will find whoever did this."

Rick could only shake his head back and forth on the pillow. From under the bandages on his eyes seeped the tears of rage and frustration.

"How long have I been out?" Rick's voice was dry and raspy.

"Eight hours. It's Christmas Day. You had better get some rest now," said the doctor as he slowly squeezed the intravenous tubing vent, allowing a dose of morphine to run into Rick's veins to ease his pain and mercifully suspend the torment in his mind.

* * *

"Try to look like you're alive, for Chrissakes!" The thug with the dirty, stringy hair didn't need to lean over to yell at Danny. The boy was scared, not deaf.

"Shut up asshole. Yelling at the kid ain't gonna make it better." The larger and calmer of the two men turned to Danny. "Now look. All we want you to do is hold this paper a little higher and try to give us a half smile."

Danny rolled his eyes at him nervously. He did not like these men. They frightened him and he hated them. He thought that if he hated them enough, like all other bad things in his life, they would go away.

"We'll let you eat as soon as we get this done." It was too late for gentle persuasion. Danny had been locked in a closet all night and fell asleep crying on a musty smelling blanket. Breakfast had been a soggy piece of cold toast. Offers of food would not be a sufficient bribe if that was the quality of the menu. He shook his head back and forth and glared at his captors. But Danny was overestimating his position. The more reasonable of the two, the large man that Danny thought of as 'Dummy,' grabbed him around the collar and shook him.

"Look kid. You can make this easy, or make it hard. Do you want me to let Mike persuade you?" He nodded to his partner that Danny called, in his mind, 'Greasy.'

"Okay. Okay." Danny still had some fight left in him. Hunger and hopelessness would drain it from him in the days to come. "I'll smile, okay."

"Don't be a smart ass. Hold up the paper higher."

It was more of a grimace than a smile, but Danny did at least look alive as the flash went off.

"Good enough. Tape him up," said the pale man who had been standing in the corner. Danny surmised that he was their leader. Whenever he was around, the other goons jumped at his every bark. Danny thought of him as

'Ghost Boss.' His cold, silent stare scared Danny as much as the shouting of 'Greasy' and 'Dummy.'

'Greasy' approached with a roll of electrical tape just like the kind they had ripped off his tender face for the photograph.

"You said I could eat."

"Supper ain't ready kid." 'Greasy' was laughing as he pulled a long strip out from the roll and moved his hand to Danny's cheek to line up the tape.

Danny was furious. He wanted out of here. He wanted Christmas. As the kidnapper's hand moved by his mouth, he reached up, pulled it to his teeth, and bit as hard as he could. As the startled man jerked back his hand in pain, Danny was off like a bolt past the equally surprised 'Dummy'.

"Son of a bitch. Get him."

Danny headed down the hall. He had been blindfolded when he was brought into the filthy place, but he could sense his way out. He saw the front door and sprinted for it. He turned the knob with both hands and yanked. It popped open and then wrenched out of his hand. He looked up at the security chain that was two feet above his reach. As he stared at it a pair of arms tackled him from behind and slammed him against the door. He was hit with a hail of hard slaps from 'Dummy'.

'Greasy' came across the room in a rage, holding his hand, a slight trickle of blood oozing between the fingers. "I'm gonna kill you, you little fucker." Danny cowered into a ball as he was pummeled on the back and head.

"Stop it. Stop. Stop," shouted 'Dummy' as he physically restrained the other. "Keith says we got to keep him alive."

'Greasy' stiffened and stopped swinging. He reached into his pocket and pulled out a knife. With a click the thick blade flashed forward. "I'm going to kill him."

"Settle down, you idiots," hissed 'Ghost Boss,' striding into the room. They did.

'Ghost Boss' walked up to Danny who stood with his chest heaving, fighting back tears of fear and frustration. He returned Keith Carney's stare, but unlike the big man, he shook uncontrollably.

Carney bent over and moved his hand to Danny's ear and locked his thumb and index finger on a tender lobe. Danny tried to jerk away, but the pain stopped him. He squirmed and whimpered. 'Ghost Boss' bent over and whispered, "Do that again, punk, and I'll let my friend cut you to pieces. You hear me?"

Danny nodded, eyes swelling with tears. Carney gave the ear a sharp twist for punctuation.

Danny crumbled to the floor. With tears streaming down his cheek, he looked upward at Carney and shouted in a voice more controlled than he felt, "Go ahead. I hate you. I want to die so I can tell Jesus to make you go to hell."

Carney stepped back, astonished that a mere child would defy his threats that made men crumble. He was not used to dealing with children, certainly not this one. And then it struck him who this kid was. Even though 'Ghost Boss' had no convictions whatsoever on religion or the possibility of afterlife, a shudder of revulsion, as if he had been manhandling a corpse, ran through him. Speechless, he blinked at Danny before regaining his composure. "Kid, you're fucked," was the best retort he could muster. As he turned and left the room he muttered to 'Greasy' and 'Dummy,' "Keep an eye on him, you fools."

They shook their heads up and down.

Danny lay motionless with tears silently rolling down his cheeks as 'Dummy' roughly taped his arms behind his back. His stomach growled.

* * *

Jen walked through the mall, hand in hand with Danny, like they used to in the days before the discovery of the bloodline. Her mood was light, and she was willing to indulge Danny's side trips into his favorite shops. Danny excitedly pointed out the newest line of toys. She patiently listened, looking proudly at her mannish little son. He could be such a gentleman, yet such a rebel. He was the spitting image of his father. They took their time. No one in the stores recognized them. They were a normal mother and son on an afternoon outing.

In the pet store Danny intently watched the tropical fish for over fifteen minutes before moving to the puppy pens. Danny had always wanted a dog, but with their hectic schedules the adult Mantons had never had the inclination. Today, however, Jen ached to buy him a dog. She would talk to Rick about it when she got home. When the dogs finally tired of Danny tapping on the window, Jen and Danny left.

When they stepped into the mall, the air seemed stifling to Jen. She labored to breath, not knowing what was wrong. She looked down at Danny. He seemed fine. Then she looked around and noticed passer-bys in the mall looking at her and Danny. *What are you looking at?* she wondered angrily. Across the hall a mother ushered her children to the side wall and whispered something behind her hand.

Walking quickly, they headed toward what appeared to be the end of the massive building.

"What's wrong, Mom?" Danny pleaded, alarmed by the rough grasp of his mother's hand.

Jen did not answer and increased her stride. The shoppers they overcame from behind seemed to be warned of their approach and stepped to the side. As Jen and Danny passed, the shoppers would turn and stare. Jen glanced back and saw a crowd of onlookers matching her pace, following them.

"Mommy?! Slow down." Danny was tugging with all his strength, but Jen could barely feel him. The footsteps of the people behind her drew closer. She stretched out her stride until Danny began to run.

"Mommy. Please."

The faces multiplied and pressed closer as Jen pushed a path through the mall. She began to run, dragging Danny behind her.

Up ahead she saw the sign for the escalator going down. Feelings of paranoia swept her. *Out. Out, now.* She shoved aside staring strangers who held their hands up. She vaguely heard them telling her to stop. Bursting through the last line, she surged forward.

Her feet stepped into thin air. As if in slow motion she pitched forward and began to fall into a void where the escalator should have been. She could not see the bottom. As her heart went into her throat she felt Danny's hand. He had stopped short on the edge of the overhang. His sweating hand held tight as she fell.

"Mommy, Mommy," he screamed in terror.

Their hands held tight until their arms reached their furthest extension. A stabbing pain seared through Jen's shoulder as she felt Danny's hand wrench away. She clawed at the air, reaching for her son as she slowly fell down and away. *Don't let go. Please, Danny ... I'm sorry, I'm so sorry.*

Each split second was an eternity in Jen's mind. Danny was getting smaller and smaller, but she could still clearly see the agony in his eyes as he leaned over the edge, arms held out for her. His voice echoed into the cavern, "Mommy, don't leave me."

Jen burst with a blood-chilling cry. "Dannnyyyy!" As he disappeared from sight, Jen hit the ground.

The hospital bed shuddered as Jen's body spasmed. Her piercing scream was heard throughout the wing.

Jen wildly looked around her. The sterile hospital environment soon told her where she was. She blinked. She was sweating and panting. But the nightmare was not over. She was awake, and her Danny was really gone. Her anxiety peaked and she clumsily swung her feet out of the bed.

"Mrs. Manton. Mrs. Manton. Please, don't get out of bed."

A large red-haired nurse had her in a gentle bear hug. Jen was tangled in a web of tubing that ran from her arm. A searing pain shot through her shoulder, and she collapsed into the nurse's clutch with a pitiful groan.

"It's all right, Ma'am. Just lay back, now." A male voice was now talking to her. Jen heard the voice tell the nurse that it was time for "another dose." The nurse gently guided her back to the edge of the bed and firmly sat her down.

"Rick? Are you here? Where's Rick?" Jen began to panic again as the pain ebbed.

"Mr. Manton is fine. He's right next door. He was in to see you earlier. Do you remember, Mrs. Manton?" The nurse swung Jen's feet up into the bed.

Jen did remember. And she recalled she was told that Danny had been kidnapped. He was gone. She began to struggle against the nurse's hands, but a soothing warmth spread up her arm and oozed into her brain. Jen began to weep, "Danny. Danny. Oh, my poor Danny." Her words slurred. "Rick, get him back. Get him back."

As the morphine released her body and mind Jen lay back in bed.

"Mr. Manton is resting. Everything will be fine. You must rest now, and not worry."

The room was spinning. Jen could not keep her eyes open. The faces of the doctor and nurse began to blur. She was flooded with a calm and peaceful feeling as she realized she was back in the mall with Danny. And no one knew them.

* * *

The Newsroom

"Hey, Jim, you better come look at this." Jerry, one of many Times copy editors, was leaning over the now rarely used telefax machine watching a page mechanically spit out.

"Be right there." It was Gilliam's first day back in the office since the kidnapping five days earlier. The publisher had ordered him to Philadelphia to cover the events, but there was nothing happening other than the news crews running into each other at the hospital hoping for anything that could be stretched into a soundbite for the evening broadcast. The kidnappers had virtually vanished into thin air. The abduction was on film from a dozen different cameras that had been at the church that night, but they showed nothing that could help the FBI. Nothing but the eerie sight of the mask-clad terrorists, dragging Danny toward the waiting car and firing a few rounds over the heads of the camera crews. The car was found within hours, a burning hulk in a parking lot next to the 580 freeway.

"I think you'll want to see this."

It was impossible for Gilliam to get excited about any new 'religious' development that he was supposed to be screening for use in the paper. What he had witnessed over and over again on television had left him drained. As a beat police reporter twelve years earlier he had seen crime scenes of some pretty gruesome murders, but this was different. It had actually happened in front of his eyes. And he felt responsible. He had grown to like these people. It was his story that put them in the spotlight. Made them targets for this assault.

"It just came in on the fax with a cover sheet for you." Jerry was being uncharacteristically insistent. What could be so important?

Gilliam looked at the telefax Jerry handed to him. The cover sheet was typically bland, but oddly styled:

> *To: Gilliam of NY Times*
>
> *From: Your Friends*

But the second page shook him from his fog. Half the page was a black and white photograph of the skyline which, from the onion-shaped spires appeared to be a Middle Eastern city. In the middle of the photograph was a small child holding a newspaper, headline facing out. Gilliam leaned over and squinted.

"Oh, my God." It was Danny. The picture was clear enough to see that he was alive, but very unhappy. The newspaper was not clear, but Gilliam could tell from the oversized banner headline that it was The Times' edition the day after the kidnapping:

CHILDREN OF JESUS ATTACKED

Gilliam was not proud of his newspaper for that headline. He quickly pulled up the last fax page and began to read.

Mr. Gilliam,

As you can see, the Grandson of Christ is alive and well. <u>For now.</u>

The peoples of Israel have been in a struggle for survival since we were abandoned by all Christians to fight the entire Arab world by ourselves. We won without your help, even defeating the weapons you gave to them.

If you want your Grandson back Christians must pay $100 million to the agencies that directly support the resettling of our recaptured homelands on the West Bank. Payment can only be to such organizations. Donations to the Jewish Defense League and other old clubs that are merely the lackeys of gutless American politicians will not be credited!!! GILLIAM- Your paper must account for the donations and the houses on the Plains of Jericho will grow like mushrooms in the spring.

Pay the money, and we will return the Grandson of Christ.

Don't pay the money and find out if he can rise from the dead.
Friends of Pure Judea

Gilliam was stunned by the letter. He had never heard of any such terrorist group, let alone a legitimate organization, with such a tortured purpose. The name was certainly unfamiliar. In the past few days, dozens of crackpots had surfaced, claiming responsibility for the kidnapping, many, perversely, citing Biblical authority. But no leads had been developed based on these claims, as far as he could discover.

But as Gilliam flipped back to the ghostly image of Danny he knew that, somehow, this demand was genuine.

*   *   *

6

When we do evil, we and our victims, are equally bewildered. -- W. H. Auden

The leaves were beginning their colorful celebration of death in the autumn of 1209 when the Albigensian Crusade approached the outskirts of Rennes-le-Château. The horde numbered thirty-five thousand strong, including battalions of mercenaries from the German principalities. The dust from their column darkened the sunset for days, announcing their arrival. Having conquered the coastal plains, Simon de Montfort found it more difficult to maneuver in the erratic valleys leading into the Pyrenées. Rocky peaks where castles had wisely been perched by Goths and Merovingian lords of the first millennium still provided nearly impregnable forts centuries after their construction.

Like their northerly neighbors, the defenders of Blanchefort were gravely outmanned, numbering barely six hundred fighting men. They were defending another eight hundred women, children, aged and lame who were unable to fight, huddled within the manor walls.

Lancel stood on the castle balcony, assessing the situation. Joseph stood at his side, copying his broad stance. Though the endless line of combatants weaving through the valley sent a chill up Lancel's spine, he did not believe that all was lost. Numerically the odds were insurmountable. But there was only one path up the mountain to the castle and, despite the multitudes the crusaders held in reserve, only hundreds at the front of any charge would be able to assault the castle walls at one time. Few more would be within striking distance with their crossbows. Far ranging "long bows" had not yet been invented. Combat was still a relatively close and personal affair. Blanchefort was defensible.

For Joseph it was a time of great excitement. He believed that the coming battle was the quest for which his father had been preparing him all these years. To a eight-year olds' mind, this was the noble purpose for which he had been held to such pure and virtuous standards. As Lancel gazed at his wiry and handsome son he prayed that this boy would be spared seeing the darkest side of mankind in the bloodshed that he anticipated.

"Father," Joseph asked gravely, "do the invaders have catapults?"

"Yes, Son, we hear that they do." Afraid that such technology would put fear into Joseph he began to explain, "But we need not worry ..."

"Because our mountain is so steep that there is no place where a catapult can reach the walls. They will be throwing their boulders straight up. And onto their heads," Joseph uncharacteristically interrupted with pride.

"We shall pray that they are so foolish," added Lancel with pride. Someday his son would be an astute warrior.

On the rutted northern road leaving Rennes-le-Château, a procession of villagers, headed by Delacroix and Jacques Boulanger, met the approaching force. The anxious locals prominently displayed every banner possessed by the parish to proclaim their fealty to the same God and religious code that had sent forth these intruders. The display had been organized by Boulanger in an attempt to save the village, as well as himself. Word had spread that the craving of the onrushing crusaders for plunder was becoming less voracious as the total of their booty overwhelmed their returning supply lines. Although Delacroix had grown to dislike and distrust Boulanger, he saw that the overture was wise if the devout people of the village were to be spared.

The lead soldiers knew their duty upon encountering the contingent. They had seen similar demonstrations at each village throughout their march. Without ceremony, Delacroix, Boulanger and four of the attending monks stepped forward. The remainder of the nervous villagers in the greeting party were put under guard in the shade of a tree by the side of the dusty trail. They watched forlornly as their leaders were escorted away and marched into the advancing column of foot soldiers.

Delacroix was not afraid for himself as he first entered the ranks of the long-awaited Lord's avengers. But they were a scraggly, unorganized lot. They looked the part of mercenaries. Their clothes were filthy and their language crude, although there were no remarks directed to the villagers. The soldiers who were leading the greeting party to their commander were neither welcoming nor rude. They knew no better than their escorts what disposition would be ordered by their volatile leader.

Boulanger froze when he heard the thunder of approaching hooves. The soldiers briskly moved to the side and turned their faces to the noise. Around the bend in the trail galloped a knight in full regalia. The ostentatious trappings of the armored horse and glistening steel of the shield and lance of the rider that approached clearly indicated his prowess in battle. He was flanked by knights with broad, heavy, iron swords drawn and raised high. Behind them rode archers, crossbows pulled tight and arrows placed. It was a demonstration to remind the greeting contingent that this was not a force to be taken lightly.

Unable to control the dread building within him, Boulanger fell to his knees in the dust. He raised his arms in submission and waited for the horsemen to rear their mounts to a stop in front of the assembly. Boulanger cried out, "Mercy, our lord. We are at thy service as true followers of His Holiness, the Pope. Have mercy."

The lead knight pulled up his metal visor and looked from side to side at his staff, appalled at the premature display of cowardice. He addressed Delacroix. "Tell your lowly servant to rise. He has mistaken me for a Cathar who imitates Our Savior."

Delacroix was also embarrassed by Boulanger's actions, and did not assist him in rising from the dust where he had fallen. He looked directly at the warrior. "I am Father Bernard Delacroix of the parish of Rennes-le-Château. The armies of the Pope are welcome here to do His Holiness' bidding." Delacroix dipped his head slightly, maintaining eye contact with the leader.

"*The* Father Delacroix. I am honored to at last make your acquaintance. The Holy Father spoke highly of the reports that you have provided. Forgive me my manners. I am Simon de Montfort l'Amaury, commander of the Albigensian Crusade as directed by His Holiness, Pope Innocent the Third."

The sound of the commander's name caused the welcoming party to shudder. The reputation of Simon de Montfort for bloodthirsty ruthlessness to heretics and faithful alike had been well-publicized by word of mouth of southbound refugees. The stories were exaggerated in their total number of victims, although accurate upon occasion. They hoped that the presence of their Father Delacroix -a favorite of the pope!- was sufficient for merciful treatment.

De Montfort saw that his thunderous arrival had achieved its desired affect and continued. "Please. You have nothing to fear. We are here to cleanse Languedoc of the heretics and nothing more. Our mission has been thus far successful, and we hope to complete it upon reaching those distant mountains," he declared, pointing his gloved hand toward Blanchefort and the Pyrenées behind.

De Montfort swung down from his horse and removed his helmet. In deference to Delacroix's spiritual position, he bowed slightly. Despite the sinful excesses of the crusaders, de Montfort and his men were devoutly religious, approaching superstitious, in their practices prior to entering battle. Upon obtaining victory, the call for divine observation was usually suspended.

"How may we assist you?" asked Delacroix.

"Your reconnaissance of the heretics shall abet our task." De Montfort was accustomed to full cooperation.

Delacroix hesitated, uneasy in the role being thrust upon him.

Boulanger was not so uncomfortable, and stepped forward to tell all that he knew. "Your Lordship, may I assist?" He continued without pause. "Cathars and Knights Templar are holed up in the castle Blanchefort, about a half day's ride north of here. Heretics, one and all of them. They claim to be gods and spit on the figure of the Blessed Virgin Mary."

De Montfort immediately obtained a distrust for Boulanger that the man seemed to engender. "Ah, we have seen it many times before. Is this correct, Father?"

Delacroix spoke hesitantly. "These people are misguided. If given time, I could convince them of the wrongfulness of their ways."

De Montfort laughed. "You are too modest, Father. I have heard your reports of these pagans. They swear an unnatural allegiance to the whore Mary Magdalen. They claim royal and holy blood. They refuse to eat meat or swear oaths. And chastity!" De Montfort snorted his disdain. "I will certainly relay to His Holiness your dedication in offering to continue to fight for the souls of these demons, but he has sent me with a commission to speed the process of their salvation."

"I see." Delacroix had not expected the messengers of the pope to be so sanguine.

"Why of course you do. You are not saying that there is hope for these people, are you?"

"Perhaps." But Delacroix did not see hope as a possibility. "Will you offer them terms of surrender?"

"Surrender! They have seen the dust of my armies approaching for five weeks. They have had time to repent. Ha. The time has come."

"And if they were to repent?"

"Then I should have to slay them as proven heretics." De Montfort was accustomed to the bloodshed, but preferred the contest of the battle to mass execution. His terms usually insured that there was a struggle, at least initially.

"All?" Delacroix asked.

Normally de Montfort had little patience for the squeamish, but he mistakenly believed that Delacroix was a favorite of the Holy Father and decided to back pedal slightly. Besides, his men were tired. Terrified by reports of the merciless treatment of the soldiers, each village in the southward path of destruction had multiplied their efforts to raise defenses and store provisions to withstand a siege. Those who were not Cathars either fled north to lavishly welcome the army in hopes of mercy, such as Boulanger now hoped to do, or they joined the Cathars and Knights Templar in the fight to the death. As a result, the booty and plunder no longer came so easy and many of the mercenaries, obligated only for forty days service as was the custom of the age, took their treasure troves and returned to their homes. They had been replaced by new, untrained fortune seekers and de Montfort was seeing his army become a massive but disorganized rabble. He would not generate more turmoil today.

"Come, come, my gentle Priest," de Montfort soothed. "Perhaps all shall not need death. But if they do not repent, it is for their salvation that they must die."

That heretics must die, Delacroix accepted as logical and divine. The flesh was spoiled, but the soul could be saved. Still, the consequences were painful to contemplate as he thought of heretics that he now counted as friends, huddling fearfully behind the walls of Blanchefort. "It is in God's hands," he said softly.

"Certainly." De Montfort was relieved. He quickly changed subjects to prevent any further troublesome meddling by Delacroix. "Now we were hoping that the fine village of Rennes-le-Château would have some extra provisions to provide for weary Christian soldiers prior to battle." It was said loud enough for the soldiers to hear. They shuffled their feet impatiently.

Boulanger took that as his cue. "Why we most indeed do! Fresh hare captured and fattened. Autumn squeeze of the early grapes. Yes. Yes. It is waiting for you."

"Well then, let not tarry. We have the Lord's work to do." The soldiers began a cheer that spread up the ranks as its meaning became clear.

Delacroix looked at the dust of the road as the soldiers began milling past.

"Come Father. I have many stories to tell you," de Montfort called. They were not stories that Delacroix would relish.

With a heavy burden on his heart, Delacroix slowly turned to make the journey back into his village. He rightfully feared that it would never be the same after de Montfort had finished his work.

*   *   *

Delacroix stirred on his burlap covered straw mattress long before dawn. He could not sleep. The face of de Montfort dominated his mind. He sat up in the bed, panicked. He would have to speak with Lancel. He did not know what he would say. It did not appear that this cup could be passed. He prayed that Lancel would at last receive his hand and confess his sins and request absolution. Maybe mercy would be shown, if not to the knight, then to his innocent son.

As the first rays of sun broke over the distant plain, determination in each step, Delacroix hiked up the winding cart path to Blanchefort. He had left the monastery on foot, not wanting to wake the stable hands. To the sides, in the woods, makeshift encampments held refugees fleeing the crusaders to the safety promised by the Knights Templar behind the sturdy white stone walls of Lancel's castle. Although no one approached Delacroix, he could hear murmurs of reproval, perhaps hatred, directed at him, the symbol of the Church which had sanctioned this pending travesty.

It was mid-morning as he cleared the final rise. Crews of frantic workmen were clearing the dry moat of shrubbery that would conceal attackers and chopping at any vines that climbed the walls and could possibly provide a foothold for invaders.

Despite the air of urgency, the stout drawbridge was not raised. If needed, it could be pulled into place in seconds. Delacroix crossed it, unchallenged, he believed. He looked high above him at the pointed stakes of the metal and wood trellis of the raised portcullis. He had never noticed it before. Soon it would be lowered along the grooved walls, a further barrier to the outside world. An attentive face stared down at the priest through the meurtriere, the "murder holes" in the roof of the entryway where sharpened missiles or boiling water could be dropped onto trespassers. Delacroix shivered. The once friendly face of Blanchefort was putting on its makeup of warfare.

Inside the walls, the lower bailey was teaming with activity. Delacroix surveyed the preparations. Carts of ripe wheat and corn were lined up to be unloaded into the granary, food for both people and livestock during the anticipated siege. Acrid smoke billowed from the blacksmith's forge as an assembly of bare-chested men hammered on what Delacroix knew to be instruments of death. He finally spotted Lancel on the alure, from where he could oversee the activities on both sides of the wall. His leg muscles burning, Delacroix climbed the steps to the walkway.

Lancel had been informed of the visitor's arrival and waited for him at the head of the steep stairs. He called out for the benefit of the vassals surrounding him, "Father Delacroix, hast thou come as a spy for the Holy Father, or perhapst thou comest to administer last rites to an unworthy knight."

Lancel roared with laughter and his entourage joined him. But there was no humor in his biting tone.

Delacroix had not known what to expect, but was taken aback by the caustic mockery. He chose to speak formally. "Sir Frederick, willst thou beseech the Lord's forgiveness of thy sins?"

"And what sins hast I committed that thou hast not committed before me?" The vassals laughed.

"Confess thy ignorance in professing an unholy bond to Our Lord." Delacroix did not mean to be self-righteous, he was pleading for a man's soul.

It was painful for Lancel to mock Delacroix's sincerity. He walked to the far end of the alure to the cool shade of the rectangular tower keep and motioned for Delacroix to follow. Lancel's back was to Delacroix as he faced the distant wooded valley and the hazy mountains. He surveyed the hills that he had tramped as a boy at his father's side, and until late, had shared the same fatherly pleasure with his son. Delacroix approached his side and also studied the aerial view of the region he had come to embrace. The wind was warm in their faces as it had been on his arrival years before.

"Bernard," Lancel spoke in a soft tone, "save those of the true royal line will understand what we do here. By blood we have been chosen. We could say that we have been mistaken, but that would betray what we were born to be, what we are. We cannot confess a sin. We are free of sin on this matter."

The two men, the most powerful in the valley, each in their own manner, stood mutely side by side. They knew in their hearts that on that balcony they could not resolve the differences of the world that had pitted them against one another.

Lancel continued. "We have tried to live side by side with the Church, you know that most of all. Now we have no choice but to stand by who we are. In the battle to come the will of God shall be done and our claim will be justified. And then perhaps you and I shall again raise a tankard to Our Father."

Delacroix tried to protest and was cut off.

"Your Grace, I cannot guarantee you safe passage if you remain longer. I must request your leave."

Delacroix stood in silence. The love between these men could not overthrow the circumstances of history. He understood. He turned to the stern profile of Lancel. "Godspeed, Sir Frederick Lancel. May He guide you in what shall come."

Lancel turned to face Delacroix. The muscles in his jaw twitched. "And you."

*   *   *

Franklin Memorial

Rick lay in his hospital bed, fully clothed in jeans and a pull-over shirt. He stared vacantly at the television screen. The sound was off. A pile of newspapers from across the country were strewn around the room. The door opened. Rick did not shift his head even though he detected movement.

"Mr. Manton, I'm not supposed to do this, but I've got a telefax for you from Jim Gilliam at the New York Times. He has been pestering the front desk for two hours to get through to you. He claims he knows you."

"That's okay, I'll take it." The Mantons had been secured in a separate wing of Franklin Memorial since leaving the emergency room on Christmas Eve. City police had initially cordoned off their wing, but had given way to the FBI the next morning. It was unclear whether another attack was expected or whether these precautions were taken to hold off the press. Other than the hospital staff, a few close friends and Jen's family, Rick's primary contact with the outside world was the three agents assigned in shifts around the clock. "What's going on?" Manton asked the stone-faced agent.

"Nothing official, of course ..."

"Of course." Rick was frustrated with the lack of progress reports from the FBI. There seemed to be lots of activity, but if anything was coming of it, the FBI was not telling him.

"The buzz is that The Times has some verifiable information on an organization that claims responsibility." The agent spoke in the bureau's typically cryptic jargon.

"Such as ...?"

"Can't elaborate."

Can't or won't? Rick thought disgustedly. He was fed up with this treatment.

Rick was worried about Jen, across the hall, still hooked up to an intra-venous antibiotic due to the possibility of infection from the trauma caused to her left kidney. When she was first brought into the emergency room her condition was listed as critical. She was unconscious, and the extent of internal damage was unknown. Hours later, when she regained consciousness, her condition was upgraded to stable. They were relative terms. Her kidneys had shut down, and she had lost a life-threatening amount of blood. The deep cuts on her right shoulder had been tricky for the surgical staff to cleanse and stitch. She would have thick purple scars for the rest of her life, reminders of this nightmare. She was stiff and sore. Miraculously, there was no permanent damage to the ligaments or tendons in her shoulder. Her only lingering injury was the emotional trauma of the realization that her precious son had been stolen. Jen had been delirious in her anguish. With heavy sedation that had turned her into an uncaring zombie for four days she was eased through the initial shock.

Rick's injuries were less severe, although they had been much bloodier at the scene, feeding sensational photospreads and subsequent reports that he was near death. The kidnapper had fired at point blank range. The bullet grazed Rick's scalp and tore off a piece of his ear. The concussion of the blast had knocked him unconscious. Combined with a broken and bloody nose, probably from the exploding airbag, Rick appeared to be quite dead when the first photographer opened his car door, long after the attackers had sped away, and he had slumped to the ground.

Rick could deal with his injuries. What he was finding intolerable was the feeling of helplessness as he held Jen's hand, and listened to her drug induced moaning for her missing son.

Rick took the telefax from the agent.

"I'd like to be alone," Rick requested. 'Alone' meant the agent sat in a chair outside the door.

"Yes sir."

"Could you shut the door?"

"Sure."

Rick quickly dialed Gilliam's number from the sheet.

"Jim, Rick Manton here."

"Great. Thanks for calling."

"No thank you. What the hell's going on?"

"I received a ransom note at the office from apparently some fringe pro-Israel group. They have Danny."

"Jim, they let me watch the news here. Every religious fanatic from here to Peru is claiming responsibility." Rick had been dismayed by the vicious nature of the reaction to Hershner and Fahey's findings and further shocked by the verbal attacks on him and his family, but he was still not prepared for what appeared to be glee in some corners that he had been shot and his son stolen. Were these people human? he wondered when he read such news.

"Rick, listen. They sent a picture. It's Danny, I'm positive."

"Oh God, is he ..."

"He's alive. He looks okay. A little pissed off, but fine. They have him holding a newspaper from the day after the kidnapping."

Rick slumped in his bed. He hadn't wanted to admit it, but he knew the more likely possibility was that Danny was dead. His rage was tempered with relief. His eyes welled and his throat tightened. "Why? What do they want?"

"They claim to be seeking donations to Israeli organizations dedicated to settling the occupied lands on the West Bank. Those areas are being returned to

Palestinian control according to the recent peace accords. The turnover is strongly opposed by many in Israel and they believe the best way to stop it is to build homes and settle Jewish families there."

"Whatever it is, I'll pay it." Rick would gladly give all of his new-found wealth to make this nightmare end.

"It's not just you. They want payment from all Christians. One hundred million dollars."

Rick's head fell to his chest. Danny had been taken by lunatics.

"Rick, we've given this to the FBI. You know they have agents working on this case from every possible angle. But there is a major problem. In the photograph, behind Danny, the background of a city is visible. One of our staffers recognized it from a trip last year. They didn't try to hide it. He's in Jerusalem."

Jerusalem. To Rick, it was just a name in a Sunday school book and the national news. Overseas the FBI had its hands tied. How could Danny be rescued from there? Rick shook his head. This was almost as bad as not knowing. He was already trying to formulate how he would tell Jen.

"How long do I have before this is on TV?" Rick asked. He was getting the hang of how the world of electronic media worked.

"You know I'd hold this if I could. The editors negotiated with the FBI and have agreed to hold it for twelve hours as long as there is no hint of a leak." Gilliam fudged this point. The twelve hour hold coincided with the next edition's run, but realistically it was the most for which they could ask.

"Can I call you for updates? The bureau isn't telling me shit here."

"I'm not surprised. I didn't anticipate this during our series of interviews last November, but you have some powerful enemies out there besides the religious fruitcakes. This whole descendent versus the message debate has become a political hot potato. It isn't just the zealots and the bagladies that would like to see you disappear. You're sort of the new abortion issue that every politician fears."

Rick had no concern for politics. He had none for religion until three months ago. "Well, I'll gladly disappear as soon as we get Danny back. Can I call you?"

"Any time. Really." Gilliam gave him his home telephone and cell numbers.

Rick looked at the receiver after Gilliam had hung up. Jerusalem! Israeli terrorists? The events of the past two months had been surreal enough. This was mind-numbing. He slowly rose from the bed and walked into Jen's room, his emotions a tangled combination of anger and helplessness. The reassuring hum of his wife's monitors filled the room. She opened her eyes as he approached her bed. For a change she had a half smile. The doctors were weaning her off the sedatives. She was tough. He knew she would bounce back.

"I'm feeling better." she said weakly.

He knew that his news would not bolster her recovery. "Jen. I talked to Jim Gilliam." He paused to see if she remembered him in her haze.

"Yes." Her expression said that she recognized the name, but she must have read Rick's expression and feared the news was not good. "What does he say?"

"He received a ransom note for Danny at the Times. It also came with a picture. Jim says Danny looks fine."

"Oh, thank God." Rick could hear strength in her voice at the news.

"But Jim says that it appears he is in the hands of some kind of Israeli terrorist group and they have taken him to Israel."

Jen drew a deep breath and laid back, closing her eyes. Rick had feared she would begin crying uncontrollably as she had done the previous days. He watched her face twitch and contort into a pained expression.

"I'm okay, Rick." She sighed. "We've got to get out of here and find out what the hell is going on."

Rick was relieved to hear her determination. "I'll make some calls and see what else I can find out. You have to start eating some food."

She opened her eyes and looked at him with a resolute air that was familiar to him. When she had that look, she was ready for a fight. She nodded. His Jen was back.

* * *

The first week of the new year had not been a good one for Ben Dailley's administration. Before adjourning for the holidays, Congress had dropped a number of bills in his lap that had unilateral public support, but contained riders and amendments that were not widely understood. But Dailley understood that the hidden expenditures ran exactly in opposition with his campaign pledges. Sooner or later those in his own party would use his non-veto to "prove" to the primary voters that he was soft on eliminating pork barrel legislation. He was damned if he vetoed. Damned if he didn't. He rued his party's failure to push the line item veto legislation last term. They could have pushed it through when they had control of both houses, but they had backed off because, at the time, a Democrat held the Oval Office reigns. They smugly thought they could wait until they had control of the executive as well. Now the shoe was on the other foot.

So here sat Dailley, his entire cabinet and top advisors seated at the huge, wooden conference table, gathering to strategize the content of his upcoming State of the Union address. They were not discussing the precipitous fall of the dollar, the revolution in Mexico nor global warming or China's counter trade sanctions. His staff was urging him, no, they were ordering him, to finally take a public stand on this insane Manton tragedy that was playing out on every television screen in America. Nothing else seemed to matter. Dailley did not appreciate the added pressure.

"So what do you want me to do? The kid has been abducted to Israel. They're thumbing their noses at us, aren't they? Pat, what's our status with Israel?" Dailley wanted answers, not questions.

Patrick Hindman, the Secretary of State spoke up. "We're in constant touch with the Israeli government on the Manton search. The Israelis pride themselves on internal security. This is quite an embarrassment. Not a trace. Not a clue. And the Israeli government is feeling the heat from the minority parties that don't think the ransom for further settlements is a bad idea. So publicly the prime minister has to take the position that they will handle it internally and we should not interfere. Ron," he continued, nodding to FBI Director Ronald Shultz, "has some questions about the Israel connection, but hasn't located any leads as of yet. It's baffling."

"So." Dailley's theatrical sigh and raised arms told his cabinet that he wanted a solution. He glared around the room at a number of cabinet officers who were purposefully studying their empty notepads. "So we can't seem to find Danny Manton, let alone rescue him. Anybody got any bright ideas on how we address that?" The silence in the room was deafening. "Great. Just great."

"Mr. President, if I may?" The Reverend Johnny Hanner sat forward. His surface politeness masked the fact that he had advised the past eight presidents based not on his standing as the titular head of the Protestant church, but on his potential to deliver thirty million votes to either party in the next election. Since Dailley had emerged as the front-runner in the primaries eighteen months ago Hanner had full access to his ear. He was a regular at Oval Office staff meetings, having made sure that the new chief of staff had been promptly informed that he had held this privilege through the last four cabinets.

"Certainly, Reverend."

"On addressing this bloodline claim. It doesn't seem that this is a matter of believing, or not believing, these unproven *theories*. A true follower of Jesus will, and should, continue to spread the message as he is instructed by the Bible. The existence of a family descending from Christ is contrary to its teachings. A true believer will never see anything that could disprove this point."

The entire cabinet squirmed uncomfortably in their chairs. Dailley, who owed much of his political acumen to being a shrewd judge of character, never had gotten a good read on Hanner. Did the minister truly believe what he said, or was he protecting his position as the leader of those spreading the message? If it was the latter, Dailley could certainly appreciate the posturing, his career had been guided by a similar principle. But he wasn't sure which it was. The air in the room was stifling. Thorne, doing his job, helped out his boss.

"So the President should be ...?" The long pause by Thorne was clearly Hanner's cue to fill in the blank.

"I'm suggesting that the President state that the theories surrounding this bloodline, while interesting, and the spur of much good theological debate, are still just that, theories, and the Mantons should be treated the same as any American citizen. That, of course, would mean that every usual effort would be made to secure the safe return of their son." Hanner looked challengingly from face to face in the room. He was used to having his suggestions followed.

I could take lesson from the good Reverend, mused Dailley. He looked around his suddenly timid staff. Down turned faces were finally lifting up from the table. They looked nervously back and forth. No one objected.

Dailley was satisfied. "That sounds like wise counsel. Thank-you, Reverend. Thank-you. Well, that about wraps it up for this morning. Let's get together this afternoon to discuss the rest of the world's issues, if that is all right with y'all." There was a general chuckle in the room. "Reverend, a pleasure as always."

"My pleasure, Ben." Hanner had outlasted eight presidents. He believed he had earned the right to call this one by his Christian name.

"Joe, Ron, could I see you for a minute. Now." Dailley was working through lunch again.

*   *   *

Dailley, Thorne and Schultz could now freely talk. The three of them had constituted an "inner circle" for years and each was not afraid to speak his mind, that is, when not being observed by the staffers outside their cabal.

"Ben, we're toast whichever way you go on this. I think the pompous ass reverend is right this time though. Let's just wash our hands of the whole affair," said Thorne.

"Very Biblical, Joe. That's probably what the Times headline will read, too." Dailley paced to the window and looked out onto Pennsylvania Avenue. No protests. Maybe it wouldn't be such a bad day after all. He swung to face the room. "How can we shut this thing down without appearing to be running a reversal? Any bright ideas, Ron, now that you've got the whole damn Bureau assigned to it?"

Schultz sat forward and jabbed a pen into the air in Thorne's direction. "Keep in mind that you guys were the ones that wanted this high priority. 'Let's solve this,' you said. 'Show the country the administration can do something ...'"

"Fine. Fine." Thorne jumped in, defending his strategy. "We made the wrong call. But we did think you'd be able to solve a crime that was filmed by twenty-eight news crews!"

"Enough you two." Dailley wanted to keep the discussion under control. "None of us have been able to predict where this Manton issue has been going since day one. Let's just find a way out of this swamp. Ron, are you anywhere close to finding the kid?"

"As you know, if he is in Israel the Bureau has no jurisdiction. It would be in Pat's hands over at State, and he can't do squat to put pressure on Israel with all the pending talks with the Arabs. There is one thing, though." Schultz paused. He didn't know if he wanted to open any other can of worms.

"What? What!" Dailley said impatiently.

"Well, strange as it seems, preliminary reports from our computer analysts indicate that the ransom photo has been doctored. It's the kid for sure. But the background was blended underneath his photo. He could be anywhere. And probably not Jerusalem or whoever has him wouldn't have gone to the trouble to make us think that."

"Just great, as if we could locate him when it was narrowed down to Israel." Dailley returned to the window. He leaned over on the knuckles of his clenched fists.

"Mr. President," Schultz felt it was proper to be formal under the circumstances, "there is the possibility that the kid might still be right under our noses."

"Fantastic. And we can't find him," Thorne jabbed. "Better off that he'd be in Israel."

The room fell silent. Dailley hung his head and looked at the floor. "Maybe the Rev's right. Try this on. Tell the public that it isn't our call whether this kid is related to Christ. Tell them that we're taking all the normal steps to investigate, but that it appears that he is in Israel so our hands are tied. We're pressuring the Israeli government to do everything it can, blah, blah, blah." Dailley looked up. "Joe, how's that shake out?"

"Let's see." Thorne would put on a show with his analysis. He leaned back in his chair, clasped his hands behind his neck and stared at the ceiling as if deep in creative thought. "Point one. Dodges the religious issue, yet supports the Religious Right that Manton's bloodline claim is an unproven theory. That's acceptable. Point two. Takes the heat off the FBI. We need that."

Schultz bristled at Thorne's sarcasm.

"Point three. Sort of a bonus. It puts pressure on the Israeli prime minister. Since he has been refusing to come to the table with Syria we could use this, covertly, to get his people to at least try to act civil at the peace talks. Wrangle a concession or two. That would make us look good."

"What's the downside?" Dailley asked.

Thorne took his time. He knew Dailley would not interrupt. "Minimal. Liberals and universities like this Manton bloodline claim. They don't vote for us anyway. And American Jews want us to find the kid. They're in the proverbial hot seat now. If Manton is related to Jesus then this is the second crucifixion pinned on them. They took enough lumps the last two thousand years for the first one. So they'd like it resolved. But the Jews never vote for us either. Screw 'em. I can't think of any other potential gripers we should worry about."

"Ron, can you scale back the investigation?"

The head of the Bureau nodded grimly. "There will be some questions, but I can handle them."

"How far can we reduce it?"

"How far do you want, Mr. President?"

Dailley looked around the room, making eye contact with each of them to insure that he had a consensus. "Shut it down. As far as we're concerned, Master Manton is in Israel. Nothing you can do. If he happens to show up later get your boys out to the site as soon as possible for the photo shoots. If there are some FBI hats in the evening news, then no harm is done, right?"

"Sounds good." Schultz looked relieved.

"I'll handle the press." Thorne was pleased.

Unbeknownst to them, the Mantons were on their own.

*   *   *

7

Oh my Father, if it be possible, let this cup pass from me: nevertheless, not as I will, but as thou wilt.
--Matthew 26:39

"Rick. You awake?"

"Yeah. Of course." The Mantons both had been constantly tossing and turning, each making sleep impossible for the other. They didn't want to take any sedatives, they needed to be ready. The phone could ring at any second. They would be there for Danny. It had been over two weeks since the kidnapping. They were at home, under close guard, and had healed, physically, from their injuries. Yet here it was, two in the morning, and they were still awake, as usual.

"Hon, I can't stop thinking of how Danny must feel." Jen was positive that Danny was alive. Rick could not stay so optimistic, but was careful not to let her know.

"He's a tough little guy, Jen. These people are terrorists. They want money. They're not the religious fanatics, thank God. They get a benefit out of Danny being alive. He is their golden goose. They won't do anything to hurt him. He's looked all right in all of the pictures." Rick tried to sound confident for both their sakes. He was less anxious about the present than the future. He believed that what he had told her was true, or at least logical. What he couldn't voice was his fear over how this all would end. What happened to Danny when the terrorists had wrung all of the money out of this that they could? Why would they risk leaving a witness alive? His main concern now was the inaction of the FBI. What the hell was it doing? It was as if Danny had vanished.

"Damn it, I want to do something. I can't stand just waiting day after day." Jen shared his feelings. Her maternal instincts had replaced her depression as she had recovered from her injuries. She felt like a mother bear. She wanted to lash out and protect her cub. But there was no one to lash at. "How are you doing?" she asked.

"I keep going through the crash. Over and over. Something keeps recurring in the dream that seems important. It's very specific and I feel myself crying out 'Who are you? ... Look at that! ... Look at that!' Then poof, I'm awake and it's all gone." Except the pain.

"Rick, you can't sleep anyhow, right?" Jen didn't wait for an answer. "I want to try something. Some of the docs at the hospital are using hypnosis for recall of latent memories. Usually long term repressed stuff. They swear by its accuracy. I've never had a need for it, but I've heard enough about it at the seminars that I think I could do it to you. Maybe you saw these kidnappers before? Maybe the bastards were following us for days? Maybe that is why this is haunting you?" Jen looked at Rick, imploringly. "Who knows? Let's try to find out what it was, okay?"

"Hey, you don't have to sell me, I'm game. It might be something like that. Something in the dream is bothering me. Do you know how to do this?" He turned on the bedside light.

"I've read about it and saw a demonstration last year at the Atlantic City seminar. It seems pretty straightforward. I'm sure I can do it. I don't know whether you're the right type, though. It's worth a try."

"Sure is. Just don't make me quack like a duck."

Jen decided to go into Danny's room for the experiment. She didn't have any reason why this would help, but it seemed like the best place to establish sober, reflective settings. A collection of well-worn stuffed animals peered down from the shelves. Their eyes seemed even sadder that they first did when their master had stopped playing with them a year ago. The bed was made when it should have been rumpled with skinny white legs sticking out of the covers at a cock-eyed angle. A Philadelphia Eagles pillow stood at the head against the wall as a mute tombstone to their youthful fan.

Rick sat on the bed facing Jen. She followed the procedures that she recalled. Looking deeply into his eyes, she started speaking in a rhythmic cadence.

"Relax. Let your muscles go. Deep breathes. Feel your muscles warming and melting." On and on she droned in a low, singsong voice. Occasionally Rick's eyes flashed with alertness. She kept trying. This is getting nowhere, she feared. She continued a few more sentences before breaking her cadence and asking her husband, "Are you even getting a little sleepy?"

"No, not at all." He spoke in a flat voice. No disappointment, no emotion. His eyes didn't move.

He's not blinking. I've got him...we're there.

"Close your eyes, Rick." He did. "Now are you sleepy?"

"Very, very sleepy."

"I want you to dream. I want you to dream about the kidnapping. I want you to tell me about the crash. I want to hear what you remember."

Rick gave a long, low groan. It had a ghostly, inhuman quality. "Ooooohh. I see lights. Here come the lights. Here they come again." He rocked in the bed nervously.

"Go on. I'm listening."

"What are you doing? Stop. You're going to hit us! You idiots. Stop. Stop. Stop! Ahhh." Rick grimaced and his body jerked involuntarily as if he was in the car again as it was rammed. He stopped talking and his head moved side to side.

"It's all right. Go on."

"Damn you. Damn you. You've hurt my family. Where's Danny? Jen? Are you all right? Jen? Jen? Answer me! Jen."

Rick fell quiet. Jen waited. She was unnerved by the pain in her husband's voice. After all these years with him, she was used to his macho belief that men should rarely, if ever, show their true emotions. It shocked her to see this side of him.

"So many lights. Too bright. Turn them down. Help us. Please. Please help us." Rick was pleading. His body then went rigid. "Hey, you're being too rough with Danny. Be careful, he's hurt. Who are you anyway? Stop that you jackass. You aren't helping. Stop ...What? What's that? Who are you? What are you doing? What is that? What is that?" By now he was screaming.

"Rick, what do you see? Tell me."

Rick calmed down. "His arm ... above the glove. Grabbing Danny. I see his forearm. Something on it. A tattoo. Green and blue. I don't know what it is."

"Think, Rick. Tell me, what does it look like?"

" A symbol. A cloverleaf. But lopsided. Pushed over. And writing underneath."

"Can you read it? Rick, what does it say?"

"On a banner. It says 'Death.'...'Death.' Rick's voice had a resigned tone. Again his body jerked. "A gun. Why? Why? You bastard. Ugh." Rick jerked again. He doubled over, grimacing silently, wincing over and over. His body spasmed, but he did not cry. Jen had heard enough.

"Rick, wake up now. It's over Rick. It's over."

Rick slowly opened his eyes and let out a huge sigh. "I remember now."

"I know."

"I want to kill them so bad."

"I know."

One nightmare was over. They had hoped for some greater revelation, but at least, in their minds, they had finally done something. They had taken a positive step to help their son. Perhaps the tattoo could be used to identify a suspect, if there ever was one. They'd call the FBI in the morning with a description of the tattoo that Rick could now clearly recall. For now they could go to bed and, in spite of themselves, they collapsed into a deep sleep.

* * *

When Rick called the FBI the next morning and described the tattoo he now recalled, the agent was unexcited and non-committal. Rick resented the attitude. He knew it wasn't much, but it was more than the FBI had found. The agent said he'd have the field operative pick up their drawing of the tattoo later that morning. There was still security provided outside the house. It had been offered by the FBI and Rick saw no reason not to accept. It turned out that it was more for appearances than protection. "Security" meant a car with two agents sitting in it, usually on the end of a double shift and half asleep.

The state highway patrol was doing more work controlling the barrier at the end of the block that was now more of a vigil than a picket line as it had been before the kidnapping.

The phone rang. It was Gilliam. "Rick."

"Any news?"

"Always lots of news. We should talk sometime. But for now, you guys take care of yourselves and don't forget to fill those prescriptions." Gilliam sounded uncharacteristically carefree. His comments were inappropriate for the situation. Gilliam had talked to him numerous times since the ransom note had arrived and he never sounded so flippant.

"What are you talking about?"

"I'm just saying that you wouldn't want any of those pain pill prescriptions to lapse, so why don't you go down to the drugstore or wherever and get them refilled. You can call me from there while you wait. Understand?"

Rick slowly responded. "I think so." Why wouldn't Gilliam talk to him over the phone? Was his house wiretapped?

"Call me?"

"Uh-huh."

Rick walked out to the parked car and was about to rap on the window when he saw his protectors sound asleep. He motioned Jen toward the garage. Surreptitiously they backed their new van out and slowly pulled away. A handful of their supporters stood huddled together around a makeshift can with a fire in it on the sidewalk at the end of the block. A pair of state troopers sipped steaming cups of coffee in their car. The engine was running and the heater was on. Having received no alert, neither group noticed the van drive by. It was a residential area and vans were commonplace.

Keeping their eyes cast to the floor, the Mantons snuck into the far corner of the local pharmacy. Rick dialed Gilliam's number. Jen pressed her ear close to his and kept a lookout on the office supply aisle. Gilliam answered. "Jim, what in the world's going on? Am I being bugged?"

Gilliam knew that the Times phones were regularly "cleaned" for wiretaps. They did it not due any longer to fear of government spying, but to protect against leaks of the coveted scoop. "Are you at home?"

"No."

"Good. Look, I don't know if you're being tapped or not, but I've got to play it safe. I'm having a hard time figuring out exactly what's going on in Washington. My sources tell me that Schultz has kiboshed the investigation." Gilliam didn't see the need to inform Rick that his "sources" was an old police beat friend of his who was now fairly highly placed at the FBI. The source didn't care for this gutless order. Neither did the field agents on the case. They could care less if Manton was related to Christ or was Christ himself. They saw an innocent boy kidnapped on national networks and they wanted him back.

"How the hell can he do that?"

"Apparently approved by the White House. It looks like the whole bloodline issue has made the ransom too hot for them and this is how they handle it."

"Those sons-of-bitches." Rick had been as naive about politics as he had been about religion. It had never occurred to him that the government, his government, would bail out on him like this.

"I'm going to blast those gutless bastards," Rick said through gritted teeth. "Will you help me raise a stink about this in the press, Jim?"

There was a pause on the line. "Rick. I can't burn my source. Besides, anything the Times says won't hurt Dailley or the FBI anyway. Most of the voting public sees you as a publicity stunt and wouldn't mind hearing that you're not getting special treatment. The White House is going to present to the public the angle that they will take all normal steps to investigate and negotiate with Israel."

"But Israel doesn't know who's got Danny either."

"I know." There was a long silence on the line.

"We're screwed."

"It stinks. Typical Ben Dailley head-in-the-sand attitude."

"What are we going to do?" It was more of a rhetorical question than a plea for help.

"I've got some friends in law enforcement. They want to keep the investigation going, but they have no authority. They're going to have to do it under the table, for now. If they get any leads they'll let me know. They're embarrassed by this chickenshit move too. In the meantime, I've got a meeting this afternoon with Joel Cohen, the senator from New York who has some pretty powerful ties with Israel. His staffers called me to set it up. I hope it is more than just a publicity move to soften the public pressure on Israel, but they wouldn't say. I'll let you know."

Jen tapped Rick on the forearm and mouthed 'tattoo.' It didn't seem too important in the scheme of things.

Rick nodded at her. "Jim, something else, it probably won't matter, but last night I recalled that there was a tattoo on the son-of-a-bitch that took Danny."

"No kidding?" Gilliam's voice indicated more interest than the agent had earlier. "That might be helpful for identification. You didn't remember it before?"

"Naw, just came back to me." Jen gave him a thanks-for-the-credit look.

"If it's odd enough maybe they can track the guy. What'd it look like?"

"Hard to describe. Like a smashed shamrock. Underneath it said 'Death'."

"Well, it's a long shot, but why don't you draw a picture for me. I can give it to my contacts, see if they can round up someone. Can you scan it to me?"

Jen looked around and nodded. "Yes," she interjected. She had the drawing in her purse.

"Good. You have my email on the card I gave you. I'll wait for it and call you when I'm done with Cohen."

"Jim, thanks. Really."

"Save your thanks, we've got a long way to go." The line went dead. Gilliam wasn't one for long goodbyes.

Jen looked up. Her eyes reflected her helplessness.

"C'mon. We've got some shopping to do," Rick said.

*   *   *

Sunrise

At dawn the onslaught began. As designed, the plain before the castle gate provided no cover for the attack. Behind the swordsmen and ladder bearers a row of archers stood impotent until a hail of arrows from the upper castle walls forced a disorganized, stumbling retreat. The eager foot soldiers regrouped and assaulted the entrance wall in wave after wave in a futile, deadly desire to raze the gate and pillage their prize. By day's end the defenders of Blanchefort had repelled each offensive. As the sunset sent its rays through the lingering cloud of dust that shrouded the castle, Lancel stood on the wall above his cheering troops and stared at the path where he had first paused to show his bride, now many years ago, the home of her children-to-be. Now it was littered with bloody bodies, arrows rising from them like the stems of cherries. The red stain that drained from the corpses marked a gruesome path to Rennes-le-Château. An eerie stillness replaced the cheers of the day's victors. To Lancel it was an ominous silence.

Over the next four months there were sporadic frontal assaults at the gate that seemed half-hearted and were easily repelled. Lancel, against his better judgment, allowed himself the hope of withstanding the siege. The knights had stored enough supplies that they could survive captivity for many more months. The water was supplied through a well which had been dug at considerable effort over three hundred years previously. He knew that certainly his knights were better trained than the hastily assembled armies of the north. They also had the superior advantage of the castle walls towering above the encampments of aggressors. Admittedly the Cathars were of little help in matters of combat. But Lancel had pledged his support to them and a good share of his knights were among their members. By honor, he would not abandon them.

Seven months into the siege, Lancel was inspecting the repairs to the iron pot which was used to pour boiling animal fat over the edge of the wall onto the invaders attempting to scale the wall on wooden ladders. As the blacksmith was explaining the difficulties of patching the crack with the unstable materials available in the fort, a sentry on the wall rose to obtain a better view of movement he spied on the trail. In a weed thicket at the edge of the clearing around the castle lay an eager bowsman who had crawled to his concealed post and was waiting for such an opportunity. He had been instructed not to indiscriminately shoot his arrows. An arrow which fell in the fort without breaking its shaft would most likely be shot back later in the day. But in this case the upper torso of the guard was exposed. Adrenaline rushing from this rare chance, the young bowsman pulled his bow tauter than ever, skillfully aimed and quickly fired the arrow which he had meticulously dipped in cow manure that morning. It rose high and true, but from fifty yards distant, and with the swirling winds that constantly encircled the hilltop, only fortune could make the arrow find its target. With the hum of a large bee it whistled over the guard's head causing him to topple backward from his perch. The errant dart continued its arch upward until it was deep into the compound. As Lancel rose from inspecting the crack in the pot, the arrow, seemingly guided by the hand of God, sailed into the unsuspecting cluster of men and pierced his upper right shoulder. Lancel lurched forward, unaware of what had struck him until the first spasm of pain surged down his arm.

The arrow had little power at the end of its flight and was not lodged deeply into Lancel's flesh. It had slightly penetrated the muscle and veins between Lancel's neck and shoulder. Blood freely flowed down his chest and back. As his servants dutifully held Lancel erect and pulled the arrow from his body, flecks of cattle dung broke loose from the tip and lodged in the wound.

Within minutes the castle physician was summoned. He quickly curbed the bleeding and patched the wound. The injury was superficial and would not harm a strong and healthy warrior such as Lancel. Although in the thirteenth century the treachery of poison arrows was appreciated, knowledge of germs and the spread of infection was still centuries away. Had Lancel not had special status as the leader of his people, and had he not received immediate attention deserving of a person of his rank, his wound would have bled itself free of the dung flecks. Instead the best known medical care, the capping of the entry site, sealed his doom.

Three days after the archer's freak strike Lancel first felt the fever. It was slight at first, but the chills and sweats worsened until he was forced to stand down from his command position and retreat to his bedchamber. The physician was again called. As he examined the red streaking veins running down Lancel's arm the physician's face told him all he needed to know.

*   *   *

Against the physician's advice, Lancel had been carried to the chapel. He was feverish and weak. If he were to have any chance, he must rest and allow the physicians to drain the poisonous blood from his body.

But Lancel was a strong-willed man, and he was not to be denied his request. In the flickering glow of the bank of votive candle, Lancel appeared to have more color in his face than he did in his chamber. Perhaps divine intervention was the only solution.

"Please let me alone here," Lancel said softly to the four men that had carried his stretcher. They assisted him to a broad bench and propped him in a sitting position on three large goose down pillows. The men bowed slightly and backed outside the door to await his call.

He looked up at the oil portraits on the wall, hanging on twined rope below the rough stained glass windows. The Virgin Mother. Mary Magdalen. He nodded in respect to them. Rising weakly, Lancel shuffled from the small chapel into a smaller grotto off to the side. It was familiar territory to him. When he had to pray, when he had to think, he came here. He knew in his heart that it would be his last trip.

He looked up at the portrait of his departed wife. His hand gripped a smooth wooden bar in front of the shrine. A dozen candles flickered in the faint breeze he had caused. He sank to his knees and stared at the floor below the candles. Molten drops had fallen onto previous piles, forming a waxy mountain range, not unlike the view out his chamber window. Mesmerizingly, the drips splashed down, drop by drop.

"Solange," he whispered in agony.

Because of his royal blood, Lancel had put his son, their son, in mortal peril. He could not look up at the portrait, darkening with age and the smoke of candle fat. He could not face the reproving eyes, still vibrant as if alive.

"Solange, my dear. Please forgive me."

Lancel knelt in the shadows, alternately mumbling and lapsing into long silences. He cursed the ego within him that would not let go of the bloodline mantle that he had worn with pride, upholding the traditions of generations before him. The cloak that he desired to pass down to his son as much as he desired life itself. But now that desire, that stubborn pride, could cause the bloodline to perish. Tears ran down his cheeks and spattered in unison with the candle wax.

"Please help me, my Love," he cried at the foot of the image of the wife that he planned shortly to rejoin.

* * *

Delacroix was not surprised to see the messenger, a young boy in filthy rags standing in the doorway, head stiffly bowed.

"Your Grace." He held up the sealed envelope without lifting his head.

Delacroix took the note and administered a blessing on the waif who sprinted home to tell his parents of his good fortune.

Delacroix was shocked to see the wax seal on the letter imprinted with the signature ring of Lancel. The circle around the castle was not so tight that messengers and even enterprising merchants could not easily sneak through, but he had not anticipated ever communicating again with his lost friend. He expectantly broke open the wax and unfolded the paper.

Dear Father Delacroix,

Sir Frederick Lancel has been wounded and fallen mortally ill. He humbly requests the grace of your audience.

The letter was concluded with an ink stamp of Lancel's ring.

Of course Delacroix would go. He hoped that this was a sign that Lancel would repent prior to his receiving the sacrament of last rites. If so, his soul could be saved from the fires of hell. Perhaps the bloodshed could be avoided. Certainly Joseph could be spared. After all, the Church sought only absolution and obedience, not death. Certainly there would be a price to pay to appease the brigades of soldiers from the north, but it would be a mere pittance compared to eternal salvation.

At dawn's light Delacroix set foot for the castle. This time he did not wear his priestly raiments. There would be too many questions to answer if word got back to de Montfort, as he knew it would. He pulled the wool hooded cape he had taken from the stable close to his face. The pungent smell of horse manure completed his disguise. Now the pathway to Blanchefort was deserted. The refugees had completed their flight to the castle. Some had continued to flee south into the Pyreneés and even onto Spain.

Exhausted from his charge up the hill, he approached the castle. The fields were cleared for a hundred yards and he felt the presence of hundreds of eyes watching his every step. At the foot of the moat where normally the drawbridge rested, Delacroix pulled back his hood and stood silently, looking at the dark slats in the wall where only furtive movements could be detected. After a minute, a rope ladder was lowered along the wall to the side of the gate. The drawbridge gate over the dry moat had long been barricaded and could not be lowered. Not a word was called out.

Delacroix clambered down the dry bank into the moat. Each step grew spongier. At the top of the mountain, there was no way to fill the moat with water except in the heavy rains of spring, but in these dire circumstances, precious water from the well had been diverted to soak the bottom enough to make it slippery and unstable for the anticipated siege apparatuses. Delacroix sunk into the muck. Although still rotund, Delacroix was now fit from his years of mountain excursions. He slogged forward to the rope, his feet make sucking sounds as he pulled them upward. Clumsily, he climbed the ladder to helping, but wary arms at the top of the wall.

Delacroix was escorted across the bailey to the manor. At the manor a new contingent of armed guards led him down a hallway leading to the bedchambers of Lancel. The lead escort pulled open the heavy wooden door. Lancel had been apprised of Delacroix's first approach and now called out. "Father Delacroix, please enter."

Delacroix entered slowly, his eyes unaccustomed to the darkness.

"I'm sorry. I cannot get up. Will you please open a curtain?" He waved away the guard who stood motionless for a second, then departed.

Delacroix crossed the floor and parted the drapes that hung from the ceiling. The late morning light flooded the room. This wing of the manor abutted the castle wall and the window, high on the exterior wall and on the steepest part of the mountain, overlooked the entire valley.

"Do be careful standing there. The Norman archers have keen eyesight and their arrows seem to be tipped with fortune." The tone was bitter, but not unfriendly.

Delacroix turned from the window. He gasped as he saw his formerly robust confrere, gaunt and pale with watery eyes sunken into dark sockets. Despite his appearance Lancel managed to flash a weak, but broad smile at the sight of Delacroix. "Thank you for coming."

"You knew I would. I do the Lord's bidding, Sir Frederick." Delacroix looked around the room. He had never been in this chamber before. Hanging above the unlit fireplace, on the wall opposite the bed, was an oil portrait of Lancel's deceased wife. She was indeed as beautiful as her descriptions.

"Please, at this hour of my life, when I am within sight of our Lord, call me Lancel."

"Certainly." Delacroix paused as Lancel coughed, his lungs rattling. "You are not well, Lancel."

"I am better this day but my blood carries the poison of an arrow. Nothing but God's will can stop its spread."

It seemed like an opening to Delacroix. "Are you ready to receive the Lord? Shall you confess your sins?"

"Ah, my good and impatient friend, Bernard. I knew that you would offer your services, but I called for you for a different purpose for I still have no sins to confess."

"But you must. You cannot die in this state. For your heresy you ..."

Lancel interrupted the sermon he knew by heart. "Please don't go on. We have discussed this before as men of wisdom, and of God. I understand that you cannot accept the vision I see. My judgment day is nigh upon me. If my beliefs are heresy, I shall soon know and accordingly receive my punishment. But I cannot now relinquish what I believeth."

"Why have you called me here? I cannot condone what you utter. I cannot prevent your damnation." Delacroix was in physical pain from the turmoil caused by Lancel's denial of his assistance.

"I have requested the honor of your presence to beg, not for my soul, but for the life of my son."

The room fell silent as the humbling words were spoken.

"How is Joseph?"

"He is fine. He misses you. And we all miss your fresh fish." Lancel smiled again and wheezed.

"I have not been fishing without him." Both men looked uncomfortably at their feet. Delacroix spoke first. "He must repent this belief that he is the offspring of Our Lord."

"He shall." The admission was not given lightly by Lancel. "He is young and he will obey the order of his father. I can die for my convictions, but I cannot sacrifice my son. But before this is done I am compelled to demonstrate to you that I am not a fool." Pointing across the room to a large jewel encrusted chest Lancel croaked, "Please bring to me the satchel from the ark."

Delacroix walked to the table and opened the lid. Inside was a soft leather satchel. Embossed in gold script on its covering flap was a Latin phrase, Et In Arcadia Ego. Delacroix lifted it. It was heavy. Cradling it in his arms he brought the satchel to Lancel and laid it by his side.

Lancel dropped a hand upon the bag. The once powerful limb hung limply. "Bernard, there is no Holy Grail. That is but a myth arising from the true account of Mary Magdalen who arrived on these blessed shores bearing a vessel that held the Sang Raal, the Royal Blood of Christ. But that vessel was not a stone goblet nor a metal chalice as relayed by legend. It was the human receptacle of Our Lord's children."

"I shall not hear this," asserted Delacroix as he turned to leave.

"Please, hear me. I understand that by your faith you can never accept my belief that I am the descendant of King David and of Christ. I shall not ask you to. But you should see the revelation to which I was born. Judge for yourself whether I should die unrepentant of this creed."

Reluctantly Delacroix turned to face the bed.

Struggling to sit forward, Lancel pulled from the satchel three leather bound volumes that appeared to be Bibles, each older than any Delacroix had ever seen. He then cautiously withdrew four scrolls. He unrolled the one which appeared most fragile.

"You are a man of words and languages. I cannot fully read this, but for what I was told by my father. For my soul, proceed."

Delacroix reluctantly took the scroll and squinted at it.

"Here, take these." Lancel handed him his eye spectacles from the chest by the bed. "I won't be in need of them any longer."

Delacroix gingerly held the rare glass and metal device and slipped them on. He blinked at the book which was suddenly clearer and larger. He turned to what appeared to be the first page. The text was written in ancient Greek. Delacroix had not read in that language since coming to Rennes-le-Château. He looked skeptically at Lancel, and returned to the pages. At first he deciphered the script slowly, but soon the tutelage of Brother Mihiel came back to him. It was a letter addressed to a person of honored position that the author called 'The Faithful One.' It went on to inquire of the health and growth of the followers of Christ in face of the persecution by the Roman occupiers of Judea. It appeared to be a missive from an apostle. To Delacroix it was unmistakably in the style of Saint Paul, a prodigious writer whose letters formed many books of the New Testament. But it was not a passage from the Bible that Delacroix knew. He was certain of that. Nonetheless, he was fascinated by the verse as his fingers moved over the words, guiding his weak eyes. He began to tremble as he read aloud.

"The growth of Our Lord's congregation at Antioch confirms God's blessings. But such tidings of joy are tempered by the sad news that the Blessed Wife of Our Lord ..."

Delacroix squinted at the Greek words. In all his experience the translation for the offending word had never been anything other than 'spouse' or 'wife.' He continued, slower.

"... has died on the shores of her refuge lo these many years, and has left this Earthly domain for the Palace of Heaven to take her seat beside our beloved Christos."

Delacroix's brows furled in revulsion at the words. He glared at the page and he could no longer read aloud.

Raising Her to Her reward were the arms of the Sons of Our Redeemer. His daughters wept as they did upon His Ascension. Surely the Holy Family will heed the Blood within them and spread His Message to the world.

This fraudulent attempt at authenticity angered Delacroix all the more. "Lancel, you are a learned man. How can you allow yourself to be swindled by this?"

"Please reserve your judgment. There is more. Behold the scroll wrapped in skin. It is written in Hebrew, I believe." Lancel handed him another ancient roll of parchment which was not as stiff as the first.

Delacroix strained to read the text. It was a genealogy of the male descendants from the Jewish King David. It was familiar to Delacroix. The New Testament began with the lineage of King David down through Joseph, the husband of the Virgin Mary when she was bearing the Holy Child. It had never occurred to Delacroix to question why this royal lineage, which ran to such an insignificant principal in the blessed story, would have such a prominent position in the New Testament. The text of the scroll he held continued from where the Bible was truncated. The next entry was 'Jesus Christ.' With no further explanation other than the word 'begat,' his lineal descendant was listed. And then another and another and another of names unknown to Delacroix.

"What of this scandal? This is not the Word of God," Delacroix insisted.

"These relics, and others like them which you can examine, support the oral traditions that have been in my family since the Resurrection. The items themselves were retrieved from diggings in the Stables of Solomon which lay under the Temple of David in Jerusalem. They were brought back by my forebearer, Godfroi de Bouillon, upon his great crusade to liberate the Holy Lands."

Delacroix knew well the story of Godfroi as did all French children. He had taken the message of Christ back to Palestine and reclaimed Jerusalem for Christendom. Years later he returned with the Knights Templar and for years had encamped on the Temple Mount, the ruined remains of the grandiose temple built by King David which had stood for centuries until 70 AD, when Moslem forces overran Jerusalem. Faced with capture, the Jewish priests of the temple had buried treasure and artifacts sacred to Judaism below the temple floors. Further beneath the temple were the Stables of Solomon which held two thousand horses. When the invading Moslems razed the temple, the rubble, and the fabled treasure, collapsed onto the stable. In had long been rumored that the Knights Templar had excavated the site of their encampment until untold wealth was found. Legend also claimed that the Holy Grail, a fabled chalice that held the blood of Christ, was unearthed.

"Bernard, the crusades of the Knights Templar were their quests to prove their heritage. But even after they found the proof that I show you here, and there was much more at one time that has been lost through the ages, the bloodline was not accepted. So we have allowed the senseless myth of a search for a holy grail to persist. It is far better to be thought a dreamer than a heretic. But the proof that we Brothers of Zion know cannot be refuted. We are the descendants of Christ."

Delacroix was stunned. He gravely looked at the remaining scrolls. He leafed through the opening pages of the Latin Bibles which contained relatively more recent lineage of Lancel's family. The names in French were more familiar and linked to Merovingian kings of France known to Delacroix. These lines traced backward to the lines detailed in the scrolls. He could not have been more shaken if someone had just attempted to prove that the sun did not circle the flat Earth.

Lancel saw the look of bewilderment on Delacroix's face. "You can see my friend, when presented at birth with the mantle of royalty, it is a cloak that cannot be shed."

Delacroix nodded mutely. He began to place the items back in the sack. He pointed to the gold lettering. "What does it mean?" he asked. It was unclear whether it was a rhetorical question directed at all that had been revealed to him or merely to the Latin words, Et In Arcadia Ego.

Lancel shrugged. His response was equally ambiguous and evasive. "You are a man of words and wisdom. And you also know that sometimes meanings are hidden until wisdom allows one to see the true words." They mutely stared at the bag.

Lancel continued. "We are not like the Cathars. Yes, they, too, are secondary descendants of Christ, but they have been foolish in their strange practices. They denied the divinity of Our Lord. We do no such thing. We accept the Holy Catholic Church. But we have knowledge, given to us as our cross to bear, that the Church fathers cannot receive. So Bernard, as I prepare to leave this world, I ask no pardon. I only beseech that you assist my son in surviving, not as a descendent of Christ, but as a boy who likes to fish and hear the birds sing in the forest. He will repent that which we know is true. I ask no obligation of you in that regard."

Lancel was winded from his plea. Breathlessly he urged, "I beg you my friend, will you grant my son thy quarter?"

Delacroix contemplated the mortal request. Numbly he responded, "I shall." He looked out the window over the valley. "When the time is nigh, Joseph shall be delivered by my hand."

"God bless you."

There was nothing more to be said. Whatever they had once was gone. Forbidden by codifice to grant absolution to one who refused to repent, Delacroix could be of no service to Lancel. "May God ease your path, my dear Lancel."

Delacroix's mind was numb as he was escorted out of the manor. This assignment to the God-forsaken outpost of Rennes-le-Château had turned out to be paradise. For once, Delacroix thought of himself and mourned the destruction of his peaceful life.

Tangled at every rung, he climbed down the rope to the mire below. Tears filled his eyes. He plodded to the far side of the moat and climbed up on all fours. He turned to look at Blanchefort. The white walls glistened in the sun, a vision of heaven.

Delacroix turned his back to the castle and pulled his hood over his head and mindlessly started his trek down the hill. As he crossed the open field, he did not notice a pair of wary eyes peering from the bottom of a pile of shrubbery cuttings.

* * *

Hart Senate Office Building

Senator Joel Cohen's waiting room was richly paneled with dark walnut. The walls were filled with large, framed prints of scenes of colonial life along the banks of the Hudson River. Not much self-aggrandizement for a politician, Gilliam thought. He didn't have to wait long. A staffer led him to the senator's office and closed the door behind him as he left. It occurred to Gilliam that it was unusual for him to get to speak to a politician alone, without a note-taking aide who would lend deniability later to any unfavorable quotes. Cohen was known as a bit of a rogue who was not as concerned with appearances as he was with results. That was probably why the voters had reelected him twice.

Cohen immediately rose from his chair and came around the polished wooden desk to shake his hand. "Mr. Gilliam, thank you for taking the time to come down." Cohen had a firm handshake and a warm aura. He was a large, gangly man, with a long forehead that sloped to a prominent nose and piercing eyes set close together. His hair was tousled, yet his suit was impeccably tailored.

"No problem," replied Gilliam. He was wary of being used.

"I've admired your work recently with the Times. Very scholarly. Where did you go to theology school?"

Gilliam bristled slightly at the common mistake. "Actually I've got no educational background in religion. Just filling a desk for now."

Cohen didn't miss a beat. "Makes sense. Well, you've done a fine job. I'll tell you what I've called you here for. It isn't about your original series, it is about the Manton kidnapping."

"I suspected as much."

"As you know, it is no secret that a large and powerful percentage of my constituency are also strong financial backers of Israel." He was correct, it was a well-known fact.

"The work of Hershner and Fahey was very scholarly, but of no particular interest to the Jewish community. Oh, there was some secret smugness about the portions of the work that confirmed Jewish doctrine that Jesus was a human prophet, but not necessarily divine. But for the most part it didn't involve us. Christians are always feuding amongst themselves. The Manton kidnapping is a different matter. It is wrongly being blamed on the Jews."

Gilliam had expected this slant. He must have looked disappointed. He didn't have long to wait, however, for Cohen to give him a real news angle.

"My counterparts in Israel took the allegations that Danny Manton was smuggled into their country very seriously. They pride themselves on security. Their whole existence has been a struggle for survival amidst sworn enemies. To think that a person of such visibility could be brought in under their noses was an outrage to the Israeli people. If a boy whose picture was on every magazine in the world could be slipped in, why not a terrorist with a nuclear bomb? We don't let just anyone wander in." Cohen randomly spoke as if he were Israeli himself.

The senator rose to pace and continued. "The whole ransom business smelled. The last thing the Israeli settlers in the occupied territories want is publicity. They want to move in as quickly and quietly as possible. They establish roots and when it comes time to swap land in the latest round of peace talks the settlers scream 'Never! This is our home, we have as much right to it as the Arabs.' I'm not saying this is right or wrong. That's how it is done. The old riddle is, 'What is the first thing the Israeli Army builds after conquering new territory?" Cohen paused for an answer from Gilliam.

Gilliam played along. "I don't know."

"A kindergarten!" Cohen snorted at his own joke and continued. "So suddenly these organizations want to resort to terrorism and kidnap the relatives of Jesus? That stinks like rotten fish. So the Israeli government starts checking out these so-called non-profit agencies that are supposed to get the ransom payments and what do they find?"

Gilliam saw that he was to be the straight man. "I don't know."

"Basically two tiers of organizations. A few that have been around since the creation of Israel, and a flurry of others that have been created in the last two to three years. Both tiers get a lot of money from the United States. But the old ones spend theirs on new land, lumber and carpenters as fast as they can get it. These new ones, as far as anyone can tell, have taken in contributions but haven't done squat with them. And unlike the old organizations, there seems to be very little actual Israeli presence other than a storefront operation to answer the phone and collect the money. The PLO has operated like that for years. Billions of dollars in Arab money pours in, but other than a few random bombings each year. And what does that cost? Not much. The PLO doesn't do anything other than cater to the lifestyles of the terrorists. So the question is, were these organizations, which are getting the grand majority of the ransom donations, legitimate or were they set up by someone who wanted to tap into the profitable terrorist industry?"

Gilliam took a breath to answer, but Cohen was on a roll and did not wait.

"It had to be someone outside. The true settlers build houses, they don't establish endowments. So the Israelis looked into the target corporations. Israel has looser restrictions on corporate privacy than we do in America. We like to think of it as tighter accountability. What do you suppose they found?"

Gilliam shrugged. He just wanted the point.

"Straw men. Nothing but pass-throughs. These corporations were supposed to be the organizational and financial equivalent of a large American housing developer. There was nothing there. The officers were barely more than street peddlers. But they were good at what they were hired for. They were ignorant. They just knew that the funds were transferred to America through banks in the Cayman Islands. Obviously laundering the checks for their anonymous clients."

"So you're saying that the Israelis have nothing to do with the kidnapping."

"Couldn't. Wouldn't. Goes against everything they've done in the past. And the investigation is thorough. The Israelis tried to give the State Department their entire investigation, but they were told that the White House didn't want it. Dailley is making too much political hay with Jewish guilt over the kidnapping to give it up with the resumption of the peace talks next month."

Now the recent events were beginning to make sense to Gilliam. "So what can you give me that's concrete?"

"I've been authorized to release Israel's investigation and conclusions to the press, and you're the logical choice because of your past work." Cohen didn't need to mention that Gilliam also worked for the newspaper with the largest daily circulation on the east coast.

"What about the pictures of Danny in Jerusalem? It seems like that establishes a solid connection with Israel."

"Hogwash. You can do anything nowadays with a computer and a couple of snapshots. Last year I was on the cover of National Investigator leaving a nightclub arm-in-arm with that supermodel Kristi."

Gilliam recalled the photo and headline proclaiming the torrid affair. He had been surprised at the time because it went contrary to the Senator's reputation of being a straight arrow.

"Thank God my wife knows I'm a zombie after ten o'clock or there would have been hell to pay," Cohen confessed. "It was a great photo though. Cute girl. My God she could be my granddaughter. I got better press out of that rumor than any speech I ever gave on the Senate floor."

"Wouldn't the Bureau be able to tell if the photo was bogus?" Gilliam pressed.

"That's the other part of the story I'd like to give you. And I wouldn't mind spilling the beans on our spineless President. He has terminated the investigation into the Manton case. I can't tell you how I know that though." News traveled fast. Gilliam didn't have the only angry source that was squealing. Then Cohen dropped a bombshell. "The Bureau has known practically from the start that the picture was doctored. They can't admit that or else they'd lose their trump card at the table in Vienna."

Cohen ceremoniously heaved a thick file onto Gilliam's lap. Raising a finger into the air, Cohen declared, "Dailley wanted to shove this on Israel. Well, Mr. President, the Jews are shoving back!"

*   *   *

During the afternoon the Mantons made four calls to Gilliam, all from different locations, before finally getting connected. They were anxious for any information.

"Any luck?" Rick spoke into one of the half dozen prepaid cell phones he purchased at a 7-Eleven. Jen slightly leaned against his shoulder to listen.

"Quite a bit. Senator Cohen has done a lot of digging. He has a pretty good pipeline from Israel. They have strong evidence that there isn't any Israeli involvement at all. They're convinced that the kidnap plot was hatched here in America. But best of all, Cohen says the FBI believes that the photo of Danny is fake."

"Fake?! I've seen it. That's Danny. What do you mean? " Jen's distraught voice said that she had misunderstood what Gilliam had said.

"No, Jen, not Danny. I meant the background is forged. That's Danny, we know that, but his picture was superimposed on that sweeping landscape of Jerusalem. I guess the FBI has known that for a while. It wasn't too difficult to analyze in the computer lab."

"Those bastards. Did Cohen tell you anything else that the FBI knows?" Rick's anger was being redirected from the kidnappers.

"That was about it. He confirmed that the investigation has been put on the back burner. Word is getting around. Cohen is pissed too."

"Good. Stick it to them. You are going to publish this, aren't you?"

"Some of it. Cohen will trumpet his findings to whoever will publish it so it may as well be me. But he won't give any confirmation about the FBI being ordered to stop so I've got to hold that for now."

"Jim, this is our chance to pressure them."

"It just won't help. The White House has already pretty much announced that they are scaling back. That is fine by the majority of the public. If I do a story on the real reason for the bailout I couldn't attribute it, but the FBI would be able to figure out where the leak was. I'd blow my source, and it wouldn't do us any good. An unattributed allegation like that isn't much better than a rumor, and there have been plenty of those flying around already. No one would listen."

The line was quiet with disappointment. They knew that what Gilliam said made sense. But it was hard to resign themselves to more inaction.

"Hey, I'm on your side you know." Gilliam said matter-of-factly.

"Believe me, we know. It's just frustrating."

"I'm not done yet. Hang in there. I'll call you if I hear anything. Anything."

"Thank you so much," Jen leaned in and said. She didn't want Gilliam to think that they didn't appreciate what he was doing. He seemed to be their last hope.

"No problem. See ya." *Click.*

* * *

8

At times, in the silence of the night and in rare, lonely moments, I experience a sort of communion of myself with Something Great that is not myself.
-- H. G. Wells

"Keith, he's over there."

On the far side of the enclosed parking ramp, fifty yards away, Keith Carney and his driver saw a flash of flame from a cigarette lighter. Carney swiveled his head and looked out all of the darkened windows. It was late, there would be no one around.

"Keep your fucking eyes open. If you see anyone, lay on the horn and get your ass over there. You got it?"

"Yah, boss."

Carney slammed the car door of the eight-year old Buick as a signal of his approach. He didn't want to spook the guy.

Night was Carney's preferred time of day. His pale, thin skin didn't tan well. And his business was usually conducted when the sun was down. He was dressed in an expensive dark, double-breasted suit and crisply starched white shirt. His multi-colored, silk tie matched the fluffed handkerchief protruding from his pocket. He spent his money on clothes, not cars. Clothes could not be traced.

Carney's slow footsteps echoed from the concrete floor and ceiling. He could see the orange glow of a lit cigarette. A man came out of the shadows to greet him. "Thanks for coming, Keith. You know I could have met you at your office. It's damn cold tonight." He wasn't wearing a coat. He had been told not to.

"Security is a little tighter now, Mario. We can't be making any slips," Carney explained.

"Yah, I know. This thing is all over the news. They don't have a friggin' clue, do they?" Mario laughed.

"Not a clue. And we have to keep it that way." Carney didn't want to address the business they were there to discuss until he had allowed Mario a chance to get sufficiently nervous. It was a negotiating ploy that Carney used, even when dealing with insiders. It worked. Mario began shifting his weight from foot to foot, hoping for Carney to continue the conversation.

Mario took a drag on his cigarette and cleared his throat. "I read in the paper that we asked for a hundred million."

Carney stood rigidly and did not speak.

"That's why I told Tony that I thought I should have gotten more than a thousand dollars, ya know?"

Still Carney did not speak.

"I mean, a hundred million. That's great, Boss. You're a fuc ..., a genius, man. But, ya know, I says to Tony, hey that's me on the news running around in that stupid Dailley mask. How'd I know the stinking press was going to be there? Now if anybody goes down on this thing, it's like me, ya know? So I just thought maybe I should get a bit more when I heard it was a hundred million bucks. That's all. Ya know?"

As Carney continued his silence, Mario looked like he was going to explode. Carney finally nodded. Mario breathed a sigh of relief and continued. "So when I says to Dick I want fifty thousand, I'm just like kiddin', ya know?"

"I'm glad to hear that," Carney said in a friendly voice. He enjoyed negotiating, but he enjoyed crushing his opponent even more. "Because we really don't expect to get that much, and frankly, so far, we haven't received a god damn dime."

"Really? I didn't know."

"Of course not. But I decided that you were right, and we should have given you more for the job." Carney reached into his jacket pocket and pulled out an envelope. "Five thousand, to say thank-you."

Mario was ecstatic. It was not all he had expected to get when the conversation had started, but now he was thrilled. "Thanks, Keith. Really."

"Count it. Make sure the bank teller didn't screw me."

"Sure." Mario ripped open the envelope and pulled out ... baseball cards. He squinted at them in the darkness. "What's this?" he said looking up at Carney, still smiling, but confused.

Carney held the pistol two feet from Mario's face. *Thhhwwp. Thhhwwp.* The silencer muffled the sound of the two bullets. They entered Mario's head, one above each eye. The confused smile slowly drained from his face as he crumpled to his knees and pitched forward onto the concrete.

Carney walked away, looking around the ramp. It was still empty. Behind him, Mario lay face down. His hand still clutched the baseball cards. Carney knew that the only fingerprints the police would find on them were those of the nine-year old he had bought them from that afternoon. He smiled ruefully just as he had when he wrote the ransom note. He loved these high-stakes games.

By the time Carney reached his waiting car, a pool of blood had gushed from Mario's head, and formed around his bare outstretched arm, framing a colorful tattoo of a Celtic cross and the words, "White Death."

Carney settled into his seat. The driver was excited. "That was real quiet. Couldn't hardly hear a thing."

"Good. Drive, you moron."

The car pulled away. "He tried to blackmail you, didn't he Boss?"

"Yes."

"I always said we shouldn't let them spics into the blood. This proves it."

"He was half spic," Carney clarified.

"Same thing."

*   *   *

The Mantons' kitchen

The ring startled Rick and Jen who sat in front of untouched now-cold coffee, staring aimlessly out the window.

"Excuse me for disturbing you, sir," a woman's polite voice said.

"Yes," said Rick.

"I'm calling from the FBI's Office of the Assistant Director. If now would be a good time, the Director would like to speak with you."

The assistant director, thought Rick. They're having the god damned underling call to pacify me.

"Fine," Rick replied tersely.

There was a very brief pause. This was not an impromptu call.

"Mr. Manton?"

"Yes."

"Sir, we haven't had a chance to meet. I'm Gary McClure, assistant director here at the Bureau."

"Yes." Rick was like a pot about to boil over.

"Sir, I'm just calling to assure you that we're doing everything possible here to get your son back."

"Bullshit."

This was not fitting into the assistant director's script.

"Pardon me."

"You heard me. Don't hand me some line just so you can get on the news and assure the world that you have assured me of anything."

"Mr. Manton, I ..." he wanted to say 'assure,' and groped for another word, "promise you that we are checking all leads."

"Okay. Then tell me what you are doing to investigate the tattoo I saw."

McClure hadn't heard about that line of investigation. But he knew that they either had it covered, or hadn't chosen not to. "We're looking into it, just like we're looking into all legitimate leads that can trace this to Israel."

The blood surged in Rick's blood. He was just a pawn now, it was clear. He spoke low, the anger and sarcasm apparent. "Mr. Assistant Director, when you make your press release, be sure to say that Mr. Manton told you to tell your gutless President to stick his head up his ass." He slammed down the phone. He was not used to losing control, and any reply would have pushed him over the edge.

*   *   *

"Damn him. Damn him. When this is over I want the world to know what a spineless bastard Dailley is." Rick was so angry at the news he had just received from Gilliam that he could not control his rage. Jen was feeling the same, but held hers in coldly.

He beat his hands on the steering wheel. They had not yet left the grocery store parking lot. "He was just going to let us fly off to Israel thinking Danny was there. Yet they know he is still here somewhere. Still here." He put his head down on the rim. "Jesus Christ."

They had been deluding themselves that Danny was in the hands of a profit-motivated terrorist, if there was such a thing, and that money could solve the problem. This latest news destroyed that framework of thinking.

Jen spoke in a deadpan tone. "So one of those fringe groups could have him. The sick bastards." She began to quietly cry. They had received hundreds of hateful letters from persons claiming religious justification for their venom. Most were obviously demented. The Mantons knew that the indignant, self-righteous ones like

Reverend Hanner, that blasted them and the bloodline theory publicly, were only doing it for their own personal gain. They were irritating, but not dangerous. It was the anonymous antagonists that they feared. Now the possibility was back that it was them that had Danny.

"What about the ransom, though? That just doesn't make sense if there isn't some way for them to get the money." Rick was groping for a target, something or someone concrete, so that he could focus his hatred. "God damn that Dailley."

The van windows were steaming up. It was freezing. Rick turned on the engine to get some warm air circulating. They were both deep in thought, problem-solvers by nature, they were stumped. He looked at Jen. "Can we go to Montoursville?"

"Now?"

"Yeah. I need to."

Jen looked at her husband lovingly. In her pain it was easy to forget that he too was suffering. She understood. "Let's go. The drive will do us good. There isn't any snow forecast so we should be able to make it in three hours."

"I can do eighty-five. What cop is going to give us a ticket? Two and a half hours, tops." He felt better just thinking about the drive. Movement.

*   *   *

It was good therapy for the Mantons to get on the road. They hadn't gone on a road trip just for the pleasure of driving since the bloodline discovery. The hum of the tires on the road relaxed them as they discussed the many possibilities that rose from Gilliam's last call. The weather report was correct, it hadn't snowed, but a steady wind blew swirls of snow across the highway.

It was well after dark when Rick stopped the van. They had passed the wrought iron entrance gate, and it had been chained shut so he had driven further down the two-lane asphalt road to a spot where the stone wall surrounding the field was only three feet high.

Rick pulled off the road, careful not to get wedged in the line of dirty snow piled along the side. He turned off the lights and was plunged into darkness. The nearest streetlight was three miles back in the center of Montoursville. "I'll leave the engine running, it's pretty cold," he said.

"Do you want me to come?" Jen asked.

"No. I'll be fine."

Rick was surprised at how frigid the air had become since late afternoon. The north wind blew in his face. He slipped on his leather gloves. He had not brought a hat so he pulled the thick collar of his coat as high up on his face as he could. He crossed the slick road and inched down a small ditch, his feet crunching through a thin layer of ice that had formed from the days runoff of melted snow. He climbed up the other side of the ditch to the wall. The moon was full and reflected brightly off the blanket of snow that had not fully melted from last week's storm.

Finding a low spot in the wall, Rick sat down and swung his legs over onto a crusty bank of snow. As he stood, his feet broke through and sunk deep into the drift. As he pulled each foot out, the sides of his shoes filled with snow crystals. He shivered as they melted and the cold penetrated his warm socks.

He walked toward a bank of pine trees. The field was silent in a way that it never was in the suburbs. He could hear only the sound of the ice-crusted tree branches creaking in the wind and the crunch of his steps. He walked to the last tree in the stand and turned his back to the road. Here, during the day, the shade of the trees had protected the snow from the sunshine, and it was deeper and softer. Rick lowered to one knee and began to dig in the snow. He scraped methodically at first, then, as his fingers felt the cold, he dug quicker.

It has to be here somewhere, he bemoaned as he began scooping frantically.

"Where are you?" His yell echoed into the night.

Rick had cleared an area twice as large as his reach when, with a wide sweeping arc, he finally brushed off a metal corner. He slowed his pace and reverently cleared off the rest of a bronze marker. He rubbed the plaque clean with his glove, and stared down at it as he huffed torrents of frosty breath at the raised names of his parents. *Beloved husband. Beloved wife. Beloved parents.* The letters were so permanent. The words were so…insufficient.

Rick sat back in the scattered piles of snow he had just created. There was no sound other than his labored breathing. It was on this peaceful, wind-swept hill where he had gathered each time to bury his parents. He only vaguely recalled the words of the ministers that were spoken over their caskets. He knew that they were phrases that were intended to comfort, but he had found little solace in them, and, with each subsequent death, he heard them less. Now, the only comment he could recall was the shocking refrain, *'Ashes to ashes, dust to dust.'* He couldn't remember how the sentence finished. Those few words brutally summed up his feelings at the time.

Deep in thought, Rick looked around. There were a few other Mantons buried within a dozen yards, relatives of his father, but their flat markers were also covered in snow. Rick had not known any of them as a child anyway, and their plaques had elicited no emotions when he had first seen them at his father's funeral. Ironic, he thought, how little his own bloodline had meant to him. He had given it more thought lately.

Montoursville was his father's home town. Even for Pennsylvania, the landscape was striking. From here, he could see three valleys converging and a frozen river rigidly pointing toward the town. It was beautiful, but his memories on this spot were only those of shattering tragedy and unrestrained grief. It was the place where he had vainly struggled with his true beliefs on what the lowering of those coffins had forebode. If there was ever any place in the world that he felt that God possibly existed, it was here.

Under the protection of the tree the air was still. The digging had warmed his blood. His breathing had calmed. He balled up a wad of snow and vacantly threw it at a nearby tree trunk. The snow was too dry and the ball disintegrated in the air. The flakes drifted to the ground.

Rick looked at the grave marker. "Mom. Dad. Can you believe this?" he sighed softly, and paused as if waiting for an answer.

Shifting to his knees, he leaned over and put his palms on the plaque. He spoke into the ground. "They've got Danny. They've got our boy." He took a deep breath as if summoning courage. "And I don't know how to help him. Oh God, I don't know how to help him." His tears dropped straight down onto the raised letters.

"Did you know about this? This bloodline? Jen and Danny are related to Jesus." He laughed sarcastically. "Jesus! I know it sounds crazy. I didn't believe it either. I sure didn't ask for it. You know that I could care less about any of it."

The wind began to blow harder as Rick stared at the snow. "The only thing I ever wanted in life was to have a family. Now ... I'm afraid that I am going to have to bury him, too. I can't bury anyone else." His voice was desperate. "Can you please help me find him? Rick's voice broke and his head slumped down. He cried uncontrollably with the thought of burying his son in the ground beneath him.

When he had stopped crying, Rick was numb from the cold. He had hoped that he would feel something. But there was no other worldly presence. He snapped back to the reality that there was no one here to help him. All he felt was cold. He trembled.

Rick looked forlornly at the grave, and pushed himself back onto his haunches. Raising his puffy face to the stars that were shimmering brightly in the cold higher altitude, he called out, "God. God! Do you hear me? I don't know if you are up there...down here....or what. All I know is that because of you someone has my son." Rick was looking upward, his head thrown back. But the sound of his voice dissipated into the air, and he felt foolish and frozen.

Rick continued to stare upwards and blew out a long breath. His shoulders slumped and he lowered his voice. "OK. You win." He stood stiffly, looking deep into the milky stream of stars. He couldn't remember ever seeing so many.

Rick took a cold gulp of air. "Let's try this God. If I can have Danny back, I will know that you exist. If I can just hold him again, just one more time ... I will devote my life to you. I promise." His voice trailed off. "I swear by the soul of my son."

The only reply was the quiet rustle of the wind through the tree branches.

Rick stood and deferentially looked at the grave of his parents. They were not here. It was only an ice-crusted plaque on a lonely hill that represented that they had once lived and were now dead. This was not how he thought of them. But it was all he had. Inwardly, he mumbled good-bye. Drained of emotion, he turned and trudged back through the cemetery. He did not look back. There was no one there to look back to. Stepping in his tracks, his feet felt like blocks of cement. His limbs had lost all feeling from the cold. Yet he also felt a sense of peace and relief that he couldn't explain. A weight seemed to have lifted from him.

He fumbled with the door of the van and quickly slid into his seat. His nose was red and dripping. Jen looked at his face in the moonlight and reached out and gently took his hand. It was as cold as the corpses she had worked on in nursing school.

"Are you okay, Rick?"

Rick looked at the pale, troubled face of his wife, and remembered that not everyone had been taken from him. He felt the pain that the woman he loved was also feeling. He wished that he could console her. But he had learned from his lessons on the hill that words alone could not soothe her anguish. He gently squeezed her warm fingers.

"I think so," he said simply. Moving his hand, he shifted the van into gear and flicked on the headlights. "Let's find somewhere to eat and figure out what we are going to do next."

* * *

The Bloodline

Frederick Lancel's bedchamber

Joseph Lancel entered his father's darkened room. The air was pungent from the ineffectual herbs and salves the physician had been administering for days. The musty gloom filled the boy with apprehension. As his eyes adjusted to the dim light, he was shocked to see his father's condition worsening each day. Lancel's face had a yellowish pallor and his eyes had sunken into dark sockets.

"Father, you have summoned me. How may I serve you?" Joseph stated firmly to cover his apprehension. He bowed his head. He was doing his best to be a brave knight in training.

Lancel gazed at his brave son, his soul bursting with love and sadness. Joseph had his mother's flashing eyes and full lips.

Lancel had not allowed Joseph to participate in the fighting that had been ongoing sporadically for months, but he had used his assistance in supervising repairs to the defenses and replenishment of armaments. As Lancel's son, his mere presence, more so than any orders issued, insured that the tasks were performed diligently. To Lancel's chagrin, the boy had also seen the butchery of battle, dead knights and villagers strewn grotesquely upon the walls, wounded that would suffer slow and hideous deaths, and the wrenching sorrow of the loved ones left behind in a never ending nightmare of fear and want. A makeshift graveyard had risen in the shadow of the rear wall. The carpenters no longer attempted to build coffins for the dead. The mounds of the fresh mass graves registered the ongoing carnage. As trained, Joseph had observed it all, unflinchingly.

"Please come to me, Joseph."

Joseph's eyes adjusted to the gloom and he approached the bed. "Are you going to be all right, Father?" he asked, standing rigidly at his father's side.

"I fear not. The poison in my blood remains strong. I need to talk to you of the future."

Joseph wanted to cry out 'no,' but his eagerness to meet all standards of a knight stifled him. "Yes, Father," he replied stoically.

"I have asked Father Delacroix to lead you from here."

Joseph's face gnarled with contempt for the suggestion. He stepped back from the bed. "I shall not leave Blanchefort! I shall stay with you, Father, until the last infidel is dead."

Lancel had known that his son would utter these words. He was proud to hear them delivered so forcefully. But his fatherly devotion demanded that he protect Joseph, even in death. "Son. You must obey my orders."

"I cannot. I will not! You have taught me that a knight does not leave another on the field of battle. The death of one knight calls for the death of all. To give one's life to liberate one's soul is the meaning of freedom. Was it not you who taught me these truths?" Joseph had learned his lessons well.

"Joseph. Please sit."

Joseph sat on the edge of the bed. Boyish tears of anger and frustration filled his eyes.

Lancel coughed weakly and haltingly continued. "There are some matters that are larger than those of knighthood. The Order exists to serve its master, and for no other reason. Should our master not exist, the Order has no purpose. I have also instructed you thus, have I not?"

"Yes, Father."

"And I have also discussed with you that we have two masters." Lancel's tone was gentle.

"Of course."

"What are they?"

"The Order of the Knights Templar shall do the bidding of the Holy Catholic Church. The Order of the Knights Templar shall always defend Truth and Right." The tenets were ingrained in the youth.

"As you have seen, the Holy Church has been misguided by worldly elements. They can no longer see what is the Truth and what is Right. It is up to us to insure that the Truth, as told to us by God, is preserved. That is a knight's duty. And it is for that reason that I must order you to safety."

"But why Father? I would rather die at your side," Joseph pleaded.

"My Son. My beloved Son. I have no doubt but that you would be the bravest and strongest of all my knights."

Joseph's chest swelled with the praise. Lancel could clearly see that he was now a young man. It eased his pain of knowing that he would soon be leaving him on his own.

Lancel continued. "But you are more than a mere knight. You were the holy product of your sainted mother. You are the blood of Our Savior, Christ the Lord. You were christened with the name of the blessed father of Mary Magdalen. For the royal bloodline to survive, you, Sir Joseph Lancel, must survive this ... madness." Lancel could no longer hide his bitterness. He sat forward in the bed. His voice was edged with determination.

"Joseph. God has placed His Son's blood inside of us for a purpose which only He understands. It is our destiny to continue the bloodline. And now it is you who must do so. My time has come."

Joseph sat on the bed, looking at the wall away from his father. He did not want him to see the tears flowing down his cheeks and dripping to the floor. He did not know how he would live without his father. He did not believe that he could ever be the knight that his father was.

Sensing Joseph's misery, Lancel placed his hand on his shoulder and whispered, "I shall reach peace with God when I know that my son has carried out His will."

Joseph sniffed wetly. "I will obey you, Father," he said, his voice cracking. "But one day I shall return to Blanchefort and excise these walls of the heretics that you deem will prevail."

"Son, it is God's will if we are defeated. If it is God's will that you return, then He shall give you a sign. Until then, I order that you conceal from all others on this earthly realm that which you know is true. Do not reveal your bloodline. To do so will place you in indefensible peril. As a child of Christ, your duty is to survive. And to have children."

Lancel's throat constricted with the thought of grandchildren that he would never see. He took a deep breath and squeezed Joseph's shoulder, more to muster his own strength, than Joseph's. Lancel was helpless for the first time since he had been a child. He could not protect himself, let alone his son or his future grandchildren. Now, he could only pass his wisdom.

"My Son. Raise your children to revere Our Lord. But do not tell them of their holy blood."

Joseph raised an eyebrow and looked at his father. Stories of his lineage had been the overriding theme of his life and his relationship with his father.

Lancel looked hard into his son's eyes. "It will be the only protection you can give them once the brotherhood is destroyed. If God deems that they should know this secret, He will unveil it to them in ways that we cannot foresee. You must swear to me on this matter."

Joseph was silent for a long time. The words came hard to him. He knew that his father had correctly spoken his duty, but he could not deny his grief. Under the eye of his father, he said softly, "I swear, Father. I swear by Our Father, Jesus Christ."

Lancel lifted his arms out weakly to the sides. Ignoring the dogmas of his training, Joseph leaned over resignedly onto his father's chest, allowing the once powerful arms to encircle him lightly. Lancel's chest heaved with deep breaths, attempting to stave off tears that would reveal his weakness at a time when only courage should be displayed. Staring at the fading portrait of Solange, he stroked the long, soft curls of his beloved son and prayed that Joseph would live to do the same to his children.

* * *

The Mantons arrived home from Montoursville very late that night. The next morning they were still asleep when the phone rang. Rick picked up the phone as Jen rolled over and opened a sleepy eye.

It was Gilliam. "Good day to go out for breakfast," he said. "I'm having mine at home."

He didn't need to say more. "We will," replied Rick.

Hanging up the phone he gave Jen a look and she sat up. "Gilliam?"

"Yes. Let's go."

They crowded into a Rick and Jen huddled on a bench at the local mall. The FBI agents assigned to them for the morning shift had trailed them. The Mantons didn't mind the security as long as they kept out of ear shot, especially now that they weren't sure if the government was on their side or not. It was early and no one else was around except the cleaning crews. Rick was on one of his prepaid cells.

"Jim, any news?"

"It looks like it." Gilliam hesitated. He didn't want to be misinterpreted again. He knew the Mantons were on pins and needles.

"What?" The Mantons spoke in unison.

"It's preliminary, so don't get your hopes up yet. I ran your tattoo by my police contacts. They figured that if you saw it, it had to be on film from one of those cameras on the scene. They had the techs zoom in on every arm on the film. Everyone has been focused on faces since this happened. Sure enough, they found about a tenth of a second when the asshole, excuse my French, backs out of the car with Danny, and his sleeve is up. You were right, Rick. There's a mark just about as you described it. They ran it through a centralized computer hook-up that tracks and identifies gang activity and catalogues gang symbols. The one you drew, the smashed shamrock, a Celtic cross is actually what it is, is a white supremacy symbol. By itself, that isn't too distinctive. But they found that there is one group that uses that symbol, along with the words 'White Death,' with the word 'White' on top of the cross, and the word 'Death' down below. Matches up almost perfectly with what you saw except you didn't see a top word."

"That was covered by his sleeve," Rick offered, not sure if he was remembering or presuming what he must have seen.

"That's what I thought."

Rick looked at Jen. Despite Gilliam's warning, their hopes soared. This was the break they were hoping for, the first real lead, tentative as it was. "What do you know about the gang?" Rick queried.

"We're looking into it. I've got a copy of the surveillance file on it. Call themselves the 'Sons of Odin' after some Nordic god. Located in New Jersey. Newark area. It appears to be fairly sophisticated as gangs go. Not just a bunch of pimps and drug runners. It is a known race hate group, all white, of course. But the members aren't quite skinheads. Law enforcement fears these kinds of gangs more because they don't stick out. Harder to monitor. And they are more creative in their schemes to get money. As likely to commit mail fraud or scam an old lady as they are to knock off a liquor store. Don't get me wrong, these guys are armed to the teeth. That is what they use their money for ... assault rifles, extended clip handguns, even grenades ... they're planning for an upcoming race war. And making money while doing it."

"How can we help?"

"I can't think of anything right now."

"Can we contact them? You name it. Jim, you know we have to be involved in this."

"I knew you'd say that. What could you do, though? You two stick out like Mr. and Mrs. Santa Claus. Everyone in the world knows you."

"We'll take care of that," Jen said. "When can we meet?"

"Okay. Okay. I've got some things I've got to do. Tomorrow, any time."

"We'll be there by nine."

"Make it ten."

"Jim, is this going in the papers?" Rick really couldn't guess how Gilliam would interpret this bit of information.

"Hell, no. The kidnapper would see that in the papers and the tattoo would be burned off and then we've just got another dead end. Tomorrow."

Rick looked at Jen. "Finally."

"Thank God," she responded. Then added, "We've got some shopping to do."

*   *   *

The woman's brow was furrowed with concentration. Her jet black hair was straight and cropped severely at her shoulders giving her a Cleopatra look. Her green eyes squinted, but did not waver as she peered down the short barrel and aimed her .38 caliber Remington pistol. She calmly squeezed the trigger.

Crack, crack, crack, crack, crack, crack. All six shots tore into the heart of her target. She relaxed and lowered her weapon. She smiled sinisterly.

Her prematurely graying companion began to turn the crank that would pull the silhouette up to them. "Damn good shooting, Jen," he whispered.

"Thanks Old Man. A few more practice rounds before we go. It's starting to feel comfortable."

"Yep. Women will fool ya." An overly enthusiastic and underworked range operator stood behind the pair, and was offering unsolicited commentary. "Men think chicks can't shoot 'til they get out here. But ladies don't drink as much as men. Take better care of themselves. They've got steadier hands and reflexes. They're surprised too 'cause they ain't never held a real piece. Seen it hundreds of time. Never shot before, eh?"

Jen didn't answer. If she told him of the hours she and Danny had spent on the computer game joysticks he never would go away. The lonely man didn't seem to mind her silence. She was the best-looking woman he would see here in a month. After being obviously ignored, he headed back to the range control booth. With binoculars, the view would be good there, too.

Rick smiled. His eyes couldn't help but linger over Jen. If he hadn't been married to her for eight years he wouldn't have known her. Her long, curly reddish-brown mane had always been her pride and joy. The black dye and hair straightener totally changed her appearance. Normally his conservative wife would have been appalled with this punk look. 'I feel like a call girl,' had been her first reaction. Frankly, except for their circumstances, Rick would have been aroused by the fresh sexy look resulting from the drastic changes. Extreme measures had to be taken for the current first couple of the grocery store magazine racks to drive to Philadelphia and purchase two handguns incognito. Even without being recognized it had taken them hours longer than anticipated to purchase the pistols without proper identification. Improperly purchasing a firearm was the least of their concerns now.

Jen sure-handedly loaded another round and glanced at her husband. She was amused by the short haircut and the graying temples they had given him. It added fifteen years to his age. To her surprise she hadn't minded the new look either. She liked mature men. The fake mustache was a little silly, but also necessary to hide his now famous face.

Jen raised her arm and extended the pistol forward. This time she alternated her shots from target chest to head and back again. All landed within inches of dead center. It would have earned her a million points on 'Alien Invasion.' This was not a game to her. Whoever had her son should know that. She took a deep breath of the sweet gunpowder-filled air. "Let's go. We don't want to be late."

*   *   *

Gilliam stuck his head out into the large, but usually cramped waiting room of the New York Times and looked around. Seeing no one familiar, he started to turn back in.

"Hey Jim. Over here," a female voice directed. The Mantons couldn't help but grin shyly. They felt like it was Halloween and they were glad that their costumes had fooled Gilliam.

"Holy shit." Gilliam knew the eyes, but hadn't recognized either one. "Get in here."

No one looked up as he walked through the pressroom with the most coveted interviews in America. A minute ago he expected this march would create quite a stir, but now it only received a few lecherous glances at the backside of Jen's well-fitting black jeans.

"This is great. Anyone recognize you?" Gilliam asked as he closed the door to his windowed lined office.

"Nope. We could kiss Johnny Hanner's ass and he wouldn't have a clue," said Rick.

"No kidding. Is this permanent?"

"For now."

There was a little small talk, but everyone was ready to get to work. Gilliam closed the mini-blinds to his windows and opened a file on the table in front of them. They intently leaned over and examined it.

Rick gave out a low whistle. It was a surveillance file of the FBI. Rick looked at Gilliam, his eyes asking permission to open it.

"Go ahead."

The left side of the file held dozens of rap sheets listing government indictments and convictions. These thugs might be creative, but they weren't necessarily efficient. Rick flipped through the pages. On top, Greg Dopson ... armed robbery, drug sales. Currently upstate, twelve years for second degree murder. Jack Reynolds ... armed robbery, battery, weapons possession. The stack went on and on. Racketeering. Burglary, many times.

Lots of drug and weapons possessions. Conspiracy to commit mail fraud. Even one count of computer fraud. There were a few convictions under the recently enacted "hate crimes" legislation. They covered the whole gambit.

Jen leaned over and put her finger on a page so she could fully read the entries.

Michael Hendricks, booked for murder. A merchant who refused to pay for 'protection fees' was gunned down in front of a store full of lunch time customers. The charges were dropped before an indictment was returned when all of the prosecution witnesses had severe, inexplicable memory lapses in front of the grand jury. The murder was listed as 'Unsolved.'

Lee Borman. Battery. Extortion. Across the left cheek was an ugly, raised hook-shaped scar. Rick shuddered as he thought what may have caused that.

Keith Carney, lewd conduct. The victim had been raped. Two months past her eighteenth birthday. But 'witnesses' had testified that she had gone into the back room willingly, even suggestively. The DA couldn't file those charges. Rick stared at the mug shot. A fierce and angry face peered back. The eyes were not unintelligent. Mail fraud. Some scheme that had targeted the elderly. Plea bargain accepted due to inconsistent memory from the ancient victims.

So here was the enemy.

Rick glanced at Jen. She was intently studying the photographs. Clinically analyzing each face. But, unlike her patients, she had no intention of helping them.

"Who's the leader, or whatever they call it?" Rick asked Gilliam.

"They aren't sure. The past head guy just went to prison. God knows how they sort out who will run things," Gilliam shrugged.

On the bottom left of each rap sheet was a block for recording any identifying marks of the suspects. Each report had a rough sketch of the Celtic cross that Rick now remembered. In the diagram, it was sandwiched between the words 'White Death.' The reports all read, 'Right forearm.'

The right side of the file had surveillance tracking logs. The section concerning confidential informants had been blocked out. It didn't appear extensive. The FBI had not been successful in penetrating the organization with a plant. Rick was impressed with how much information had been assembled on this gang. At least the FBI could still gather dirt on their foes. It made Rick realize that Gilliam's fear of wiretapping was not all paranoia.

"What do you hear from your police contacts?" Rick asked as he continued to flip through the file.

"They are willing to help, but all of this is off-the-book stuff, so they can't devote all day to it. Most of their shift commanders are willing to nod and look the other way to their sniffing around the files and computers, but taking unauthorized trips to New Jersey is another matter. They're contacting cops in the Newark area to see if there is any sympathy there. There probably will be. It takes time."

Rick appreciated what Gilliam was doing for them and the amount of effort he was putting into this, but it was no time to pull punches. He looked Gilliam directly in the eyes. "Danny may not have time. Can we get a copy of this file?"

Gilliam sat back. "I can guess what you're thinking. Rick, you can't go out there alone. These are animals we're dealing with. The police are armed and even they are hesitant to cross these types without some good backup."

"Maybe their son isn't out there with the animals," Jen added to show that her resolve was equal to, if not more than, her partners'.

"I'll go with you then," Gilliam offered.

Rick shook his head.

"We're not sure what we're going to do yet." That was half true. He and Jen had discussed some possible courses of action. The detail in the file was better than they had hoped for. Rick believed it might give them even more options. They knew that they weren't going to sit still any longer. "We'll have to let you know."

"Rick, Jen, I've covered the streets before. I'm serious when I say it's a war zone out there where these guys are. They're scum. They wouldn't think twice about killing you. Look, I'll level with you. My source is in the FBI regional bureau headquarters. He can pipeline to me anything his staff can dig up. And aside from that I've got friends from my police beat days that are willing to help."

"When they can. Jim, we can't thank you enough for all of this. And I'm not saying we won't use your help. But other than you, everyone else has bailed out on us. We finally have a lead. Someone has to keep pushing this. Who is going to pursue it night and day? It has to be us. If we find anything, we'll be on the phone to you in a flash. We won't do anything to risk Danny."

"I know. I just don't like it. Be careful. You have my home number, too. Use it. Any time."

"Deal."

Thirty minutes after they had come in, the couple walked back through the pressroom, again without fanfare. They had a quick, determined step. Rick had a copy of the file, still warm from the copier, tightly pinned under his arm, wedged against his jacket-covered holster. Gilliam watched them leave from his office doorway.

Jerry walked up next to him. "Jimbo, You've got another cop holding for you on line seven. They've been calling all week. What's up, you going back to the beat?" Jerry asked, not expecting an answer. He always welcomed a reprieve from copy editing, especially if it involved women.

Jerry watched closely as Jen exited. When the door closed he gave a low whistle. "Who is the babe with the Sugar Daddy? Not your typical Bible-banger interviewees."

"No, you wouldn't say so."

*   *   *

Danny winced as the tape was ripped off his mouth. He didn't cry from the pain. There were no tears left. His face was blank. A tattooed arm held a chipped white plate out to him. It had a hot dog and potato chips on it.

"C'mon kid, you got to eat something." The voice was tinged with frustration.

Danny slowly picked up the bare hot dog and took a small bite, chewing slowly as children do right before proclaiming they are too full to eat any more. In medical terms Danny was not in physical shock, but emotionally his system had shut down. It was a blessing that he was barely registering any external stimuli. He had spent the last week in a closet after spending the week before that at another filthy apartment in another closet. At first he had thrashed and squirmed. Then he cried for days on end. Now he stared blankly at the walls.

Danny had not been violently abused, but the wrenching separation from his parents had been terrifying. The terror continued with each of the minimal contacts that he had with these rough and threatening men. If he cried, they yelled. If he spoke, they bellowed. He was afraid to wiggle. Mercifully, his weakened body no longer yearned to move.

"Look. I'll let you watch TV if you keep eating, Okay?"

Danny nodded and walked across the room where some of his captors slept. His parents' bedroom was nothing like this. Blankets lay piled on the floor next to a foul smelling pile of clothes and dishes encrusted with dried bits of food. There were no curtains on the windows, and no pictures on the walls. A spider lazily spun a web in the low corner of the ceiling.

Danny sat cross-legged in front of a small television that was on a wobbly metal stand in the corner. The man turned on the set and adjusted the antenna. A fuzzy black and white cartoon appeared. Danny stared vacantly at the screen and continued to chew slowly. The man stomped out.

"Ron, you letting him watch the damn tube again?" A male in his mid-twenties with a pock-marked face and shoulder length greasy hair was registering his displeasure. He had his hand deep in the potato chip bag.

"Hey, screw you, Mike. The little shit is starving to death. Keith told us we've got to keep him alive. He ain't a god damn pet fish, you know." Ron Williams was not soft-hearted. He just followed orders.

"Chill out. I just don't want him making any noise."

"Christ, like anyone would notice around here. I hear that squeeze downstairs beating her brats every night. Our kid hasn't made a sound for a week."

"I just want to keep it that way." Mike Hendricks wiped his oily hands on his jeans. "Keith says the ragheads should be getting some big bills coming in any time. He said he's going to turn the heat up on the holy rollers real soon." He was not particularly careful about applying his racial slurs. He hated anyone from the Middle East. Not that he'd ever met an Israeli or Arab or Persian that had wronged him. They just weren't white enough for him. They weren't American. "Keep the kid alive for a few more beauty photos and maybe we can get out of this rathole like we were supposed to when Keith set up those Jew-loving companies."

They were supposed to have gotten rich three years ago when Keith Carney was introduced to the scheme of setting up non-profit corporations to launder funds for a mob syndicate in Brooklyn. Carney was supposedly the brains of the Sons of Odin. Not that it took much to be valedictorian of the bunch. He was intelligent, however, and had his life been different he may have been a stockbroker or an accountant. But he never knew who his father was, and his mother's greatest accomplishment was introducing him to the seedy side of upper Manhattan. When he was ten they moved to Newark. 'Time for a new jurisdiction,' was the only explanation she had given for the move. He learned his entrepreneurial and negotiating skills from watching her handle her nightly customers.

Carney's first money laundering scheme was a clumsy attempt. The paper trail to and from the syndicate had been easy to follow, and Williams, manning the front office, had taken the fall. He was relatively clean, as Sons of Odin went, and the judge was lenient with the 'time served' sentence that he was given for mail fraud. Carney had learned some lessons from the fiasco. He set up websites soliciting white supremacists donations to a non-profit corporation. Almost legal, and much harder to trace. Always self-taught, he moved on to other phony charities. It was amazing how easy it was to form a company with the online legal forms. And could just as easily disappear before it could be traced.

With years of trial and error, Carney's masterpiece was the phony Israeli charity scheme. His Sons of Odin cronies, those who were out on parole anyway, had heartily approved Carney's plan. It had the twin appeal of shifting the risk to low paid computer geeks in Israel to take in the money at Tel Aviv post office boxes and wire it to veiled accounts that could be tapped into Carney. The bonus to the Sons of Odin was that all of the money was supposed to be coming from the Jews that they despised.

But the scheme was better on paper than in actuality. Contrary to their twisted beliefs, American Jews would not throw their money at an unknown organization, especially one whose only purpose, slightly veiled, was to build illegally in occupied territories. The Sons of Odin had spent over ten thousand dollars on newspaper ads soliciting for the various 'Jewish Freedom Charities,' but were largely unrewarded. What contributions did trickle in were eaten up by the costs of incorporation, advertising and a few crumbs for their despised operatives in Israel. Having put the charitable corporations in place, Carney and the Sons of Odin were loathe to shut them down until they had turned a profit.

What the Sons of Odin needed was handed to them when Jen and Danny Manton hit the supermarket tabloids. If they couldn't sweet talk the Jews into supporting their own charities, by God, they'd force the Christians to do it for them. Carney had learned enough to be wary to diffuse the paper trail this time. By demanding the donations go to a narrow base of charities, not all concocted by him, he thought he could spread the focus of the anticipated investigation. It grieved him that some real Jewish charities were actually going to benefit from the ransom, but for the millions of dollars they were going to reap they could overlook it.

As it stood, this would go down as the most brilliant of Carney's plans, or so he thought. The kidnapping was a breeze. It was amazing how the rich and famous in America took no precautions to protect themselves until after it was too late. A couple of expensive trips to Israel to eliminate any funny business in the storefront offices, and the money should be rolling in. The FBI was too incompetent to catch Keith Carney twice, he bragged. And apparently they had given up trying, if the newspapers were to be believed.

The door to the apartment swung open. Three more Sons of Odin barged in. They were all talking at once.

"Are we good or what?" said the skinny one. With a theatrical wave of his arm he swung a brown paper bag onto the couch next to Hendricks. He grabbed it and looked in. It was packed with baggies of granular white crystals.

"How the hell did you get this?"

Hendricks pulled out a baggie and held it up to the light.

"Some crackhead on 78th tried to jack us up on the price. We convinced him to donate to the cause." The new arrivals all laughed at their grisly humor.

"Whack him?" Hendricks threw out, still more interested in the goodies.

"Naw. Too many people around. Gave him a nice facelift in exchange. Joey made sure he don't use his wanger tonight." They all laughed again.

"Let's see if this shit's any good."

"The Knicks are on. I'll get the TV."

"Sure. Kid's watching it. Stuff him back in the closet. I don't want my retirement policy to get loose."

"Babysitter of the year."

"Bite me."

9

The good news is that Jesus is coming back. The bad news is that he's really pissed off.-- Bob Hope

Rick backed their van into the space between the two cars and shut off the engine. It was dark. There was a lamppost on the other side of the street but the bulb was broken out. He looked at Jen. There was enough illumination from distant streetlights for him to make out her features. Her face looked strained. He had wished that she hadn't come along, but he knew that she wouldn't even consider such a proposition. He had fallen in love with her years ago for her determination and passion. She still had those qualities though they hadn't surfaced recently in their mundane lives.

They had debated possible plans of action all afternoon. They knew they had to move quickly, but cautiously. If it were only their own lives at stake they could have been bolder and taken riskier and faster methods. Initially they had to discover if Danny was even in this country. Maybe these Sons of Odin were just the low-level, low-lives hired to make the kidnapping. They were certainly the logical place to start since they were the first to put their hands on Danny. There was much to uncover and, as far as they knew, little time.

They pored over the various reports of the investigative file, absorbing its details. It was a gold mine. The file listed a number of businesses that were known to be either owned by or regularly frequented by Sons of Odin members. They were all located in areas of Newark that the Mantons never would have entered but for this mission. It was urban blight at its worst. One hundred years ago these areas might have been fashionable suburbs of New York City. Now the streets consisted of deteriorating brownstone walkups interspersed with high rise tenements. The sidewalks seemed busy for a cold night. Homeless men gathered around a fire they had built in a garbage can. Women with makeup caked on to hide the years and mileage walked along Van Buren Avenue, tight minidresses exposing the length of their fishnet covered legs to the frigid air. Teenage boys stood on the corners nervously shuffling their feet. Selling drugs or buying drugs, the Mantons could not know. Each intersection seemed to have been staked out by a different race, cautiously coexisting at a distance. To the Mantons it didn't matter who controlled the intersection, they felt equally uncomfortable in each. It wasn't their race that caused their anxiety, it was their class. This just wasn't a world that they inhabited, where arguments were settled with knives and agreements were enforced with guns. Morality was suspended. Rick cursed his government under his breath, not for the plight of those he drove by, but in anger that its desertion was the cause of their being forced to enter this hell to search for their son.

The Mantons looked down the street at their next selected surveillance post. Their first attempt had been fruitless. They had already gone to a diner on the other side of the city that supposedly catered to the Sons of Odin. "Louis' Place" was filthy and dark, but the Mantons weren't out for fine dining. But not only were there no gang members there, there was no one else. They quickly learned why after their dinners arrived. The "house special" pasta was over boiled spaghetti with a canned sauce dumped liberally on top. They were careful in questioning the elderly waitress who was the only sign of life in the place other than a foul-mouthed cook they could hear in the kitchen.

"Ever have any problems here?" Jen asked the haggard women, dressed in a stained, light blue uniform. It was the most innocuous question they could think of that wouldn't seem suspicious.

"Yeah, honey. That's why it's so dead here now. You probably wanna hear the story. Why else would you be here?" The woman seemed glad for the diversion from the kitchen.

"What happened?"

"Big tough gang hangs out here for years. No problem, long as you'se white anyway. Couple a weeks ago one of dem punks gets all hopped up and starts bitching about the food. Same thing he's et here forever. He starts cussing at the cook. Real bad stuff. Louis, he was the cook, he tells him 'Shove it up his ass.' Next thing you know this guy's got Louis bent over the counter and slits his throat." She turned toward the empty counter. "Right over there. Took us a week to get all the blood out." She gazed at her handiwork and shook her head slowly at the memory.

Jen's appetite was totally gone now. "He's all right, isn't he?" she asked, throwing a look toward the kitchen where the cook was cursing at the top of his lungs at a shipment of meat gone bad.

"Oh hell no. He bled to death right where he landed. That jackass in the back is his son, Pete." She leaned over to Jen. "He ain't half the cook his Dad was." That was obvious.

"Did they ever catch the guy?"

"Uh-uh. That kind of dirt can disappear anywhere. Ain't none of 'em been back. That would be fine with me 'cept tippin's bad now. Enjoy your meal folks."

Minutes later when they left Louis' Place, Rick left a five dollar tip next to the untouched "house specials".

So their precious file hadn't been up to date on Louis' Place, but it was accurate as to who had frequented it. According to the tracking logs, the most Sons of Odin nightly activity occurred at the Bright Paradise, a bar and strip joint on Van Buren and 98th Street where they were now parked. Bright Paradise was a misnomer if ever there was one. It was neither bright nor a paradise, but its owners thought that the name echoed with racial purity. It was a one story, square concrete block building. Where there once were front windows there were now cinder blocks. A neon sign rhythmically flashed "Girls, Liquor, Girls." From the FBI file they knew this meant topless waitresses and "semi-nude" dancers, whatever that meant. They hadn't expected to find the Sons of Odin at the Symphony Hall.

"Are you ready to go?" Rick felt a primitive protectiveness toward Jen ever since the kidnapping.

"Let's do it."

They jaywalked together across the street toward the entrance. Contrary to etiquette in rural Pennsylvania, and most other civilized areas, Rick pulled open the metal door to the bar and entered first. A steamy blast of warm air hit him in the face, a mixture of smoke, spilled beer and body odor. Jen followed closely. They had decided for this spy mission to dress down. Rick wore a faded pair of jeans and worn baggy flannel shirt with his fifteen year old hiking boots. Jen was dressed about the same except for a pair of more fashionable black boots. With her hip makeover she still stood out, the modern cut and heavier makeup completing the tough girl image. Both wore their oldest bulky winter coats.

A bouncer in the entryway stepped in front of them. It was obvious why he had been hired. He stood almost six-foot, six-inches tall. He looked like a football player ten years after his prime, still strong but carrying forty extra pounds. Even though he wore a black tank top his bulk caused his face to drip with sweat. Rick looked up at him. One of his eyes had a cloud over the pupil and it seemed to look off in a different direction from the other. "It's twenty bucks admission. Each. That gets you coupons for two free drinks. Shows run every half hour all night long."

Rick was relieved that there was no frisk at the door for weapons. Apparently the Bright Paradise had adopted the same policy that the world had used for decades for nuclear weapons. Mutually assured destruction. His senses jolted as he began to hand the guard two twenties and he saw the words "White Death" tattooed on the large forearm. Rick involuntarily hesitated. The bouncer was looking Jen over with his one good eye when he turned to Rick and saw his eyes glance away from the tattoo. "Don't allow niggers in here," he explained. It was said with a tone of pride. "Too many fine looking ladies like you," he said toward Jen. "Wouldn't want 'em bothering you." He tried to continue the eye contact with Jen, but she looked down and fumbled with her gloves.

"Good idea," was the best Rick could mumble as he composed himself and they squeezed through into the bar.

He and Jen crossed through the smoky room and slid into a booth in the rear. A number of pairs of eyes had watched Jen cross through the room even though a black haired young woman, wearing only a skimpy pair of red satin thong panties, was slowly dancing on a platform stage. She was of above average good looks and, as required, white, but the sparse crowd, almost all men, seemed nonchalant. Music blared from large dusty speakers suspended from the high ceiling. The music was geared for the crowd, angst-ridden and without any hint of ethnic flavor. The dancer began to gyrate seductively to a song that was released before she was born.

Are you a lucky little lady in the city of lights ...

She stepped forward, threw back her mane of black curls and seductively rubbed her crotch against a pole that was placed in the spotlights. She cupped her breasts and shook them at the onlookers who were beginning to warm to her act.

Or just another lost angel ...

Jen looked around. There was no waitress in sight. "Ugh. That was Miller," she leaned over and whispered.

"Which one was he?" Rick asked. Jen had the photographic memory.

"Acquitted of manslaughter."

"Right, right, him." Rick recalled the work up. Anthony Miller. Arrested for allegedly shooting a black man to death while on door duty at another Sons of Odin bar. Some of the witnesses said that he shot him through the heart as he lay on the ground pleading. But more witnesses testified at trial that the victim lunged with a knife prior to the shooting. The district attorney's office hadn't identified the Sons of Odin as a gang worthy of tracking at that time and never knew that the witnesses were all members or somehow owed a favor to the strong-arm organization. The jury bought the story. Miller was involved in a similar shooting the next year, but this time he was slashed with a buck knife across his right eye.

Anticipating another tale of self-defense the DA hadn't even bothered to press charges

A waitress interrupted their whispers. "What'll it be?" She stood nonchalantly in front of them with her round tray braced against her hip. She wearing only red hot pants. Her tanned, firm breasts were eye level with Rick. Her name tag, "Cindy," was pinned to her shorts.

"Just Cokes, please."

"First two drinks are free. That includes booze."

"Cokes will be fine."

"Suit yourself." Cindy wasn't talkative. Rick watched her turn and walk away.

"Looking for tattoos?" Jen asked as she kicked him lightly under the table. Their marriage was secure, but this was a new experience that Jen wouldn't let repeat once their mission was accomplished.

As the seats filled up they felt less conspicuous. Jen was surprised at the number of women accompanying men. She found the atmosphere tawdry and demeaning. The night dragged on. Rick and Jen had their faces pointed toward the various amateurish and lewd shows that were being performed, but their eyes were constantly scanning the growing crowd searching vainly for tattoos. In winter most of the men wore long sleeves. At the pool tables at the back of the bar they spotted a few tattoos on players with their sleeves rolled up. They couldn't tell about the rest of the seedy audience, but to the Manton's middle-class mind set the grand majority of the people looked like criminals anyway.

After two hours they knew they had to make a move. They hadn't known what to expect, half hoping to hear someone with a tattoo bragging of the kidnapping. As reality set in they admitted that it wouldn't be that easy. They picked up their second glasses of soda and moved to the bar.

"Freshen those up?" The bartender was a gorgeous blond woman in her late twenties. She wore a white halter top and stand alone black bow tie around her neck, her relatively conservative attire apparently in deference to her position as head bartender.

"Cokes are fine." She gave him a puzzled look, but returned shortly with the drinks. "Eight dollars."

Rick was slow in pulling out his wallet and fumbled for his money to allow an opening for conversation. "We're opening up a bar in the Philly area next month and we are kind of looking around for employees that would be willing to relocate." Rick offered her a twenty dollar bill and motioned for her to keep it. "Mind if we ask a few questions."

The bartender paused and looked to Jen then looked back at Rick. "I don't strip anymore."

She was tall with the posture of a model that held her shoulders back and her breasts high. It was probably a proposition she had been given many times. Rick shook his head. "It won't be that kind of place. Things are a little tamer where we come from."

"No kidding," she said, nodding toward the colas.

"We're looking for bartenders, bookkeepers, bouncers, the whole bit." Rick was fishing. "Do you think anyone here would be interested?"

"Yeah, I'd listen. But look, gimme your number, I can't talk now, I wouldn't want the boss to get wind of this. I need the job."

"Sure." Rick made up a number and scribbled it on a cocktail napkin and slid it across the bar. He was still trying to prolong the conversation. "Who is your boss, maybe I know him?"

"I don't think you'd know him, he's not your type," she said as she stuffed the napkin into a front pocket of her tight black satin shorts.

Rick kept stalling and exploring. "I'm sorry, I didn't ask your name."

"Dorothy. Friends call me Dot."

"Well hi, Dot. I'm Bill and this is my girlfriend ... Rhonda."

"Glad to meet you." Dot glanced around again to silently explain why she didn't offer a handshake.

Rick continued. "How about bouncers? You've got some guys in the back room that could handle the whole town where we're from."

"I really don't think they're what you want." The bartender welcomed the possibility of moving up from this dive so she darted her eyes around the bar and started drying glasses in front of Jen. She spoke out of the corner of her mouth to both of them. "I don't know who sent you here, but isn't it kind of obvious that most of the men in here are ... members. You two aren't part of this white supremacy stuff, are you?"

Rick paused. They were at a crossroads. He looked at Jen. Her eyes gave him no clue which direction to go. "No, not at all."

"I didn't think so. You act like nice people, but you can't be too sure these days. Look around you. Most of them," she gestured toward the backs of the men, now banging on the stage and cheering lustily for the stripper who was half out of her schoolgirl outfit, "are members of this local white supremacy gang. They're like any other gang, just a bunch of hoods that have to stick together to be any kind of threat, but they take joy in beating anyone that isn't white. I've heard them brag about some of the attacks. They give me the creeps. Yeah, I'd be interested to get out of here. The boss is one of them. High muckty-muck with them, however they work it ... he's never around, thank God for small favors. He just sets the places up and lets his accountants and lawyers run them."

"What's his name?" Rick would try again.

"Keith Carney." Dot wiped a glass with a damp rag and watched Rick's face. He hid his recognition of the name.

"See, I told you, you wouldn't know him," Dot said.

"The name is familiar. Where does he live?"

"Jesus, I don't know. Some snake hole."

Rick scrambled to think. They were getting lots of information, but they needed more. Something specific.

"Let me grab this customer. I'll be right back."

Rick breathed a sigh of relief. As the bartender moved down the bar he whispered to Jen, "I feel crummy about this. She's a nice kid."

"So hire her to wash the dishes when we're out of here. How did you come up with the name Rhonda!?" There was an edge to Jen's voice. The bartender was working her way back. Jen hissed, "Ask her about Cyclops at the front door."

"Sure I can't get you anything? On the house."

"No thanks. How about the big guy at the front door? Do you think he'd be open to move?"

"Tony? Oh no. He's in real tight with Carney, the boss. Acts like he's his brother or something. Anything Carney wants done a particular way he asks Tony to do it. He'd never leave Carney. Please don't even ask him, or he'll get suspicious of us talking. He's not too bright either, you know? He's one of the biggest racists of that gang I was telling you about. That ugly tattoo he has on his arm is their thing. 'White Death.' Jeez. How do those guys ever expect to get a date? You'd have to be crazy to go out with one of them."

As Dot was finishing her comments, Manton's eyes glanced by the television screen suspended above the bar behind her. The Knicks game had been on with the sound turned down. It was half-time, and a news break was filling the time. His eyes jerked back to the screen and the banner that flashed the bullets for the nightly newscast. "Danny Deadline Set ... Weekend Snowstorm ... Details After Knicks"

"Oh, my God." Jen saw the horrified expression on his face and looked at the screen. She caught a split second of the promo before a commercial cut in.

"Did that say what I saw?"

"Yeah. Let's go. Excuse us Dot. We'll be in touch."

"I'll call you," she said expectantly. She too had looked at the television in response to Manton's reaction. She shrugged. *Weird people to let a little snow freak them out.*

*　　　*　　　*

The Tavern

"Father Delacroix. I am so pleased you could make time in your busy schedule to see me," called out Simon de Montfort, drunkenly, from the head of the long, crowded table at the inn. The crusaders had commandeered every shop and home in Rennes-le-Château.

Delacroix squinted into the candlelit dimness, replying, "As you serve the Holy Father, so shall I serve you, Commander de Montfort." He nodded slightly.

De Montfort grinned sloppily. He knew that Delacroix was here only because he had sent his men to the monastery with an order that he appear, voluntarily, or otherwise.

Delacroix had maintained his distance from the crusaders, not because of their goals, but because of the hedonistic and ungodly activities that surrounded them. Fueled by donations of locals, such as Jacques Boulanger, who hoped to remain in favor with their formidable visitors, the muddy campsites throughout the village were orgies of drinking and debauchery. A constant flow of beer, wine and willing, and not so willing, women kept the crusaders contented in a manner that Delacroix could not approve. Tonight was no different. De Montfort and his lieutenants were inebriated. Each had at his side a female companion, ages ranging from thirteen to thirty. From the looks of their disheveled clothes and hair, and the glassy smiles on their faces, the party was well under way.

"Father," de Monfort yelled theatrically, "are my scouts correct when they tell me that you have visited the mighty Blanchefort?"

"That is correct, Sir," Delacroix replied firmly. Obviously he had been discovered. Lying would serve no purpose. Despite the uncomfortable surroundings, Delacroix felt no fear.

Turning to the man next to him, de Montfort asked satirically for all to hear, "Lieutenant, did I give permission for anyone to go inside Blanchefort?" He belched for punctuation. The women tittered.

"Not without a battering ram, Sir," yelled his minion, gleefully.

Turning back to priest, de Monfort's eyes flashed with anger. "What business did you transact there, Father Delacroix?"

"I was called by Sir Frederick Lancel."

De Montfort rose from his seat and roared, "The mighty heretic Lancel? You went to him at his call?"

"I went to administer the word of God."

A strong fist smashed forcefully onto the table. "I am the word of God now."

Delacroix looked at the angry man dispassionately. He was drunk. There was no purpose in challenging him at this time. The silence in the room sobered de Montfort. He knew his pronouncement was crude, and he retreated.

"Forgive me, Father," he said quickly. "But you see, we have been here for months, and the Holy Father is impatient for us to move on. We do not wish to be delayed any longer and spend the winter in the Pyrenées."

Having regained his composure, de Montfort became serious. "For what purpose did you meet with Lancel?"

"He was stricken by arrow. He is deathly ill with fever." The room erupted in simultaneous comment.

"Silence," yelled de Montfort. The room quickly quieted. "Does he wish to surrender?"

"No. I am afraid that he does not repent of his beliefs. I could not persuade him."

"Clear the women," growled de Montfort to the innkeeper. Amid high-pitched protest, the room was cleared of women and villagers. Delacroix faced de Montfort and his staff.

"Father, does he not realize that his situation is hopeless?"

"He seemed to know." Delacroix saw no reason to provide details.

"What is the appearance of his soldiers?" asked one of the men at Delacroix's side.

"I did not look to see," Delacroix replied truthfully.

"Eeiii" moaned de Montfort, batting his forehead. His eyes moved nervously around the table. His lieutenants looked at their goblets.

"Father," said the crusader in a soft voice. "I do not like to slaughter women and children. We have seen enough of this." The lieutenants nodded. "But we are sent here to do the will of the Pope. If Lancel does not repent, we have no choice but to do so. Does Lancel not understand this?"

"I fear that he does, Commander de Montfort."

De Montfort slammed his hands flat on the table and looked to his men. "The efforts must be increased tenfold. We must take this damned castle Blanchefort and move on."

De Montfort looked at the priest and continued his instructions, "They are all heretics. They are infested." Then he squinted at Delacroix and hissed, "No one is to be spared. No one. If they demand martyrdom, they may have it. I wash my hands of their self-destruction." He spit into his hands forcefully and rubbed them together in front of him.

Delacroix nodded remorsefully at de Montfort. In resigned silence he turned and walked toward the door. He could not change Lancel's will. Nor that of de Montfort. And certainly not that of God.

*   *   *

Outside the Bright Paradise

Rick and Jen walked to the car as quickly as they could without drawing attention. Rick speed dialed as he walked. Gilliam picked up on the first ring.

"Jim, what's going on?" There was urgency in Manton's voice.

"It didn't get sent through me this time. They wired it directly to NBC, and it was on the air before I'd even heard the news." Gilliam was defensive.

"What news? What was sent?"

"Don't you know? It has been on the air for three hours?"

"We've been busy. What was sent?"

"Another message came in. The Friends of Judea are getting jumpy. The money isn't pouring in like they hoped, and they've given a deadline of forty-eight hours to either double the donations or for some Christian leader to step forward and sanction the donation process."

"Forty eight hours or else what?"

"They'll kill Danny."

"Oh Christ. Oh Christ." Rick felt pressure in his chest and struggled to breath. Anger and panic surged through his blood. Jen had her ear pressed to the receiver and heard Jim's report. She grabbed the receiver.

"Is it legit, Jim?"

"Yeah, they sent another photo. He looks good. Holding headlines from three days ago." They could see it on the news that night along with the rest of the world.

"I'll kill them. I'll kill everyone of them." The veins in Jen's neck stood out. She had never known such rage.

"Jen, Rick, you have to calm down. I've been trying to play through this to see how we can put some pressure on Dailley to move again. Maybe we can go public with what we've got on the Sons of Odin and close the net." Gilliam was throwing out ideas. Rick was back on the line.

"There's no time, Jim. We can't count on any official help. You know that. And we know that none of the preachers are going to step forward. I wouldn't trust them anyway. We better find a solution here."

"Where are you? Are you in Newark?"

"Yeah. We had to do something. We've been mixing with the Nazis tonight. We might have a lead."

"Tell me what you've got and I'll pass it on. Surely the locals can authorize action with this new info. They can get warrants."

There was a long pause in the frigid car. Rick and Jen's eyes met. "I don't think that would work, Jim. Look, we better think about this before doing anything rash. Don't go public with the Sons of Odin story. Give us a day to see what we can dig up."

Gilliam was skeptical about the mood shift he detected in Rick's voice. "Are you sure?"

"Yes."

"You'll keep me posted. I can't get hold of you."

"We will. Thanks."

Rick pressed the off button.

"My bag is in the back," Jen said evenly.

"What do you think?"

"We're out of time."

"I agree."

* * *

De Montfort was true to his word. He would not skirt around this castle. He intended to take it and move on. For the two days the activity at the base of Blanchefort intensified. Assault weapons were sharpened and stockpiled. Armor was tightened and polished. Horses were shod. And on the cliff below Blanchefort's southern walls, villagers adept at climbing the local rock formations guided the crusaders in surreptitiously fashioning a stairway of ladders and ropes for an assault on the rear.

On dawn of the third day, the castle grounds were jolted awake by a chilling scream of a sentry, followed by the roar of a wave of crusaders charging the front walls. Simultaneously, brawny swordsmen, who had spent the night climbing the cliff, began scaling the back wall. The defenders of Blanchefort were all on the front ramparts, believing that it was the only direction that they could be pierced. The back wall was breached before the intruders were even spotted.

Frightened by the small, but startling, contingent at the rear of the compound, panic ensued. Archers on the walls mistakenly shifted their attention toward the rear of the compound where the crusaders were raising havoc, but remaining under cover. Without Lancel's calm and experienced leadership, the response to the surprise was slow and uncoordinated. Unfettered by the usual rain of arrows, ladders were raised on the front wall and the tide of attackers surged up. The knights fought valiantly, slashing and stabbing the encroachers. But the numbers were overwhelming and, in the end, for every crusader the swordsmen felled, two more pushed up and over the wall.

In close combat, the archer's weapons were cumbersome and ineffective. They were soon routed off the wall and tried vainly to find other positions of height. They were tracked down and killed one at a time. Only the manor was being feebly defended. That ended as well when the gates were opened wide and the bloodthirsty mobs in the rear stormed through by the thousands.

Lancel could hear the sounds of battle, but he was too weak to rise. At first his subordinates ran in to give him reports. He was too feverish to offer advice and soon they stopped coming to his room. He could hear the howling of crusaders as they ran through the halls of the manor, killing anyone in their path.

Lancel sat up in his bed and reached for his broadsword propped in a wooden rack by the head of the bed. It was too heavy for him to raise, and as his door burst open he could only watch, his sword drooped to the floor, as they drug him from the bed.

Lancel was the coveted laurel, the leader of the infidels of Rennes-le-Château. The crusaders were ecstatic that he had been taken alive and called out jubilantly as they entered the courtyard.

Stumbling forward, Lancel cursed that God had not granted him a warriors' honorable death. The jeering faces pressed in around him as he was pushed toward the front gate.

By the battle's end the moat was littered with the bodies of the slain invaders, but victory was theirs. The victors would show no pity. Most of the Templars and Cathars were killed where they fought. Those that were injured or had surrendered were herded into a group with the quaking wives and wailing children, to be marched to the village for sentencing.

The sides of the path down the mountain dropped precipitously on the outward side. Many of the captured were shoved over the side as they were marched to the village. Their deaths were a combination of glory to God and the depraved sport of their captors. Lancel heard the cries as he lurched down the path. He could not see Joseph nor find the sergeant assigned to protect him and keep him from the battle. He did not see Delacroix. He was in agony over what God hath wrought upon him.

As Lancel was marched into the square the mob that had assembled called for his blood. The infidel was to be burned. Rennes-le-Château was to be cleared of heretics. He was thrown on the ground and strapped to two wooden posts which were tied together in an "X". He could smell the smoke from the fire that was being ignited in the center of the square to the howls of delight of the mob. He prayed the prayer of his blood father as the crowd hoisted him in the air and surged toward the growing fire. "My God, My God, why hast Thou forsaken me?"

The crowd lowered Lancel so that the feet of his cross were at the base of the fire. In the middle of the fire was a pole with a cross arm. He was pushed backward until the arms of his cross fell against the cross arms, suspending him at a slant high above the fire. The crowd wanted visible vengeance. They wanted to see the heretics burn.

Lancel felt the flames against his pant legs. Pain seared through his limbs as he smelled the stench of his own flesh burning. He heard the crowd screaming. They were demanding that the bloodline be ended. They wanted his son! They were calling for Joseph!

From the back of the mob a voice boomed in delight, "I got 'im. I got the little devil bastard. Found 'im hiding in the castle venison cooler, I did."

The crowd turned its back to the growing fire and pushed toward the arrogant man who stood over a small filthy boy lying limply at his feet. "That's 'im. Ain't it? The son of that heretic Frederick Lancel."

Surprisingly, no one in the cluster of villagers knew whether this battered, dust-covered child was the same boy that they only briefly saw at times when he was cleaned and dressed in finest clothes befitting a Knight Templar's son.

"They tried to disguise 'im, they did."

Delacroix had entered the square in time to see the rabble stand Lancel in the fledgling fire. He was helpless against the crazed mob. At the sound of Joseph's name he began to march through the square. A woman's voice shrieked, "It's Father Delacroix. He'll know the heretic." A chorus of supporters joined the call.

Delacroix knelt beside the miserable form on the hard dirt.

"Is it 'im? Is it 'im?" The crowd pressed closer.

The sound of the voices assaulted Delacroix's ears. They jostled him threateningly as they surged closer. They demanded an answer. And there was only one that they wanted. Lifting his hands, with palms upwards, Delacroix turned to the crowd and nodded sadly as if to say, 'He is yours.' The mob howled its delight that it had its sacrifice.

Lancel could barely see the backs of the heads in front of him, but he could fathom what was happening. As the crowd parted he faced Delacroix. Their eyes met. There was no emotion in Delacroix's. Lancel screamed at the crowd, at Delacroix and at his Savior, "May you all rot in hell."

The growing fire lapped against his stomach as his clothing began to smolder. The flames ate into the flesh of his thighs. His screams continued as the crowd hoisted the boy in the air and carried him across the square and hurled his limp body onto the base of the fire. Lancel's face was contorted with pain and rage as he stared at the figure that landed at his feet and was engulfed in flames. As the knight's hair ignited his eyes contorted wide in final shock and disbelief as he passed from his earthly hell.

* * *

Newark

This time Jen entered the bar first. It was colder now than when they initially came in, but this time her coat was unbuttoned as well as two more buttons on her flannel shirt. Her red lip gloss had been reapplied. Rick followed. Tony Miller was still on duty and loomed in front of them.

"You came back." Miller usually remembered any woman that came in. He certainly hadn't forgotten Jen in the fifteen minutes since they had raced out.

Rick stepped forward. "We just had to make a few calls."

"Well you have to pay again." Miller's boss would have been proud of him. "Maybe I could make an exception for someone like you." he said to Jen. His crude form of a pickup line nauseated her.

"That's okay." Rick stepped in between Jen and Miller. "Actually we came back to talk to you. You're Tony, right?"

"Maybe. What's it to you?" Miller's guard went up. He had too many enemies. They weren't usually white though, unless they were cops.

"Keith told us to talk to you."

"What about?" The sound of his boss' name relaxed him a little.

"This is Rhonda," Rick said, opening his arm toward Jen. "I'm her manager. She's looking for work. Keith hasn't seen her. He said you should check her out."

Miller smiled. His yellow teeth made his face even more repulsive. Carney had always entrusted him with important jobs, but he had never given him a task that would be as fun as this was going to be. "You mean as one of the girls?"

"Don't I qualify?" Jen asked with as much seductiveness as she could muster.

"Sure do, Baby. But I'll have to see the whole package before I can recommend you." Miller was acquiring a sense of importance right in front of them. "Let me get one of the boys to relieve me and we can go in back."

"Tony," Jen purred, "I've got a van out front that we could use."

Miller raised an eyebrow and looked puzzled. This seemed like a come on line, but he wasn't used to having them used on him.

"Keith said you'd give him a report on me to determine what my salary would be. I thought maybe if I was, well, nice to you, you'd say nice things about me."

The sweat rolled down Tony's puffy face. "We can do that upstairs."

"Well Tony..." Jen hesitated and, for effect, looked around. She leaned over close to Miller so that her hair brushed against his shoulder and whispered in his ear, "I've got some toys in the van. We could play."

Rick thought Miller would pass out on the spot. The giant of a man left without a word and hurried toward the pool room to get someone to replace him, leaving the entrance open.

"I think I'm going to vomit," Jen groaned.

"Hang in there."

Miller came back with one of the thugs, nearly as big as him. "How long I gotta stay here, Tony? I was winning."

Miller was in a state of excitement and wasn't going to miss his once in a lifetime chance. He didn't want his authority challenged in front of this willing woman who was apparently impressed with his status in the organization. "Shut up. Just shut up. You stay until I get back, you understand." The replacement shook his head in wonder at Miller's sudden moodiness and sat down on a stool by the door.

Miller was opening the door to charge outside when he remembered Jen and awkwardly held the door for her. Jen smiled pertly and walked through. Rick started to follow. "What you doing?" Miller growled.

"Don't worry, Tony," Rick said confidently. "I'm not going to watch. But someone has to hang around outside in case you two get a little noisy in there. We don't want to draw a crowd." Miller smiled and shook his head up and down. He would have agreed to dance in a tutu on Van Buren at this point. It never occurred to him that there might be danger. He wasn't carrying any money and these people weren't niggers or spics.

Jen pulled her coat lapels together as they headed to the van. Miller hadn't stopped for a coat, but was impervious to the freezing wind. As Jen and her escort walked in front of him, Rick looked the thug over carefully. The only place he could have a weapon was in his western style snakeskin boots which were partially covered by his jeans. He and Jen had assumed that he'd be armed when they were finalizing their plan in the van after the phone call. Miller's past record indicated he wouldn't go far without either a handgun or very large switchblade.

They reached the van. Jen entered the side door and slid over on the middle seat. "Come on in, big fella." Miller grinned nervously, ducked his head and stepped in. Rick was behind him motioning to Miller's boots. Jen nodded. She had figured as much. "You can shut the door ... Bill."

Rick's brain screamed with anguish as he shut the door of the cage that held his wife and this animal. The van had windows tinted so dark that he could see nothing inside. They had purchased it that way after all this bloodline business came up thinking that they could have a little anonymity when running errands. It hadn't worked.

Now all Rick saw was his angry reflection in the side panel window.

"I can't see you Baby." Miller didn't want to miss any part of this fantasy.

"Ah, Tony. We can turn on a light later. But before I give you the show I thought you'd like me to warm you up."

"Uh-huh. Yeah. Sure."

"Why don't you pull those tight old pants down?"

Miller's fingers nearly ripped his belt buckle apart in his hurry to get it undone. He lifted his butt off the seat and pushed his pants down and paused, almost obediently. Jen reached out and pushed the pants a little farther so that they wrapped up the tops of his boots.

"Good." Then Jen raised her voice slightly. "Will you check the door? I feel a draft."

As Miller shifted and turned toward the door, Jen's hand slipped into the side pocket of the van seat. Tony tugged on the door. He scootched back around. "It's ..."

The blow of the hammer nailed him between the eyes. It landed hard with a sickening thud. Miller gave out a half shriek of pain as Jen shouted, "Rick. Now!"

The door flew open instantaneously and Rick filled the door with his pistol drawn. "Freeze!"

But Miller didn't freeze. He sat still for a moment, eyes unblinking. Then slowly, without uttering a sound, he slumped forward and wedged in between the seat and the floor. Jen held her hammer poised to strike. Rick pointed his gun at his head. After a moment, when Miller made no movement or sound, they glanced at each other. Rick leaned over and vigorously shook the body. There was a slight groan. After holstering his pistol, Rick roughly pulled the unconscious man's arms behind him and slapped on a pair of handcuffs. He had been practicing with them for only a day since their purchase and was pleased not to fumble on his first attempt. Jen was wrapping wide, silver-colored duct tape around Miller's face, sealing his mouth shut.

"Jesus, did you kill him?"

"No, he's breathing. I didn't know how hard to swing. I wanted to make sure."

"I'm not complaining. I just hope he can talk."

Rick helped Jen over the packaged figure and slammed the door. Looking up and down the dark, cold street, he circled the van and jumped in the driver's seat. They were moving as soon as the engine turned over.

* * *

Twenty minutes later, on another dark, deserted street, the van was parked and the Mantons crawled between the front captain's seat into the back. The rear passenger bench had been removed and Miller was lying on the floor bed. Rick pointed a large flashlight into his face and slapped his cheek with short, rough blows. "Wake up, Anthony. Wake up."

Miller opened his eyes and squinted them tightly against the light and roared a grunt of pain and rage. He started to sit up. He tried to kick, but his legs were duct taped together and all he could do was thrash around.

"Settle down." Rick flicked his knuckles against the huge knot rising out of the middle of Miller's forehead. It was lucky that Jen hadn't killed him. Her adrenaline had given her the power of a carpenter swinging the hammer. Miller grunted a high shriek of pain and laid back. He tried to talk through the tape. They could tell it wasn't a friendly message. Rick saw the evil in the eyes that was probably the last sight of many of Miller's victims. Rick didn't have an ounce of compassion in him for this pig.

"Look, Tony. We can do this easy or we can do it hard. We are not the police. You don't have any rights anymore," Rick said deliberately.

Miller closed his eyes. "Look at me you asshole." Rick didn't realize that Miller couldn't see through the blinding light.

Miller grunted. Through the tape they could clearly make out, "Fuck you."

Rick pulled out his gun and placed it on Miller's nose. He pressed it hard into the bridge of Miller's nose. His voice was strained and high. "You aren't listening to me, scum." Miller settled down as much by Rick's apparent loss of control as the gun aimed between his eyes.

"You are looking at the parents of Danny Manton. And you have our son." Miller's dumbfounded blink told his surprise.

"We want some information about where Danny is at. We want our son back. If you don't give us that information, we will kill you. Do you understand?" Rick explained impatiently.

Miller blinked again. His nostrils flared.

"Now listen. I am going to take this tape off your mouth. I don't want you making any noise or I'll let Danny's mother have another whack at you. And we're a long ways from nowhere so all you'll get is a headache. Do we understand each other?"

Again Miller grunted the familiar insult of the uneducated. Now Rick was surprised. Miller had just been knocked unconscious, hog tied, and threatened with his life by people who had every incentive to kill him. Yet he was still defiant.

"This guy is dumber than we thought," Rick said under his breath to Jen.

"Let's give it a try anyway," she said.

Jen snipped the tape with a pair of surgical scissors, and in one yank, ripped the tape off Miller's mouth. He had not been listening. He was like a cat in a bathtub.

"You bitch. I'm going to cut you up, bitch and ..."

Rick stiff armed Miller on his swollen forehead, knocking his skull to the floor of the van.

"You aren't listening ..."

Miller raised his head off the floor and yelled, "Fuck you, you bastard. You ain't got the balls to shoot me. We'll dump your ass in the Hudson ..."

Rick stiff armed him again on the forehead, harder this time. Miller wasn't a quick learner. As Miller sucked in a breath to counteract the searing pain in his head, Rick slapped on a fresh strip of duct tape. Miller was still kicking fruitlessly against the duct tape on his ankles.

"Hand me that hammer," Rick said evenly. It had the desired effect, and Miller stopped thrashing.

Rick got up on his knees above Miller's head. "You're not so smart, Anthony. My wife here wants to talk to you. Keep in mind that your people have her son when you question what she'll do."

Jen got on her knees on the other side of Miller. "Hello, Mr. Miller. I'm Jennifer, Daniel Manton's mother." Jen had put on her clinical voice. The contrast with her seductive voice earlier was chilling.

"I don't know if you can read the papers, Mr. Miller, but you can probably watch a television, and somewhere along the line heard that Daniel's mother was a nurse. So a little blood is not going to deter me from getting my son back. Do you read me so far?"

Miller blinked. The voice above him was as cold as the night air.

"But you're right about us not killing you. We aren't like you. But I'll tell you what I could do without losing a minute of sleep." Jen reached into a bag. Rick moved the flashlight beam so Miller could see as she pulled out a four-inch hypodermic needle.

Jen's steady, skilled hands held the needle inches from Miller's eyes as she pulled the plunger back. His eyes were transfixed on the silvery spine of the needle, glistening in the beam of light. Belonephobia. The fear of needles. Jen knew it afflicted many men who were supposedly afraid of nothing.

Jen continued in her clinical voice. "You know, I read your rap sheet, Mr. Miller. I see that you had to spend some time in jail waiting for your trial. When you were there, did you run across any sex offenders?"

Miller slowly shook his head up and down. She had his attention.

"Good. Then maybe you heard them talk about a new treatment that has been developed for repeat sex offenders. Some of them actually like this new treatment, because if they take it, the parole board looks at them differently. Do you know what I'm talking about, Mr. Miller?"

"Uh-uh," came the grunt. It didn't matter if his response was yes or no.

"It's called cyproterone acetate." She pulled out a small glass vial and inserted the needle through the rubber stopper. She flipped the bottle up and pushed the plunger in, causing a long line of tiny bubbles to rise to the top. Jen slowly pulled back the plunger and filled the chamber. "This wonderfully powerful drug is an antiandrogen. Do you know what that means?"

Miller fearfully grunted.

"It is a chemical castration agent." Jen knew that fear of castration exceeded all other men's fears combined. "It has some good purposes. Would you like me to explain them to you?"

Miller frantically shook his head no. He wouldn't be doubting this woman's capability for vengeance anymore.

"I will anyway. I think you should know. Mr. Miller, a small dose of this will take away your ability to achieve an erection." While Jen's words concerned a sexual topic, lust was the furthest thing from Miller's mind. His eyes did not leave the needle. His chest was heaving.

Jen leaned over so that her face was inches from Miller. She changed the tone of her voice. It was low and sinister. "Tony," she whispered, "I am going to give you enough of this stuff to turn you into a woman. Permanently. And I am damn well going to enjoy it. The next time you look at those girls shaking their ass in your face, your dick will be as limp as a day old plate of fettuccini. All you will be able to think about is your next crochet project. Your friends might even make you wear a dress. Now do we understand each other you piece of shit?!"

Jen started to move the needle toward Miller's arm. Not all of what she had said was true, but her manner and delivery was convincing. Miller gave a series of high-pitched screams through the tape, and shook his head violently back and forth.

"I believe the patient wants to talk politely with us now," Rick said, getting into the role of assistant. "Am I right, Mr. Miller?" Miller bobbed his head rapidly up and down.

"Okay then. Let's try this one last time." Rick ripped the tape off again. Miller winced, but did not make a sound.

"Mr. Miller," Jen had gone back to her clinical diction, "glad to finally have your cooperation. Before continuing I note that you're a mighty large person, and we are having a hard time controlling you. I am going to give you a muscle relaxant so that we can talk in a more conciliatory manner. It will also make you more comfortable. I give you my word that it is not cyproterone acetate. May I proceed?"

"Not the castration stuff? Right?" Miller sounded very relieved.

"Not if you help us." Jen waggled the needle.

Miller nodded. "But not that stuff." Miller was getting more pliable.

Jen handed Rick the first needle. Miller's eyes followed it. Jen filled another needle with sodium penathol. Known as the "truth serum," Jen had no such belief in its popular, but mostly fictitious, powers. But it was used by doctors and dentists to relax patients, and it had been known to enhance candor due to the calming effect it caused. At a minimum, it would tranquilize this beast. Jen drew an amount three times the clinically recommended dose. She wasn't concerned with malpractice. She didn't care if Miller's liver rotted. She was careful only to keep it under a lethal dosage. Miller's face was aghast as she inserted the needle into a vein in his forearm, but he did not struggle against the handcuffs. Jen noticed other needle marks in the same vein. The son of a bitch will probably enjoy this, she surmised.

The drug immediately took effect on Miller. She could see his body slump back to the floor of the van. The furrowed crease in his forehead relaxed. His breathing slowed dramatically. The sodium penathol was working well. Between it, and the base of fear Jen had established, they could begin the interrogation.

Rick took over. "Miller, we know that you're a member of the Sons of Odin. Are we correct?"

"Yes." Miller's speech was thick and slow. He had a half smile on his face that made him look even stupider than usual.

"And we know that you have our boy, Danny Manton. Right?"

"Oh ... I don't know." Miller's head rolled around. The denial wasn't delivered with any conviction.

"Tony! Don't get my wife mad at you. Do you have Danny?"

"Well. Yeah, we do." His voice was happy.

The Mantons' hopes soared. Their hearts were racing. Bingo. They were on the right track. Rick reeled in his excitement. "Tony," he said evenly, "where is he at?"

"I can't tell you that. Keith would kill me." Miller looked like he would cry even though he still had a drugged smile on his face.

Jen leaned in. "Mr. Miller, do you want me to turn you into a woman?"

"Oh no, no, no. Please don't say that."

"Mr. Miller, I am going to inject you right now if you don't tell us the truth." She put a hand on his forearm where the other shot had been given.

"Okay, I'll talk. I'll talk. Don't tell Keith I talked."

"We won't tell Keith." It was like talking to a drunk.

"Where is he?" Rick stated deliberately.

"At the apartment. At my place. Where me and some other guys live."

"Where is it? Give us the address."

"Number 702. Seventh floor."

"The address, Tony."

"1642 Goff Avenue."

They sat back and looked at each other, their eyes wet with tears of tempered happiness and relief. Rick continued. There was no time to waste. "Who is guarding Danny?"

By now Miller had no will or reason to keep any secrets. "About eight of us live there off and on. We take turns watching him."

It was time to enter the next phase. "Where do you keep him? Which room?"

"In the bedroom in the back. In the closet."

Rick fought his urge to smash the hammer into Miller's face. He held his composure. Through gritted teeth, he persisted. "How many people stay in the apartment to guard him?"

"We come. We go. Just someone. We're usually all there." That was not what Rick wanted to hear.

"Is there any time that there is only one ... or two guards?"

"Really ... no one keeps track." Rick paused to think. He remembered the most recent demand.

"What do you know about the forty-eight hour deadline? The deadline for more money?"

"Oh, is that what Keith decided? I didn't know. Honest." Fear crept into Miller's stupor when he felt he was not giving the right answers. He stammered, "We're having a meeting Saturday night to talk about what was going to happen. Getting together for a big supper at the new place we're opening. I didn't know, I swear." Rick didn't trust Miller's oath, but the drugs insured his truthfulness.

"Where will Danny be during this meeting?"

"Same place. We don't move him much. He might yell."

"Who is guarding him during the meeting?"

"Whoever loses. Nobody wants to miss the free food. Keith says it's better than Louis' Place."

"Tony. Listen to me. What time is the supper? What time?" Miller was obviously fading from the hefty dose.

"Six o'clock."

It was late Friday night. It was a long time until tomorrow. Should we get Gilliam involved? Rick thought not, but he'd have to talk to Jen.

"Tony, if you're not telling us everything, you'll be wearing pantyhose next week," he stated coolly. "We aren't letting you go until we can verify all of what you told us."

"It's true, it's true."

There was one more question from Jen. "Is Danny all right? You haven't hurt him, have you?"

"He's okay. He cries a lot. What has he got to whine about? I never had a room of my own when I was a boy. And he gets new clothes ..." Miller was blubbering.

Jen didn't care about his childhood problems. "You can shut up now, Tony."

Rick put the strip of tape back on Miller's mouth. He didn't fight. He closed his eyes and fell asleep.

*   *   *

10

Yea, though I walk through the valley of the shadow of death, I will fear no evil: for thou art with me.
-- Psalms 23:4

The Mantons were tempted to set up watch all day to the entrance to the Goff Avenue apartment building, but they were afraid their van would be too conspicuous. It was too new and undented. This wasn't the suburbs and it would have been noticeable. They didn't think it would be safe to stroll by the entrance either. They had sat in the midst of the Sons of Odin for hours the night before and at least one of them saw the Mantons leave with Miller.

Their reluctant, but now docile, prey was still cuffed, taped and drugged in the back. Rick had also taped him to the seat supports and secured his legs so he couldn't kick to make noise. It was an extremely uncomfortable position, painful after a few hours, but that was not their concern. Jen kept Miller only so drugged that he was pliable.

They debated whether to call Gilliam and get the police involved. Any plan to free Danny themselves was fraught with danger. But official involvement hadn't proven itself reliable so far. If the police were involved would they even act? There were so many variables. Would there be a jurisdiction dispute between federal, state and local officials? How much time would be wasted deciding? The Mantons had done in two days what should have been done weeks ago. Of course the police did not have access to Jen's unusual methods. Nor would the police have blanket freedom to move in to save Danny. They would want a search warrant. A judge would have to be found on a Saturday. Would the judge disregard the coerced confession? There were just too many obstacles and no trust that the law enforcement agencies involved could or would overcome them. Failure to clear any one of these hurdles might mean that Danny would be whisked away, or worse, dead. No, they would do this themselves.

During one of the intervals when Jen allowed Miller to come out of his coma they obtained the names of the other roommates in the apartment. Some of the names were familiar from the file. Ron Williams. Lee Borman. Mike Hendricks. Bob Crockett, on parole from a child pornography conviction. David Allen, extortion. Allen was the flunky who had replaced Miller at the door. There were two others that surprisingly had no criminal record, not that was in the file anyway. The Mantons studied the photographs that were available, memorizing every detail of the faces staring grimly back at them.

By five o'clock another cold winter night had set in. Converse to what they would normally feel in such an area, the darkness provided security and they moved their van into a position where they could see the front of the building. The entrance had the makings of having once been a grand hotel. There was a concrete canopy with decorative scroll along the face. But now the door was no longer attended by an obedient bellman. Glass doors had been replaced by more durable wooden ones painted battleship gray. The address, 1642, had been painted in orange above the door.

The Mantons had to fight their temptation to charge in the front door, to attempt get to Danny as quick as possible. He was so close. Or at least was supposed to be so close. They sat in the van with the engine running to keep warm and in case they needed to move fast. After what seemed like an endless half hour they saw Hendricks and Allen enter the building. But no one left. At least Miller's recantation was panning out so far. This was the nest of snakes. Was Danny in there?

Jen spotted them first. Fifteen minutes before the hour two groups of men came out. They pulled up the collars of their coats against the wind and crossed over to the side of the street where the Mantons stood watch. The Mantons hearts jumped into their throats.

"Let's stay cool," Rick warned as the group stepped up onto the sidewalk and veered toward their position. They heard a slight shuffling from the back as Miller was beginning to squirm.

The men had room to walk three abreast and continued quickly toward the van. Rick and Jen slunk slightly in their seats. The first row walking toward them had two familiar faces, definitely Sons of Odin. Jen couldn't forget that scarred face of the rapist Borman. The others were Williams and Crockett. Neither Rick or Jen looked up as they approached and walked by the van. The second row was a short distance behind. It was Allen and two others that were unknown. They must have been the "virgins." As the line approached one of the two unknowns glanced up at the vehicle's windshield and noticed Jen's shiny black hair hanging down as she pretended to look at a map. Next to him Allen stopped short. "Hey, Dickhead," he shouted, "you're driving." He spun around and walked to the car parked in front of the Mantons.

"I drove last time," 'Dickhead' whined.

"Well don't almost get us killed again," yelled Allen. He glanced briefly in the direction of the van, hesitated, and ducked into the beat-up Ford Escort.

Not a word was spoken in the van. They didn't want to tip off Miller how close his compatriots were. The Escort pulled away. From behind them down the street a Lincoln pulled out and the other three drove by. The Mantons knew from their afternoon questioning that the restaurant was six blocks away.

Rick let out his breath that he had subconsciously been holding. "Whew." He checked his watch. The boys would be on time for their free dinner. He hoped they choked to death. To Jen he said, "It's time."

The Mantons crawled to the back of the van. The risk of a passer-by was too great to open the door in back. Miller was starting to gain consciousness. He was blindfolded. Jen had not given him a dose of sodium penathol for two hours. They needed him awake. Jen leaned closer and spoke low. "Okay, Tony, wake up. Let's do this just like we practiced and maybe you'll live to use that little pecker of yours." Jen chose not to use her clinical voice. She was not in a mood to mess around. To Miller's misfortune, he did not pick up on that.

Rick ripped the tape away. Had Miller known where he was he may have screamed. Instead his voice was defiant, too much of the drug had worn off. "I'm not doing this. Go to hell."

They had come too far. They were too close to be thwarted now. Jen's rage surged and she picked up the hammer. "You miserable excuse for a human being," she cried as she smashed the hammer into Miller's knee cap. Miller never saw the blow coming and lurched forward and screamed.

Rick quickly clapped his hands on Miller's mouth. "Jen! Jen! Don't." Miller twisted his head and bared his teeth. "Miller, don't even think of biting me or we'll break your other knee." Rick didn't necessarily disagree with what Jen had done, he was just shocked that she did it.

"Okay. Okay." came the muffled, pain-filled response.

Jen had sat back and Rick could tell she was talking to herself. Jen never was out of control. She took a deep breath. "I'm all right now, Rick. Sorry."

Rick looked up and down the street through the tinted windows. The muffled scream hadn't penetrated the closed windows in the neighborhood. There was no activity on the street. Had they heard, no one would have responded anyway.

"Look Miller, we've got a problem. If you don't help us we may as well finish with you now and find some other way to do this. Have you thought about what your life will be like when the whores you hire are snickering at you behind your back? Do you really want to be a eunuch?" Rick slowly removed his hand.

"I'll do it. I'll do it. Just keep her away from me."

"Sorry, no deal," Jen declared. "We can't afford anymore funny business like that again. I'm going to put this needle in your arm. I've got enough cc's of cyproterone acetate in the barrel to turn you into Lady Gaga. If you so much as breathe funny, we're hanging up and I'll slam that plunger to the hilt. Then I get to sit back and watch your balls shrivel. There will not be a second chance. What do you want to do, Tony?"

"I'll make the call."

"Good. Sit tight for a second. Don't make me slip." Jen inserted the needle into Miller's vein. His body stiffened. "Remember, you pull any stunts and this needle comes out of you empty."

Rick started to dial the phone number they had squeezed out of Miller earlier. On the third ring he heard someone pick up and quickly moved the phone to Miller's ear and mouth. He pressed his ear to the other side of the receiver.

"Yeah." Phone presence was not a strong suit of the Sons of Odin.

"Hey, this is Tony. Who's this?"

"Who the hell you think it is? It's Mike you dumbshit. Where the hell you been? Everybody's looking for you. Allen says you ditched him at the door to bang some broad."

"Listen, I can't talk. Keith told me to call you. You got the kid, right?"

"No, I ate him, you idiot. Course I got him."

"You alone?"

"Damn right. Everyone else is stuffin' their fat faces. Why? You ain't gettin' queer on me are ya?"

"No. Keith says the heat is on to us and we got to move the kid real quick, like now."

"No shit. Where to?"

"The armory."

"I gotta drive to Albany tonight? Christ."

Rick nudged Miller and pulled the receiver back and whispered in Miller's ear, "Now." Jen tapped the needle as a reminder of his precarious position.

"Mike, Keith says this is coming down now. You got to move the kid now. Don't wait for nobody. Move the kid now." Miller had most of his senses back and was responding fully to directions from his captors.

"You okay, Tony. You don't sound right." He had probably never heard Miller speak an entire sentence without cursing.

Jen squeezed his arm. "I'm fine. Will you move him, now?"

"I'm going, okay? Don't be such an ass, man."

"Get outta there in five minutes."

"I ain't deaf. I'm going already. Jesus."

Rick pushed the off button. "Good enough."

"Take the needle out ... please."

Jen wanted to ram the plunger deep into him anyway. She was under control now, however, and realized they might need some more dirt from Miller and didn't want to use up their only effective threat. She pulled the needle out. "You do have to stay with us a little longer. Back to the regular stuff."

Miller started to whine as Jen injected a small dose of sodium penathol, but he did not fight. Rick taped his mouth again. "Let's move."

* * *

Jen exited the van by the side door and looked up and down the street as Rick followed. Without a word she went one way and he went the other and circled in front of the van to cross the street. Jen had tucked her hair up into a knit hat. She didn't want to have anymore close calls like they just had with anyone recognizing her. In ne pocket was her cell. In the other coat pocket she had transferred her Remington .45. She kept her ungloved hand in that pocket and on the handle. Her finger tapped the safety as she debated whether to have it on or off.

Rick crossed the street and headed for the entrance to the apartment building. Jen would be keeping watch on the street and could text him if any Sons of Odin unexpectedly came back. His phone was on vibrate. But he also had his hand in his pocket on his pistol. His safety was off.

The lobby of the building was only slightly warmer than outside. Any trappings of the wealthy were decades gone. Dirt and dust lay in circular piles where the wind had swirled them. It smelled of urine. Along one wall were banks of tin U.S. Postal Service mailboxes. As Rick walked by them toward the elevators he noticed a stack of paper with a rock on top. They were flyers advertising a new pizza parlor. Rick grabbed a handful of them.

There were two elevator door frames, but one of the doors had a faded 'Out of Order' sign taped on it. Rick pressed the 'up' button and waited. It was extremely slow in arriving. He looked around. Above him was a large circular mirror, certainly put in for safety and not for the expediency of rounding corners. The mirror was cracked and had graffiti sprayed on the bottom half, but in it Rick could still see most of the lobby and half way down a rear corridor. Rick stepped over and looked down the hallway. It led to the stairwell and a back exit to the alley. He and Jen had driven down the alley earlier in the day, suspecting an alternative exit. There was nothing back there except garbage bins and a few burned out hulks of cars. Even the bums wouldn't hang out there. It seemed unlikely that Danny would be brought that way so it was agreed that Jen would remain in the street and, if Rick couldn't get close to Hendricks for some reason, she would try to supply a diversion. She would get in front of the car if she had to.

Rick heard the elevator arrive. He lingered in the hallway waiting to see who, if anyone, would exit. It took the doors another three seconds before they opened. Even three seconds seemed to drag.

Upstairs Mike Hendricks was grumbling and trying to collect what he needed for his trip. It wasn't that the drive to Albany was so far, but he knew that the armory didn't have the comforts of the apartment, dump that it was. The called in an armory, but it was just a glorified warehouse where they stored the weapons before they were sold. He was loading a duffel bag with beer and whatever food he could find in the cupboards and refrigerator. He eyed the television wondering if he could carry it all. He decided against it. Better have a free hand for his hostage. Aw, shit, Hendricks muttered as he remembered that his car had overheated two nights before when he had run an errand. The radiator had boiled over and steam had whistled out from all sides of the hood. He had cursed it and walked away, planning to get it fixed later. By now with this miserable cold spell it would be a block of ice under the hood. He walked out into the hallway. He paused for a moment. The kid wouldn't try to run, he hasn't moved all day. Hendricks walked down the hallway to the window. Instead of glass the window pane was Plexiglas that was weathered and scratched to the point where he couldn't see through it. He tilted it open and craned his neck to look out onto the street to see whose car was still available. He could see that Borman's car was still there. Hendricks didn't notice the chilled woman alertly walking the sidewalk in front of the building.

Hendricks knew where Borman left a set of keys for his car. He also knew that Borman would be pissed off at him for taking it. He and Borman didn't see eye-to-eye on many things. Damn, better call him. Hendricks did enjoy the thought of telling Borman that he was taking his car on Keith's authority. That would shut him up. Hendricks jogged back down the hall and ducked into the apartment as the elevator arrived. Hendricks slammed the door as the elevator slowly creaked open.

The phone rang at the front desk. "Hello, American Hofbrau House." The Sons of Odin's newest venture was named for the Munich beerhall which had given rise to Adolph Hitler. "May I take your reservation?" The nineteen-year old hostess made a good presentation to the public. She had no idea who owned the restaurant. It was her first weekend. She didn't know the Sons of Odin yet either. By Monday she would be looking for a new job.

"This is Mike. Is Lee Borman there yet?"

"I'm sorry, we don't have a Borman party. Could he be with another party?"

"Oh Christ. He's with the Carney group."

"I'm sorry, I don't show them either."

"Hear me Babe, how many parties you got there? It's the owners' party."

"Oh, I'm sorry. They aren't here yet." This was true. Carney and the carload that included Borman had just pulled up in front. They were greeting each other as they headed toward the door. "May I take a message?"

"Yeah. It's for Lee Borman. He's a big, ugly guy with a scar clear across his face. You can't miss him. Tell him Mike is taking his car to Albany on Keith's orders. You got that."

"Lee Borman. Mike is taking car to Albany on Keith's order. Got it." She was smarter than any three of the gang members combined. She was already having second thoughts about this job.

"Great, Sweetheart."

As the hostess hung up the receiver she looked up into the scarred face of a man who had to be Lee Borman. She tried not to stare at the raised gash. "Are you Mr. Borman?" she managed to gulp.

"Yes."

"I just received this message for you." She handed the note to him, eyes unintentionally locked on the scary face.

Borman looked puzzled. He turned to Carney. "Hey, Keith. Mike's supposed to be babysitting. Why you sending him to Albany?"

Carney was admiring the restaurant remodel job in a Bavarian motif. He hoped that the money he was expecting from Israel would start funneling in so he could pay for it. "What are you talking about? I haven't told him a thing. You left that lamebrain with the kid? Get him on the phone."

Borman reached in front of the timid hostess and grabbed the phone. Looking her up and down, he dialed. Hendricks was talking to "Darla," who he had met the night before at a sleazy bar in Hoboken. He had hoped to score with her later when his babysitting shift was over.

No answer. "Hell with it, get your ass back there and see what Hendricks is up to. What the hell were you thinking of, Borman?" Carney did not like his charges taking risks with his prize. He should have guarded the kid himself, but that wasn't within his position anymore. Besides, if the scheme went awry, as so many had in the past, he might be able to pawn it off onto the underlings if he kept his distance. But, obviously, he needed closer supervision. Good help was hard to find when one of the necessary qualifications was being a racist.

"Sorry boss," stammered Borman.

"Ah, Christ. I'd better go with you. Can't you knuckleheads get anything right?"

Borman looked at the ground. The receptionist looked at him, then Carney, and she looked down, too.

Allen walked in from parking the car.

"Turn around," growled Borman, needing to assert his authority somewhere. If he wasn't going to get to eat until he cleared up this mess he would at least make sure that the rookies didn't take all the appetizers. He glanced at the hostess who was studying a blank page in the reservation book.

"You better have not messed up that message, bitch," he grumbled.

* * *

As Rick stepped out of the maddeningly slow elevator onto the seventh floor he heard a door slam shut. He looked in the direction of the noise. It was Apartment 702. His pulse raced. He believed that his best shot to get the drop on the kidnapper was in public. The Sons of Odin didn't know that their cover was blown. Their guard might be down. Rick knew he couldn't just knock on the door. It had to be quick. It had to be a surprise. He walked to the end of the hall to listen for footsteps in the stairwell. It was quiet. In exaggerated slowness he began walking door to door in the straight hallway, bending over and laying a pizza flyer against the bottom of each door.

Rick slowly approached 702. He could hear a muffled voice inside. He did not hear Danny. This had to be it. Miller hadn't dared lie on any detail. The fear of Jen had insured his veracity. *C'mon. c'mon, get out here.* Rick prayed for an opening at the sole guard without Danny nearby. *What's taking you?* He continued to linger outside a door half way down the hall.

Outside Jen snapped to attention as she heard the sound of squealing tires as a car came around the corner behind her. She turned as nonchalantly as possible and to her dismay saw the Ford Escort stop in front of the building and double park. Out stepped Borman and one of the new members. *Oh my God.* This was not the way they wanted it to go. They had planned on this possibility though and Jen quickly turned her back to the car and pulled her cell phone to the top of the pocket. She pushed Rick's one digit speed dial number.

Rick was bending over in front of Apartment 705 when he felt the vibration in his pocket. This was not good. He pulled out his cell and turned his back to shield it from view of anyone entering the hallway. He pushed the speed dial for Jen and was listening to the automated beeps of the dialing when he heard the clicking of a doorknob behind him. He punched the off button as Jen picked up on the other side.

Hendricks stormed into the hallway, duffle bag over one shoulder. His other hand was covered with a stocking cap and rested on Danny's shoulder, pressing against his neck. He froze for a moment when he saw the unexpected form down the hallway. He chuckled to himself when he saw the person bend over and lay a flyer on the ground. Hendricks looked down at his own feet. "Jumbo pizza, 12 slices, $8.99." He gave Danny a push toward the elevator.

"I have to pee!" Rick heard his son's voice for the first time in weeks. Hope surged in him. He didn't dare turn yet. He didn't think Danny would recognize him with only a momentary look, but he couldn't risk it. He pulled his black cap lower over his face and turned to lay a leaflet at the door on the opposite side of the hall.

"Chrissakes. Why didn't you say something before? Of course Hendricks hadn't mentioned to Danny that they were going until he had pulled him into the hall. "Okay, okay." Hendricks shifted his load and wedged back in the door. To Rick's chagrin, he pulled the door shut behind him.

"Rick. Rick!" Jen whispered frantically into the hand held unit. "Rick, can you hear me?" She had heard the line disconnect. It had a distinctly different sound than a bad connection as she had heard many times when calling her office or home while driving through the steep valleys of eastern Pennsylvania. Rick had hung up. He couldn't talk. She had to buy him some time. Buy Danny some time. She clicked on 'Mute' and walked toward the entrance where the Escort driver still sat. She smiled at him as she turned and walked in, unbuttoning her coat. Her mind was racing. *Buy some time. Buy some time.*

The car sat at the curb, engine running. The driver was fiddling with the radio and did not notice her. The other two Sons of Odin stood at the end of the lobby waiting for the elevator. Jen approached them, pulled off her cap and shook her thick hair violently. It fell in crazy dark strands over her face. She exhaled dramatically and pushed her hair back over her forehead. By this time attention was riveted on her.

"Thank goodness I've found some big, strong men." The thugs grinned and looked at each other. It was quite a show for the lobby of this rundown place. "It's soooo cold out there and my car won't start. Daddy said a Mercedes wouldn't ever give me a problem," Jen cooed. She may have been overplaying her new youthful look, but her three admirers didn't seem to notice. Jen recognized Carney. The boss. And she couldn't help but identify Borman again. She sauntered over to Carney and took his hand in her two frozen ones. "Feel that? I'm so cold. I'd be very grateful if you could come give me some help." Carney was annoyed, but did not appear totally unreceptive to her. *Buy some time.* "It would only take a minute for someone like you." She gave his fingers a squeeze.

Carney, like Williams the night before, was not used to attention from an attractive woman unless she had been paid in either drugs or money. His ego swelled and brought forth urges in him that made him forget the menial task he was on. Hendricks could wait a couple of minutes while he checked this out. The fool was probably watching cartoons anyway. "Oh all right."

Turning to his underlings, Carney said sweetly, "Come with us boys." Might as well impress the cupcake with his benevolent power. Besides, Carney knew nothing about cars. He needed the muscle. They followed.

"What kind of Mercedes do you have?" Carney asked, sliding his arm around Jen.

Jen didn't have the foggiest idea what models of Mercedes existed. She was conjuring this story up as fast as her imagination would allow. *Where is Rick? Is he getting Danny? Clear these morons out of here!* "Oh, the big one," she answered with a giggle.

Out in the street all eyes were on Jen. She found that a toss of her hair was like a magnet to these hoodlums. "It's down this way a little," she said and flipped her hair toward the furthest intersection.

One of the younger ones broke the spell long enough to look down the street. "I don't see any Mercedes."

"Oh, it's around the corner." She put her arm behind Carney and started leading him down the street, away from the rescue she hoped was ongoing. She glanced at the car at the curb. She wasn't supposed to know Carney had arrived in it. "It might be the battery, you know?" she said innocently.

Carney at least knew enough to jump start a battery. "No problem, Babe." He waved for the driver to follow them. None of them would admit to feeling the cold if their damsel in distress could handle it.

Jen looked at the car in mock surprise. "Oh, good."

On the seventh floor Rick was nervously continuing his charade of distributing flyers. It only should have been a minute before they reappeared. He quickly dialed Jen. *Why won't she answer? What's going on down there?* He didn't dare walk down the hall so far from 702 and the elevator to look out the window. Had he done so he would have seen his wife leading the Sons of Odin in a parade down the street like the Pied Piper of Hamelin. He waited in anticipation, not knowing that while Danny was in the restroom Hendricks sat down to catch the last two minutes in regulation of a tied Rangers game. It would be a long two minutes. There would be three faces-offs and a timeout with a commercial break before Hendricks was to move again.

When Jen was half a block away from the building she slowed her pace. The exit was clear for her family. Now she had to stall. She asked Carney all the mundane questions a couple ask during an interested first meeting. When they exchanged names, Jen, now 'Rikki,' stopped and flirtatiously plucked at his lapel, repeating his name which, surprisingly, he had given truthfully. When they arrived at the corner the freezing and hungry Borman again noted that there was no Mercedes in sight.

"Did I tell you around this corner? Oh heavens no, it is around that corner over there," she said pointing down the street to the next intersection. The siren continued to lead her men as the car turned the corner and crept alongside the walkers. Jen did everything except drag her feet to slow their arrival at the next corner.

"Hey boss, there ain't no Mercedes here either. What's going on?"

Jen feigned confusion. "This is where I left it. Or at least I'm pretty sure it was this street. Is this Jefferson? It was the name of some president I know."

By this time Carney was thoroughly aroused by Jen, but was beginning to realize that he was on a wild goose chase. "Rikki, why don't you show me the car keys?"

"Oh let's just forget that stupid old car, it really doesn't matter ... we could go have a drink. That would warm us all up." Jen held open her arms to welcome Borman as well.

"Show me the keys." Carney was perturbed. He didn't like people playing games with him.

Jen looked at her hands and held them up with a shrug. "Silly me. I must have left them in my purse in the car. Let's go get a drink."

Now Carney was pissed. He didn't want a drink. He wanted this woman. He had been willing to do some silly dating dance for a few minutes, but now he wanted to call the shots. He grabbed her arm roughly. "What's your game, bitch?" Carney's prior sexual assault arrest flashed through Jen's mind. It had been particularly violent. The victim was lucky to have lived to testify.

"Keith, I was just looking for some company with some real men. Let's go have a drink, we could do some dancing." Jen's voice was pleading.

"I haven't got time for that, Nikki. We got things to do. But you got me all worked up." Carney was walking her back up the street to an alley they had passed. He waved at the car to back up. The signs were ominous to Jen.

"Please, Keith. Maybe if we just get to know each other a bit ..."

"Shut the fuck up. You aren't going to tease me and walk away." He turned her into the alley. The car backed past the alley then pulled in and cut its lights.

Jen thought about the gun in her pocket. She doubted that she could hold them at bay with it. Surely they were all armed. She wouldn't be able to shoot them all. If she tried that they would kill her for sure. Carney roughly plunged a hand inside of her coat and squeezed her breast hard. For the first time Jen's thoughts went from buying time to survival. "Please don't do this. Please, Keith."

Carney ripped open her shirt, exposing her lace lined bra. "Nice titties. I thought they would be." He paused to admire his view in the dim light of the alley. His breath was a cloud of white air firing from his nostrils. Jen wrenched free from his grasp and turned and ran. Carney and Borman laughed heartily behind her. She froze in place as she realized what they knew, that the alley was a dead end. She spun around to see all three of the Sons of Odin spread across the alley coming for her as if trapping a scared cat.

Carney tapped Borman and he moved forward and called out, sarcastically, "Come here Nikki. You said you wanted a good time." Time seemed to standstill for Jen as her attackers advanced step by step. She couldn't run. She didn't dare shoot. *What are women counseled to do in this situation? Be firm. Don't play into the man's power game.* She mustered her nerve. "Enough is enough guys. If you're going to act like this, I'm leaving."

Jen stepped forward confidently into the advancing line. Two sets of arms grabbed her firmly. She shook her shoulders, but the clutching fingers dug into her flesh. "Get your hands off me. I want out of here." Her arms were twisted behind her. "I'm telling you ..."

Jen's head jarred with the blow of the slap with the heel of Carney's hand. "Don't tell me what to do, bitch." Her attempts had angered him. Again he rudely mauled her breasts, pulling at her bra and pinching her nipples. Borman and Allen held her arms and kneaded her buttocks through her jeans.

There was one other approach known to forestall rapes, and it now came natural. Jen began to cry as her head was yanked backwards by her hair and Borman tugged at the belt on her jeans.

*   *   *

They have got to get out of there now. Rick could not believe how long it was taking for Danny and Hendricks to reappear. Danny was a little boy. A 'potty' stop only took seconds. Rick had been waiting in the hallway for minutes. He didn't know what was going on with Jen and couldn't run to the window for even a peek. What could he do if he saw trouble anyway? He was committed to this course of action to rescue Danny. He fretted that this delay would blow his cover as a leaflet delivery boy. He had no choice but to risk it. He stood facing the elevator, saying a silent prayer to a God he didn't dare not believe in at this moment.

The apartment door swung open hard. Hendricks entered the hall in a foul mood, muttering out loud. "Three freaking seconds left. Lose to the god-damned Canucks. What the hell is a Canuck?" Hendricks glared at Rick standing by the elevators. In his anger over the Ranger's loss it did not occur to him that this meathead had been in the hallway for over five minutes. He again had the bag on his shoulder and a hat over his other hand placed against the base of Danny's neck. Rick only braved a scant glance. To anyone uninformed of the situation the hat on hand would look peculiar, but since it was cold outside it wouldn't particularly denote danger. Rick deduced that Hendricks was holding a weapon to Danny's throat. He could not tell if it was a gun or a knife. *Please make me kill you, you bastard.* Rick's prayer had become self-serving.

Danny looked down and shuffled to the elevator. Rick felt compelled to say something to cover his extended presence. "Elevators take forever." He tried to disguise his voice so Danny would not recognize it.

"You gotta push the button," Hendricks growled in exasperation as he kicked the down button with his boot. The cover worked. But the elevator did take forever.

*   *   *

The cathedral in Rennes-le-Château

Delacroix stood in the shadow of one of the pillars that held the great cupola over the altar, vacantly supervising the six peasants who had been hired to move the ambo, the massive raised pulpit, and dig a small undercroft at its base. He was deliberating the events of the past year. It had been only nine months since the siege at Blanchefort. The horrors he had witnessed would haunt him for the rest of his life, were still vivid. Even in an age of such bitterly harsh life, the recent events were overwhelming. The massacre seemed so senseless to him. Delacroix was constantly trying to find a holy justification for what occurred. Such good and supportive people whose only fault was their misguided, foolish belief in a bloodline that, to Delacroix's mind, could not exist. If only he had had more time to steer their rudderless souls ashore.

Not long after the capitulation at Rennes-le-Château, messengers returned the word that the so-called Albigensian Crusade was fulfilled, and from the Pyrenées to the Mediterranean, from Albi to Avignon, the Cathars and their heretical beliefs had been eradicated, along with any Knights Templar who had dared defend them. The enormous wealth confiscated was apportioned among the conquering barons and their armies, and the Church. To the relief of the Knights Templar outside of Languedoc, their Order, liberators of Palestine, symbols to the civilized world of the Christian empire on earth, had been cleansed of its radical elements. They could not know that in the next century they too would be disbanded in a power struggle with the king of France, and resigned to be merely a curious footnote to history. Divided, they would fall.

Delacroix's standing in the eyes of the Church's regional hierarchy was elevated with the success of the crusade in his village and, in particular, his part in the subsequent fervent spiritual vengeance. Word of Delacroix's fanaticism, meant in the most honorable sense, had been relayed to the Archbishop and praised to the Pope. The Archbishop was inwardly amazed that this pudgy, bookish bishop was truly the subject of the heroic deeds ascribed to him. Deeds whose description Delacroix himself would not have recognized. He had proven his devotion by his righteous display of loyalty when he apparently had delivered the doomed heir into the crazed hands of the frenzied mob. That act assured that the blasphemous claim to a bloodline of Jesus would end, at least for the faction of the Brothers of Zion that supported Sir Frederick Lancel's claim to the holy throne. Similar claims throughout the targeted villages of southern France were all likewise thought to be eliminated. The Church believed that finally all seeds of the claimed bloodline, and of discontent with the growing power of the clergy, were terminated. History would reveal that it was wrong. While the murder of the adherents to the bloodline silenced the current believers, their martyrdom gained credibility for the Cathars' creed, and its supporters returned as it went further underground. In the century to come, more purges would be necessary. Drastic measures were justified, leading the Catholic Church to institute the Inquisition, for which it would gain eternal condemnation.

Where there was a void caused by the absence of the previous power structure, scavengers jumped in to fill it. Jacques Boulanger had lobbied himself into the position as new captain of a group that was essentially a rehash of the scattered Brothers of Zion. He had served Simon de Montfort solicitously during the months of the siege, for which he was richly rewarded with Blanchefort and all of its surrounding lands. While de Montfort could barely tolerate the sniveling Boulanger, he also knew that the word of his generosity with collaborators would spread to the next village, again easing the path of his army. With his newly acquired wealth Boulanger was able to occupy Blanchefort, and live a shallow semblance of the life that Lancel and the Knights Templar had once led there.

The accolades Delacroix received only deepened the wound that was in his soul. He was a man who had studied the words of Christ. What had transpired was not consistent with his understanding of the teachings of his Lord. He had read that Jesus instructed that the strays of the flock were to be returned to the fold and treated with compassion. Mercy and forgiveness were the groundstones of the Savior's message. He agonized over his failure to avert the tragedy. What had been his role in this dire play? What penance could he pay to receive peace?

He recalled graphically the day the siege had overwhelmed Lancel's defenders. Beginning at dawn, the excited villagers had watched the carnage from afar until the outcome was apparent. Late in the morning an elderly man was spotted attempting to slip the circle of attackers that ensnared the castle. He was one of the very few that had even endeavored to escape, but his flight was strange indeed. He was burdened with a mule laboring with a large leather bound satchel. Even in his terror he could not spur his mule to out ride the vengeful pursuit of the crowd. After a harrowing chase down the mountain and into the nearby woods, he was captured. He was lustily dragged back to the village square and sacrificed to the fires which had already consumed the vanquished survivors to the battle. The satchel for which he had given his life was untied. The captors howled with the prospect of the riches they would find. To their chagrin, they found a number of hide-bound parchments and scrolls wound in lambskin. Even the illiterate villagers knew that these were books, but the strange markings were indecipherable to them.

As the bag and its contents were about to be hurled onto the pyre to stoke the flames, Delacroix interceded, and authoritatively placed his hands upon the satchel. At first the arsonists coiled, ready to strike at whoever interfered with their mindless orgy of destruction. When they saw it was the Bishop, who, since the deliverance of the boy into their hands, was now elevated to sainthood in their eyes, they passionately offered him the books, and charged off to new destruction amid demented cries.

Smoke was still pooling high above the valley floor as Delacroix walked in a stupor back to the rectory, cradling the satchel in his arms, as if it were a child he was saving from the bewildering apocalypse. He passed through the vespery, but he could offer no prayer. He had no words. He felt only numbness.

Delacroix entered his study, and in the early afternoon sunlight he began emptying the satchel, one piece at a time. He handled each volume reverently. He had known that the satchel had contained Lancel's heretical 'proof' when he saved it. He had been moved by many emotions. Respect for Lancel, his inner love for the written word, still a rare, almost mystic, object in this century, and his disgust for the ongoing pillaging. He was also curious to study them, to reveal their flaws and disprove their claims. Here it was. The blasphemous documentation of the bloodline claimed by the smoldering corpses in the square. It hardly seemed worthy of all the death. "My God, what have we done?" he lamented.

Delacroix began to decipher the texts. He did not know if what he held was genuine or forgeries made to continue the hoax which had now persisted for generations. It went against the grain of his teaching that this bloodline claim was not inspired by evil, yet the writings were detailed, minute and logical. The volumes traced the family histories. In Hebrew the tree grew from Christ. The French and Latin went back through the eradicated Cathars, to the French Merovingian lords, and on to kingdoms foreign to Delacroix. At the top of the tree was his deceased friend, Lancel, the inheritor of the throne of David. The branches of the tree beyond Lancel were blank, stark testimony of the violence that had just passed. In distress over his young wife's death on Joseph's birth, Lancel had never filled in the boy's name. It was an oversight that Lancel could not now bring himself to correct.

Delacroix slid the incredible accounts back into the satchel. His hand ran over the objects inside. What did any of it matter now? He tied the bag tight and went to the window and looked down the road. The village was still resounding with grisly festivities. Boulanger was leading a host of villagers in exhorting the crusaders for their successful slaughter. The sickly odor of burned flesh seared Delacroix's nostrils. He closed the window and went outside. He quickly walked through the cemetery, passing under the hand-crafted iron framework which proclaimed salvation for those who rested within. He kept walking into the setting sun toward the mountains and streams. After hiking for an hour the air became clear and he could breathe deeply again.

Soaked in sweat, Delacroix arrived at the most productive of all the streams he and Joseph had fished. He knelt and drank the cold water. He saw the reflection of a tormented man looking back at himself. He sat back on a rock, and looked at the small trickle of water cascading over polished rocks. In spring there would be a hundred times more water. But he would not fish in it again with Joseph.

Delacroix began to whistle a hymn that had been a favorite of Joseph's as they would march the mountain trails. After whistling for five minutes he heard a nearby bush rattle and spun around. He took a deep breath and called out. " You are safe now. Come. Come to me."

The branches of the bush parted, and Joseph stepped out into the opening. His face was dirty, the cheeks streaked with white where tears had fallen. Delacroix held his arms open. Joseph ran into his arms and hugged him around his stomach. His body began to shake. Delacroix whispered softly, "God's will has been done! All have perished." Despite all of the indoctrination against showing emotion each had received in his life, they cried and held one another as darkness closed in around them.

When the day's siege had begun, Delacroix went to the front of the troops, ostensibly ministering to their spiritual needs. Shortly after the walls had been breached, Delacroix joined the confusion and rushed into Blanchefort. He knew his way around the manor grounds from his nights of entertainment there. He had supposed correctly that Joseph would be held in the smokehouse with the other children. It was an unobtrusive yet solid brick building near the back of the grounds, adjacent to the castle walls. Joseph at first had refused to yield to Delacroix's urging that he accompany him from the castle. He consented when reminded of his father's order. Veiled by the smoke and dust, Delacroix and Joseph surreptitiously passed through the gate. Outside the walls they were brusquely stopped, but when the troops saw that it was the bishop with whom their commander had dined, they allowed him and the quiet boy to pass without explanation. Once past the advancing pillagers, they left the trail and ran deep into the woods. Safely beyond discovery, Delacroix instructed the boy to flee to the stream that they both knew so well. As he had promised Lancel, Joseph was delivered from the holocaust.

Delacroix's acts that day in the village square would always haunt him. The doomed boy who had lain at his feet was the son of another of the Knights Templar, also a Brother of Zion, though not a claimant of royal blood. Delacroix only vaguely knew him. Delacroix could justify that he had spoken no words that encouraged the boy's demise. The mob had taken his silence as acquiescence to their demands. Had he told the truth of the boy's identity, no mercy would have been shown, and the boy would have been thrown into the fire anyway. The search for Joseph would have begun in earnest. So Delacroix had taken no steps to save the misidentified boy. He rationalized that his sacrifice was sanctioned by the all-knowing Church. An all-knowing God. Elimination of the heretics was the purpose of the crusade. It would provide him little comfort at night in years to come.

As Delacroix stood in the forest holding the sobbing Joseph, he knew that a just God would forgive the heresy he had committed in saving this youth. As the sun sat behind the trees, he was not so assured of absolution for his other sins.

Delacroix knew a distant hamlet, a cluster of huts actually, where he could deposit Joseph with unknowing, hard-working serfs who would consider it a blessing to raise a select orphan of the Church. It would not be the kind of generous life to which Joseph was accustomed, but he could grow up there. He would live. That was the best Delacroix could provide.

* * *

In the alley

Tears flowed down Jen's cheeks as she sobbed yet coherently tried anything she thought would turn off her attackers' lust for power. "Don't. I have children. Don't do this. My mother will die. What would your mother say?" She had squirmed and kicked enough that Borman was unable to get her jeans down past her thighs.

"Shut her up, Dickhead," Borman grunted at Allen. "Hold her still." Carney slapped her hard again and Jen stopped struggling. Dazed, she knew they would kill her if Carney didn't get what he wanted. She went limp and slumped toward the ground, held up by her handlers.

"Screw this," Carney proclaimed. "It's too cold for this shit, bitch." With that Carney unfastened his belt and let his pants drop to his ankles. He pushed down his shorts to expose himself. Grinning, he reached into his jacket pocket and pulled out a pistol, twice as large as any Jen had seen at the gun shop. He placed the barrel of the gun firmly against her temple. "Do it now and do it right, baby, or I'll spread your brains around this alley." He pulled the hammer back.

The gunshot blast exploded in Jen's ears. She flinched and clamped her eyes shut. She felt Carney surge forward, the cold metal of the gun gouging erratically across the back of her neck. She opened her eyes as he pitched forward onto her as his face erupted in a gusher of blood and flesh. His body stiffened and the gun dropped to the ground as he slumped onto her.

"Freeze. Freeze. Freeze." The alley echoed in a torrent of screaming voices. Still dazed, Jen vaguely realized she was not hurt. *I'm alive.*

"Police. Police. Get your hands in the air scumbag or you'll join your buddy there. Up, up, up."

Jen felt a hand on her arm. "Are you all right Jen?" The voice was familiar. She unknowingly wiped a piece of Carney's brain from her face and looked up at Jim Gilliam.

"I told you you'd need some help." She threw her arms around his neck and pulled him tight.

"Thank God."

"No, thank my buddies here. Wally, Len and Roger." Gilliam pointed each out and they nodded. "Friends of mine from the police beat days." She looked around at three men in dark overcoats that were in the process of indelicately handcuffing the remaining two Sons of Odin who were already sniveling their innocence. "Jim, have you helped Danny and Rick?"

"Now, where is Rick?"

"Right around the corner. We think Danny is there."

"Wally, can you handle these two?" asked Len.

Wally held the rifle that he had used to destroy Carney's head. "If they fart I'll consider it an escape attempt," he said.

Gilliam helped Jen stand on wobbly legs. She pulled up her jeans. She buckled her belt as she looked at her assailants spread eagled on the icy ground. Pulling her coat together she took three choppy steps forward and drove her pointed boot into the crotch of Borman. His head banged down on the asphalt as he screamed in pain. The officers tightened uncomfortably in their firing stances, but none of them moved to stop Jen, who was now standing over her attacker, her hands clenching and chest heaving.

Gilliam put his arm around her shoulder. "C'mon, Jen. Let's go."

Two squad cars were coming up the alley, silently and without flashing lights. Jen climbed into the opened door of the back seat. Composing herself, she dabbed her eyes with the sleeve of her coat.

"God, thanks, Jim," she said softly, trying to refocus herself as the car slowly backed out.

"No problem," Gilliam replied tersely, his adrenaline pumping furiously.

"How did you find me?" Jen asked with a final sniff.

"It looks like Senator Cohen called in some favors. This morning the Israeli Shabak, essentially their FBI, confirmed with him that they had penetrated higher up in the sham charities that Carney had set up in Tel Aviv to skim off a percentage of the ransom donations. The Israelis are, shall we say, a little better at getting information out of people than we are and the scam operators were quick to rat out their middlemen who in turn ratted out Carney's group of thugs to save their own skin." Honor among thieves, after all, was just a saying.

"So we knew it had to be Carney in charge," Gilliam concluded.

"Yeah, we knew that too," Jen said, neither bragging nor complaining.

"Which way, ma'am," asked the driver, reaching the street.

"That way," she answered, pointing and looking at the intense eyes in the mirror. "1642 Goff."

"I figured you knew, the way you were acting," Gilliam nodded. "But I also knew that even if I told you that I could come with help, you still wouldn't have told me where you were."

"You were right," Jen agreed. "Sorry," she added.

"I understand. It's not like the FBI was helping. So the last time I called, I kept you on the line while my friends here triangulated your cell phone to get your location. We knew that Carney owned at least five properties in New Jersey under his own name, and that it was likely Danny was at one of them. Sure enough, we traced you here, and that matched up with Carney's deed for the building on Goff. When we got here I saw you leading this parade of characters down the sidewalk. It didn't look too good so we followed you."

"Obviously, I'm glad," Jen said, looking at Gilliam with admiration. Her eyes said 'thanks' enough for him.

"Let's get Danny," Gilliam said to the cops up front.

"You bet," came the calm reply as they silently pulled over around the corner from their destination.

*   *   *

The neighbor's hallway door opened as Rick, Hendricks and Danny waited for the elevator. Out bundled a short, stout woman with her pre-teen daughter.

They too walked to the elevator and lined up.

Of all the times they could have come out, why now? lamented Rick. He did not want a crowd. He hoped to follow Hendricks to the getaway car and get a drop on him when he put Danny in the car. Rick calculated that Hendricks would have to move his hand from Danny's neck at some time to get the car door open. He hoped he would also let down his guard. It would be the optimum time to move. Rick was fully prepared to shoot to kill if he had to. His only reluctance was the danger of hitting Danny, certainly not from a lack of hatred of his son's tormentor who was pressing a weapon to the little boy's head. Rick didn't worry about legal repercussions. It was his son. It would be justifiable homicide or self-defense, he didn't really care.

They heard the elevator finally grind to a stop on the seventh floor. It sat for its customary pause and the doors jerkily opened. An excited black woman stepped into the door jamb. "Lillian," she said to her neighbor, "there was a shooting over on Madison just a couple a minutes ago. Some white woman gettin' raped by some of those ..." The woman paused and looked sidelong at Hendricks. She decided to say something else. "Anyway, some other white guys come up and started shootin'. Lordy, Lordy, this neighborhood goin' to hell ..."

"Ya mind." Hendricks spat as he pushed his way into the elevator. The woman turned up her nose, but quickly stepped out into the hallway. Rick had been standing with his face away from Danny and closely followed Hendricks and Danny into the elevator. Hendricks guided Danny into the far right corner, keeping his right hat-covered hand across his body on Danny's shoulder. Rick went to the back of the elevator and stood next to Hendricks, keeping a socially acceptable space between them. It was easier to be shielded from Danny in this position. "Lillian" and her daughter backed into the elevator.

Rick did not like what he had just heard. Someone was raped and apparently the woman thought the attackers were white thugs like Hendricks. *Was it Jen? Is she hurt?* He could only give a fleeting thought to his wife now. He had to focus on Hendricks. His senses were on full alert. The elevator slowed and bounced to a stop on the fifth floor. It paused and opened. Three more people stepped in. The elevator was fairly large, a carryover from the building's grander days. Still, it was beginning to feel crowded. Rick noticed that Hendricks had allowed his right hand to drop slightly away from Danny. Rick's fingers caressed the pistol inside of his coat pocket. *That's it. Let your guard down.* In his left hand he was still holding some pizza flyers when he felt the vibrating in his pocket. He took it as a sign that Jen was alive. *Thank God. But I can't talk now, Honey.*

"He's not answering." Jen, Gilliam and the two policemen were running to the corner when Jen had speed dialed Rick's cell. She stopped her party before rounding the corner and leaned over to survey the street. She had been explaining their plan as they ran. "Rick might be out in the street by now." She looked up Goff Avenue. There was no activity.

"Let's go." Jen wasn't sure if the original plan with Rick was still in effect. There must have been some reason why her attackers had come back. *Had they been alerted somehow? Were there more there now? Why couldn't Rick answer the phone?* Either he was in trouble or he had made contact with Hendricks. In either event, they could help if they approached undetected. If she got to her husband before he made contact with Hendricks they could let Gilliam's friends provide cover. They were better trained for this and she could trust them now. They were there, not sitting in an office finding reasons why they couldn't help. And Borman's blood splattered on her shirt proved the extent they would go to save Danny.

Jen was out of breath long before she reached the entrance. She raised her hand to signal the others to wait while she opened the door and glanced around the lobby. It was clear to the three men that Jen was in charge. This lady was tough.

"Clear. There are probably stairs. Can one of you go up them?" The tall cop nodded. "Great. Can you cover the front?" she said to the other one. He also nodded obediently. "Okay. Make yourself invisible. Hopefully we'll be coming back this way with our original plan once we check out Rick and let him know we're here. We'll take the elevator." It seemed like a prudent plan. If Rick needed back-up she just couldn't sit outside and wait. Too much had gone awry already.

The elevator door closed and the car dropped slightly, jolting the passengers who let out a collective groan. It began its descent. Four, three, two. It slowed and stopped prematurely on the second floor. "Someone too lazy to take the stairs?" one of the passengers mumbled under their breath before the door opened. The common sentiment evoked a chuckle from others.

As the door opened onto the second floor the wailing sound of emergency sirens filled the elevator. Out of the corner of his eye Rick could see Hendricks bristle. His hand moved back, slightly closer to Danny's throat. Someone must have called the police at the sound of the shooting the woman had just described.

In the hallway a middle-aged man in a wheelchair asked peered in at the unmoving mass of people. "Got room?" The now embarrassed passengers began shuffling backward. The man wheeled forward. He stuck momentarily at the lip of the elevator which did not always stop exactly even with the floor. "Damn thing," the man said in a mild tone as he gave a hard push and rose into the elevator. The door closed.

Hendricks was clearly getting edgy. From years of drug usage he was fidgety to begin with. Now his eyes darted around the elevator. He leaned over and in a barely audible voice said to Danny, "We're going out the alley. I don't want a sound." No one else in the elevator was listening. No one would have cared, but Rick hung on every word. They were going out the back! He knew he couldn't follow them inconspicuously into a deserted alley. Beads of sweat rose on his forehead. He knew he had to act soon. It was too crowded to try anything in the elevator. He would have to confront Hendricks in the hallway to the alley. It wasn't as good as the initial plan, but he didn't have a choice. Once in the alley Hendricks would certainly be on alert to any other presence.

As Rick calculated his options, Danny unexpectedly raised his face and looked directly into his father's eyes. Rick looked away, but it was too late. The recognition had been instantaneous. Danny started to lurch toward him, but Hendricks tightened his grip painfully on Danny's shoulder. Rick could see the movements out of the corner of his eye and sensed that Danny recognized him. He looked up to see Danny's terrified eyes. Rick put a stern and troubled look on his face and slowly shook his head. He hoped Danny would pick up on his attempt to convey the dire need for silence.

It worked. Danny did not blurt out. But the frightened six-year old in him yearned to be taken from this nightmare. Too often in the next agonizingly long seconds he turned his head time and again to glance at Rick as if to assure himself that this was really his father.

"Settle down," growled Hendricks to Danny as he shot a glance toward Rick to see what had drawn the boy's attention. Rick looked down and shuffled his pizza leaflets.

Jen and Gilliam strode quickly across the lobby to the elevator. She had been so glad to see him that it only now occurred to her that he might not be the best one to be going upstairs with her. "Are you armed, Jim?"

Gilliam patted his coat pocket. "Do you think I'd come in this neighborhood without protection." Their conversation was cut short was the weak ding of the elevator arriving at the ground floor.

"Quick. Down this hall." Jen pulled Gilliam around the corner into the hallway to the alley. "Act natural," she said as she threw her arms around his neck and pressed her lips to his. Embracing, their eyes peered toward the lobby where they could hear the elevator door finally opening.

Inside the elevator, the passengers impatiently began leaning closer to the door. Much as they all wanted to push forward, they waited for the man in the wheelchair to exit. The man paused at the inch differential between the elevator and the ground floor. He was used to this decrepit lift. "Could I get a push?" he announced.

As one of the passengers assisted, Rick looked out of the door into the lobby. He was about to glance back to Hendricks when his eye caught movement in the circular mirror in front of the elevator. What in the world? It was Jen. It certainly looked like her anyway, but some man had his arms around her. Rick could not quite make him out. *Who the hell is that?* Jen's eyes met his. He could only make out surprise, or was it fear?

"Thanks," said the disabled man as he rolled away. Rick had a split second to think. *He is taking Danny down that hallway. Is that one of the goons sitting in wait? Is Jen a hostage now?* He feared that Danny would also recognize his mother and that it would be too much to continue his silence.

The other passengers were shuffling out as Rick's adrenaline surged. *Now!*

The woman from the seventh floor was the last to leave. Hendricks was waiting until the end, not out of politeness, but to insure no one was behind him. Danny turned and looked at his father. Rick took a large step forward and to his left. As he moved forward he swung his left hand forward with the flyers and fumbled them into the air toward the far wall of the elevator. Hendricks could not defeat human nature, his eyes shifted to the colored papers as they hit the wall. At that instance Rick shot his left hand forward and slammed Hendricks' weapon arm upward with as much of a jolt as he could muster. It caught Hendricks by surprise and his arm flew up in the air, throwing the stocking cap against the ceiling and revealing Hendricks' pistol. Danny hunched forward.

There was no doubt what Rick had to do. In the same motion he charged Hendricks and clutched at his wrist with his left arm. As Rick was pulling his pistol out of his pocket, Hendricks struggled with Rick to lower his arm as he began to squeeze off shots wildly over Rick's shoulder. But Rick had the element of surprise and power fueled by pure rage. Hendricks fired a shot over their heads into the ceiling and clawed Rick's face with his other hand. Hendricks' arm was coming down as Rick pressed the muzzle into Hendricks' stomach and pulled the trigger. Hendricks convulsed and doubled over, his strength increasing in reaction to the pain. Rick squeezed the trigger again and again and again until his senses registered no more strength at all coming from Hendricks' body which he was still clutching. Rick allowed the body to slump to the floor. Rick looked at it in horror and then saw Danny folded into a ball next to Hendricks. He heard Jen scream and reflexively crouched and spun, pistol ready to fire.

"Rick, it's me,. It's me!. Don't shoot." Jen charged into the gunpowder filled elevator and fell to her knees. "Oh Danny!"

Rick turned and dropped with her next to the tightly coiled little body of their son. Blood was pooled under his elbow and head. Jen touched him gingerly. She was frantic. "Danny. Oh Danny."

"Mom?" A weak voice came from the floor. The boy slowly lifted his head and looked up.

"Son. My boy." Tears welled in Rick's eyes. Danny began to reach up to his mother. "Don't move, Danny, you're hurt."

Danny reached up anyway and hugged his mother, crying. Rick realized in was a cry of joy and exhaustion and relief, not pain. He looked down at the pool of blood. It was growing wider as it drained from the corpse of the fallen Son of Odin. Rick leaned forward and put his arms around his family and hugged. "Are you all right? Jen?"

"Yes, oh, yes. It was Jim, you know?" she sobbed. "He brought help. He's out there." Rick looked up to the hallway to see a man he did not recognize kneeling next to Jim Gilliam who was propped against the wall. Gilliam's eyes were closed and his white shirt soaked in blood where Hendricks' last shot had entered his chest.

*   *   *

11

The best blood will sometimes get into a fool or a mosquito. -- Austin O'Malley

"Dad, why did those men want to keep me? Because I'm related to Jesus?"

Rick and Danny Manton creaked along the loose wooden planks of the pier. Rick didn't like to fish. Never had liked it. Neither did Danny. But they both were curiously interested in the comings and goings of the boats at the dock. The slow pace in the harbor set a good tempo for father and son discussions. Rick placed his hand gently on his son's shoulder.

Rick was very sensitive to Danny's questions ever since the kidnapping. It had only been two months since the rescue in Newark, and he and Jen feared that the scars of his captivity would linger forever. But, other than a justifiable distrust of strangers and a few nightmares, he had recovered remarkably well, so far. Rick was careful with his comments.

"Sort of, Son. They thought that people would pay lots of money for them to return you to us. But they wanted more money than anyone had, so we had to come get you ourselves."

Danny thought about this as they stopped to watch a weathered fishing boat pull up to the dock. He was fascinated with the crusty fishermen and the pungent odor of the day's catch. "Wow. Smell that, Dad."

"They caught something." They watched the boat bump along the rubber car tires that were tied to the sides of the dock.

"At Sunday School the teacher said we are all Jesus' children. Is that right?"

Rick turned to the thick, rope railing and paused to watch the old fisherman loop his tow line around a post rising from the murky, lapping waves. Before the kidnapping, he and Jen had shielded Danny from much of the controversy over the bloodline partly because questions such as these were difficult to answer. It was time to stop hiding.

"When people say we are all Jesus' children, they mean he loves us all, and we are his children like at school when they said all of you in Mrs. Smith's class were Mrs. Smith's children. They didn't mean you were actually her son. But she cared for you and taught you, so that is just how people describe it."

"So why did they take me?" Danny asked.

"Well, Mr. Gilliam printed a story that proved that your great-great-great grandparents actually came from Jesus just like you came from Mommy and me. Those bad men thought that would make you worth a lot of money. But they were wrong. You can't put a dollar value on what a human is worth. To Mommy and me, you are worth more than all the money in the world. Does that make sense?"

"Sort of. Did they want *a lot* of money for me?" The fisherman was getting to Danny's favorite part. He was hefting the wooden slatted "pots" on end and shaking out the lobsters into a large water-filled bin. It had been a bumper crop on this trip.

"Yes. Quite a bit."

"How much?"

This was more detail than Rick really wanted to face, but he decided that it was no time to start hedging. "One hundred million dollars."

"That's a lot, huh?" Danny was happy that he was worth a lot of money even despite his Dad's speech to the contrary.

"That is a way, way lot, Skipper," Rick replied in the boy's vernacular.

Danny thought for a minute as he watched the fishermen begin to unload the squirming catch. "Have you ever met Jesus?"

"No, he lived a long time ago."

"That's what I thought. But I heard the guy on church TV say he had seen Jesus. He was only old like you." Danny looked puzzled.

"I'm pretty sure he meant that he really believed in Jesus, and wants you to believe too."

"That's not what he said."

"Sometimes grown-ups say things in blown-up ways so people will listen to them. Remember, we had that talk about exaggerating." He rustled Danny's now short hair.

"Zaggerating. Yeah. Like make believe."

The fisherman reached his gloved hand inside the pot to untangle a lobster. "Are those men coming back, Dad?"

"No, they're going to prison. You're perfectly safe now. And nobody else bad will come here either because no one here knows who we are. That's why we made all these changes." Nonetheless, Rick had his pistol in the shoulder belt under his jacket.

"Good. I didn't like being related to Jesus."

"Well, Son," Rick was still not used to calling Danny by his new name and didn't risk calling him by his old name anymore. It was confusing enough. "You still are related to Jesus. It's that bloodline you've heard us talk about. That means that you and Mommy have a tiny bit of Jesus' blood in you." He and Jen had fully accepted Hershner and Steinman's theories. At least they hadn't heard a factual contradiction as of yet.

"But we're not telling nobody."

"Right. It's our secret."

"Good." Danny still looked troubled. "Dad, I feel bad for the lobsters stuck in those traps. Why do they do that to them?" Rick could understand Danny's sympathy with the captured crustaceans.

"People have been eating lobsters for hundreds of years. I guess we believe God put them on earth for us to catch and eat."

"I still don't like it."

"Just because it's always been that way doesn't make it right. It's okay if you don't like it."

"And they taste weird, too."

"That's true. You might get used to them someday."

The cold ocean wind was kicking up. "Thanks for saving me, Dad."

Rick squatted down on the dock and took his son's shoulders in his hands and looked into his innocent face. "Son, you don't have to thank me. Your mother and I were not going to let those men hurt you. We were so sad when they had you."

"I was too. Did Mommy cry?"

"Yes, she did. And I did, too."

"Really?" Danny thought about that. "It's okay. I cried, too."

"Danny, you should know that your mother and I love you very, very much, and we are so sorry that this happened. We both thank God every day that we are all back together." Rick was glad he was having this talk.

"I don't believe in God."

Rick looked at his determined son. "Well, that's okay not to believe in God, but you should think about how things come to life and what makes the world so beautiful if there isn't God."

"Oh, I think there is someone who runs all that stuff, but the boys at my old school said they went to an art painting place and saw a picture of him. They said he was in a cloud and he was big and hairy and didn't wear any clothes. I don't believe that."

"I agree. I don't think that is quite right. But everyone can have their own opinion on what God looks like, because no one really knows."

"I think God is all over, like a feeling, like when you say I feel good."

"That's a good way to think of God." Rick hadn't forgotten his graveyard promise. He now believed that something had been looking out for them. He didn't know what to call it. Providence. God. But even with weeks to reflect on it, he still didn't know what it was that he now believed in. Danny's concept was as good as any he had come up with.

"Can God be a woman?"

"That's possible. Your mother would say 'yes.'"

"Could God be a lobster?" Danny grinned. He had learned years ago how to effectively tease his father.

"Now you're pulling my leg. It's getting cold. We better get going." Rick stood up. He looked at the gathering gray clouds. White caps were forming on the waves coming around the quay into the bay. Rick thought that his family would like Maine, but it seemed that spring came awfully late.

After Danny's rescue, the FBI had been quick in offering the Mantons a new identity and full relocation for what the FBI and Dailley administration was characterizing as "witness protection." It was true that Rick and Jen's testimony played a key role in securing the grand jury's indictment of a number of the Sons of Odin. Their cool, unimpeachable recitation of the facts that constituted the required elements for kidnapping, assault and attempted rape had caused those supposed "life-long" blood brothers to roll over on each other as fast as their lawyers could cut deals. The Sons of Odin was functionally obliterated and the Israeli government was shutting down their "charities." Keith Carney was buried without fanfare a week after his death. His mother had been located and identified his body at the city morgue. After hearing that any assets he might have had were going to be seized by the authorities as fruits of a multitude of crimes, she disappeared. He was buried by the state.

      Despite their indispensability to the prosecutors, Rick knew the actual reason that he and Jen were now Mr. and Mrs. Paul Stonehill living on a peninsula on the central coast of Maine was that President Dailley was desperate for their silence. By whisking them underground they weren't able to hold the damning press conference that Dailley's chief of staff feared, which would have revealed to America that Dailley had again ultimately opted for inaction over action in leaving little Danny Manton helpless in the hands of domestic kidnappers. Whether the public supported the bloodline or not, it would have been a public relations disaster. Yes, Rick thought, the stipend for life and new government jobs were worth missing having the final say. Rick didn't have a need to show up Dailley. When he had Danny safely in his hands, his only concern was to take his family away from the nightmare as soon as possible. The FBI's offer dove-tailed perfectly into his desires. Their house in Norristown was packed for them, and they vanished.

"*Holy Ghosts*," the tabloids said. A great, inaudible sigh of relief emitted from the White House.

The New York Times had not been so forgiving. In a series of articles the failure to pursue leads on the Manton kidnapping and subsequent cover-up was detailed under front page headlines for weeks as the story leaked out. Dailley's foes had a field day with the latest perceived flip-flop, and the administration's political friends chose to lay low, not wanting to risk unfavorable alliance with a President who was, by consensus, a lame duck.

The press suffered a terminal case of withdrawal when they were told they would not get to interview the Manton family in what was arguably the most dramatic story of the millennium. But soon there would be other scandals, other celebrities arising from nowhere. Mercifully, the Mantons' fame would fade.

Rick liked the two-year old Dodge van they were given as part of their deal. Its windows weren't tinted, but since he and Jen had kept up their disguises, it wasn't needed. He had finally gotten to enjoy Jen's vampish new look. Danny had been allowed to pick his own new name, a concession to the delicate psyche of a six-year old. It was believed that he would adjust more favorably to a new identity if he chose it himself. He and Jen were still getting used to 'Lincoln,' the current most popular karate-kicking superhero. Danny, was only vaguely aware that his new name also was the name of a past president.

They would keep Danny, now Lincoln, out of school and tutor him at home. Fortunately his appearance was radically changing day to day. With over four months until the new school year, and with a new haircut, Danny would be able to reenter a private school and make new friends as he had always been able to do. The last photograph the public had seen of him, and the last they would see, was the ransom photograph. He had changed quite a bit since then. Jen was more than willing to keep him at home for now. It was hard for her to let him out of her sight for even a trip to the grocery store. She could start her job at the Knox County child abuse center whenever she felt like she was up to it. It would be a while. The witness protection program stipend was guaranteed whether she worked or not.

Rick drove slowly down the country roads. Though he wouldn't admit it even to himself, he was constantly checking his rear view mirror to insure that he was not being followed. In many ways the countryside was like Pennsylvania. Green pastures with cows peacefully grazing on grassy knolls, weathered wooden fences keeping them from meandering onto the road. Then he would drive around a curve and the rocky, barren beauty of the rough, gray ocean would spread in front of him. If they survived the winters, they would love it here.

Maine had the perfect populace in which to disappear. 'Live and let live' should have been their motto. Rick was casually accepted by his neighbors and the downtown merchants. For the few who were so bold to inquire, he told them that he wrote articles for technical magazines and worked out of his office at home. It was enough explanation. Rick had selected this new profession when the FBI was establishing their relocation program. He would get started at it as soon as his family was acclimated to its new surroundings. His stipend was also guaranteed. If he wrote articles and got them published, he was allowed to keep the money. He too would take his time. It had been a long, upsetting four months. It seemed like a lifetime. Now they were secure for life. It was no longer necessary to appear on talk shows to make ends meet.

Rick pulled down the quarter-mile, tree-lined driveway to his new two-story white Cape Cod home. "We should get a dog," he thought out loud, looking at all the property they now occupied. They didn't actually own it, they had a rent-free lease on it for his life and Danny's too. Jen's new car was in the driveway. She must have gotten home early from her doctor's appointment.

The house was warm and steamy. Jen was trying to get into the foreign role of stay-home mother. Cooking had never been her forte. Rick was afraid that the stress of the recent past had taken quite a toll on her. She just didn't have her old spark. It was still too close to the traumatic events, he reasoned. He was glad to see that she was on the phone and looked quite relaxed, even happy.

She held out the phone. "This character wants to talk to you."

Rick gave her a puzzled look and took the receiver. "Hello."

"Paul Stonehill?" The voice was familiar, but Rick Manton hadn't been Paul Stonehill long enough to be able to hear a familiar voice using that name.

"Yes. What can I do for you?"

"You could subscribe to the Times and keep our circulation up now that we lost our number one story."

"Jim Gilliam? How in the world are you doing? It's great to hear you."

"The doctors have been a pain in the butt. No booze, no juicy steaks, no all nighters to meet a deadline. They give medicine a bad name."

"We've been following your progress in the papers. You know we came to see you before we left, but you were still out of it."

"The nurses told me. Hey, don't worry about it. I'm glad you could get out of this mess. I was beginning to feel a little guilty that I got you into it in the first place." Gilliam sounded weak, but otherwise good after two surgeries to repair the damage caused by the bullet that had just missed his heart and lodged in his lung.

"Well, you warned us. Sort of," Rick joked. "So we read that you're moving up."

"Can you believe it? Kicked me up to national news. Editor. Wouldn't you know. I never wanted the religion page job to begin with. So after I break the biggest religious story since Jesus, no offense to your relatives of course ..."

"None taken."

"... then the publisher sees my true abilities are back in the real news where I started. Such geniuses they are. But I'm glad Jen called today. You'll love tomorrow's headline that we're working on now."

"What is it?"

"Something like, 'Memphis Call Girl Claims She Has Reverend Hanner's Love Child.' Kind of has a ring to it, doesn't it?" Gilliam and Rick laughed heartily together. There was relief in both voices. "Looks like they're all coming down together. Serves them right."

"I'm not shedding any tears."

"Jen tells me Danny's doing well ... as well as can be expected anyway."

"Yes he is. Jim, I can't thank you enough for what you did for Jen, Danny, all of us ..."

"Aw, knock it off. I couldn't let my best story get too far away. Besides, now you owe me one. When you come out of hiding, I'm the exclusive interview, right?"

"You bet. You might even get a few while we are in hiding. We didn't sign a vow of silence. But not yet."

"I understand. You know I'm not asking."

"I know."

"I better get a swing on here. I've got the Reverend's denial to analyze. He says his accuser is under the influence of the devil. He should have paid her better. You'll keep in touch, won't you?" Gilliam asked.

"As soon as it's safe we'll have you up for a visit."

"Up? Sounds like a hint to me," Gilliam said jokingly.

"Go chase your story somewhere else," Rick responded. He knew Gilliam would appreciate it.

"Will do." Click. Gilliam hadn't slowed much.

Rick looked at Jen. "We really do owe a lot to him," he said. "The Times' articles were too modest in emphasizing his role. It seems insulting to say to him, 'you can interview us,' but that is what he'd want the most."

"Believe me, I agree. But when we do tell our story, we'll make him the hero. The only thing I could think that would be more fitting would be naming something after him to honor him."

"Like a dog?" Rick thought Gilliam would get a chuckle out of that idea. He was looking out the window at the new buds on the willow tree.

"Honey, I was thinking more along the lines of naming our next child after him. Hopefully Jamie." Rick's head snapped away from the window and stared at Jen. She nodded, her eyes squinted in a smile.

Rick's eyes misted over as he took Jen into his arms. "Oh, Jen. That's great. Great, great, great."

Seeing his happiness, Jen couldn't hold back her tears of elation and she didn't try. "Danny should have a brother or sister. We wouldn't want to leave him alone after we're gone," she sobbed on his shoulder. Through her tears she looked up and smiled. "There is some bad news, though."

He could tell by her face that it wasn't truly bad. "What?"

"The projected due date."

Rick looked up, counting months. "I give up. When?"

"Christmas Day." They both laughed in ironic delight.

Danny stomped into the kitchen. "What's going on?" he said in mock horror at all the visible affection as he headed for the snack pantry.

"You are going to have a brother or sister. Your mother is going to have a baby."

"Oh, maaaaaan. Dad?" he said pleadingly.

"What's wrong? This is wonderful."

"Does that mean we don't get to have a dog?"

"Oh. No, it doesn't mean that. We have room for a dog, too."

"Good." Danny held up a bag of cheese curls and waggled them at his parents for permission.

"Go ahead." Danny left before he got a warning about not spoiling his dinner.

Rick took Jen back in his arms. "You're right," he said as he squeezed her. "He should never be alone."

* * *

The village road

"Oh your Lordship, are you certain that this is necessary?" The younger monk protested the trip into the village. Father Bernard Delacroix, at age fifty-two, was feeble and his eye-sight so dim that he could hardly see his feet, but he was still a man of determination. He took the arm of the monk and shuffled to the door to begin the half-mile walk to the stonecutter's shop.

"Kind of you to say, Brother Francois, but I know that the time of seeing my Lord is near and I must prepare." It was a sunny day and the warmth would ease his aching joints.

The stonecutter saw the couple shuffling toward his shop and greeted them at the entrance in the rock wall. "Right this way, your Highness," he proclaimed as he brushed dust from his leather apron. He led them around the side of the stone hut that was his home to his open air workshop. "I hope it meets your pleasure."

On a wooden platform lay a large slab which was to be used to enclose the bishop's grave. It was common for men of power and influence to commission a sarcophagus to hold their remains in public view to insure that they would be remembered long after death. As instructed, the stonecutter had sculpted a life-sized statue of Delacroix, fully draped in ceremonial robes, lying in peaceful repose. His eyes were closed, the face solemn. In his hands he clutched a large book so that the parishioners would remember that Bishop Bernard Delacroix paid highest respect, second only to God and the Church, to the written word.

Delacroix ran his hand over the polished figure. It was a poor quality marble, but Rennes-le-Château was a poor parish now, and even the price of cheap marble had depleted the coffers. Since Jacques Boulanger had been given Blanchefort by Simon de Montfort, the donations to the Church had steadily dropped from the levels maintained by Lancel and the Knights Templar. Boulanger did not command the respect or allegiance of the serfs that farmed his land. They would only pay minimal rents, and hid the portions of their crop normally owed to the lord of the manor. The feudal yoke had been removed from them, as it was lifting throughout Europe, and they were not willing to allow its return. It was not surprising when Boulanger's broken and lifeless body was found one morning in his ill-gotten castle's horse pen. His few sycophantic supporters said that he had been trampled to death by a spooked stallion, but for years after his passing, the laborers seemed to reap the fields with extra vigor and furtive knowing looks.

Delacroix bent over his marble likeness as if examining it. The stonecutter-turned-sculptor stood proudly to the side. Everyone who had viewed the work in progress had commented on how well he had captured the Bishop's likeness. He could not hold his self-satisfaction. "Looks just like you, Sir."

"Yes. Yes. It does," Delacroix replied absently. But he wasn't looking at the face. His fingers were tracing the words chiseled into a banner that lay in a semi-circle above the high bishop's cap. He smiled as he registered the feeling of the grooves in his fingertips. *ET IN ARCADIA EGO.* He chuckled as he recalled the days he had puzzled over the meaning of the phrase, Lancel's cryptic non-explanation echoing in his mind. When he finally realized its hidden meaning, he was astounded that he had never seen it before. With a simple rearrangement of the letters, a mere anagram, the unfinished phrase became a Latin sentence. *I Tego Arcana Dei.* Its translation would be a fitting epitaph. *Begone! I conceal the secrets of God.*

Still chuckling over the riddle that would mark his grave for eternity, Delacroix turned to leave. Francois and the stonecutter proudly mistook the chortles to be Delacroix's expression of pleasure with the fine work.

Back at the monastery, Francois assisted Delacroix into his bed. The short walk had exhausted him. His breaths were quick and shallow. He knew that his body had run its course, and he accepted his demise. His soul was prepared. "Brother in Christ, please repeat my last testament."

"Your Worship, we did it this morning. I shall not forget."

"Please honor an old soul."

"Yes, m'Lord." Francois carefully recited the words he had memorized. "Upon your acceptance into the Kingdom you are to be placed in your coffin. In your arms I shall lay the satchel which holds your Bibles. All else is to be given to the Church for use by the brothers. High mass shall be held for three consecutive days. Upon the third day the coffin shall be placed in the undercroft at the front of the altar."

Delacroix strained to nod his head. "Bless you, Francois. You have served me faithfully in life. I have no fear that you shall do the same upon my death."

"Don't speak such sadness, m'Lord. You shall feel better as the warmth of spring returns."

"No. My table is set. I am prepared to feast with the Creator. Please bring to me the satchel and a quill."

Francois retrieved the leather sack from a wooden cabinet along the far wall. Only Delacroix knew that it was the one saved from the fires in the square some twenty years earlier. "I will rest now." Francois, the life-long dutiful assistant, backed out of the chamber.

Reverently Delacroix widened the drawstring of the satchel and withdrew the newest of the Bibles. He opened it to the page where Lancel's genealogy had terminated. He looked at the blank line following Lancel's name.

True to his vow to Lancel, Delacroix had delivered Joseph from the destruction. The family that received him raised him as their son. It was a poor family and that meant back-breaking work in the fields just to insure survival. It was also a pious and God-fearing family that, although shocked by the violence that had occurred fifteen miles distant from the castle, had understood that the crusade had been God's will. Delacroix had explained that the boy he was asking them to raise had witnessed such atrocities that, even though they were committed with a holy purpose, should not be mentioned around the boy. Likewise they were instructed that he should never return to the village. The family accepted the conditions of the honor bestowed upon them.

Joseph never forgot his father nor the heritage that had been instilled in him since birth. But he heeded his father's last bidding, and kept the matters a secret known only to himself and God. The manual labor of the farm was not a hardship to him. He loved working outdoors, and grew to welcome the challenge of the vineyards, the most temperamental, yet rewarding, of the crops. He was wise beyond his years, and had inherited his father's gift of making even the most lowly feel worthy of respect. He grew to be a strong and handsome man, admired by all that knew him in the hamlet which was the limit of his world. When he turned sixteen he married the most charming and beautiful maiden in the valley.

Delacroix did not forsake Joseph as the years passed. The hamlet was not technically part of his parish, but he had served it upon odd occasion in the past upon request from the neighboring parish, and could therefore have reason to make the journey. His heart was warmed to see the orphan grow, mirroring the traits of his departed father. Upon Delacroix's visits, Joseph would take the late afternoons off, and together they would race to local fishing holes that the growing boy had quickly discovered.

They would talk for hours as they once had. Joseph would ask questions about his father and the Knights Templar as time dimmed his memory. But keeping the pact they had silently made, they never discussed the belief in the bloodline for which his father had been martyred. To Delacroix, the continued silence on this heresy justified the fact that he never asked Joseph to repent and recant his beliefs.

As Delacroix lay on his deathbed, he thought of his last visit with Joseph. His lovely wife had prepared a delicious supper of rabbit and vegetable stew as she teased Delacroix with her keen wit. She was the perfect mate for Joseph, and Delacroix wondered how similar she would have been to Joseph's mother. Their seven auburn-haired children kept their small hut in a cheerful ruckus. They had been blessed with one child per year. Surely God did not carry His disfavor any longer.

In his reverie Delacroix became certain of his next act. He looked at the accursed genealogy written in the Bible. He could not destroy a holy book. It was only within God's power to do so. But should this bloodline fall into the wrong hands, those of men who took it upon themselves to render God's judgment, the curse could begin anew, and it would afflict Joseph, or his children, maybe even his children generations and centuries away. As promised to Lancel, Delacroix would grant deliverance from this shackle. For eternity.

Dipping his pen into the inkwell, Delacroix began to fill in the blank lines. Next to Lancel's wife he scribed 'deceased in childbirth.' Next in succession, where Joseph's name should rightfully have been placed, had it not been neglected at his mother's death, he entered 'Mary.' Joseph had no child by that name, but to cover the bloodline a common name was best, Delacroix mused. Every third girl these days was named Mary. Below that, where 'Mary's' spouse was to be entered, he penned in

'Andre Vassimont. Rennes-le-Château.' Delacroix sighed. *Andre.* Such a pity that the quick-witted vineyard worker with the remarkable memory had perished with so many other young men and women that horrible day so many years before. Or at least Delacroix believed he had. Andre had never been seen again. Delacroix was satisfied that with Andre's name now inscribed into the family Bible, the bloodline could be tracked no further. *It is over.*

But what Delacroix could not know was that indeed Andre Vassimont had escaped, using his wiles to disguise himself as a peasant girl, slink past the advancing crusaders and flee the bloodshed. He ran as far from Rennes-le-Château as his feet would carry him for ten days. And as chance, or was it fate, would have it, he quietly settled down in a far off town and married an equally quick-minded maiden who not surprisingly was named Mary. Together they began a handsome and industrious family. It was not royal. It was not holy. But, unfortunately for the Mantons, this would not be so apparent centuries later when Delacroix's fake genealogy was unearthed and traced forward from Andre and Mary Vassimont to Jen and Danny.

For Father Delacroix the sad events in his village were many years behind him. After all, it all been God's plan, and, as often was the case, the purpose behind it was a mystery to mere mortals. Delacroix still puzzled over the fate of those who had nobly struggled for decades to complete the holy Albigensian Crusade. Simon de Montfort l'Amaury died in battle during the siege of Toulouse, some nine years after marching through Rennes-le-Château. And, even more confusing to Delacroix, the crusading general had been excommunicated shortly before his death following a dispute with the abbot Arnaldus Amalrici over the control of Narbonne which had broken into armed conflict. What could have caused that was foreign to the politically innocent Delacroix.

And, finally, even the revered abbot himself had died, simply, of old age, in the monastery where he had first taken his vows, at age sixty-five. Delacroix smiled, allowing himself a rare ration of worldly pride for having out lived them all, truly a sign of virtue. But, presumably, they were now with the Savior, though Delacroix often wondered at the affect on de Montfort's soul of the Church's banishment. It was another riddle that he would not solve in this lifetime.

In the years after the capitulation of Blanchefort, Delacroix had many afternoons to reread and study the heretical texts. Try as he might, he had never found a flaw that disproved their authenticity. But he could never bring himself to consider that what they stated was true. But he resolved his intellectual conflict, as he always did, by accepting it as one of God's many shrouded mysteries.

After the ink had dried, Delacroix closed the book and replaced it. He folded his arms over the satchel, and lowered his head in silent prayer. *Oh Lord, I shall hold Thy secrets. If these holy books are ripped from my arms while in death, Thy secret shall be safe. I beseech Thee to grant forgiveness to Joseph and his progeny.* Delacroix had reached peace. Wearily he closed his eyes, content in knowing that when he next awakened he would be in Heaven with his Risen Savior.

*   *   *

A vineyard in Southern France

The weathered, sturdy man deliberately chopped his hoe down through the dry, rocky soil around the base of the grape vine, searching for weeds that he knew could spring up and infiltrate his crop. He was deep in thought and did not notice the gathering of storm clouds over the range of hills on the far side of the valley. He was not contemplating great problems. It had been hours since he had eaten his lunch of cheese, wine and a long loaf of crusty bread under the shade of the lone tree at the far end of his vineyards. He was speculating what dish his wife of thirty years would prepare for the gathering of the family this coming Sunday. He should urge her to make his favorite, her pan-broiled trout, laced heavily with cloves of garlic and stewed tomatoes and celery. It was a favorite in the southern provinces of France, influenced by the Basque culinary tastes from the other side of the Pyrenées that rimmed his village.

He had been a grape-grower all his life, but he only did it because it was the best paying crop in the area. Actually, he hated farming, but a man has to make a living, he reasoned. His true passions were riding horses through the beautiful hills and catching fish in the cool streams.

He was one of eight brothers and sisters. His father had come from a family of ten siblings and his father's father likewise sprung from a large family. He had more cousins and second cousins in the region than anyone could calculate. Every other Sunday a small percentage of the relatives would gather after mass at one of the family homes for an informal, noisy feast. Everyone contributed, but it was a matter of pride for the rotating hostess to provide a generous, and flavorful, entree. His brother would be disappointed if his wife did not serve the *truite a la Dieu*, the Trout of God, bathed in roasted tomatoes and garlic cloves, as he would jokingly proclaim after three generous helpings, washed down with an equal number of goblets of home grown and bottled vintage Bordeaux.

At the sound of a deep rumble he paused from his labors. He painfully straightened his legs and arched his back, stretching his tired muscles. Cupping a heavily callused hand under the short brim of his beret, he looked skyward toward the dark eastern horizon. He squinted, causing the dimple in his cheek to deepen. *Was it thunder or a sonic boom?* he wondered. He grumbled at the thought of rain and uttered toward the heavens a short prayer, which was more of a statement to the clouds, "Surely you can come another day?"

The man wanted to ride his favorite mare into the hills to catch fresh fish for the gathering. The cold spring rain would make such a foray miserable. The clouds grew darker. His shoulders slumped, relinquishing hope. *Ah well. I'll have to tell Marie to take the fish down from the freezer. Too bad. Frozen is not as good as fresh.*

Hitching up his jeans in resignation, he leaned over and began to hoe, quicker than before. Unknown to him, or anyone else, he and his myriad of cousins were the true descendants of Lancel and Joseph. Not Jen or Danny Manton. When he had heard of them on the news he had shrugged. It did not concern him and he hadn't really believed it. *If Jesus had fathered children the school's nuns certainly would have told us.* Yet it was this modest man's family that were the relatives of Christ. The carriers of the royal bloodline. A heritage that was now untraceable due to Father Bernard Delacroix's forgery eight hundred years earlier. Lost to history.

The next rumble of the approaching storm was louder. The farmer sighed. *I suppose He knows best. The grapes need the rain more than I need trout.* He chopped a little faster as the first sporadic drops fell on the dirt before him. *After all, who is man to try to change the path of God.*

The Bloodline

-fini-

Made in the USA
Charleston, SC
23 August 2012